A Rainbow
Murder Mystery

Praise for *Biotechnology Is Murder* —

"Nifty, light-hearted and deadly."
— Edna Buchanan, *Garden of Evil*

". . . a potent mix of science, business and crime."
— *Publishers Weekly*

". . . a very well written and clever second addition to the Ben Candidi series. Dirk Wyle is able to paint a vivid picture of Ben Candidi's world. . . . Halfway through this book, I reached the point where I happily lost track of time and had to remind myself to breathe. Wyle followed through with a stunning ending that felt realistic and complete."
—Andrea Collare, Charlotte Austin Review

". . . a combination of white collar crime medical thriller hardboiled mystery. . . . Ben Candidi doesn't carry a gun or have a PI license. He's witty, complex and a very different sleuth."
— Lane Wright, Mystery Books Review at About.com

". . . Wyle writes a heck of a good novel . . . keeping the reader hooked as he proceeds."
— G. Miki Hayden, *By Reason of Insanity* and *Pacific Empire*

BIOTECHNOLOGY

IS

MURDER

Praise for *Pharmacology Is Murder*, first in the Ben Candidi Mystery series (1998)

". . . Wyle skillfully pairs the tone of the hard-boiled mystery with the intricate scientific detail common to the medical thriller. The result is an excellent whodunit. . . . a first-class mystery that combines elements of Michael Crichton, Patricia Cornwell, and even Edna Buchanan."
— *Booklist* Mystery Showcase (American Library Association)

". . . one fine debut mystery, combining scientific method with a quirky, humanistic scientist/detective and resulting in the perfect compound . . . inventive, intriguing, and, most importantly, evocatively drawn. If you like a puzzle, you'll love this one."
— Les Standiford, author of *Black Mountain*

"Dirk Wyle fuses Miami's cosmopolitan setting with academic intrigue, scientific discoveries, romance and murder to create a unique read. . . . this book delivers. . . . Wyle explains scientific jargon and theories in clear layman's terms, mixing investigations with in-depth character studies to explore all aspects of the crime."
— Devorah Stone, The Quill

". . . a good solid interesting mystery in the traditional style of literate storytelling. . . . very smooth and intelligent."
— Sharon Villines, Archives of Detective Fiction

". . . so easy to pick up and so hard to put down!"
— Reviewer's Bookwatch

". . . written for the intellectual who loves mysteries . . . characters well presented."
— Under the Covers Book Reviews

"Wyle demonstrates a breezy style, a flair for drawing vivid and memorable characters with just a few deft strokes. . . . I've found myself thinking about it and admiring it in retrospect over an over again."
— Joe Lofgreen's Detective Pages,
Judged **Best First Detective Novel** of 1998

". . . step into the scientific world, the Mensa Society, be led down a heady path of suspense, and witness in our main character an emergence of love and vulnerability." — Linda Tharp, *The Snooper*, Snoop Sisters Bookstore

"The reader is amazed at the author's ability to create tension, introduce a little love-making along the way, and tell a good mystery story."
— Kathie Nuckols Lawson, BookBrowser

DIRK WYLE

BIOTECHNOLOGY

IS

MURDER

A BEN CANDIDI MYSTERY

RAINBOW BOOKS, INC.

Library of Congress Cataloging-in-Publication Data

Wyle, Dirk, 1945-
   Biotechnology is murder : a Ben Candidi mystery / Dirk Wyle.
    p.   cm.
   ISBN 1-56825-045-2 (alk. paper)
   I. Title
   PS3573.Y4854B56   1999
   813'.54--dc21   99-27225
                                         CIP

Biotechnology Is Murder © 2000 by Dirk Wyle

ISBN 1-56825-045-2

Publisher
      Rainbow Books, Inc.
      P. O. Box 430
      Highland City, FL 33846-0430

Editorial Offices and Wholesale/Distributor/Retail Orders
      Telephone/Fax: (863) 648-4420
      Email: RBIbooks@aol.com

Individual/Retail Orders
      Telephone: (800) 431-1579; Fax: (914) 835-0398

Cover and interior design by Betsy A. Lampé

This is a work of fiction. Any similarity of characters to individuals, living or dead, is purely coincidental.

Second Printing 2000
Printed in the United States of America.

This novel is dedicated to members of that small subset of biomedical scientists who have labored, fought and schemed to develop their scientific discoveries into pharmaceutical products.

AUTHOR'S NOTE

In common with legal thrillers, courtroom dramas and other forms of white-collar detective fiction, this novel contains examples of authentic professional dialogue. Business and scientific terms are limited to those found in *Webster's New Collegiate Dictionary* and are explained in the novel within their immediate context. No specialized knowledge is required to solve the murder(s). Have fun!

ACKNOWLEDGMENTS

I would like to thank Betty Wright, my publisher, for her unshakable belief in my work and for her suggestions on its fine-tuning. I am also deeply indebted to Betsy Lampé for imaginative cover design and for tenacious promotion of my work.

I also thank the many readers who have written and e-mailed their reactions to *Pharmacology Is Murder*, the first novel in the Ben Candidi series.

The present novel benefited from the early-stage critiques of Yvonne, Ed, Charlie, Paddy, Ira, Mary-May, Harrison, Karl, Gisela, Carlisle, Brant and Douglas (Miami bicyclist, historian and photographer). I would also like to thank Mike and Deborah for input on fire-rescue procedure, Dawn (Historical Museum of Southern Florida) for help with historical facts, and José and Marta Julia for authentic rendering of Cuban Spanish.

BIOTECHNOLOGY

IS

MURDER

PROLOGUE

I once read that the Great Houdini was making almost a thousand dollars a week with his staged magic around July 7, 1912, when he invited a crowd of reporters, photographers, and skeptics aboard a hired tugboat to witness his most famous trick. He was handcuffed, manacled and placed in a packing box together with 200 pounds of lead. After the lid was nailed down, snugly-boxed Harry Houdini was lowered into the East River. Two minutes and 57 seconds later he emerged to a cheering crowd.

When I accepted an offer for a consulting job paying almost a thousand dollars an hour, I never thought that performing the old Houdini trick would be part of my job description. I didn't get a cheering crowd, either. I just got a couple of gangsters shining a searchlight on the water to make sure I stayed down there — dead.

Of course, the little skeptic living in back of my brain had done his best to warn me that the consulting job was too incredible to be true. I didn't listen to him. I was just overjoyed to find a client ready to pay me big bucks for four days of scientific advice. With the client gambling $20 million on those anticancer compounds, he could afford to pay $24,000 for my newly-acquired scientific expertise. I knew enough about the business to play the part, and I would figure out the rules of the game as I went along. But I didn't know that the logic of the game would turn out weirder than *Alice in Wonderland*. I had no inkling that it would turn into a game of "crack the whip" where built-up momentum is transferred down the line to snap out the man on the end — Ben Candidi.

A VOICE FROM THE PAST 1

My white rabbit came in the form of a telephone call from my old mentor, Dr. Geoffrey A. Westley, Chief Dade County Medical Examiner. Dr. Westley was a living legend in Miami, Florida, celebrated in the media for his ability to pinpoint the exact cause of death, whether by cocaine, heroin, or designer drugs, or by mundane agents like insecticides and rat poison, not to mention his ability to differentiate — by mere examination of the wounds — between all the garden variety methods of violating God's Sixth Commandment.

For over 30 years, Dr. Westley had stalwartly directed the Medical Examiner's Office, all the time retaining his Oxford/Cambridge accent, a lordly demeanor and a consistent air of cultural superiority. He had certainly paid little attention to me over the many years I had worked as a technician in his laboratory, until three years earlier, when he had unexpectedly taken an interest in me and offered me a special project.

Dr. Westley had invited me to dinner where he announced that he was firing me for my own good. The old aristocrat explained that this would free me up to study for a Ph.D. in pharmacology at nearby Bryan Medical School. He said that a 28-year-old "Mensa genius", such as myself, should not be squandering his talents doing cocaine analyses on cadaver blood. Would I consider his proposition? Yes? Jolly good! He was so pleased. And while I was at it, would I be so good as to investigate — clandestinely, of course — one of the professors there? Seems that the chap may have murdered a colleague. By poison, of course.

Back then, I took up the offer, "acquitted myself well", and also made an anonymous contribution to Dr. Geoffrey Westley's legendary reputation. As a secret payoff, he arranged a lucrative part-time job for me with another branch of Dade County. And now, three years later, I was 31 years-old, much wiser, and about to be awarded a Ph.D. in pharmacology.

Today Dr. Westley's call interrupted an interesting handcuffing experiment. Chemical handcuffing, that is. Just as a private detective will capture a pair of illicit lovers on videotape, an astute scientist can trap a pair of copulating molecules by chemically handcuffing them together. After that, the molecules can neither escape nor deny their act.

This is not to say that the molecules have any sense of shame. They live in a state of submicroscopic innocence. They spend half their time drifting around, waiting to bump into a properly built partner. And they spend the other half of their time in writhing copulation. I caught them in the act and handcuffed them — Adam-calmodulin and Eve-tyrosine-phosphatase. I threw them on the gel electrophoresis slab, turned on the electricity and marched them down the lane.

It was a pleasant enough lab on the fifth floor of the Bryan Medical School. My dissertation advisor, Dr. Rob McGregor, Research Assistant Professor of Pharmacology, supplied everything I needed: chemicals on the shelves and new hypotheses on the blackboards. The coffee pot was always full. The window had nice view of the Miami River and of downtown Miami, farther south.

Was it incurable perfectionism or force of habit that brought me back to the lab for just one more experiment? My doctoral dissertation was already written and handed in. I should have been making projection slides. Should have been rehearsing my oral presentation. High noon before the examining committee would be next Monday, seven short days from now. If all went well, I would graduate a couple weeks afterwards in late May.

I picked up the ringing telephone and said, "McGregor Laboratory."

"Ben." One syllable was enough to identify the speaker as Dr. Westley: The mildly percussive "b", the softly reverberating "e" that rose and dipped ever so slightly before resolving into a final "n" which was so perfectly tapered that it seemed to fill the ensuing seconds of silence. Dr. Westley's next tones were formally cordial.

"Ben, I hope I have not rung you up at an inconvenient time."

He was undoubtedly calling from his Medical Examiner's office, located about five blocks away on the periphery of the Miami Medical Center. I could imagine his pudgy, sixtyish frame sunk into his soft leather chair, his face displaying an air of distracted bemusement, a shock of thin white hair partially obscuring the plump hand holding the receiver against a cheek so pale that it resembled blue cheese in cellophane. His other hand was probably playing with the cord or fiddling with his antique, brass-rimmed magnifying glass.

Yes, we had gotten to know each well during our last project. But over the last three years, in the absence of a project to pull us together, our social distance had increased to a new equilibrium value. Dr. Westley now sounded incredibly autocratic and remote. And he was announcing that he wanted something, whether it was convenient for me or not.

"No inconvenience, Dr. Westley. I have a few minutes left on my electrophoresis experiment."

"Wonderful," he replied. "An experiment that can be switched on and off at will."

After getting me to admit that there was no rush, he engaged me in a linguistic game of trivial pursuit. It was something like a cricket match. He pitched me clever puns on topics dear to him, and I was supposed to swing at them with my bat. Playing the fuddy duddy was his way of being friendly. I moved to the window and rested my eyes on the green of Miami. Five minutes passed, and Westley came to the point.

"Ben," he said earnestly, "I would like to make a little proposition. I was wondering if you might drop over for a cocktail, *circa* six o'clock. If Rebecca could come too, I would be most delighted, although it will be primarily a business matter."

Dr. Westley was so polite.

"I'm sorry, but Rebecca is in Jamaica, doing a fourth year clinical rotation."

"Yes, I remember your telling me something of the sort. If I have my chronology straight, she will receive her M.D. this June." As Westley rattled on, I rested my eyes on the narrow, tree-lined Miami River. "The clerkship is in Kingston, is it not? Should be good training for her internship. Probably more knife wounds and fewer gunshot wounds than here at Dade General."

Rebecca was actually in Montego Bay, and her patients came from coastal villages and the Green Mountains. But it made no sense to interrupt the Old Boy when he was in a talkative mood.

My eyes had been following a dot growing between two tall cumulus clouds over Biscayne Bay to the southeast. Now it had grown into a jetliner that was lowering its wheels and descending for its final approach to Miami International, three miles due west.

"Rebecca is more interested in other preventable conditions — like infection," I explained. "Regarding our cocktail engagement, it would be a pleasure to drop by. And I'm sure you have something in mind."

"I would like you to meet my physician friend Brian Broadmoore, a compatriot from Boston, a fine chap whom I have known since public school." I half expected Westley to tell me — for the thousandth time — that "public schools" in England are equivalent to private prep schools in the United States. But he didn't — this time. "Dr. Broadmoore would like to make a little business proposition. Very short notice, I am afraid, but a rare opportunity."

"I appreciate your thinking of me, but I do have a problem. I must defend my dissertation in exactly seven days."

"The matter shouldn't take that long. As I understand, the job should require exactly four days. Brian needs someone of your qualifications — biomedical science background, high intelligence, Mensa caliber and the like."

Westley could never resist a gentle jab about my connection with Mensa. When I was younger, the Society had been an important part of my life. But in the last few years I improved my navigational skills in normal society and became less adherent to elitist doctrine. I attended maybe three monthly meetings a year.

"The job," Dr. Westley continued, "the consultancy, actually, will entail sniffing around and ferreting out certain scientific details."

Dr. Westley personified the upper-crust mentality that had no qualms about sending out the lesser sort to do dangerous and dirty work. And he often used understatement as a linguistic device for getting around obstacles.

I had to ask: "Will I be required to walk through walls?"

"Nothing supernatural. No clairvoyant skill required. Nothing clandestine, and certainly nothing illegal. You would simply be required to make a diligent effort in a due diligence audit — if you can excuse my redundant use of the operative word diligence. At any rate, Broadmoore is in a position to pay twenty-four thousand dollars for four days of your services. Although you have proven worth your weight in gold, I would wager that you have never yet received six thousand dollars per day for your services."

"You're right there. I would be very interested."

"Very well. Present yourself at my apartment — Faire Isle, you will remember — at six o'clock, and I will arrange the introduction. Of course, you already know how to conduct a scientific-technical due diligence audit — or will have familiarized yourself with its requirements before arriving."

Hell, I didn't know anything about due diligence. "What is this due diligence for?" Maybe an ambiguously posed question would tease information out of the Old Boy. With a little bit of luck, he might wind up defining the term for me.

Westley cleared his throat in disapproval. "Broadmoore is investing in a local biotechnology company — BIOTECH Florida. Due diligence must be completed before making the final commitment." He raised his tempo and pitch. "But since you are a Mensa genius and your neurons signal at the speed of light, whereas we normal folk must be satisfied with a mediocre one hundred and twenty meters per second — providing that we remain properly myelinated — you will not have the least problem in bedazzling us with your newly acquired knowledge."

Well, so much for getting any help from him. "I'll give it my best shot," I answered.

Two halves of a bascule bridge had parted over the Miami River and were rising at a steep angle to make way for a mid-sized freighter.

"And I would hope that your first impression will be commensurate with the aforementioned rate of compensation. You must dress the part, so wear your business finest. You have not reverted to a ponytail, have you?"

"No," I answered quickly. Westley almost made me ashamed that I was wearing blue jeans and a polo shirt. But comfortable clothes are a must for anyone who is serious about working in the lab. "I'll see you at six, Dr. Westley."

"Good show. Incidently, I must explain that the twenty-four thousand dollars is not a previously agreed-upon figure, but rather my assessment of what you should reasonably demand. Cheers." (Click)

Whether by design or by habit, that was how old Westley operated. He used voice inflection and word choice to get what he wanted at the least inconvenience to himself. No matter that his every sentence generated five questions. I'd just have to be a good soldier and muddle on through.

Westley's opportunity was very welcome; I was worried about how much money I would be able to earn with the Ph.D. that was about to be granted. My plan was to follow Rebecca to whatever medical center she chose for her residency and pick up a $27,000 a year postdoctoral position in one of the labs. Low-paying postdoc positions are easy to find; regular faculty positions are not.

Of course, I was a hell of a lot better off with a Ph.D., viable job or not. And I had Dr. Westley to thank for giving me the kick in the butt that made me go after it, together with his clandestine "special project" that got my butt kicked quite a few times more before I finally succeeded. But I did remember fondly the dinners with him and his wife, Margaret.

I recalled the little travelogues on England and monologues on English culture which they recited for their "fine young visitor". Oh, I had been so saddened when I learned of dear Margaret's death. And I remembered those hours on the balcony with Dr. Westley — "Wessie," Margaret had called him — racking our brains to solve that murder-by-poison and learning about Nature and human nature in the process. Yes, I would like to work with Dr. Westley again. And, yes, I could use the money. But I still couldn't believe anyone would be willing to pay me that sum of money under any circumstances . . .

My thoughts were interrupted when my dissertation advisor, Dr. Rob McGregor, lumbered in. He was wearing a diffuse grin that told me he was in a mood to chat.

"Say, Rob, have you heard about a pharmaceutical company called BIOTECH Florida? It's supposed to be a Miami company."

"No, but you could check on it with the Strategic Biomedical Alliance. You know the outfit — the biotechnology 'incubator' downtown. I've got their Website written down somewhere." He waddled off and returned in a few minutes. "It's http://www.strategic-biomed.com."

"Thanks, Rob."

"Thinking of buying stock?"

"Nope. Just taking stock."

"What do you mean by that?"

"Just a hyperinflated play on words," I answered, hoping he wouldn't press me further. Rob McGregor was a good friend, but his curiosity was invasive. I just didn't want him to give me any friendly advice about not being able to spare a few days on this Westley/Broadmoore proposition. Hell, I'd given McGregor three good years of work. We had already published four scientific articles together.

Rob leaned his heavy frame against the lab bench and frowned at the floor. This was always his prelude to a scientific discussion. I made a show of glancing at my watch and told Rob I had to leave. I hurried over to the other side of the lab and flipped off the electrophoresis machine. Put the gel slab in the refrigerator. It was 4:30 p.m., and I didn't have much time to spare — especially if Dr. Westley expected me to be properly attired.

AN ECOLOGICALLY SOUND WAY TO GET THERE 2

Five minutes later I was at home — staring into the closet. Home is the apartment that Rebecca and I share on the 10th floor of the Medical Towers Building on Twelfth Avenue, along the west side of the Medical Center. Staring into the closet where our clothes hung together made me feel all the more lonely for Rebecca. Her idealistic choice of clinical rotation had already cost us three months of togetherness. But it was no time to think about such things, not now.

I had to suit up to play the businessman in biotechnology for $24,000 in prize money. And I was up to it. I found my dependable polyester blue blazer and a not-too-wrinkled, white, button-down Oxfordcloth shirt. I put on the most regimental of the five ties that Dad mailed me from New Jersey for the last five Christmas's. I attached the sterling silver clip that Mom sent from Scottsdale, Arizona. After symbolically reuniting long-divorced Mom and Dad, I selected a pair of tan Dockers slacks to complete my ensemble. With my black penny loafers, I would look passably preppy. Some day I would break down and buy a pair of cordovans.

Adjusting my tie in the mirror and going through my repertoire of serious faces, I fell into daydreaming. It's my all-too-frequent pastime. Yes, Ben, you are almost good-looking. A few inches short of the six-foot masculine ideal, but no runt. Vigorous, thick, Italian-black hair, regular features and a nice smile. It shows a couple of slightly crooked teeth, but it's a good smile nonetheless. It had won the heart of Rebecca, the girl you had picked to last a lifetime. So stop daydreaming, Ben. Get out there and win one for Rebecca!

My first decision was how to get to Westley's condominium.

A cab would be expensive, maybe unreliable and always against my general principles. No, today's trip would use a most excellent combination of Metrorail and bicycle. I grabbed my Metrorail photo-ID bike pass and attached it to the front brake cable of my 10-speed. Wheeled it out the door.

I've been an ecology freak and conservation fanatic since an early age. You might say I was an ecologist before ecology was cool. Bikes save money and fossil fuel. Rebecca agrees with me completely. She comes from New York and never developed the bad habit of owning a car.

One elevator ride, a skip and a jump, and I was down on Twelfth Avenue, looking up at the elevated Metrorail station whose massive concrete underside resembles an Empire Battlestar. I bent the rules a little by taking my bike on the escalator to the first level.

While trying to focus my mind on the upcoming interview, I realized that a cab ride might have been less distracting. On the mezzanine level a brawny Wackenhut guard made a big point of checking my bike pass. On the open-air platform level, I was distracted by the occasional roar of semitrailers 50 feet below and the screams of frequent jetliners a couple of thousand feet above.

As I was stowing the bike in the wheelchair area of the rear car, a northside passenger broke into a panoramic, golden-tooth-capped smile and made fun of me. He called out to everyone that I was all duded up like some kind of yuppie, but was driving a bicycle. I ignored him. But it got me thinking. He might have scored a few points by "diss-ing" me, but that kind of crap is just a "negative-sum game" — the type of game where everyone comes out with less chips than when he started. People get mad at each other, the neighborhood becomes a slum, and everyone suffers. That's how an *Atlantic Monthly* article described it.

Of course, the corporate science game I'd be playing was a "positive-sum game" — the type of game where everyone comes out with more chips than when he started. A scientist discovers a new drug, a businessman invests in it, a disease is cured and everyone comes out ahead. The elevated train sped me toward downtown Miami. At that point, an influx of office workers made it standing room only and disturbed my concentration.

I gazed out the window, trying to think about how I'd play this game to win. It's always been a problem for me, playing to win. I had excelled in college and in graduate school where they reward you for coming up with the right answer. But real world jobs involve dealing with people and battles of will. That type of game is so foreign to my nature that I often have trouble keeping my mind on it.

Maybe I'm rebelling against the fact that so much of life *is* a game. Once, after an evening of deep-probing introspection, I was rewarded with a flash of insight into Ben Candidi — the soul of a teenager and the mind of a cynical 40 year-old occupying a 31-year-old body.

Unresolved personality problems were coming back to haunt me, now that I was getting a Ph.D. What would I do with the Ph.D. in "real life"? Would I spend my next five years in the normal academic career pattern, staking a claim to a small patch of turf in basic scientific research, while working in an established lab and subsisting on a $27,000 a year postdoctoral fellowship? Hell, this Westley/Broadmoore job would pay me the same money in *one week*. Face it, Ben: You're auditioning for an important job. Give it all you've got!

As the train crossed over the Miami River, I couldn't resist contemplating the scene below. Two tugboats were maneuvering a Panamanian freighter through the narrow gap between the tilted halves of the Seventh Avenue bridge. Some jobs require great responsibility. The tug up front was pulling the freighter straight through, and the tug behind was maneuvering the freighter's stern. Its massive pilothouse cleared the parted ends of the bridge with only a few feet to spare. Hats off to the two tugboat captains. They know how to keep their minds on the game.

The approaching high-rises of the Brickell Avenue Financial District brought to mind another type of responsibility — taking care of other people's money. For this consult job, I would have to give advice on whether to spend big money on a new technology. Up to now, I'd never thought about such questions. I'd always joked that the Financial District was a center for questionable loans to Latin America and for money laundering.

I really didn't know how to do the job that I was interviewing for. What exactly is a "due diligence" audit, anyway? From Westley's context, I guessed it involved making a diligent effort to determine the value of the company you are buying — before you lay your money on the table. This deal probably involved a lot of money — probably more than it would take to replace a bridge or buy a new freighter. Hopefully Westley's friend didn't need a *licensed* tugboat captain. I could only pass myself off as a good first mate.

I probably shouldn't be thinking of the Brickell high-rises as unnecessary structures that blocked our view of the Bay. Maybe I should take a cue from our previous mayor and regard them as examples of "tropical elegance". One was a flat, 500-foot wall of wavy glass. It presented a distorted reflection of cumulus cloudscape. Another was a wall curved inward, its blue-tinted glass arranged in jewel-like facets. It looked like a giant Christmas tree ornament. But the one next to it was a heartless black glass monolith. Its black, latticed base was actually a disguised parking garage, probably full of black Beemers.

I fell into contemplation. At the foot of this financial Land of Oz was an expanse of tree canopy, several blocks wide. Under the trees were wooden houses built from Dade County pine, some covered with clapboard and some with tongue-and-groove, most dating back to the 1920s. Snaking toward us through the treetops was the concrete guideway of the elevated MetroMover. Its low-speed robotic trains brought office workers from the high-rises to the Brickell Avenue Station, our next stop.

Our car received a large influx of Brickell passengers now, and we reached Tokyo subway packing density. Crowded next to me were systems analysts, international bankers, business people, and their secretaries. Audible volume rose to cocktail party levels. Executives in three-piece suits talked about Eurodollars and South American finance. Impeccably dressed Super Moms pulled out cellular phones and issued instructions for dinner or piano lesson pickups, using Spanish, English or any practical mixture of the two. Obviously, these people knew how to keep their minds on the game of life. Maybe I should be taking my cues from them and start playing the game *to win*.

But spiritual life and appreciation of nature are important, too. That green blur whizzing by was Simpson Park. How many of my fellow passengers had ever visited it? Behind those high fences stood the few remaining acres of Miami's virgin forest — tropical hardwood, dense undergrowth and solution holes — that had managed to escape the developers' bulldozers.

When I maneuvered my bike toward the door, I received a wink from a kindly looking businessman on the high side of 50. He meant it sympathetically: If I kept working hard, I would soon be able to afford a nice car.

I smiled back, sympathetically. I really need an emblem to keep people from getting the wrong ideas. One of these days I'll laser-print a bumper sticker for my bike's rear fender: "My second bike is a sailing yacht."

I thought about him while pedaling over U. S. Highway 1 on the glassed-in pedestrian bridge — his generation and mine, the Baby Boomers and Generation Xers. The Boomers really did make a mess of things with their deficit spending, suburban sprawl, cannibalistic law suits and careerism *über alles*. Day after day, they sacrifice their lives to careers to afford an "upscale" lifestyle. It's a vicious circle. The lifestyle requires the career, the career requires the lifestyle. Expensive clothes and luxury cars have become necessities. It's a negative-sum game that isn't really working for anyone. The proof could be found on that six-lane highway directly below me — an endless stream of air-conditioned Mercedes, Jaguars and BMWs spewing exhaust and moving slower than a middle-aged jogger.

Not that I won't drive a car when necessary. In my shirt pocket is a little black book containing phone numbers of seven car rental agencies. Tucked in the back of the book are my driver's license and American Express card, garden green variety. People can call me a bicycle nerd if they like. But when I flash my little green card, I can match them, automotive ton for ton. And I can match them faster than you can say Hertz or Avis. Yes, I will rent a guzzler when I really need one. But when it's all over, my greatest satisfaction is strutting up to the counter and handing back the keys.

My overpass ramp descended into the stand of live oaks. The air was warm but not unpleasant. This time next month, it would be sweltering. I glided past the Museum of Science and up to Bayshore Drive, which was also jammed with traffic.

Sight of the James Deering Vizcaya estate and mansion fed my thoughts on ecology and the meaning of life. With minimal environmental impact, Deering had built an Italian mansion in the tropical hammock on the edge of Biscayne Bay. He filled it with art treasure and lived there, in harmony with nature — a century ago. Vizcaya survives as a museum. Its neighbor to the south is a hospital that always keeps expanding. Its neighbors to the north are an action movie hero and a pop icon. They would like to transform the area into a "gatehouse community".

While moving south on the bike path along Bayshore Drive, I kept mulling it over: Everyone wants to live in paradise, but few can live there without trashing it. Nine years ago I gave up on the idea of owning waterfront property and settled for the next best thing. I bought and restored a 36-foot Cheoy Lee ketch, the *Diogenes*. Before I met Rebecca, the sailing yacht was my home. Now, every free weekend, it is our summer house. We sail down to Elliott Key and anchor under the stars. It really isn't expensive, since I do my own maintenance work. I think that moving by the power of the wind and your mind is the best way of getting there . . .

There? I was almost *there* and still hadn't mentally rehearsed for the interview!

Well, maybe I didn't need any rehearsal for this "due diligence" job. I had been developing a dilettante knowledge of business, with an idea of getting a job in the pharmaceutical industry. I had watched the public television shows on Friday night. I had bought some used textbooks on business administration. I'd even surfed the business discussion groups on the Internet.

A couple of my old Mensa friends were becoming business administration gurus. So I occasionally tried out my knowledge on them. It went well until they got tired of listening to me and deliberately lost me in a thicket of jargon.

These recollections cheered me on as I passed slow-moving cars for the next 10 blocks of Bayshore Drive. Inspiration often comes to my rescue.

How many times, back at Swathmore, had I aced exams for which I was incompletely prepared?

ЛАТЕ VIЛT 3

I turned left off Bayshore Drive and descended to the Bay. Across an expanse of water, Dr. Westley's Faire Isle condominium complex came into view. His complex exemplified Commercial Man's approach to the environment. A few decades ago some developers filled in several acres of the Bay to make their own island, a quarter of a mile out. Behold their creation: five enormous high-rises, associated swimming pools, tennis courts, and clubhouse.

I pedaled along the private causeway and over the bridge, arriving at the little house where the residents' cars receive daily admiration from a pith-helmeted guard. I rode up to him and stated my business. He consulted a list, then told me, in Jamaican-accented tones, that I was among The Expected. I chained my bike to a convenient out-of-sight tree. I walked to the "motor entrance", past a couple of pimply faced teenagers who collected tips for racing luxury cars according to the unwritten rules of a social phenomenon called valet parking.

I tried to get into a businesslike state of mind.

Little had changed since my last visit two years ago: The elevators still played Muzak; the 43rd floor hallway was lined with the same indestructible sharkskin-like plastic material of hypnotic design; Dr. Westley's custom-made oaken door looked as dignified as ever. He opened it at my third bang of the heavy brass knocker and ushered me into his virtual English country house — 400 feet over Miami.

In the background, orchestral music was playing, reminding me of previous visits. Westley had always played records to furnish background music for our conversations. His actual purpose had been to indoctrinate me into classical music. Today it was an orchestral piece with military overtones. I guessed it was something by Sir Edward Elgar.

"Ben, so kind of you to come." Under bushy, white brows, his eyes quickly and politely scanned me. A subtle nod indicated that my clothing had passed muster — but just barely. Dr. Westley's own collar was open, revealing flaccid skin around his sternum. In a hushed voice, he said, "Remember, not a penny under twenty-four thousand dollars. Be a good choirboy — willing but not submissive, clear and confident, but neither brash nor brazen."

Westley was proud of having been the lead choirboy at Exeter Cathedral, 50-some years ago. He often used choirboy analogies as a means of offering fatherly advice.

He laid a soft, pudgy hand on my shoulder and led me through his dining room. It was elegantly appointed with a hardwood table, and a glass and wood cabinet displaying expensive crystal. He guided me in the direction of the music and into his living room, dominated by an oversized sofa and well-stuffed leather chairs.

"Brian, I would like to introduce my erstwhile protégé and present colleague, Dr. Benjamin Candidi." Westley's eyebrows twitched as he looked back at me. He was probably warning me not to say that I had not yet formally received my Ph.D.

Dr. Broadmoore slowly rose from the couch. Maybe it was the influence of the British march music, but Broadmoore seemed vaguely reminiscent of an English field officer in one of those 1950-1960s World War II movies. To a sound track of a muted orchestra playing variations on English folk songs, the film Colonel would speak softly and encouragingly to his assembled men. When he was done the trumpets would pick up the melody, and the assembled troops would climb into half-tracks and ride bravely into the sandstorm to do battle with *Feldmarschall* Rommel.

Broadmoore's physiognomy could command that type of respect. In fact, his whole body could be described by the simple word that was part of his name — broad. His broad hand completely encircled mine as we clasped, and his broad shoulders provided a solid platform as his muscular arm pumped mine. Broad chest and hips supplied weight and inertia. And his broad forehead crowned an open face, now bearing a friendly smile.

"I am so pleased to meet you, Dr. Candidi. Geoffrey has told me so much about you. Such a glowing description." Broadmoore's English accent was also broad, in marked contrast to Westley's carefully controlled Cambridge/Oxford variety. Broadmoore's large-boned, muscular vigor also set him apart from the more sedentary, pudgy, yet polished Westley. I wondered if Broadmoore was from northern England.

He shook hands with the standard formality practiced by old school Englishmen, leaning forward and extending his arm while shaking my hand, thus retaining the greatest distance between our centers of gravity. It would have been awkward to have stood this way for very long. As our hands disengaged, he rocked back onto his heels, regaining social equilibrium at a comfortable distance.

Dr. Westley interjected, "As I told you, Dr. Broadmoore is the founder of the Broadmoore Medical Holding Company. He is also the principal of B.M. Capital Company."

"I plead guilty on both counts," Broadmoore said, smiling to himself. He took a small step backwards, turning away from me slightly.

The music took on a more martial tone.

Westley continued with the introduction. "Brian and I share a number of delightful commonalities, not the least of which is having succeeded in making a living among the Americans for over thirty years."

Was I being called upon to bad-mouth my country? It was hard to think up an answer, but I did. I took a deep breath before replying, "Well, I would rather think that one would find the endeavor more gratifying in Boston than in Miami." My delivery would have been perfect, except that I didn't hit on the right intonation for the most important word: "rather". I winked at Broadmoore and raised eyebrows to Westley.

Westley's white jowls took on a slight blush. If he made a sarcastic reply, I would make some kind of joke about him having "gone native".

Broadmoore turned to Westley, clicked his tongue and said, "Bright lad, that."

I tried to move the conversation to friendlier territory. "You also attended the same public school, I understand."

"Yes, we had a number of delightful years together," Dr. Broadmoore replied.

Westley recovered quickly. "Of course, English public schools are not to be confused with the truly public schools of America." Westley was never satisfied, unless he had the upper hand.

The march ended in equestrian parade tempo. There were a few seconds of scratchy silence before the next cut. Then, the string section of the orchestra played in stately tempo the first notes of a vaguely familiar fanfare. The concert audience immediately joined in applause of recognition.

"*Rule Britannia*," volunteered Westley. "An auspicious moment. Calls for a touch of sherry." Brass and woodwinds answered the marching strings. Westley handed me a faded album cover. "Perhaps you will be interested."

On the front cover was a full orchestra posed in Royal Albert Hall. The back cover had a close-in action shot. A serious-looking conductor — perhaps Sir Edward Elgar himself — was directing from the podium. Between him and the first row of violins stood a wide-mouthed, full-bodied female vocalist. Her every ounce seemed dedicated to the musical moment that was captured on the grainy film.

I listened intently to the complicated, violin-dominated prelude, but I could not find a recognizable melody among the frills and curlicues. Dr. Westley padded over to his ancient mahogany-cabinetted phonograph and turned a large brown plastic dial to double the volume. Dr. Broadmoore took another backstep and quarter turn. I sensed that this was to be a solemn occasion and that further conversation would be inappropriate. Broadmoore sank into one end of the soft leather sofa, and I sat in the other.

A melody finally emerged. A tuba gathered the orchestra together for a rendering of the last four bars of an unmistakable chorus: Da, DAA-DAA, Da-Da-Da-Da, DAA-DAA, Da-DAAA!

With the orchestra dutifully marching behind at a majestic pace, the full-bodied and full-voiced alto instructed a hushed audience in the glory of Anglophilia:

"When Britain first, at Heav'n's command,
"Arose from out the azure main,
"Arose from out the azure main,
"This was the charter, the charter of the land,
"And guardian angels sang this strain —
"Rule, Britannia! Britannia rule the waves;
"Britons never, never, never will be slaves."

Broadmoore was looking down on his shoes and nodding his

head in rhythm with the melody. Obviously it would be just as important for me to listen appreciatively to their anthem as it would be to give the right answers in the upcoming interview. But the damn song seemed to drag on for ages. Each verse took a century. The culprit was those damned fanfares. They had one after each line of each verse! The different sections of the orchestra took turns playing the fanfares. Sometimes they paired up sections, like the strings and woodwinds. How many permutations would they go through?

The jacket notes indicated there were six verses. At the beginning of the third verse, Dr. Westley went to the kitchen. The fanfares in the third verse gave him plenty of time to organize a tray with three glasses and a bottle of sherry. In fact, the third verse left him ample time to return, open the bottle and pour the three glasses with great ceremony. The music's pace was so slow that we were able to punctuate the last beat of the third verse with a simultaneous clink of our glasses — which we did with great ceremony — toasting Miss Britannia's schoolmarmish admonition that Britons never, never, NEVER shall be slaves.

In the middle of the fourth verse, Dr. Westley appeared agitated, as if he wanted to sing along. The two Englishmen seemed to be in imperceptible rhythmic communication, although each was staring at a separate patch of the rug. Perhaps the song did rouse in them a "generous flame" (which haughty tyrants could not tame). For my part, I tried to act respectful and send out the right vibrations.

Meantime, I stole glances at Dr. Broadmoore, augmenting to my initial mental picture of him. He wore a finely woven white shirt and a tie of somber paisley design. His herringbone pants were obviously part of a suit. He sat in a relaxed posture with his stomach protruding a bit.

At last, the well-enunciated Anglo-Wagnerian contralto was triumphantly concluding the sixth verse. Now both Englishmen's chests were swelling with pride. The chorus sang in *fortissimo*:

"Rule, Britannia!
"Britannia rule the waves,
"Britons never, never, never, WILL BE SLAVES."

The audience responded with thunderous applause which the recording engineer skillfully ramped to a low level before cutting it

off. For a painfully long time the two Englishmen sat silent, immo-
bile and mesmerized. Would it be heresy to break the spell? Or were
they waiting for me to pay homage?

I mentally rehearsed a comment for a couple of seconds. "That
'Britannia rules the waves' has certainly been true for centuries — "

Dr. Westley snapped out of his trance, frowned and interjected,
" — although the lyric is actually 'Britannia *rule* the waves', which
is an exhortation, not a statement of fact."

"Quite," Dr. Broadmoore concurred.

Westley could be such an asshole, correcting me in front of his
friend. He continued, "The exhortation, penned by James Thomp-
son in 1740, did have its intended effect, until the Continental Bar-
barians put an end to the Empire."

He probably meant the Germans in World War II, but I wouldn't
say anything for fear of committing another *faux pas*. But I already
had: Dr. Westley leaned forward to refill my empty glass. His and
Broadmoore's were still half-full.

Dr. Westley went on, "I am sure you gentlemen have much to
discuss. For my part, I must retire to my study to work on my latest
article. It describes my noninvasive, magnetic resonance imaging
study of the mummified Madonna of Loulan — discovered in the
desert north of Tibet, south of Mongolia. Beautiful creature . . . exquisitely preserved in the desert sands. Superior to all the beauties
of ancient Egypt. And thirty-eight hundred years old, you know."

Glass in hand, Dr. Westley disappeared into his study to pursue his passions — leaving me alone to make my pitch to Dr.
Broadmoore.

4 PROPOſITION, TWENTY-FOUR THOUſAND

It took us a while to get into the job interview, since I kept waiting
for Broadmoore to make the first move. After a couple of exchanges
of meaningless small talk, I started asking him leading questions
about the companies he had founded.

"My *modus operandi* is no more complicated than that of an Arab trader at the bazaar: buy on the cheap and sell dearly. Of course, I deal in a better class of property — improved medications for the good of Mankind."

"At what stage do you buy?" I asked, slipping into a journalistic mode that has always worked well for me when dealing with things I knew absolutely nothing about.

"Usually at the lab bench stage where the commercial potential is relatively unevaluated. There the technology may be worth fifty thousand dollars. Sometimes at the idea stage where we have nothing but the inventor's enthusiasm. There the technology may be worth ten thousand dollars."

"At what stage do you sell the technologies?" I asked, hoping to set up an instructional rhythm and learn a lot in the process.

"We generally sell it as a clinically tested technology. We usually exit after a successful IND but before multicenter human testing."

I wasn't sure what an IND was, but I had some conception of the magnitude of "multicenter human testing". I asked, "How many patients do you test in the IND stage?"

"Sometimes as few as a dozen, sometimes as many as one hundred, depending on the drug and its application."

"And when you sell the technology after a successful IND, how much is it worth?"

"Between three million and hundred million, depending on the application."

I suppressed a whistle. "Buy it for hundred thousand and sell it for over a hundred million! That's some spread."

"Yes, but we have to invest heavily and attract investment capital."

"And you have been through this process three times already? Which drugs?"

"You may be familiar with *Hirudo-plastin,* our anticoagulant peptide from a South-Asian leech."

No, I hadn't heard about it, but I kept nodding.

"Or *Invertoprofen*, the nonsteroidal antiinflammatory agent? It has some specificity for glutamergic pain transmission."

I nodded. No, I hadn't heard about that, either.

"Or *Cardionostic*, the new cardiac infarct imaging kit. It works with gamma scintigraphy and highlights borderline ischemia."

This time I could nod my head with honesty. "Yes, I've heard quite a lot about that one."

I asked leading questions, and soon Broadmoore was speaking fondly of his companies. I thought of an English rose gardener as he rubbed his big hands together and lovingly described the process of nurturing the technology with the right mixture of chemical and animal tests, and getting it ready to exhibit to the FDA.

Then Broadmoore suddenly stiffened, as if waking up to the fact that I'd made him do all the talking. "I understand from Geoffrey that you are an expert on intracellular signalling." He wrinkled his brow. "He also described you as a bright lad who learns quickly everything put in front of him, which I cannot now doubt."

It was time to stop playing the interested student. "What is the intracellular signalling mechanism of the technology that you want evaluated?"

For an instant Broadmoore seemed surprised that I had matched his abruptness. He sank back slowly into the sofa. "BIOTECH Florida, the company for sale, has proposed three anticancer drugs. All three work by inhibiting of the so-called protein kinase C pathways."

Protein kinase (rhymes with "line-maze") C is an enzyme that tags other enzymes with a phosphate, speeding them up in the process. Runaway activity of protein kinase C can produce tumors. Compounds that inhibit protein kinase C can slow tumor growth. Actually it isn't that simple. There are other enzymes called "phosphatases" which remove the phosphate tags from enzymes and are also important in controlling runaway cell growth.

I knew the story from my general reading and was actually working on a related enzyme for my dissertation. I thought up a question that would show Broadmoore what I knew about this stuff. "Would it be down-regulation of protein kinase C activity, causing down-regulation of oncogene promotion factors?"

"Yes, I believe so, although you are taxing my memory," Broadmoore replied.

If that was true, then I was sure as hell qualified to be his scientific advisor. "Back in the lab I have a thick file on these mechanisms. I know of eleven kinds of protein kinase C . . . " I stopped myself, figuring my point had been made. Broadmoore said nothing. After a long silence, I asked, "How can I help you with respect to the three compounds and protein kinase C?"

"We have an unexpected opening in our due diligence team — evaluating the technology and the company. Our specific concerns relate to the mechanism of action of the three candidate drugs. We also require a determination of the appropriateness of the patent and an estimate of the likelihood of success in the planned clinical trials."

We sniffed each other's tails for a while. Broadmoore had no idea about oncogenes and protein kinase C, and I had no notion of how to conduct due diligence. And neither of us became the wiser.

"When will the effort start?" I asked

"Tomorrow morning."

I tried to show no surprise. But Broadmoore volunteered no explanation.

"Can you tell me about the business parameters?" I was making up my own terminology as I went along.

"Yes, I will explain them. But you must consider the financial details confidential. Some months ago we purchased an option to buy a ninety-percent interest in BIOTECH Florida for a lump-sum payment. The option agreement specifies the development contract and purchase agreement. If we exercise the option, sign the contract and purchase the technology, we will be obligated to take the three anticancer compounds through the FDA process for approval as new drugs. We have until Friday evening at 5:00 p.m. to complete the due diligence, at which time the contract and purchase agreement must be either signed or declined. The payment is also due at that time."

"So by Friday evening you have either plunk down a lot of money, or you pay nothing and walk away from it," I summarized, hoping the plain language wouldn't hurt.

"We have already paid some. Nine months ago we paid eighty thousand dollars for the option to buy the company. And we invested an equal amount of in-house effort."

The heat was really on. Broadmoore had already paid $160,000 just for the chance to buy BIOTECH. And he had until Friday to decide whether it was worth buying. Hell, he'd already thrown around enough money to keep me going for five years!

I needed to know how deeply they had looked into the science of the project. But I could not ask directly. I pussyfooted around the questions. "Would I be right in assuming that most of your in-house effort was directed toward scientific questions?"

"No, the majority of our expenditure was for legal expenses to frame the option agreement and to work out the details of the contract and purchase agreement."

I was having a hard time in believing what I was hearing; he'd spent nine months and $160,000 to have lawyers work out a contract to buy a pig in a poke.

Pussyfooting a step farther, I remarked, "The contract must specify a sizable investment."

"Yes, but before we go into that, I would appreciate your signing a confidentiality agreement."

What the hell was that?

Broadmoore bent over his side of the couch and pulled out a thin black leather attaché case. He opened it and handed me a duplicate pair of two-page documents, headed, "Confidentiality Agreement". I skimmed one quickly, acting like I'd signed a hundred of those things. The Agreement was full of legal gobbledygook about keeping each other's secrets for five years, except for what was already public information or could have been learned from other parties and so on. Interestingly Broadmoore had already entered my name at the top and had signed the second page. I pulled out my 49-cent ballpoint pen and signed both copies with a flourish, returning one to him.

My deft enactment of the signing ritual must have boosted Broadmoore's confidence. "Our ninety percent share will cost ten million dollars. Also, due upon signing, we must make a ten million dollar capital contribution for support of clinical trials of at least one of their three drugs in the cancer area. Thus, we will be investing twenty million dollars this coming Friday. Your job, Dr. Candidi, would be to render an opinion as to whether the existing scientific data on the three compounds are sufficient to warrant this level of expenditure."

The numbers were making my head spin. The $20 million was, of course, nonrefundable. You could repair a lot of freighters and broken drawbridges with that kind of money. Was I qualified to tell him to toss in $20 million after he had gambitted less than one percent of that sum? The meek and honest part of me wanted to tell him he'd better get someone else. But the mercenary part of me said that with this one lucky hunt I could bring home a year's supply of meat to Rebecca. But I would have to stalk carefully and make no false moves.

I worked hard at keeping a poker face. Broadmoore volunteered nothing more.

I took another pussyfooting step. "Is the technology based mainly on patents or trade secrets?"

"Some of both," Broadmoore equivocated. "Although the patent is the ultimate defense."

"And you will not require my services beyond these four days? I have an important commitment next Monday and for several days thereafter."

"No, it will end with a 'yes' or 'no' decision in four days."

"Under whom will I be working on your scientific due diligence team?" I asked.

"Under no one. You will be working by yourself."

I suppressed a gasp. I felt the blood draining from my face. The job was for a tugboat captain, not a deck hand. Quick, Ben. Ask a question. "Will I be starting from scratch?"

Broadmoore avoided my eyes. "No, you will be furnished with the notes of the previous ... errr ... from Dr. Yang; he left us in a bit of a lurch."

"Did he quit on you?"

"In effect, although one does not know what to expect when one visits Miami," Broadmoore said, staring at the coffee table.

Fat cat Englishmen have such fine linguistic devices to avoid questions. Well, no matter. It wouldn't do me any good to make him show his dirty laundry. There was only one thing left to say: "It sounds very interesting. I would like to take on the job."

"I am so pleased," Broadmoore said warmly. He clasped his big hands together, looked at me and smiled. Then he moved forward and refilled both our glasses with Dr. Westley's sherry. He lifted his glass to me and said, "Cheers."

I returned the toast. There was only one matter left to decide, and I couldn't bring it up myself — my pay. I sipped sherry and waited through a long amiable silence.

Broadmoore finally broke it. Frowning, he said, "There is only one matter which we must discuss."

I was determined to make no mistake here. "Yes?" I said with a smile.

"I must inquire as to your rate."

"Twenty-four thousand dollars for the whole project." The words came with a steady voice, and I didn't bat an eye.

"Well, I wouldn't think that . . . " He dropped both his voice and the sentence, as if expecting me to finish it.

I would wait him out. I would not bid against myself.

Broadmoore said nothing but viewed me obliquely. He was probably waiting for my resolve to weaken.

A ringing phone distracted us for a second. Westley apparently picked it up in his study on the third ring.

What could I do to get the ball rolling again? My picture of Broadmoore as a rose gardener was no help. Now he seemed more like a country squire. What did that make me? A simple farmer. I would be subservient but proud.

"Dr. Broadmoore, please be assured that I am not taking up your offer lightly. I will put into your service every bit of scientific knowledge, all of my critical abilities, and absolute loyalty, twenty-four-hours-a-day — until the job is done. As Dr. Westley has probably told you, I put myself into these projects wholeheartedly. My fee is only one-tenth of one percent of the twenty million dollars that's at stake. For working eighteen hours per day, my fee comes to around three hundred dollars per hour — the cost of a good lawyer. I hope that you will see fit to . . . " I dropped my voice and the sentence, copying Broadmoore's tactics.

Broadmoore looked at his crossed leg for a moment. He pulled on his sock. Then, his eyes darted up and caught mine quickly. "Yes, I agree. Twenty-four thousand it will be. I shall write you a retainer check for two thousand, the remainder to be paid after completion of your duties and upon receipt of your due diligence report."

He leaned toward me. Once again my hand was buried in his, and he was pumping my arm, this time heartily. Swiftly he turned, half-rose on one knee, and pulled two oversized metal briefcases from behind the sofa. They looked suitable for an Army major serving as a U.N. peacekeeper in Bosnia.

"The combination is fifteen aught three plus the last two digits of the present year. The fifteen aught three is easily remembered as the Ides of March."

"Thank you. Do the briefcases contain a list of the other members of your team?"

"I am not certain, but you will meet them tomorrow."

Broadmoore recited names of several team members faster than I could register them. He issued cursory instructions while writing my check. "The team meeting starts tomorrow with a breakfast at 8:30 a.m. Please appear at my suite, number twenty-eight thirty-two at the Biscayne Bay Marriott Hotel. Come with a suitcase packed for a four-day stay, suitably dressed." How was I to interpret the frown that accompanied his last two words? "The suite will be our command post. We have taken the liberty — that is, we will reserve a room for you."

The big brass knocker sounded, and Dr. Westley crossed the room to open the door. He returned with a medium-size brown bag stapled shut at the top. He handed it to Broadmoore.

"Sunshine State Messenger Service," Westley said, pronouncing the name, as if it were an oddity.

I said, "They support our only classical music station, WTMI." Neither Englishman responded.

Broadmoore extracted a blue box from the bag and opened it; then he reached in and pulled out a box of business cards. He opened the box and handed some to me.

It read, "Benjamin Candidi, Ph.D., B.M. Capital Company," followed by a Boston address, telephone and FAX number.

Westley was now wearing a prankish grin. "We took the liberty of initiating the process before receiving your formal acceptance."

Broadmoore kept a few cards and threw the remainder of the box into Dr. Westley's rampant-lion-embossed leather wastebasket. "You shouldn't be needing more cards, given the short duration of the assignment. We will present you to the other side as a team member of some three year's standing, living in Boston, of course. Other details of personal background you can ad-lib as necessary."

Westley was bouncing subtly on the balls of his feet. "You have your work cut out for you, as they say in this country."

Broadmoore stood up, indicating this was the end of the interview. As I got to my feet, he looked me over carefully — from head to toe — and shook his head. Turning to Dr. Westley, he said, "There is one remaining matter — sartorial."

Westley turned to me and chimed in, "And not in the sense of developing your sartorius muscles which must have already reached their full potential through your bicycle riding."

I smiled. Those guys were as well-coordinated as a pair of vaudeville comedians.

Dr. Westley frowned to indicate that the matter was not to be taken lightly. He ambled off to his study and returned with a slip of paper. "Please present yourself to this address within one-half hour." It was a men's clothing store. "Wu will be staying late for you. Please do everything that he says and ask no questions."

My preppy blue blazer didn't pass muster — after all.

Once more, Dr. Broadmoore looked me up and down. "Of course, this particular expense will be borne by Dr. Candidi." Dr. Westley nodded in affirmation.

Broadmoore set the phonograph to play the other side of the Elgar record, while Dr. Westley showed me to the door.

5 MONTEGO BAY CALLING

A few minutes before eleven, I was rolling my bike through the front door of our apartment. It was loaded like a pack mule with the two metal cases tied together and hanging in back like saddlebags. A shoebox was clamped in the rat-trap carrier. My attaché case rested on the handlebars, over which was draped a fancy zipper bag containing some very expensive clothes. I had presented myself at Barclay's Clothiers and had done what Mr. Wu, the tailor, had told me, spending $1,542.79 in the process.

It had been a considerable setback, letting them roll my green card for one and a half big ones, using up three-quarters of my retainer in the process. Whether a necessary business expense or not, it felt like a waste of money. Well, to get proper value for my money tomorrow, I had better rinse the formaldehyde from the shirts and air out the herringbone suit tonight. While I was doing it, the phone rang. I rushed to the living room and grabbed the receiver on the fourth ring, narrowly beating the answering machine.

"Will you accept charges for a call from Rebecca Levis from Montego Bay, Jamaica?"

"Yes, of course . . . Rebecca!"

"Ben, darling," she greeted in lilting soprano. "I've been feeling lonely and just had to talk to you."

"We must have been looking the same time at the moon. I feel that way too." Thank God for satellite transmission and for sending me the perfect girl.

"Is that what you've been doing? Looking at the moon? I've tried the last three evenings and only got the machine." She was sounding serious now. "You've been out all night, and there wasn't any answer at the lab, either." Then, she giggled. "I was afraid you'd broken faith with me and were looking at the moon with a Latin beauty."

Rebecca liked to tease me about my fluent Spanish and about the long-haired dictionaries I used to consult before meeting her three years ago. Rebecca's offering of repartee was like an invitation to dance. I sat on the floor between the sofa and coffee table.

"No, I'm satisfied with you, my *schoene maedl*, even if you are too far away to hug. And I couldn't dump you, my Jewish Joan of Arc, even if I wanted to. I have too much invested in you."

And this was quite true. And it wasn't only love I had invested. Over the last three years I had "lent" Rebecca about $40,000, which she applied to her medical school tuition. My intended marriage to her would be the easiest way to get the money back. Rebecca was very straight about it, though. She had insisted on drawing up a formal loan agreement which went as far as specifying a repayment schedule and lien against her future income. And she took out a life insurance policy, naming me as beneficiary. A very modern arrangement. She was quite sensible that way.

"Well, I hope you love me more than the bank, Ben. I've been getting more love letters from them than from you." She owed the bank about $110,000.

"That might be, darling. But mine's free love. And I don't charge interest."

"My hero!" she swooned in soprano, a humorous imitation of a melodrama heroine.

"But seriously, darling, I really miss you," I croaked.

"I wish you were here with me, Ben. It's so beautiful. But so darn lonely."

I was stretched out on the floor. I'd been leaning on one arm too long, and it had gone to sleep. I pushed myself up, leaned my back against the couch and stretched my legs under the coffee table. "Tell me about your moon and palm trees, and I'll tell you about mine," I crooned. It was a waning half-moon, I remembered.

"Oh, the moon is shining down on a lovesick maiden who's stuck on the top balcony of a thin, narrow hospital on the side of a little mountain. The moon's rays are casting deep shadows on the steep ravines on either side."

Rebecca has an inborn sense of poetry, and she really knows how to push my fantasy button. I gazed at her photo in the plastic holder that sat on top of a pile of magazines on the coffee table before me. She was standing behind the binnacle of the *Diogenes*, one hand on the wheel, the other gesturing toward the camera, her head slightly cocked, beaming a demonstrative and photogenic smile that seemed to say, "Look at me, I'm sailing Ben's boat." Her straight black hair blew in the wind.

My eyes moistened and blurred, merging the photographic image with the one permanently imprinted in my brain. Holographically, Rebecca's image seemed to move and speak in magical synchrony with her voice. Her dark green eyes twinkled, and her thin, fine-featured Mediterranean face dreamily and honestly delivered her romantic message. I found myself running my fingers through the telephone cord, involuntarily stroking her hair in anticipation of a kiss.

"Tell me more of the idealistic damsel in the tower," I moaned. I could almost see her silhouette on the tower, lit by the half-moon. The shadow danced with the graceful movements of her head and the gentle wiggle of her ponytail as she talked.

"When she looks down the side of the mountain toward the Caribbean, she sees nice little sailboats bobbing in the yacht club basin. And she wishes that her young prince will sail his *Diogenes* to her."

I could imagine Rebecca's svelte figure, leaning from a high balcony, her broad, angular hips pressed against the railing, her thin, shapely legs braced . . . My mind was wandering.

Summoning bravado, I quickly said, "Yes, darling. Sindbad would willingly sail around the whale-shaped island to make love under the stars with the maiden of his dreams." I remembered the magical evenings we had shared under the stars on the *Diogenes,* anchored off mangrove islands.

"Ben, every day the maiden sees an enormous metal bird swoop down along the coast. Maybe it could carry her to the young prince's arms." The Montego Bay airport was along the coast and behind a hill.

"Yes, please come home. The young prince is presenting a treatise before a coven of wizards next Monday morning at ten o'clock. The maiden's charm would be helpful."

"Oh, Ben," she sighed, abandoning our fairy tale. "I think they will let me off. But I can't be one hundred percent sure."

Our narrow band of microwaves fell silent for several seconds.

"What are you doing at the hospital tonight?" I asked.

"A little boy presented with malnutrition and a bloated stomach." Rebecca's poetic lilt was now replaced by a clinician monotone. "We treated him with *mebendazole*. He's been passing worms. It's so painful, I can't leave him." As I listened to her case report, I felt the waning of her professional detachment and the waxing of her compassion. Compassion for Mankind. I couldn't change it in her. It came from the same wellspring as her passion for me.

I pushed the coffee table away. Visions of Sindbad the Sailor and *Arabian Nights* evaporated as I imagined the gut-retching process taking place in the Jamaican hospital. Everyone knows that squalor is the grim reality for three-quarters of the world's population. But why had Rebecca chosen to share this hell? Why, after running the bloody four year gauntlet of medical school curriculum, had she now chosen to bury herself under a mound of Third World filth?

Once again, the microwaves were silent.

"Ben, why weren't you home tonight?"

"I was out buying one-thousand, five-hundred dollars worth of clothes under orders from Dr. Westley."

"What?"

"You heard it right. It is a necessary business expense. I'm doing a four-day consult job for one Dr. Brian Broadmoore, an old buddy of Dr. Westley. He already gave me a two-thousand retainer check." I was sounding like a businessman already.

"How much are you . . . going to get for this . . . four-day consulting job? Rebecca asked cautiously.

"Twenty-two thousand more, for a total to twenty-four thousand . . . to be applied to the Rebecca Lavis national debt."

"Aweseome!" She was genuinely impressed. "But did you have to go out and buy a new wardrobe?"

I steeled myself to play the gallant. "Direct orders from Dr. Westley to buy exactly what his Chinese tailor selected for me. Business meeting tomorrow morning with a lot of big muckety-mucks. It's a twenty-million dollar decision they want my advice on."

The thought of Westley and Broadmoore recalled the scenes where they take James Bond down to the armorer. "The one and a half Gs are for a power suit — the uniform of the mighty. This body armor is capable of deflecting the most powerful attack of logic that any business opponent can launch." Rebecca giggled. "Look. Tomorrow with this suit, I'll possess the power of Siegfried's Magic Cape. This will complete my apotheosis to the godlike status of executives and lawyers — the captains and pirates of industry."

Rebecca laughed. "But Ben — all that money for a suit?"

I kept it light. "To match the suit, you need the right Italian shirt. Can't have pockets. And then you need the right tie, and thin-soled shoes."

I told her about the job — as much as I knew.

"Ben, I hope that this job isn't going to be . . . clandestine . . . like the one you were doing for Dr. Westley when I met you . . . and you still can't tell me about it."

"No, the Miami company has to cooperate with us. They want us to buy them out."

"I'd be very careful, " she cautioned me.

"There's nothing to be careful about. I just have to do the job right."

"What happened to the man who was working the job before?"

"Dr. Broadmoore didn't say."

"Why do you think he is willing to pay so much money?"

"Dr. Westley told me that's what I should ask for, and I got Broadmoore to accept it." Rebecca said nothing. "Look, it's a twenty million dollar decision. You can buy a lot of *mebendazole* for that kind of money."

"Ben!"

"I'm sorry I said it that way. I'd just like to think that I'm getting the money because I'm worth it."

"Yes, Ben. You're the smartest person I know. And the most resourceful. But I've got a lot invested in you, too. A lot of love. Promise me you will be careful. They may have a hidden agenda."

I reassured her. I told her I loved her. We whispered sweet nothings. Whispers became moans. It was a long time before we hung up.

The conversation left me lonelier than before. But I had to get on with it.

I finished with the clothes and then unpacked the cases and spread two dozen file folders on the carpet in front of me. The files had nothing but material BIOTECH Florida had provided to promote the sale of their company. I didn't find any notes from my predecessor, Dr. Yang. And nothing was in any particular order.

I reached over to the coffee table, picked up the remote and pressed the button. I would let WTMI do it to me. By coincidence, they were playing the *Scheherazade Suite*. A violin filled the room with a solo passage — the haunting theme of the good-hearted enchantress who knew how to use her wit as well as beauty. Like Rebecca's spirit, the violin seemed to hover in the room . . .

Would the files contain any surprises?

I went back to organizing the little stacks of files on the floor. While Rimsky-Korsakov orchestrated a gathering storm, I began roping together this flotsam of financial statements, executive summaries, business plans, corporate organizational charts, patent and scientific reports. And by the time the stormy sea of strings was tossing Sindbad from the tops of towering waves, I had lashed all the flotsam together into a raft that would hold my weight. My craft was rickety, but there was no reason to panic.

The music calmed; the storm subsided. I pictured myself sailing the *Diogenes* on Biscayne Bay, gliding silently over an underwater garden of sponges containing anticancer drugs. That's what the patent claimed: three anticancer compounds derived from sponges growing in Biscayne Bay. I asked myself why would sponges contain such magical compounds? Maybe to keep the fish from eating them. The sponges would probably make the fish sick by upsetting their cellular metabolism. How could they do this? By flipping on and off little switches for cellular control.

I could imagine the three compounds inhibiting the protein kinase C, flipping off little switches in the cell and stopping tumor growth. The study of natural science opens your eyes to Nature's magic — the quickening magic which pairs maternal and paternal genes in a fertilized egg and marshals all the genes in a preprogrammed hierarchy which unfolds and evolves in a complicated process of genetic switching — a switching that gives some genes dominance over others, causing the dividing cells to become different from each other, so they can later cooperate. The magical process of genetic switching and cellular differentiation unfolds like a lotus blossom but infinitely more beautifully. It is a divine process, a billion times more complicated than the decompression of the most complicated computer program designed by man. It is a wonderful preprogrammed sequence that continues for months, until a perfect replica of the species is made — a child is born, free of webbed feet or cleft palate.

It is a lot easier to learn the Devil's tricks than to understand God. Cancer is easier to understand than cell differentiation. Just blow cigarette smoke over lung tissue for a couple decades. Take a 60 year-old Adam, go into his cells, and start flipping switches, until the gene hierarchy is messed up. Turn on the genes that are supposed to stay turned off. Metabolically insult the cell to keep it off guard. Put nitrites in the bladder and conjugated aromatics in the breast tissue. Feed the cells a lot of junk food. Do enough of this, a few cells will forget where they came from, and you'll be growing a tumor.

While going through the files, I had no trouble imagining that inhibiting protein kinase C might slow down some types of cancer. I had no trouble imagining how any one of BIOTECH Miami's three sponge compounds might do the trick. I had no trouble appreciating the theoretical diagram presented by the inventor. He speculated that the inhibition of protein kinase C turned off so-called "promoter" genes. Yes, I could imagine his three compounds shutting down the "oncogenes" responsible for cancer. But could it be that simple?

I knew from my own scientific reading that there were at least eleven different kinds of protein kinase C. Each kind had its own favorite targets. And Dr. Moon, the inventor, well, his patent didn't tell me anything about that.

Rimsky-Korsakov's magic was gone and so was his music. I turned off WTMI. I was thinking about this stuff like a critical scientist now. Dr. Moon didn't prove any particular antitumor mechanism in his patent. He just showed some protein kinase C inhibition in cellular homogenates. In essence, his presentation said, "I can shrink tumors in rats and mice. Take it or leave it."

My decision would be either "buy it" or "reject it", depending on how tough a judge I decided to be. If my judgement was too lenient, Broadmoore might waste his money; if my judgement was too harsh, Broadmoore might waste an opportunity.

I looked back at the chemistry of the basic compound called za-grionic acid. The chemical diagrams showed aliphatic and lactone rings, an aromatic residue, a carboxyl group, and a macrocyclic polya-mide ring. The three compounds — denoted by "alpha", "beta" and "gamma" — showed some minor variations in the side chains. But nothing jumped off the page to tell me that the compounds would cure cancer.

Moon presented some other diagrams, but they were just a lot of extraneous stuff — information on how the sponges synthesize the three anticancer compounds. He seemed to be hinting that the sponges might contain even more useful compounds.

I went back over everything, looking for solid facts. The patent did show that the three compounds could shrink mammary tumors in mice. And the mice survived, while their untreated cagemates died. And the compounds also shrank prostate tumors in rats. But the numbers of animals were small, and Dr. Moon did not give enough experimental detail to satisfy me. Meantime, the biggest question remained unanswered:

Would the three compounds be good drugs in humans? Would they work without side effects? Would they flip genetic switches on and off in healthy tissue? If so, they might actually cause cancer.

I was getting this stuff under control. I put away the patent and pulled out a thick scientific report that described experiments with large numbers of animals. In the middle of a lengthy critical analysis, I happened to glance at my watch.

Holy shit!

It was 1:30 in the morning, and I didn't have an answer to the most important question:

What in the hell is a due diligence audit?

6 DIVINING INSTANT EXPERTISE AFTER MIDNIGHT

How could I learn how to conduct a due diligence audit at this hour? After several moments of panic, the solution occurred to me. Old Mensa buddy Jim Grabowski could be my fairy godfather.

Jim was a mathematical genius with a rare talent for explaining things in layman's terms. Like me, he got serious about graduate studies a couple years ago and cut back on Mensa meetings. He was working on a Ph.D. dissertation titled, "Application of Chaos Theory to Price Fluctuations in the New York Stock Exchange". He figured that a big mutual fund would hire him to program their computers for stock market predictions. And he would make private use of the fluctuation data to optimize his own investments. I remembered a late night bull session we'd had a couple years ago, and I punched up his number on the phone immediately.

Jim picked up on the seventh ring with a deep, growly, "Yes."

He sounded like a hibernating bear routed from his cave. Come to think of it, the big boned, lantern-jawed, lumbering six-and-a-half footer really did resemble a bear — a friendly one, that is.

"Jim, I'm sorry to bother you so late but —"

"— but your bike's got a flat tire in the middle of Liberty City. You want me to drive in and extract you."

He said it half-humorously. He wouldn't stay mad for long.

"No, Jim. I've got a hot lead and need your advice."

"Love or money?"

"The important stuff — money. I've been hired for a due diligence job to evaluate a pharmaceutical technology — for a Boston company buying a small Miami firm. I need your help. Tomorrow morning I've got to be out there talking this stuff — and doing it —"

"Take it easy, Little Brother. Sure, old Jimbo can help you out. But first let's have a little on-your-hands-and-knees crawling." I imagined a smile coming to Jimbo's face. "At the last Mensa Society get-together you were making a diligent effort to convince us that you knew everything about the biotech industry."

I played along, answering in a quavering voice, "Oh, Mighty

and Venerated King of Siam, I crawl to you, belly on the floor, to beseech you."

"Enough. You may rise," Jim commanded in self-satisfied imitation of Yul Brynner's deep bass. "Quickly state your problem before you further anger me."

Continuing in oriental singsong, I said, "At the Mensa celebration of Winter Solstice, I overstated my case. Although I know much science, I don't know the first thing about due diligence. Please help me."

"Enough!" Jim thundered. "You can speak normally."

"The company has a protein kinase inhibitor obtained from marine sponges that might work for cancer — "

"Cut! Spare me the details. They are completely irrelevant — worse than useless." Now, Jimbo sounded different, like an overworked graduate assistant talking to a class of dim-witted freshmen. "Look, Ben. It's late; I'll give you the bottom line. You've got to look at the company and its drugs like a piece of property. Its only value is to bring in money. Now — repeat what I just said."

I repeated his words and briefly outlined the business terms.

"Good. Now forget you are buying a biotech company. Pretend you have an option to buy a hardware store for sixty thousand dollars. The store is supposed to have twenty thousand dollars worth of floor stock. It's your job to go down every aisle, tallying up the value of every piece of merchandise and making sure it comes to at least twenty thousand dollars. Suppose they claim they've got forty thousand dollars of value based on their volume of business. You go through their books and see if they're doing enough business to net you forty thousand dollars in two years or less. And don't listen to any baloney about long-term value or customer good will. You got me?"

"Yes."

"Now tell me what your biotech company has to sell."

"Three compounds that may cure breast and prostate cancer."

"And how much are they making per year on sales?" Jim asked skeptically.

"They don't have any yet. They have to get their drugs through the FDA first."

"They aren't even doing business yet?" He groaned. "That means the Miami company's a long shot. The Boston company will have to sink major bucks into it. How do you know they won't be putting the bucks into a shithole?"

"The three compounds work in rats and mice," I answered defensively.

"Sure, Ben. And saccharin gives rats cancer. How are you going to know the compounds work in people?"

"I'll have to ask these questions in my due diligence audit."

"Now you're starting to think. What proprietary rights does the Miami company have to the three compounds?"

"BIOTECH owns them."

"Incorrect, Ben. Nobody owns compounds."

"They have a patent."

"A patent is only a license to sue anyone who tries to use the compounds without permission. Are there any big companies out there playing the same game?"

"I don't know. Probably."

"Maybe the big boys have similar compounds. Maybe one of the big boys launches a related product first. Can you be sure that won't happen?"

"I don't know."

"Well, that's part of your scientific audit. Get them to show you. Now — how do you know if the patent is any good?"

"Well, the U.S. Patent Office granted it. They must have examined it carefully."

"Negative! The examiners have heavy caseloads. Maybe the examiner spent only two hours on it. Maybe someone else published the same idea ten years ago, and the inventor is keeping quiet about it."

"But," I protested, "they still have the patent — "

" — which could be overturned when the competition finds the previous work."

Jim's aggressive questioning made me uncomfortable. Like most people, I believe in progress. It's natural to suppose that most scientific discoveries can easily be transformed into new products.

"Thanks, Jim. I'll look into the patent very carefully. And I'll audit the rat and mouse data to make sure the experiments were really done properly."

"Right on, Ben. And now for the good news. Sometimes you can draw these things out for months. You make more money that way. But when you're talking with the Boston company don't get carried away with intellectual curiosity. Business meetings aren't like goddamn college seminar courses. In business, the question is whether the widget works the way they say it will. Hell! Why am I saying all these W's? You've got me waffling. I'm going back to sleep." (Click)

Okay, I got the point. He showed me how to think like a businessman. Tomorrow when I got together with Broadmoore's team I would hit on these points just like Jimbo hit on the hardware store for sale.

I went back to the documents to make a preliminary judgement. The picture was sketchy. Sure, I had some pieces of the jigsaw puzzle, but there was no proof that this technology was worth $20 million. Worse yet, I couldn't find any useful notes from my predecessor, only a few penciled-in notations here and there.

My second spurt of energy was expended. My brain was becoming tired and inefficient. I returned the files to their steel cases.

I ironed the shirts dry, put the suit into a valet pack and filled up a suitcase with everything I might need as a "business traveler to Miami". Then, I used my last ounce of conscious effort to set the alarm clock.

I dreamt about playing on a tightly knit team. Boy, was that dream all wrong!

ROSENCRANTZ OR GUILDENSTERN 7

First day on the project.

Nestled among my suitcase, my valet pack, the two steel cases and my worse-for-wear attaché case, I sat lightly, hoping the cab's sticky back seat upholstery would not smudge my power suit.

It was a straight shot east along Fourteenth Street, past ten blocks of broken bottles, wrecked automobiles, stray dogs and mom-and-pop convenience stores with small iron-barred windows. Poor, dilapidated, but historical Overtown was once a middle-class black neighborhood. But 30 years ago, it was sentenced to a fate worse

than death. Civil engineers had drawn and quartered it with the I-95/
I-836 interchange, condemning it to eternal life as a slum.

Ahead, high crowns of royal palms heralded Biscayne Boulevard, now undergoing another type of transformation. The once grand
boulevard is now dominated by the multistory Omni International
Mall and the tall hotel connected to it. Behind it, on Bayshore Drive,
stands the Marriott, doing its best to dwarf the 1896-vintage Trinity
Cathedral and doing a great job of blocking everyone's view of
the Bay. The hotel's entrance was somewhere within its four-
story parking garage. All sunlight disappeared as my cab entered the mouth of this concrete monster and accelerated up its
steep, black asphalt tongue.

One half-turn, a jarring stop, and we had reached the end of the
cavern. With strategically placed lights, brass rails and brass plates,
they were doing their best to suggest an elegant motor entrance.
The personnel did their best, too. Rushing up to my door came a
bellboy, clad in khaki shorts and shirt with lieutenant's epaulets on
his khaki shirt. I tried to maintain a proper businessman's mindset,
holding him off until I had paid and tipped the driver.

When Lieutenant Epaulet loaded my gear onto his brass cart,
one of the metal cases fell off. After inspecting it and finding no
dent, I headed for the oversized, perpetually revolving door. Gee, it
was good to put all that engine noise and exhaust behind me.

The lobby was done up in malachite-green marble. At the front
desk, I reconfirmed Broadmoore's suite number and learned that
room arrangements had already been made for me. No, they did not
need a signature. As I put away my 49-cent ballpoint, it occurred to
me that a high-paid consultant should be brandishing fancier writing implements.

With a glance, I ordered the bellhop to stay put. I popped into
the lobby gift shop and spent close to a $100 on a Cross pen and
mechanical pencil set. It was such a shame to throw away the empty
box. Almost threw away the pen and pencil, too. I'd forgotten that
my new Italian shirts didn't have pockets. Would have to train myself to reach for the suit's inside breast pocket from now on.

Waiting for the elevator, I was pleased with the subdued image
of the young businessman in the smoked-glass mirror. I was less
pleased with the image of the smirking bellboy. It was an appropriate prelude to a crazy morning.

Broadmoore's suite was at the end of a long narrow hallway on the 28th floor. His door was opened by a short, stocky woman with sandy hair cut in a Dutch girl style who introduced herself as Sally Max, Broadmoore's personal assistant. She reminded me of a gym teacher. She showed me to my room down the hall and told me the meeting would start in one-half hour. When I asked her the names of the other team members, she promised to get me their cards.

I used the half hour to open the steel cases and review the files. I stashed the patent and the rodent experiment files in my attaché case along with my laptop computer.

At nine o'clock I knocked on Broadmoore's door, ready to jump into a spirited discussion with him and his colleagues. When no one answered I let myself in. The room was an enormous suite with a conversation grouping of two large sofas and coffee table on one side. On the other side was a large dining table — which was not set up for breakfast. Broadmoore sat on the sofa with his back to the wall, conversing with five team members. Sally was nowhere to be found.

Broadmoore's eyes met mine for a split second, but then he glanced down at the floor and placed a hand on his mouth, as if to suppress a burp. Yes, he saw me. But he didn't want me to sit down with them.

The easiest way to handle such situations is to maintain an attitude of boredom. I moved to the window that was close to them and offered an excellent view of the inner Bay. A series of small residential islands, linked by the Venetian Causeway, stretched eastward to Miami Beach. The islands were named San Marco, San Marino, Dilido and Riva Alto, if I remembered correctly. Off to the right was the MacArthur Causeway which carries the heaviest traffic to Miami Beach. And beyond that was the cruise ship terminal and the Government Cut channel.

After ten minutes, the waiting seemed farcical. Broadmoore never gave me a cue to hop in. What was the name of the play about expectant waiting? *Rosencrantz and Guildenstern are Dead.* I remembered seriocomic Rosencrantz and Guildenstern — the poor actors granted an important role in the theater of the absurd, having to wait through half the play to get their cue and having no clue as to what they should be doing.

I remembered advice Westley had once given me, based on his experience as a cathedral choirboy — advice about reading nuance, knowing when to sing loudly and when to sing cautiously. So I studied their lingo, catching and analyzing fragments such as — "life insurance on the inventor" — "burn rate" — "tax consequences of alternative accounting methods" — "adequacy of the contract language" — "eventual exit strategies" — "improvements of the invention" — and "scope of definition of the technology".

I remembered Westley's story about how he and a fellow choirboy were caught in the middle of the processional, confused about whether to skip the third verse. They just hedged their words and muddled on through. Maybe that's what Broadmoore was doing this minute. He kept staring at the carpet. He was doing a lot of listening and very little discussing.

Well, I could make allowances for Broadmoore but not for Sally. Where in the hell was she? Why hadn't she brought me those guys' business cards? Because of her, I had to play a guessing game of who's who.

Well, the fellow next to Broadmoore with the three-piece suit and tasseled loafers had to be a lawyer. He sat comfortably and quietly, head nearly motionless, but eyes darting left and right behind large horn-rimmed glasses, following the conversation and noting everyone's response. Once the ball bounced to him. It was a question about the "adequacy of the contract language". He answered in fluent legalese, skillfully modulated in pitch, volume and rate. He had to be a lawyer.

Sitting in a chair at a right angle to Broadmoore, was a white-haired man with the long nose and gaunt face. He must have been in his late fifties. His knit tie and loose tweed jacket with leather elbow patches were certainly not power clothes. He couldn't be a businessman. He probably had some irreplaceable technical skill. Probably a professor. But "Tweedy" did nothing to help me refine my guess. He just sat there, restlessly fumbling with something in his inside jacket pocket.

Sitting on the couch across from Broadmoore was a guy about my age with the physique of a football player and a go-go attitude. He didn't say anything important, but everyone treated him with extraordinary respect. Sometimes he indicated agreement by making a fist and moving his arm like he was shifting gears in a car. Finally he grunted something about "underwriting" and an "IPO". I figured he would be responsible for selling stock when Broadmoore took the company public.

I doubted whether the guy sitting next to "Go-Go" could even catch a football. Narrow-spaced, wire-framed glasses made him look cross-eyed. But he had no trouble seeing the numbers on his tape-printing adding machine that sat on the coffee table. I guessed he was a financial specialist — most likely an accountant. I was sure — after he said something about "tax consequences".

But the last guy on the couch facing Broadmoore was an enigma. He was bald-headed, plump, short and probably in his mid-fifties. He spoke unctuously, gestured smoothly, and reminded me of a funeral director. A few minutes of eavesdropping informed me that he was an expert in "regulatory affairs" — which probably meant the FDA.

Finally Sally walked in. Broadmoore looked up at her, and she gestured with an open hand and spread fingers. "Five minutes," she said.

Now was the time to focus on Sally. She must have sensed my intentions as I moved to corner her. "Dr. Candidi, I'm sorry that I didn't have time to get the cards. Room service screwed up, and I had to go down and twist the manager's arm. If these guys don't get fed, we won't get anything done."

"I understand. If you are free now, could you tell me who will be my scientific liaison with BIOTECH?"

"I'm not sure. We should find out at the luncheon."

"Great. Yesterday Dr. Broadmoore gave me two steel cases that were supposed to contain all the scientific information. You know about the steel cases?"

"Yes, I know they were given to you."

"Well, they don't have any notes from Dr. Yang . . . you know . . . the due diligence scientist you were using before me."

"Yes?"

"Well, there should have been some notes. He did work on scientific due diligence, didn't he?"

"Yes."

"Well, as personal assistant to Dr. Broadmoore, did you see any of his work?"

"No. He liked to work by himself. And he reported directly to Dr. Broadmoore."

"Well, he must have reported something, and I'd like to see it."

"I'll see if notes from him are available," Sally said. A rap on the door rescued her from further questions. A white-jacketed man wheeled in an enormous cart. Sally got everyone's attention, announcing, "Breakfast has arrived."

Broadmoore rose and swept a small arc with a broad hand to indicate that everyone was to take his place at the table. Broadmoore sat at the head. The presumptive lawyer and the accountant sat nearest to him, then the football financial guy and the smooth-headed "regulatory affairs" expert. This left a couple of places for Sally and the tweedy professor on the opposite end of the table. I took the last empty chair. It was at the end with an excellent view of Broadmoore.

The waiter brought plates under silver domes. Sally had apparently taken everyone's special order, since the waiter called out various combinations of eggs, ham, bacon, hominy grits and pancakes, and people claimed them. I took an unclaimed order of scrambled eggs and ham.

When Sally ordered for Broadmoore she must have said to "supersize it". His plate was heaped with enormous quantities of everything. I guess a stout mesomorph from the North Country needs his hearty breakfast. Before taking his first bite, Dr. Broadmoore surprised us all.

8 BEN CANDIDI — FRONT AND CENTER

Dr. Broadmoore held up a stubby finger to get everyone's attention. "As we are all assembled, may I now introduce Ben Candidi, Doctor of Science, who may not be known to many of you. He has served me well as a scientific consultant for some time now." So Broadmoore wasn't above bullshitting his own team. He pulled my business cards from the inner breast pocket of his jacket and passed them around. "Please treat him as an essential member of our team."

They all looked at me with smiling curiosity.

Broadmoore called from across the table, "Ben, I trust that you had a good flight down this morning."

"Yes," I called back. "Thank you, although the departure was on the early side."

Broadmoore introduced all the members of his team. He stated their specialties and rattled off names faster than I could stretch to shake their hands. There was no chance of memorizing their names. But my guesses about their specialties proved correct. "Go-Go" was a stock seller. "Tweedy" was an oncologist associated with the Dana Farber Cancer Center in Boston. Unctuous "Baldy" was from a "regulatory affairs" company in "suburban Maryland" — his expertise was obtaining approvals for new drugs from the FDA.

As I shook the last hand and returned to my place, Broadmoore informed the group: "Ben is our specialist for scientific due diligence."

Now all eyes were focused on me. I tried my confident smile.

After a couple second's silence, Broadmoore said, "Ben, you have the situation well in hand, do you not?"

To be truthful, I didn't have the vaguest notion. But I worked up the necessary bravado. "I can't wait to get started down here."

Broadmoore continued, "Perhaps Miss Max has already told you, our first event will be the luncheon, for which we will muster at the motor entrance at 11:15." Then, he turned to the accountant and muttered something. A couple seconds later, and he was engrossed in muted conversation with the accountant and lawyer.

It was puzzling as hell. Broadmoore introduced me to his team as a heavy hitter, but he kept me out of the action like he was dealing with a rookie. And the other team members treated me like I was straight from the farm team.

The silver-haired oncologist locked the FDA expert into a conversation which excluded me. He wanted to know something about FDA policy on "compassionate use" of some class of cancer drugs. The FDA expert turned super-unctuous, slipping from the grip of Tweedy's questions like a greased pig. He managed to get through most of breakfast without giving Tweedy a single straight answer.

The more I observed this meeting, the stranger it seemed.

How peculiar that Broadmoore brought me in so late in the game and gave me so little advice on how to play it. I didn't know Broadmoore well enough to press him, but I could sure as hell pull the information out of Sally. I caught her eye. "Regarding my predecessor, Dr. Yang. I understand he was working here last week. Did you come down with him?"

"No."

"I'd really like to get hold of his notes."

"There aren't any," Sally replied.

"How do you know?"

"I asked Dr. Broadmoore, just as we were sitting down."

"Who did Dr. Yang report to at your company, besides Dr. Broadmoore?"

"I don't think he talked to anyone else."

"Didn't he call back to Boston, while he was working here in Miami?" I persisted.

"He just called Dr. Broadmoore's secretary with instructions, like 'Look up this' or 'FEDEX that down.'"

"I find it hard to believe that he didn't make any notes. Did he use a yellow tablet or a laptop computer?"

"Laptop."

"Did it belong to him or to the company?"

"To him, I think."

Hell! The files were more talkative than Sally. I would concentrate on getting information from other team members.

Broadmoore finished breakfast and moved back to the sofa.

The lawyer and accountant quickly followed him. The FDA expert excused himself from Tweedy, who was nursing a second cup of coffee. Now was my chance to pounce. I caught Tweedy's eye and said, "I guess you are in charge of looking into the clinical trials."

"That is correct."

"What do you think of protein kinase C as a target for tumor regression?"

He blinked like I'd just trained a spotlight on him. He reached into his breast pocket and pulled out a cellular phone. After starring at it for a moment, he put it back. "It will prove a good target, if the clinical trials show tumor regression."

A fine answer: She'll be coming around the mountain when she comes.

Now Tweedy was fumbling with his phone like he was going to punch in numbers. Well, he wouldn't shake me loose that easily.

"In the most optimistic case, given the present circumstances, when would you estimate the earliest date for commencement of clinical trials?"

He answered me with a mouthful of jargon. "Clinical trials could be planned within five months of completion of GLP animal studies, provided the FDA doesn't put the IND on clinical hold."

While I was thinking up a question that would make him define "GLP", "IND", and "clinical hold", Tweedy started punching numbers on his portable phone. Soon he was talking to his head nurse about the status of his patients. I had to give up on him.

I snagged the lawyer when he drew near to pour another cup of coffee. "I was interested in your conversation with Dr. Broadmoore about whether the definition of the technology might be too narrow. How would you determine that for the present case?"

The lawyer wrinkled his forehead, as if the answer was self-evident. "It would be too narrow if the license does not include the complete medically useful scope of the invention."

"Has anyone within our company defined the medically useful scope of the invention?" I asked.

"Well, you must confer with the medical experts for that," he said, glancing at Tweedy who was still on the phone. The lawyer retreated to the sofa before I could say another word. Damn! Every team member had managed to evade me.

Sure, Jimbo warned me last night that this meeting would not be as easy as a goddamn college seminar course. But these guys weren't pulling together as a team. Okay, I would play along with this game of crazy jargon, motivated by the satisfaction of making $3,000 in a single morning. But at the end of the four days, a $20 million decision had to be made, and it had to be based on our teamwork.

The honest part of me had already deserted my body and was looking down on me from the opposite corner of the room. There stood Ben Candidi, phony expert and genuine fool, playing Rosencrantz or Guildenstern (soon he would have to choose one or the other), improvising without script, without so much as a plot outline, occupying center stage while action was brewing in the wings. There stood Ben, succumbing to civilization's ultimate terror — clueless anticipation.

After staring out the window for some time, I managed to creep back into my own skin. I turned around just in time to see the accountant leave. The oncologist was gone. So were the FDA expert and the lawyer. And Broadmoore was gone, presumably to his adjoining room, because the connecting door was shut. Only Sally and the stock seller were left. He was studying a copy of *Sports Illus-*

trated — the Swimsuit Edition. Sally's face was buried in the phone. She was probably calling room service to pick up the dirty dishes.

We had half an hour to kill. There was no use staying here and compounding my frustration. I wandered, briefcase in hand, around the hotel complex. I took a look in the restaurant on the second floor. It also had a nice view of the inner Bay. Wistfully I asked myself if we weren't all Rosencrantz and Guildensterns.

As I rode the escalators up and down between the first and third floors, I mentally replayed the last hour. If Broadmoore wasn't leading that discussion, then who was? No one.

I replayed the mental tape, this time with the audio channel turned off. Do you see a team there, Ben? No, you see a baseball team being warmed up by an indecisive pitcher. Yes, Broadmoore was always the first to throw the ball. When the ball went to the tweedy oncologist he always tossed it to the FDA expert who kept it for a long time and didn't do anything with it.

When Broadmoore threw the ball to the accountant, the guy became nervous and started punching numbers on his machine. Then the stock seller said "rah-rah" and made his gearshift gesture.

Come to think of it, the baseball analogy wasn't bad. The lawyer played shortstop, running to scoop up slow grounders and snapping the ball to a teammate. When out of play his eyes tracked the ball. They were quick eyes that always darted to pick up Broadmoore's reaction.

And what did I look like? A heavy hitter or a rookie straight from the farm team?

While walking down a hallway past a group of meeting rooms, I noticed they bore the names of the small residential islands I'd viewed from Broadmoore's window. And they were all arranged in the right order. Well, I thought, at least something went right this morning.

I returned to the third floor and walked past the ballrooms to a hallway. I passed the door to the parking garage and on toward the neighboring Grand Doubletree Hotel.

I guessed the collection of guys in Broadmoore's suite was just a pickup team. And Broadmoore had already spent $160,000 on them — his "in-house effort". And most of that was probably billed by the lawyer who wouldn't talk to me. The oncologist and FDA expert were obviously paid consultants. The accountant was probably paid by the day. Sally was probably the only full-time employee.

Maybe she didn't bring me their cards, because Broadmoore never had any printed!

It was becoming clear: B.M. Capital, Inc. was one of those "virtual companies" you sometimes read about in the financial pages of newspapers — a motley crew of hired experts assembled in one place to do a specific job on a shoestring. My teammates and I were six characters in search of an author. I'd play the part as well as I could. But I wouldn't let myself suffer any existential angst. Broadmoore wasn't paying me enough to feel that.

I still had time to spare. I wandered to the Doubletree and descended to a closed concourse of shops leading toward the hotel's marina. The occasional roar of a Cigarette boat hauling ass down the channel was the strongest reminder that we were close to the Bay. One shop specialized in expensive Chinese porcelain. Behind plate glass, a large pressed brass mural framed the shop's entrance. On one side stood a Siamese prince in bas relief. On the other side stood a matching princess. She wore a Thai temple headdress. Ornate chainwork hung from her shoulders and hips. Between two nicely rounded breasts, her hands were pressed together in prayer. At three-quarters of life size, she was quite alluring. But she would be too expensive for me to take home.

A few minutes remained before it would be time to go back and start thinking about the game.

Sitting cross-legged in a showcase was a six-inch brass Hindu goddess. Now she was within my budget. Her 18 arms seemed to minister to all of life's tasks as well as its erotic delights. Old Man Westley could probably tell me that the gestures symbolized food preparation, sewing, et cetera. I wondered what he would say about the little brass statue dancing next to her, a sexy six-armed, six-legged goddess. He'd probably tell me she wasn't meant to be sexy at all. He'd probably say it was all perfectly rational in the Hindu scheme of things — like manly Shiva and feminine Parvati on the next shelf, contemplating each other's eyes.

A glance at a French antique clock told me it was time to go.

Onward into battle as part of a motley squad of French Foreign Legionnaires!

9 DIPLOMATIC LUNCHEON

My initial impression of Broadmoore as an English Army officer in a World War II film took over again as he huddled us together in the Marriott's motor entrance. With an earnest face, he offered us quiet words of encouragement for our "forthcoming engagement". It was hard to hear him over the engine noise. His words to me were curious:

"Ben, my bright lad, please do your best to get to the bottom of it."

We mounted up to ride into a $20 million battle. Our armored personnel carriers were a couple of limousines, super-stretched to the point of obscenity. I climbed into the second one, together with Sally and the oncologist. He sat in the back, facing forward, and we sat sideways on the lounge, facing a well-equipped bar. Tweedy didn't speak with Sally, so none of us spoke.

The chauffeur drove south, skillfully negotiating the four-wheeled cylinder through downtown traffic. We crossed the bridge over the Miami River without scraping bottom and glided into that deep palm-lined boulevard known as Brickell Avenue. Sidewalks and broad stairways of the skyscrapers rising on both sides give one the feeling of driving in a groove.

Soon our trip came to an end as we pulled into the steep, elevated semicircular motor entrance of a large bank building in the middle of the Financial District. No one observed our arrival except the doormen. That suited me just fine. I didn't want anyone to see me step out of a limo equipped with bar, television, sound system and electric "moon roof". The limo was just right for delivering Madonna and Rambo wannabe's to the senior prom.

The luncheon started out as disorganized as Broadmoore's breakfast meeting. It was in an enormous boardroom on the 16th floor, loaned for the occasion by a local bank. Linen-draped tables were set up in the form of a "T" and were marked with placecards. Two groups didn't know each other and were slow to mix. At a table by the entrance, people were picking up their preprinted nametags. There was none for me. I just picked up an adhesive "Hello, My Name IS" tag, filled it in with big letters, and stuck it to my thousand dollar suit. I grabbed a Perrier from the refreshment table, poured it into a glass and strolled around, eventually taking station by the large window with an interesting view of the Bay.

A half-bald, short, stubby but vigorous man walked up to Broadmoore and shook his hand. I guessed he was C. C. King, who, I had learned, was president of BIOTECH. Curiously, he wasn't wearing power clothes, just a light blue polyester sports jacket.

Across the room, a member of the BIOTECH team was catching glances of me: a sleek-skinned, buxom blond in her early thirties. I decided against trying to talk to her because she wouldn't hold my gaze.

Feeling scrutinized, I strolled around the room, pretending to study artwork on the wall but actually checking out people's tags for name and affiliation. Besides company people, there were a lot of academics and university types. Funny that I didn't see a single name tag that said BIOTECH. But I saw many tags with "King Construction". Was C. C. King more specialized in construction than biotechnology?

Moving slowly through a crowded room reading name tags and picking up bits of conversation is not a bad way to get oriented. Our lawyer's preprinted name tag identified him as Elkins. He was talking with a middle-aged executive from King Construction. The guy was telling Elkins that a courier system like FEDEX had been in use in Bombay, India, for decades. The customers are wives who use the system to deliver fresh, home-made lunch to their businessman or bureaucrat husbands. Every morning, tens of thousands of wicker baskets are picked up and routed by train, streetcar or bus to the central clearinghouse, from which they are routed and delivered to the husband's offices. Every afternoon, the process is reversed. The wicker basket arrives home before the husband.

Elkins seemed an adroit conversationalist, interjecting questions about the Bombay Bicycle Club, Bombay Sapphire gin and trained mongooses. His eyes moved slyly behind his tortoiseshell glasses — and picked up on me. But he made no effort to bring me into the conversation as I strolled by.

A few steps away, Broadmoore was conversing with a curly-haired, middle-aged man whose name tag said Florida Atlantic University. He wore a wrinkled dark gray business suit and thick rubber-soled shoes. He actually seemed a kindred spirit. At this feet was a battered, old-style, top-loading, brown briefcase. I would have taken him for a history professor.

He was giving Broadmoore a Northerner's view of Florida sociology and economics. "The trouble with Florida . . . no, I should say the trouble with Tallahassee . . . is its redneck mentality. It started in the late 18th century when the Georgians migrated south with their hogs." While talking, he had been hugging himself at the elbows and staring at the floor. Now he frowned and jutted his head forward. "Later, they found they could throw up a motel as easily as they could throw up a pigpen."

Broadmoore smiled and said he agreed. It was more honorable to raise pastured cattle.

I caught Broadmoore's eye. He glanced away quickly and shook his head. He turned to face his conversation partner squarely and presented his backside to me.

So Broadmoore wasn't ready to take the wraps off "Dr." Ben Candidi! I was either his secret weapon or his pariah. I moved several steps back and pretended to be studying artwork on the wall.

The history prof look-alike expanded on his thesis. "In the 1940s and 1950s, they thought it was good enough to put a caged alligator at every gas station. Of course, now Florida has all sorts of attractions. And how the State Government in Tallahassee keeps track of their gate receipts! Did you know that the Department of Tourism is the only State agency that has the ear of both the governor and the legislature? When a black boy kills a German tourist and the Hamburg press starts writing that the beaches are safer in Jamaica, those good ol' boys practically send out a lynch mob."

Enjoying himself immensely, Broadmoore remained oblivious to me. "It does seem foolish to vacation where one can be held up and killed."

The university man went on, telling how Miami's Executive Rent-a-Car was placing satellite navigation ("GPS") systems in their cars so the tourist could know their location within 50 feet. The computer screen projects a little road map, with warning zones for bad neighborhoods; the cars have panic buttons to call a computerized rent-a-cop to the rescue.

Other conversations sampled around the room were less interesting: Bostonian inquiries about tropical plants and cruise ship schedules.

Caterers set up a smorgasbord along the wall. I hit the buffet after everyone was seated. Only one unassigned place was left. I asked permission before taking it. The woman nodded and smiled; the man on the left grunted his consent. He was middle-aged and looked like a manager for a string of middleweight boxing contenders. The red silk handkerchief fluffing from his breast pocket must have been responsible for the impression.

My table-mate on the right had enough charm for both of them. She laughed invitingly, after I introduced myself with an inane quip. She reacted to it with a gentle laugh and wide-eyed smile. Movement of jet black irises over a dark interior is usually hard to detect, but it felt like her eyes were sending me infrared signals.

Ahma Sharma said she was the accountant for BIOTECH but spent most of her time working for King Construction Company. When I asked her what fraction of her time she spent on BIOTECH, the man on my left grunted. Ahma hesitated for a second, then gave me an ambiguous answer. I wondered whether BIOTECH was a virtual company just like Broadmoore's company.

There was no question that Ahma Sharma viewed herself as a competent professional. She wore a dark linen business suit which complemented her black eyes and brown skin — an aesthetic statement in black and brown. Her face had a picturebook beauty with widely spaced eyes, thin angular nose and large forehead framed by flowing black hair. In half-profile, she reminded me of an illustration in a book of Hindu love poetry. She said she came from Trinidad.

I shifted my attention to the man on my left. His stick-on name tag identified him as Tony Altino and did not list a company. He was about my height and resembled me in certain features: Curly black hair, a dark complexion and a thin athletic figure. But hopefully I wouldn't slouch in my chair, as he did, when I reached my late fifties.

I tried to find out something about him. "Are you involved in BIOTECH, Mr. Altino?"

"Yes," he mumbled and returned his attention to his plate.

I tried to sound harmless, while pressing on. "Unfortunately I don't have a roster of the company. I am working hard to find out who I should be talking to." I tried to sound casual. "What is your role in the company?"

"Financial input. And enforcing logistics." He spoke like a guy from South Philly. "I keep Bud King's money from walking away."

Altino never went to Swarthmore, that was for sure.

"That's a type of an accounting responsibility," I said and glanced to my right to include Ahma Sharma. She looked away.

Tony Altino replied, "Accounting is what they do in offices. Keeping track of money at the job site is something else. That's where it walks away the fastest." He glanced at me, as if to check whether I was listening. "You see, money's like tools. Out on the job site tools can sprout legs and walk away. You'd be surprised how much money you can save by sniffing around your own job site."

Financial logistics and enforcing seemed a curious job description for a biotechnology company.

"Have you been with BIOTECH long?" I asked.

"Construction."

"Construction?"

"Yes, construction. I've been with Bud in the construction business from the beginning."

"Bud?"

"Yeah, Bud King," he answered impatiently. "The guy sitting up front in the blue jacket. He's sitting right next to your head guy."

"Right. I just didn't recognize his first name."

"Bud owns King Construction. He's also the guy that took over BIOTECH and put it on its feet. Wasn't nothing before he picked it up." He frowned and glanced at me again. "You make it in construction, you can make it in anything."

I nodded, hoping the gesture would pass for agreement.

10 REGAL PERFORMANCE

At the front table, C. C. "Bud" King clanged a glass, then stood up to play master of ceremonies. Viewed frontally, his forehead seemed all the wider under his bald crown. The close trim of the remaining hair must have been responsible for this impression.

"For those of you who don't know me, I'm Bud King. I would

like to welcome Dr. Broadmoore to Miami." King's primary tone was deep and throaty, but the words seemed to increase in pitch after squeezing through his closely set jaws. "I hope you Boston folk like it down here. Hope we're making you feel at home." The word "Boston" squeezed through with a definite "ahw", like in "Noo Yahwk". Was that where he came from? "Lots of you have already worked together — if you call talking on the phone and faxing papers work."

His quip produced mild laughter. He relaxed his mandibulars, producing a bulldog grin, and acknowledged the audience reaction with a short, right-armed jab. He smiled and pressed on. "In my thirty-eight years in business — it's thirty-eight, if you start counting the yard service I started to make money for college when I was thirteen — in my thirty-eight years, it's been a hard climb."

King delivered his anecdotes like they were part of an acceptance speech at an awards ceremony. Broadmoore's lawyer must have had similar thoughts; he was shaking his head.

"But the one thing that I learned is that the only way you can climb is when you've got a good team of people climbing with you. You need to know how to work together. You can't make fifteen million dollars mowing grass by yourself." He clenched a fist and laid in a pause for emphasis. "The grass don't grow that fast in Miami. And Coral Gables got laws against runnin' a mower past nine o'clock at night."

The audience responded with a full round of laughter. King looked slyly to the left and right. "I found that out the hard way. Coral Gables got laws against everything. But no one was going to throw a hard-working kid in the slammer."

Maybe both his parents came from New York.

He smiled as he got to the punch line, then let his arms go slack. His last quip didn't produce general applause. For a second I felt sorry for him, standing there like an ape, muscular arms dangling at his sides. He paused a couple seconds, took stock of the audience, then quickly glanced to the ceiling.

His eyes returned to us an instant later. "The trouble with Miamians is they won't invest in their own place. They don't believe in their own stuff. Not even when there's a cure for cancer." He frowned. "We had it in our family — like every family does — eventually."

Then the frown disappeared. He smiled, as if he had just thought of something. "But they believe in their own stuff up in Boston. Up there people have been making fine silverware for a couple hundred years. Lot of great discoveries at Harvard in the last couple hundred years. And, hell, it wasn't that many years ago that down here in Florida we was still up to our belts in alligators, trying to drain the swamp."

He illustrated the notion with a two-handed gesture of pulling up his breeches. Everyone laughed heartily. Some were laughing with him; some, I guessed, were laughing at him. Broadmoore laughed so hard he shook. He leaned back from the table, as if needing more room to breathe. Our lawyer Elkins laughed, though shaking his head. Our accountant seemed to be laughing through his sinuses, as he pulled out a spotless white handkerchief and polished his glasses. Broadmoore's stock seller was sharing a visceral laugh with the sleek-skinned blond who was sitting next to him. The stock seller was a real go-go guy, making time with her already.

"But I didn't get up here to convince you not to do business in Miami. Mayor García would get mad about that. The reason I got up here is to introduce my team."

Like a football coach calling out his star players, King introduced a lawyer, a financial analyst and some more business types. I guessed they were all working primarily for King Construction. With special emphasis, King introduced the green-eyed blond: "Dr. Cheryl North — my right-hand scientific expert. I put Cheryl onto that invention, and she's taking it through the roof."

I wasn't the only one who took a quick second look at the attractive green-eyed lady in her late twenties or early thirties. Seeming to enjoy the attention, she smiled confidently at everyone. I would probably be dealing with her.

After a long pause, Bud King introduced Ahma Sharma, using a pun. "She works like a charm on our company's balance sheets." Then, he grinned and gestured with an upraised open palm to indicate Tony Altino sitting next to me. "Tony's been my friend and partner since we were knee-high to a Palmetto bug.

"And that's it for the introductions," King concluded.

Funny way to present a biotechnology company, calling out the names of lawyers, "analysts", accountants, and boyhood chums who worked for a construction company. King didn't say anything about the three anticancer drugs. And except for introducing Dr. North, he hadn't said anything about the science behind the company.

Where in the hell was the inventor — the guy who made the whole thing possible — the guy who furnished the very reason for all these high-salaried people to be sitting together? The name on the patent was Dr. Tehong Moon — probably Korean and possibly Chinese. And didn't the company have other scientists and technicians?

King sat down and gestured to Dr. Broadmoore with an upturned palm.

Broadmoore did not get up. He looked toward King and started speaking in a voice just loud enough to carry through the room. "I will not attempt anything droll; you are a tough act to follow. I would be afraid of getting mired down. Regarding our cities, Boston cannot match Miami's rate of population growth. This is most probably due to the inclement weather which we must endure six months per year." Now Broadmoore addressed the rest of us, considering us with a diffuse gaze as one might contemplate a forest in a fog. "We do grow some enormous potholes in the winter. Fortunately they do not hinder our communication with Boston's several illustrious universities."

It was a dry performance. Broadmoore's only hints of special emphasis were readable from a slight elevation of eyebrows and an occasional bob of the head. I was pretty sure he didn't like King.

"And when we cannot produce our own pharmaceutical breakthroughs, we are willing to buy them from others. Just as the Yankee Traders once set sail to the tropics to buy pearls, we have embarked for Miami to sample the medicinal value of your sponges."

Broadmoore's forthright elocution lacked the elegance of old Dr. Westley's, but the figure he cut was every inch a Britisher. As for the effect of his words on most of the audience, he might as well have been speaking to those trees in the fog. Well, there was one kindred spirit among the trees: The history prof was lapping up every word of it.

I sensed that Broadmoore's purpose was to set a different tone and to distance himself from King. If true, King seemed none the wiser.

Broadmoore was now smiling directly at members of the audience. Was he stoking a warm smile to burn off the fog? "I would now like to introduce the key personnel of B.M. Capital."

He introduced us with a nod of the head. As if rehearsed, each of us nodded back politely with no more emphasis than necessary to indicate our identity. Well, almost everyone did it right: Our stock seller grinned and made a gesture over his head like he was going to throw a football.

Broadmoore announced me by saying, "And last, but by no means least illustrious, I introduce Dr. Benjamin Candidi, our scientific evaluator." His emphasis brought all eyes on me. I tried hard to look the part.

The next event was an appearance by the Honorable Raul García, Mayor Miami. King half embraced him at one shoulder and quietly introduced him to Broadmoore and to the other guests occupying the front table. Then Mayor García made a short speech, telling us how the biotech industry was good because it brought money into the community and recited all the neighborhoods that would benefit. The speech would have been equally appropriate for welcoming the cruise ship industry, casino gambling — or even money laundering, if it were legalized some day. But he struck a resonance with the audience using his predecessor's concept of "tropical sophistication". He showed good coordination between word and gesture, and maintained an air of urbanity throughout the talk. At the end, he received a standing ovation from everyone except Broadmoore, who feigned difficulty moving his chair. King made a big deal of schmoozing with the mayor while showing him the way out.

Our joint venture now had the mayor's official blessing, Latin style.

King smiled and shook his head. "Talk about a tough act to follow!" He glanced to the history prof look-alike and said, "And to tell you all about Miami's vision of biotechnology, I introduce Dr. Tom Chandler, Technology Manager of Florida Atlantic University up in Boca Raton."

More window dressing for King's virtual company, I assumed.

Dr. Chandler walked to the head of the table; it was obvious he had done this many times before. He stood in the large gap between King and Broadmoore, crossed his arms, grabbing each elbow, and stared down at a water pitcher. "I'd certainly be bringing coals to Newcastle, if I lectured you about incubation of inventions, small companies, capital formation, and marketing of technologies. The concept was worked out in Boston, then in San Francisco."

Dr. Chandler settled into a lecture on the "paradigm of technological entrepreneurship". I used the time to take stock of Dr. Cheryl North, Bud King's "right-hand scientist" who was going to take the technology "through the roof". Her outward presentation was a studied optimization of natural good looks: Thick, straight blond hair, carefully managed into graceful curves, framing a broad forehead, and pleasantly rounded face with widely spaced light green eyes. They moved slowly and self-assuredly under blond eyebrows, artfully accented with a touch of dark liner. Seldom do women in science look that good. If I hadn't known differently, I would have guessed her a seasoned fashion model now working as a buyer for a chain of expensive department stores.

Dr. North listened to Chandler and responded to our stock seller every time he whispered something in her ear. She would nod, give him a big-eyed smile, and return her attention to a sheet of paper, as if making notes.

No question why our Swimsuit Edition *aficionado* found Dr. North attractive. Her silk blouse was open at the third button to reveal a charming decolletage in the shape of reversed parentheses. This soft medallion of femininity was exquisitely shaped and lifted by the firmness of her closely tailored, deep purple, velvet jacket.

As I recalled, from when she stood to applaud the mayor, her jacket ended high on the waist. She was darned attractive. I remembered smoothly rounded hips and bottom, joined seamlessly with ample thighs, a tight skirt ending a fashionable three inches above the knee. The suit couldn't have cost less than $700.

As a guy engaged to be married to his perfect girl, I shouldn't have been looking like this at Dr. Cheryl North. But it's so unusual to find a woman scientist with so much style. Rebecca is very good-looking, but she dresses for work. Of course, Rebecca's work is seeing patients.

Still, scientific research usually means work at the lab bench where fancy clothes are a hindrance. How did Dr. Cheryl North get into such a demanding profession in the first place? With looks like hers, she could have written her own ticket in a dozen high-paying professions that are a hell of a lot easier.

Dr. Chandler lectured on, telling us that the deal between the two companies was a paradigm. As he described the first step — an inventor forming a small company — I began to notice that Dr. North was glancing at me. The eye liner and accented lashes made it easy to track her glances from across the room.

It made sense, trying to figure each other out, since we were counterparts who would be dealing with each other in a few minutes. I nodded at Chandler's words, affecting bored agreement, as if I'd been living the paradigm for years. Yes, the small company must first prove its technological concept on a small scale using venture capital. Of course, the next step is to obtain follow-on capital from sophisticated investors.

Chandler said that after a technology was further tested and proven, it could be licensed to a large company. Alternatively the small company might try to obtain major financing and do all the marketing itself — "like our own Cordis and IVAX".

Dr. Chandler looked out at us and frowned. "We are behind Boston and San Francisco in the use of this paradigm, but Miami can offer a pleasant environment, thanks to air conditioning which proved a boon to us." He wrinkled his brow, indicating that a joke had been told. No one responded to it as a joke.

Chandler slowly raised his voice as he concluded. "To paraphrase T.A. Allman's Miami, City of the Future, we offer an exciting yet controlled environment in which scientists and executives can work, create and recreate year round." He frowned and turned to the large window with the view of the Bay. "And the real estate is not too expensive. And the pot holes rarely get deeper than six inches, because the city sits on a good foundation of coral rock."

Dr. Chandler's grand finale drew polite applause. The deal between BIOTECH and B.M. Capital had received the blessing of an academic technocrat.

Next Bud King gave the floor to a bearded, bespectacled and bald, professorial-looking man, whom he introduced as the man who "put me in contact with Dr. Broadmoore's company". The corporate matchmaker was president of the "Strategic Biomedical Alliance", the organization Rob McGregor had told me about the day before. The matchmaker told us that the Alliance was a "technology incubator" which "incubated" small companies, until they hatched and were ready to compete in the marketplace. He said his nonprofit organization had "incubated" 42 companies. I made a note to visit his Website.

Finally Bud King stood up and said, "Well, now we've got enough theory to build us an atom bomb. Let's roll our sleeves up, get to work, and beat the Japs." His remark created no direct embarrassment; there were no Japanese or even Chinese in the audience.

A few minutes of confusion followed as everyone moved slowly in different directions. Small groups congealed and drifted out the door together.

Bud King went through the door with Tony Altino. Broadmoore was talking to the academics and made no effort to give me any signals. Dr. North was covering the whole room, striding from one person to the other to say goodbye. She moved around well in her high heels.

And here I stood, $3,000 richer and $1,592.79 poorer, having spent a whole morning to learn that my company was a pickup team and that BIOTECH might own nothing but fake diamonds in a locked showcase. Here I stood, without designated liaison, waiting to begin work on a $20 million decision.

Finally Dr. North caught my eye from across the room and threw me a smile. She slalomed toward me through the still-crowded room and extended her hand at midriff level. "Hi! You must be Dr. Candidi. Dr. Broadmoore gave me your card. I'm Cheryl North. I'll be your liaison for the next several days."

Her words came slowly, smoothly, confidently — delivered in middle vocal range. As she squeezed my hand, a glint seemed to flash from her light green eyes. I had trouble holding her gaze while improvising words about being pleased with her company's choice of liaison. It has always been difficult for me to deal with this variety of feminine perfection at close range.

Our go-go stock seller had no such problem. He trotted over and turned on his bovine charm. "See you around, Cheryl. I'm going to sit in on the legal session."

She turned to bathe him with her full attention. "Yes, Al. Nice to meet you."

"Same here. Great company. Won't be any trouble selling it to Wall Street, after you pass the ball to us."

Dr. North kept smiling in his direction until he was several steps away. It was an easy, natural smile. No need for that light-pink lipstick or the obvious care with which it had been applied. A millimeter added or subtracted here or there could do little to improve on already sensuous lines.

Dr. North slowly returned her gaze to me. "Now, Ben, as a good scientist, I am sure you will want to see everything we've got in lab."

Suddenly I became irritated. She had just sold Al on this fashion model thing, and now she was going to sell me on her company's lab equipment. She cast a glimpse in the stock seller's direction.

I would follow Broadmoore's example: First establish the right tone. "Sure, I can see your test tubes and instruments. But it's more important that I see your inventor."

"Well, he's in the lab," she replied matter-of-factly. "Together with the test tubes and instruments," she mimicked, using a soft tone. It was hard to fathom her unmoving, light-green eyes.

"I expected the inventor to be sitting at the front table," I challenged.

Slowly she raised her gaze toward the ceiling. "Yes, Ben," she said, as if I were a patient older sister. "He should have been there. He was invited. He may be a little *preoccupied*."

She put spin on the word, suggesting complexity. I hate it when people use words as roadblocks.

I chose words appropriate for a scientific argument. "Your use of 'preoccupied' leaves me several avenues of interpretation."

She shifted weight, bringing her left foot a bit closer.

"Well, I wouldn't feel right about speculating." She was quick. "In a few minutes you can ask him yourself." She sighed, as if to say there was no reason to be argumentive. She opened her eyes wide. "Do you need to get anything besides your briefcase?"

I reached down and grabbed it. "Have briefcase, will travel."

"Then follow me."

And follow her I did, on a spirited walk to the elevator which took us to the second floor. A couple of steps along the hall, and she pushed on a heavy metal door, opening into the parking garage. Her legs pumped and heels clicked over a large expanse of concrete in athletic tempo. Not quite a tennis player but surely athletic enough to be a golfer.

As we rounded the third concrete pillar, Dr. North pulled a set of keys from her purse. A late-model, maroon Buick Riviera whistled a gallant greeting and blinked its double set of headlights. Its chromed bumper, oval grill and high fenders reminded me of the classic roadsters of yesteryear.

As I approached the passenger-side door, it unlocked with a sharp emasculating snap. I probably flinched. Dr. North smiled primly and gestured for me to let myself in.

Soon my attractive chauffeur was skillfully zipping us through light traffic, while I sank deeply into my plush, red-upholstered bucket seat and enjoyed a stream of cool air blowing on my Italian suit. The "R"-for-Riviera hood ornament was pointing north, up Brickell Avenue. Shadows and muted images of royal palms flashed by along the tinted windows' ample surface.

It was interesting how Dr. North and I had managed to finesse the question of what my predecessor had done at BIOTECH last week. She hadn't mentioned him, and I hadn't mentioned him, either.

The Riviera's tires sang on the honeycombed steel of the bascule bridge crossing the Miami River. I would have to remember to play the Bostonian and pretend I didn't know Miami. "Nice town," I said.

"Yes, it is. And we will do everything possible to make your stay enjoyable." She said it with the professional sexiness of a flight attendant wishing a passenger a comfortable flight. "And you can call me Cheryl."

She made it *so* easy.

LAB VIƒIT 11

BIOTECH's laboratory was about ten blocks northwest of my hotel and three blocks inland from the inner Bay. It is a three-story concrete building, probably once a furniture warehouse, standing where the railroad tracks intersect Northeast Twentieth Street. I knew the neighborhood from previous explorations on bicycle. A few blocks to the north was a disused railroad switching yard which anchored a hopeless mixture of light industrial and medium-density residential real estate that is undergoing a slow transformation into a slum. The building is well-suited for the neighborhood: It has fewer windows than a concrete bunker.

Directly to the south was the historic Miami Cemetery, home of yesteryear's founders and of today's winos. South of that is a once-fashionable neighborhood of 1930s houses and three-story apartment buildings. The neighborhood now serves as ultra-high-density housing for undocumented aliens who arrive from Hong Kong and Central America. A few blocks farther south was the Omni Mall adjoining my hotel.

Cheryl parked the Riviera on a dusty strip along side the building, under a "Reserved" sign. High on the wall were large plastic signs bearing the names of BIOTECH and several other companies. Cheryl pulled out a key and unlocked a weathered wooden door, and ushered me into a dingy, unattended reception area, common to three companies.

Her second key opened the door to BIOTECH. The lab was a warehouse, converted with minimal expenditure. Along the concrete ceiling, I could see back about 100 feet to the rear wall. They had erected partitions to divide up the space into separate areas, but these reached only halfway to the 14-foot ceiling. Along one wall stood a roofed cubicle. It looked like a warehouse foreman's office, except it had no windows. As we approached, its single door slammed shut.

Cheryl seemed embarrassed as I looked at the door. What a ridiculous structure, this cubicle. Its squat roof sprouted air conditioning ducts which curved in the open space below the warehouse's high ceiling. At second glance, it looked like a climate-controlled process room. At third glance, it looked like a shipping container.

The benches and cabinets of the lab were all modular. The only sign of permanence was an occasional lag bolt, anchoring a bench to the painted concrete floor or holding a cabinet to the cinder block wall. The sink, a stainless-steel and Formica affair, stood on two improvised cinder block columns. The whole lab could have been put up in five days and taken down in three.

However, I became impressed with the lab's capabilities as the visit unfolded. The two white-jacketed technicians seemed to be working at high efficiency.

"This is the analytical laboratory," Cheryl said.

She was showing me the lab, although I would have preferred to start with the inventor.

One of the technicians was shaking a separatory funnel — a tear-shaped piece of glassware with a stopper on one end and a stopcock valve on the other, used for separating watery and organic liquid phases.

"We extract the active compounds from aqueous homogenates

of the sponge tissue," Cheryl said crisply. "We analyze them by HPLC." She seemed to have regained her composure.

I knew the jargon. Stripped down to its essentials, a High Pressure Liquid Chromatography apparatus is just a collection of small pumps, fine metal tubes, columns, and shoebox-sized light detectors. I nodded in the direction of an HPLC apparatus, sitting on a lab bench. "Yes, looks like a nice Beckman system. Tell me a little about your analytical method. What sort of separating column do you use?"

Cheryl wrinkled her forehead. "It is some sort of hydrophobic reversed phase thing," she said with a trace of irritation. She turned to one of the white-jacketed workers. "Dr. Lau, could you give Dr. Candidi the details of the assay?"

Dr. Lau turned toward us and bowed ever so slightly. "Assay is with 'C-18' column, acetonitrile water mixture, giving five point two minute retention time for the alpha compound. Effective in separating it from twelve other oil-soluble components."

He sounded competent to me. His recitation took me back several years when I had worked in the toxicology lab of Dr. Westley's Medical Examiner's Office. I got Dr. Lau to tell me about the detectors he used and how well he could resolve the elution peaks of the three anticancer compounds. He gave good answers on analytical procedure.

Did Dr. Lau understand the big picture? I cleared my throat and asked, "Is this analytical work to characterize new compounds you get out of sponges? Or are you monitoring the quality of your product?"

Lau's eyes disappeared into the far corners of their sockets. Several seconds went by without an answer.

"Are you doing animal experiments?" I asked.

"We do a little of everything," Lau said cautiously.

Cheryl took a challenge-evoking step toward me and pointed to file cabinets along the wall. "All the analytical data are logged in here and are stored in these files. They are kept under 'GLP' and are used for 'QA', and also for the 'CTM' manufacture under 'GMP.'" She speeded up purposely as she got to these abbreviations.

She was using the jargon to give me a snow job.

I pretended to understand the acronyms. "Well, maybe you can show me some of that."

"Our next stop is the 'PK' lab," Cheryl said. She lead me around a partition to the next area where they were working with rats. "All our Pharmaco-Kinetic studies are done under Good Laboratory Practices and are FDA inspectable."

So 'PK' stood for Pharmaco-Kinetic. And I knew that meant studies of how the drug moves around in the body. And I now knew that 'GLP' stood for "Good Laboratory Practices."

I paused a couple seconds to mull this over. "GMP" probably stood for Good Manufacturing Practices. This was, no doubt, the jargon that the Food and Drug Administration thought up for their demanding standards of record-keeping. The FDA couldn't let a company get sloppy that was requesting permission to test a new drug in humans. The only term left for me to decipher was "CTM".

The other scientist working in the 'PK lab' was dark-skinned and bearded. His head was wrapped in a Sikh turban. He held a rat by the tail and dropped it into a transparent cylinder filled with misty vapor. It was a carbon dioxide chamber for rendering the animal unconscious. At the bottom of the cylinder was a chunk of dry ice. Above it was a perforated plastic floor which kept the animal from touching the dry ice and freezing its paws.

"Dr. Candidi, may I introduce Dr. Singh, our pharmacokinetic specialist."

Dr. Singh greeted me with a disquieting smile featuring two perfect rows of pearly white teeth framed by a glistening black beard. Effusively he told me how glad he was to have me visiting the lab. With the rat going out quick and not wanting it to suffocate, I told Dr. Singh I wouldn't interrupt his work. Dr. Singh took half a minute to tell me about his pharmacokinetic experiment. The rat had been fed the "alpha compound" two days ago. Dr. Singh was now drawing the second blood sample to measure its rate of elimination from the body.

Finally he pulled the limp rat from the chamber and flopped it on the table. He quickly inserted a syringe into its tail vein and deftly teased out one milliliter of blood. "Short carbon dioxide anesthesia makes it easier for me to find the tail vein," Singh volunteered.

"It sure makes them easier to handle," affirmed Cheryl.

I couldn't resist adding my two cents. "Yes, it's amazing what a couple of lung-fulls of carbon dioxide can do. A small drop in blood pH is all it takes to temporarily put your brain out of commission."

Singh syringed the blood into a test tube and placed it in a table-top centrifuge.

Now was my chance to tease out of him a definition of 'CTM'. I would mix it up with a lot of other jargon in the form of a question and see what sort of answer he gave. "Are you doing 'PK' on the 'CTM' manufactured by 'GMP'?"

Singh acted like he didn't understand. Cheryl frowned and looked at me quizzically. I just acted natural and waited patiently for my answer.

Cheryl took a step closer and answered me patiently. "The compounds that we are testing in rats have been manufactured under Good Manufacturing Practices. After the FDA accepts our animal data, we would hope to use the same batch as a Clinical Trial Material."

Good. 'CTM' was Clinical Trial Material. And Cheryl had also identified another hurdle to testing their anticancer compounds in man. The FDA would first have to check out BIOTECH's GLP animal data.

Now to get control of the situation, I pointed to a lockable file cabinet next to Dr. Singh's desk. "And am I right in assuming that all the GLP PK data pursuant to an FDA submission are stored here?"

"Yes," Cheryl said. "You can find it all here, if you want to conduct a GLP audit. But the final reports are held in our Brickell office." Her voice inflection made it clear that it would be a waste of time to look in yonder file cabinet.

So far, so good. Maybe it was time for me to lighten up a bit. "What delights await me behind the next partition?" I glanced toward the rear of the lab.

"Our sponge processing area and our cell culture room," Cheryl answered. She pushed off and walked spiritedly in that direction.

Along the wall of the back lab were several stainless steel tables, the type used in restaurant kitchens. On the tabletops sat large Waring blenders and food grinders. In the center of the room stood a large stainless steel tank inside a glass enclosure.

"Are you making the batches by extraction of sponges or by growing your own cells?" I asked Cheryl, after catching up with her.

"Right now, we are extracting sponges that the boats bring."

BIOTECH's supply chain for sponges wasn't hard for me to imagine: A couple years earlier I had discovered a small sponge processing "factory" along the Miami River. I'd talked to a *viejo* who worked there, cutting them up and hanging them to dry. I bought him a beer at the open-air bar across the street, and he told me how they harvested sponges. They cut off parts of the growing sponges, using saws mounted on long poles. Of course, I couldn't tell any of this to the people in the lab; I was pretending to be a visitor from Boston.

"How many hundred thousands of dollars of drug product can you manufacture before you have depleted the whole Biscayne Bay of sponges?" I asked.

She took a step forward; I took a step back.

"The question has been studied," Cheryl answered smartly. "We are entering into discussions with the Bahamian Government for permission to harvest their waters. We are also experimenting with producing the compound in cell culture." She pointed to the food grinder and then to a large tank.

Fine. They had a well-functioning lab. Now for the most important question. "I guess I've seen everything except Dr. Moon — your inventor. Where is he?"

"He's holed up in his office up front."

"Up front?" I did not remember seeing an office.

"Yes, the office we passed it as we came in."

This was the funny windowless prefab shed where the door had slammed when we first came in.

"If you could wait here, I'll arrange for him to talk with you."

As if she needed to get his permission? "Okay," I said.

Cheryl went to make arrangements, leaving me waiting there. I had mastered their jargon; I could finally start doing my work.

I spent the first several minutes thinking about what I would ask Dr. Moon. I had read in the files that he first had a small company. Then BIOTECH bought Dr. Moon's company and the technology. The buyout was probably an example of the technology development "paradigm" that Dr. Chandler had been lecturing about at the luncheon.

Dr. Moon would be the one who would know the most about the actual compounds. I would ask him how they worked on the cellular and molecular level.

Cheryl kept me waiting so long that I almost fell into conversation with a liquid nitrogen tank. Sitting on a four-wheeled dolly, it appeared almost human — fat and cylindrical, its long flexible copper spout resembling a droopy nose. It looked like one of those obscene humanoids from a Crumb cartoon.

"Keep on truckin', buddy," I told the tank. "But keep your proboscis out of trouble."

I must have said it pretty loud, since a technician laughed to himself as he walked in. He went into the enclosure room, emerged with a rack of stoppered test tubes, and put them down on the lab bench. He donned safety goggles, a face shield, and finally thick asbestos gloves. Now bundled up, so that not a square inch of skin showed, he grabbed the tank's droopy copper proboscis; he stuck it into a silvery Dewar flask, an oversized Thermos bottle. Then he twisted open the valve on top.

The tank started rattling, and the nose roared as the first couple of pounds of liquid nitrogen expended their precious coldness to chill the copper tube, vaporizing in the process and spraying liquid nitrogen droplets into the still-warm Dewar flask where more vaporization took place. The cold hissing nitrogen gas condensed the laboratory air into roiling clouds of water vapor. The technician did the right thing, bundling up; the liquid was coming out of the tube at minus 196 degrees Celsius — cold enough to freeze your skin off, warts and all.

Stamped on the side of the cylinder was an indelible warning: "Nitrogen doesn't support life." That was probably some lawyer's idea of a product liability disclaimer.

It wasn't hard to figure out what this part of the lab was doing. They took out samples of the sponge cells they were culturing in the big tank and froze them in liquid nitrogen. They were probably storing them for later assay of the three compounds. They were likely figuring out the optimal time to harvest the cells.

Cheryl was sure taking her time setting up the interview with Dr. Moon. I wandered to Dr. Singh's area just as a Federal Express man came in with three flat boxes. They were the right size for enormous pizzas but were labelled "Live Animals, Charles River Labs."

"Is FEDEX delivering pizzas nowadays?" I asked. The delivery guy didn't think that was funny. Dr. Singh was preoccupied with signing the FEDEX clipboard, then with opening the boxes and peeking in to count the animals.

"Three boxes, six rats each," he said, half to me, half to himself. I smiled down at him and he smiled back. "Three boxes, three capitalist rats. Always has one capitalist rat in each box."

His voice was high with upper-nasal resonance. His sentences were unmodulated, except for a trace of a laugh at the end.

"What do you mean by 'capitalist' rat?" I asked.

"You will see when you look at the food block."

I peeked into the box. The supplier had provided the traveling rodents with food and drink. A translucent block was glued to the center of the box's floor. And one rat was lying on top of it.

Singh's dark eyelashes flickered. "The company gives them a block to chew. It gives them food and water for the journey. But the capitalist rat keeps it all to itself."

"A one-day trip, and they've already established a pecking order?" I asked.

My interest must have excited Singh; his answer came almost in singsong. "Yes, there is always a peck order when there are six. But very interesting is that when there are only three in the box, no rat becomes capitalist."

I had made similar observations of my own species. I was about to propose a theory when Cheryl returned.

"Long time no see," I said to her, mixing humor and irritation.

"Dr. Moon was into one of his projects. I had to tear him away," Cheryl explained. Under the makeup, her face seemed flushed. "Ben, I have to warn you that he can sometimes be a very difficult person." She eyed me earnestly and touched me in the arm with an elbow. "But I'm sure that you are a lot better than I am at handling quirky scientists."

12 KARATE FLICK

As we approached Moon's door, Cheryl put two hands on my right arm and guided me in. One step over the threshold, one pivot to the right, and I was standing squarely in front of his desk and looking down on the gentleman himself.

Moon didn't look up from the laptop computer on the desk before him. He may not have seen me: The front of his desk was dominated by a second computer, a desktop computer with an enormous monitor. I glanced to Cheryl, standing in the door. There was nowhere else for her to stand; my body occupied most of the guest space in Moon's cramped windowless cubicle.

Cheryl cleared her throat. Moon looked up, as if we had surprised him. He stood up quickly. His smile was too mechanical and came too late to be natural. He leaned to one side, so that we could shake hands around the monitor.

"Dr. Moon, this is Dr. Candidi," Cheryl said in a tone of instruction.

"Yes, I am sorry I was summarizing." he said haltingly. "I mean, I was writing." At first, his eyes seemed searching and sympathetic. But when his eyes returned to Cheryl his brows stiffened. "Please sit down. I very sorry. I very busy these days." He delivered his syllables in staccato with lots of resonance in the upper throat. He gestured for me to take his single guest chair, wedged in the corner.

I looked to Cheryl. She indicated that I was to sit, and she would remain standing. There wasn't room for two chairs. Moon waited until I was comfortably seated, before returning to his chair. The monitor hid half of his face; his eyes and flat forehead hovered a couple inches above the top. I moved my chair to correct "the eclipse of Dr. Moon". The thought must have made me smile inappropriately; Moon's eyes hardened.

Maybe a little joke would break the ice. I looked from the big monitor to his laptop computer. "I can see you are a two-computer man." Moon glared and said nothing. "You know — like in the American Western movies. Some gunfighters were two-gun men." Maybe Moon's English was the problem. To demonstrate, I made a two gun fast draw gesture.

Moon seemed irritated by my intrusion. He snapped shut the laptop computer. Maybe he thought I'd been peeking at the screen. "In Korea we don't have gunfighting cowboys. We have karate." His voice was carefully controlled now, and his eyes contained all the sympathy of a bad guy performing a ceremonial bow in an 1980s karate flick.

I wouldn't try to compete with him in a contest of glaring eye contact. My eyes dropped to his laptop computer. A telephone wire protruded; I figured he was doing modem communications with a remote site. I suppressed the impulse to call him an Internet cowboy.

We spent a few seconds in silence. Cheryl had moved to a spot that was a couple steps outside the door. Moon looked toward the empty doorway. His face softened as he turned toward me. "You have pleasant stay here? You have nice hotel?"

Clicks of spike heels on concrete announced Cheryl's return to the doorway. Moon sneaked a sideways glance at her.

Funny way to make small talk, I thought. "I'm staying at the Marriott."

Cheryl cleared her throat. "Dr. Moon, we discussed this interview last night. You are to tell Dr. Candidi everything he needs to know. And since the office isn't large enough for all three of us, I'll wait outside like we discussed." She took two steps back to where I could still see her, but Moon could not.

Moon laughed nervously, then was silent. He glanced at the empty doorway. When he spoke again it was with strained courtesy. "With what I may help you?"

What was I to make of this posturing? It was straight out of a B-grade karate flick. He was treating me like an intruder who had pissed on the floor of his *dojo*. Is that the way he had treated my predecessor, Dr. Yang? Had he killed him with a sucker chop to the neck? Was he fermenting Yang's flesh in the back room? The thought must have made me smile again, since Dr. Moon's eyes were now flashing angry.

I said, "As you know, I am doing scientific due diligence for our company, B.M. Capital. I have come to ask you some questions."

"I will try to answer your questions, Dr. Candidi, but as Dr. North probably tell you, I do not have very much time."

I decided not to contradict him. I glanced out the doorway at Cheryl. She looked up at the ceiling, as if beseeching heaven.

Moon leaned back in his chair in an exaggerated attempt to seem at ease. "Could you please state your first question."

This did not show much promise of becoming a friendly scientific discussion.

I sucked in my gut. "What is the mechanism of antitumor action of the three compounds?"

"You can find that in the patent which you should have read before coming here. Please read the Introductory Statement and the Description of the Invention in columns five and seven."

It wouldn't do to let him get away with this. I concentrated very hard on speaking in a normal voice. "Dr. Moon, I did read your patent. I do not remember it explaining how these compounds kill tumor cells. All I remember the patent saying is that the three compounds are protein kinase C inhibitors."

Moon didn't blink. "Maybe you should check patent."

Okay. I could play the game of bad manners and bad grammar. "Please excuse, while I refer to patent," I said, purposely dropping the pronoun and definite article.

I lifted my briefcase to my lap, snapped it open, and pulled out the patent. I made a big show of speed reading, running my finger over the indicated sections. It felt like a showdown scene in an ancient Fu Manchu movie played on television's Nostalgia Channel. I looked up and tried on my own version of a cruel, condescending smile. "I have — diligently — checked and have found no mechanism other than a statement of protein kinase C inhibition."

"That is correct," Moon said. "It kills tumors by inhibiting protein kinase C enzyme."

"But that doesn't tell us how it really works. Just because protein kinase C stimulation can cause cancer doesn't mean that protein kinase C inhibition can cure cancer. What genes are being turned on or off?"

"Dr. Candidi. I do not know where you come from, but I am pharmaceutical scientist, not basic scientist with five-year grant to study every detail. Where I come from it not important to have big intellectual discussion. In business what important is bottom line." He gestured with his thumb and forefinger, indicating money. "It is indisputable, my compounds shrink tumors." He overpronounced the word "indisputable."

"Indisputable in rats and mice," I countered.

"Yes, my discovery shrinks tumors in rats and mice."

"Is it a discovery or an invention?"

"It both." His eyes narrowed

"Doesn't the U.S. Patent Office differentiate between an invention and a discovery?" I asked, not knowing the answer myself.

"You try tell me I should not have patent?" Moon was now partially out of his chair.

"No, I was just interested in the issues of —"

"It not my job to discuss philosophy of U.S. Patent Office. My invention is good, and I got a patent, and no one can take it away."

Cheryl was staring off into the lab, but I could tell she was listening hard.

She wouldn't acknowledge my glance. I waited a few seconds and chose my words for Moon very carefully. "Okay, then. Let's not talk philosophy; let's talk specifics. Are there any other compounds related to or resembling your three compounds — your alpha, beta and gamma compounds — that will do the same thing?"

Moon moved back into his chair. His gaze sank to his desktop. He picked up a sheet of paper and placed it on his laptop computer. "No. If they exist, they are not discovered yet."

His answer was very important. I would cross-examine him on this point, after he showed he could behave himself for a few minutes.

My next question was chosen in hopes of regaining control over the interview. "On which of the eleven known types of the protein kinase C enzyme do your compounds work?"

Dr. Moon groaned and slumped in his chair. "I do not know," he said contritely. "I never have enough money to conduct such high-power research. If you find experts who will carry out big research program, you can find out."

I was surprised how quickly he caved in after being so defensive about the mechanism of his invention's action. Maybe I was being too hard on him. Was it important that he didn't know which of the eleven different types of enzyme his compounds worked on? With eleven types of protein kinase C tagging phosphates on an equal number of target proteins, all with different preferences, it would be hard to make any prediction on anticancer activity from a few test tube experiments. That's why they had done whole animal experiments. And they had shrunk tumors in rats and mice.

On the other hand, it's one hell of a long extrapolation from those critters to man. And Broadmoore would be gambling $20 million, using my advice from this long-shot extrapolation.

The whole damn thing would be simpler, if they had tested human tumors. But they would need FDA permission to start that kind of testing. Had they done enough 'GLP' animal toxicity testing to request permission?

As I thought this through, Moon seemed to be gathering strength in his corner. "You have more questions for me?"

I remembered a shortcut for getting human tumor information.

"Have you tested your compounds against human tumors implanted in nude mice?" This special breed lacks an immune system and can't grow hair. It is actually a well-accepted test system. Implant a piece of human tumor in a nude mouse, and the tumor will grow like it does in a cancer patient. Then inject your anticancer drug in the mouse and see if it kills the human tumor.

"Nude mouse trials are scheduled at the National Cancer Institute in about three months."

That was too late to answer our $20 million question.

"And any more questions?" Moon asked, seeming to ready himself for another tirade.

"Yes. Where do you keep your inventor's notebooks?"

"I keep them in this office. And the raw data is in notebooks outside in the three laboratories. Dr. North has duplicate copies of all my notebooks. And everything is carefully organized. It very clear which experiments go into which examples in the patent. This will help you save my time."

"I would like to return to the question of whether there are other compounds that kill tumors by working on protein kinase C."

"I say none discovered. You not believe, you look at Patent Examiner file. Maybe I wait a few minutes, while you find it in your briefcase."

I didn't remember seeing any Patent Examiner file, and Moon must have read that from my face. But I had to be sure; I opened my briefcase and went through it. The longer I looked, the stronger grew the smile on Moon's face. I had to be truthful. "I don't have it. I haven't had a chance to study it."

Now Cheryl chimed in like she had been part of the conversation all along. "We have it at the Brickell office, Ben. I can show it to you as soon as you are through here."

Moon said, "Yes, very important to look at file first to know what talk about."

I could not argue against that. But neither of them could argue that Moon was communicative. And I wasn't going to let the jerk think he was running me off. "Okay, Dr. Moon. I'll spend the afternoon looking over your files. But I'll be back at nine tomorrow morning with a list of questions."

"Please do. Nine tomorrow morning. Or else I hear from you through Dr. North."

Cheryl moved back several steps as I got up to leave.

Moon's eyes looked friendlier now. He spoke to me in a soft voice: "I think you are a real scientist. Only real scientists appreciate scientific truth and are never paid enough for it. Not like businessman that always wanting everything solid but not smart enough to really understand scientific truth."

I halted in the doorway while answering him. "There's something to be said for that."

Cheryl probably overheard at least part of Moon's comment. Her face bore a pained expression.

Moon frowned. "They want scientists to do most delicate work, but they cannot understand it. So they cannot make themselves give money for it. But they think nothing of paying many hundred-thousand dollars to businessman."

Cheryl looked much relieved after getting me away from Moon.

"Ben, I'll take you to the main office and show you the files on everything important to his patent. They are really well-organized."

I was almost glad to be getting away from the quirky guy myself. But we couldn't leave the building just yet.

A delivery man was maneuvering a large liquid nitrogen tank through the narrow doorway that led to the common reception. The tank was rolling on a hand truck with two large hard-rubber wheels. Two small auxiliary wheels kept the truck from tipping. As an additional safety measure, the man was wearing steel-toed shoes. Tilted back at a ridiculous angle, secured to the truck with a heavy strap which also kept its proboscis from flopping, the tank now looked like a straitjacketed Crumb cartoon character being hauled off to the loony bin.

Cheryl stopped and drew a breath. "Dr. Moon is so petty, so demanding. When we bought his company he insisted that we build him his own isolated office with a separate air conditioning system. Look at what we had to do." She turned around and waved a hand at Moon's enclosure dismissively.

Flexible air conditioning ducts sprouted from its ceiling and descended to an air handling system mounted on the floor in the corner. The cubicle looked like a life-support system for a captured alien from outer space.

"And the air conditioning had to be just right," Cheryl added. "Everything to Dr. Moon's specifications. And suddenly the common men's room up front wasn't good enough for him. We had to tear up the floor to put in a private toilet in the back of his office."

"So that's where the door went to — right behind his desk?"

"Yes. Charming, isn't it? He wanted everything just right, but he didn't ask for an exhaust fan. So he didn't get one!"

"I hope that's no reflection on his science."

Cheryl laughed and tossed her head. "No, Due Diligence Master, you will find his science as sweet-smelling as a rose."

I guessed Moon's problems were an overinflated ego, basic insecurity and poor communications skills. If his files were as flawless and well-organized as he said, I could forgive everything.

The delivery man was now moving the tank through the door, then toward the back lab. Cheryl led me through the reception and out the front door. She took two steps into the late afternoon heat and came to an abrupt halt. "This is just what I need," she groaned.

Her maroon Buick was blocked in against the building by an enormous, heavy hooded, flat-bed GMC truck. The situation reminded me of a street-wise cat in a defensive pose, trapped in a corner by a large dog on a leash. The Riviera actually resembled a cat with the slight rise around its rear window and fender suggesting feline haunch.

At first Cheryl handled the situation less smoothly than some cats I've seen. She let out a visceral groan. Then she walked to the back of the car for a closer look. The small space between the truck's hydraulic tailgate and the building's wall would make too tight a squeeze for the Riviera. One false turn of the wheel could scrape or even dislodge the chrome strip girdling the car's waist. "Damn truck," she cursed to herself.

Or perhaps she was posturing for me. She did a "180" and struck a forward-leaning pose, one well-proportioned leg to the fore. It was the sort of frozen action shot they use in a high fashion magazines. In a glossy advertisement, the pose could have sold to a mass audience any part of Cheryl's ensemble as well as the car. Woman and car complemented each other's lines: Cheryl's high skirt revealed a shapely leg; the Riviera's high fenders showed a lot of athletic tread and a classy hubcap. And both mistress and vehicle presented nicely upturned lines around the bottom.

Watch out, Ben. Luxury automobile fantasies can become addictive!

Framed by black designer sunglasses, gold-trimmed and opaque, Cheryl's face struck an attitude of high-intensity, focussed will-power — the type that could fetch a waiter from one-hundred paces. "Move — your — truck," she said quietly and insistently. But the driver was nowhere to be seen. Was she putting on airs for my benefit?

"He's delivering your liquid nitrogen," I said lamely.

Cheryl's immediate answer was to hold her affected stance.

Thigh muscles pulsated gently under her sleek skin. Her verbal answer came much later. "But he could take all day."

"I don't think so. He won't find any good-looking girls in there to chat with. He'll be out as fast as he can switch tanks."

Her only answer was a turn of the head in my direction. Did she actually expect me to interpret eyes that were hidden behind over-sized sunglasses? The unobscured portion of her face sure as hell didn't give me any expressions to read. I don't like to play games. Didn't bring along shades. I only wear them when I'm out there, really doing something — like sailing.

Hell, if my chatting-with-the-girls joke didn't register with her, I would focus my attentions elsewhere. I pretended to be interested in the truck. Its automotive statement was just as strong as the Buick's. It was enormous, strong, functional and professional. It must have been carrying a couple of tons of cargo in the form of liquid nitro-gen tanks and gas bottles corralled on its high-fenced boiler-plate platform. Little wonder that it needed two axles, carrying all this high-tech produce to market. And the vehicle was as spotless as the stainless steel containers it carried.

As I predicted, the driver soon returned, wheeling out an empty tank. Cheryl stood in his path and gave him a dirty look. He pre-tended to not notice but made a wide circle around her. She caught up with him at the back end of the truck, just as he pulled the lever to lower the hydraulic elevator. He waved her off, as if she might be endangering herself. Then came a curious exchange of words.

Competing with the hydraulic whine, Cheryl raised her voice to complain about being thoughtlessly blocked in. The man had wasted her valuable time and made her late for an appointment.

The man glanced at her once and shook his head like he had heard it all before. He was middle-aged and had the kind of self-assured, technical-professional demeanor I've noticed in elec-tricians and telephone linemen. First he returned his professional vigilance to the descending tailgate platform. Then he replied to Cheryl in a querulous whine in a pitch not that much different from the electric motor. He informed "the lady" that BIOTECH did not have a proper loading dock. In fact, BIOTECH didn't even have a proper loading area. By rights, the location wasn't even "deliverable".

The motor stopped whining. The man stopped talking, just long enough to pull the tank onto the grounded elevator. The silence would have been a good chance for Cheryl to retort, but she didn't seem to have anything to say.

The man turned the lever into the "up" position and the whining recommenced. The lady probably didn't know that he was actually doing BIOTECH a favor to deliver at all. And he had always taken special care to not crush their flimsy household aluminum threshold when he rolled the tank through their front entrance door. And would the lady kindly step back; insurance regulations didn't allow him to operate the lift when people were within ten feet. If the lady kept on standing there like she wanted to speak her piece, he would be late for his appointment — a delivery to the pathology department of Mount Sinai Hospital.

Cheryl seemed tongue-tied until the deliveryman's steel-toed shoes had ascended to eye level. By then, he was already busy moving the tank to the truck's central platform.

The guy was right about his company being safety-conscious. An automatic warning beep activated as he threw the truck in reverse to back it out of the corner. Mounted on the rear was a big 180 degree fish-eye mirror to ensure that he didn't back into any luxury automobiles — or well-dressed and irate woman scientists.

I was glad when Cheryl got the Riviera moving, and the air conditioning started to take over. I had started to work up a sweat, standing out in the sun all suited up. Cheryl also seemed hot under the collar. It was a silent trip downtown, over the Miami River and south on Brickell Avenue to BIOTECH's main office. Heavy shades didn't hide Cheryl's hurt and angry eyes from my first sidelong glance.

I wasn't familiar with this kind of mentality. Cheryl took the truck episode as an affront. Rebecca would have taken it as an inconvenience.

As we got into the groove of Brickell Avenue, a new question popped into my head. If Dr. Moon wanted to complain that I was wasting his time, why didn't he say that my predecessor, Dr. Yang, had gone over the same ground before?

13 GOOD LABORATORY PRACTICE

The offices of King Construction occupied the 21st floor of a Brickell Avenue building, located one block south of our luncheon venue. The elevator door opened to reveal a high, oversized reception desk. Woven into its fabric base in large letters were the words "King Construction". The huge room behind it was divided into cubicles by floor-standing partitions. The company's major interior decorating principle was gray — gray carpeting covered every inch of floor space and fuzzy dark gray fabric covered the partitions. Even the permanent walls were gray — a gray-impregnated plastic material with a rough texture that threatened to tear fibers from my suit as I followed Cheryl down a narrow corridor.

Cheryl's bailiwick was located in a suite of more permanent-looking offices at the end of the building. They were grouped around a central area dominated by a fabric-covered secretary's workstation. King's office was the next beyond Cheryl's at the far end. Ahma Sharma's was across from King's. Cheryl patted my elbow to steer me toward a conference room on the other side of her own office. "We'll be setting you up here."

A small sign on the conference room door announced "BIOTECH Florida". King Construction had sacrificed its conference room to spawn BIOTECH. The central table was large enough for six conferees. Three locked file cabinets sat to the side.

Cheryl smiled like she was doing me a big favor. "Here you are, Ben. BIOTECH's central archive. Those three file cabinets contain over a million dollars worth of data."

If BIOTECH really had spent a million dollars on the technology, our accountant would be able to verify it. I had caught a glimpse of him working with Sharma in her office across the hall. I remembered from reading the files that BIOTECH had bought out Dr.

Moon's company. That probably cost them a few hundred-thousand dollars. And the Chinese and Sikh scientists probably cost $40,000 each. How much was Cheryl making? I turned to her and said, "You can start by showing me one-hundred-thousand dollars worth of GLP animal studies."

"Coming right up, Due Diligence Master." Cheryl unlocked a file cabinet and handed me a 30-page report. I sat down and leafed through it. Concentrating was difficult while Cheryl was there. She made several trips back to the cabinet to pull out more files, brushing by me several times, until she had built a two-foot stack on the table. When she was finished she got my attention and glanced at the stack with a self-satisfied, school-girlish smile. "This is the supporting data. I'll be next door if you need me."

After she departed, I made myself comfortable. I took off my thousand-dollar suit jacket and draped it over a nearby chair. I curled up in my chair and skimmed the 30 pages. The report was authored by Drs. Lau and Singh. Their bottom line was that all three compounds produced a dramatic shrinkage of tumors in rats. Their work was an independent confirmation of what Moon reported in his patent. They repeated his experiments with a much larger number of animals.

I was enough of an expert in due diligence to know that my next step would be to audit the data in the two-foot stack. Exploring the first two inches convinced me that Lau and Singh had been very thorough. Every rat was identified by a standard toe clipping scheme. Tumor size measurements were made by different people on different days. At the end of the trial, they sacrificed the rats, cut them open, and photographed the tumors. Then they cut sections which they mounted and stained on microscope slides.

Yes, the tumor shrinkage experiments looked foolproof.

Everything was done according to a protocol that was set up in advance. The protocol spelled out everything, including what time they had to clean out the cages. I guessed this was the essence of GPL, the Good Laboratory Practices that the FDA would require to accept their data.

The study was also designed so there could be no cheating.

Dr. Singh, Dr. Lau and a technician had taken part in every aspect of the study — the tumor implantations, tumor growth and shrinkage measurements, and the drug and placebo treatments. The three men were rotated through these duties according to a prear-ranged schedule. Every step for each animal was laid out on a pre-printed form that two of them had to sign — the one who did the work and the one who checked the work.

And the experiments were "blinded" which made cheating next to impossible. The scientist measuring tumor size did not know whether the animal was receiving an active drug or a placebo. The documents identified Cheryl as the "Quality Assurance Officer". It was probably her job to make sure that everything was done accord-ing to protocol.

The report presented graphs showing that the tumors shrank.

The graphs were backed up by the triply signed data sheets. The tumor shrinkage had to be real. The only other explanation would have to be that all four — Dr. North, Dr. Lau, Dr. Singh and the technician — all took part in a falsification conspiracy.

I spent the remainder of the first hour trying to find anything wrong with the report. I found nothing wrong. Of course, there was no test tube data showing why the three compounds worked, but I couldn't expect that in this type of report.

I found Cheryl in her office, working on her computer. "The ani-mal data are very convincing, Cheryl."

"Thank you, Ben," she said. "You know, we have been spending our money on this project, too." She smiled sweetly, but her remark was a little too sassy for my taste.

"I stipulate that your data show that the alpha, beta and gamma compounds work on tumors in rats. Now for the question of whether they will work on man. You don't have any clinical trials yet."

Cheryl wrinkled her brow and moved forward in her chair like she wanted to say something but couldn't. She leaned closer to the desktop and looked up. "We have an IND document almost ready to file. We gave copies to your regulatory affairs man and your on-cologist to take back to their hotel. But if you want to study it, I have a copy next door."

It was the document they had to file with the FDA to get permis-sion to do the first human tests. "I'd definitely like to see it."

Cheryl got up, whisked past me and went to my room. She was graceful on her feet, navigating in high heels. Good flexibility in the hips helped her get around corners of desks. She could adjust the length of her stride to make turns and edge through doorways without changing speed. Her dynamic center of gravity was always a pleasant six inches in front of her chest.

By the time I had caught up with Cheryl, she was already in my room, opening the bottom drawer of second file cabinet. Over her shoulder, she handed me a three inch thick document with heavy cardboard covers and a flat wire binder. "Now keep in mind that this is only a draft."

The title read, "Cancer Chemotherapeutic Activity of Zagrionic Acid, Investigational New Drug Application (IND)".

The IND described their plan for a clinical study of the "alpha compound" in advanced breast cancer patients. This was the document that would present the drug to the FDA for the first time. It was the document that would gather strength and momentum, and raise the technology's value to many hundred millions of dollars.

After Cheryl sauntered out, I sat down to study the eight tabbed section's IND document for a half hour. Its 15-page Introductory Statement included historical anecdotes, quoting a Carib Indian legend that the juice from sponges was good for "wasting disease". The next section, "Investigational Plan", said the three compounds might be part of a greater family of compounds. If the first trials were encouraging, they would want to test other compounds. An Investigator's Brochure was supposed to tell the doc what he or she needed to know before treating the patient. BIOTECH guessed that nausea and vomiting would be possible side effects.

I should have sensed drama in this document — the document which held promise of increasing the investment's value tenfold. But I was growing tired and easily distracted. Music wafted in from Cheryl's room. Sometimes I heard Ahma Sharma answering questions from our accountant. Those two seemed to be getting along well. Every few minutes, the secretary answered the phone, saying, "King Construction." I didn't once hear her answer, "BIOTECH." King didn't seem to be in. Maybe he was checking up on one of his construction sites.

14 A STURDY PATENT

The IND's "Protocol" section had only a tentative description of the treatment plan. But it contained a lot of standard forms for recording blood, urine, and stool samples. I reviewed the "Pharmacology" section carefully. It included the report on the rat experiments. But it didn't answer the question I had asked Dr. Moon — which one of the eleven types of protein kinase C enzyme do the compounds inhibit, and why that should cure cancer. Had my predecessor, Dr. Yang, asked any of these questions? What a shame there were no notes.

I removed my laptop computer from my briefcase and typed in many observations.

Once I looked up and saw Tony Altino, Bud King's boyhood friend and construction site watchdog. He was asking the secretary, "Is Bud in?" She said he was out. I smiled to Altino. He caught my glance but shifted his eyes away quickly. Maybe he didn't approve of me. Probably thought I'd make his company's staplers grow legs and walk away.

My own legs were atrophying. Time to stand up and stretch.

The window offered a magnificent view of the Bay where all those wonderful cancer-curing sponges were growing. It reflected the mid-afternoon sun like a palette of green and blue. Across the Bay, on the southern tip of Key Biscayne, the old lighthouse was clearly visible. Hurricane Andrew sure had culled those mangroves and Australian pines. Seven years now, and they still hadn't grown back. But the 150 mile-an-hour winds had worked no lasting change on the eternal face of the Atlantic which stretched a thousand miles beyond.

A female voice, charmingly modulated in mid-range, jarred me out of my daydream. "Can I get you a cup of coffee?" It was Cheryl, of course.

"Yes, please," I answered with an awkward start. "I'd also like to see the patent files."

"Coming right up, Inspector General." She was getting sassier by the hour. How should I interpret this false subservience?

Cheryl unlocked a second file cabinet and stacked another two feet of files on the table.

I stared out the window a few minutes more, lost in thought . . . The rat tumors shrank — okay. But we don't know why the compounds work or why the inventor acted crazy when I tried to talk to him about it. I would have to go over the patent material very, very carefully.

I sat down in front of another tower of paper. I spent the better part of an hour checking the patent against the two-foot stack of data. What a pleasant surprise when my second reading of the patent showed I hadn't overlooked anything the night before. Moon's supporting data was well-organized. A computer-generated copy of the patent text actually contained footnotes referring to the pages of Moon's inventor's notebooks. A half-dozen spot checks, and I was convinced that all the experiments in Moon's patent were as real as BIOTECH's GLP animal studies. And, of course, the two sets of studies agreed. It looked really good. From this tower of organized data, BIOTECH could defend the patent, even if Moon was run over by a truck today.

The patent even had some rudimentary test tube experiments, showing that the three compounds could inhibit protein kinase C activity in cell homogenates. But it didn't show which of the eleven types were inhibited.

Most of Moon's chemistry experiments were aimed at determining the structure of the compounds. He had pages of mass spectroscopic analysis. He had a lot of unnecessary experiments using radiolabelled compounds to figure out how the molecules were synthesized in the sponge. Too many chemical structures. Dull stuff. What was the chemical structure of caffeine? That was the only chemical keeping me awake.

Deep knee bends are a good way to get the blood moving again. Okay, I would agree that Dr. Moon's invention was properly documented. What was next on my checklist? I remembered Jimbo Grabowski's midnight lecture on patent infringement. The claims in Dr. Moon's patent protected the three compounds and their use in the treatment of cancer. How could someone get around his claims? Would Dr. Moon's patent keep others from using other compounds? What if other people's compounds worked by inhibiting Moon's target enzyme, protein kinase C? Could Moon stop competitors from getting a patent on their new compounds?

It must have been the combined effect of sleep deprivation and bad indoor air; my brain was fuzzier than the fabric on the secretary's station. I went to the men's room and splashed water on my face.

Maybe, I decided, my problem was failing to feel the drama in these questions. The patent was there to defend the invention against interlopers. It had to surround the invention like a castle wall. The patent had to defend the invention by staking claims for the parts that were unique.

What about my predecessor Yang? Had he seen drama in these questions? And why hadn't he left any notes? Yang was a puzzle. I wondered about him, then shrugged my shoulders.

Returning to my room, I tried to visualize the wall of claims that the patent built around the invention. I pulled out a sheet of paper, drew a circle on it, and labeled it "three compounds". Around the circle, I drew a larger circle which I labelled "PKC inhibitors", the supposed mechanism for shrinking tumors. Could Moon's patent keep other people out of his little circle or out of both circles? I remembered from a logic course back in Swarthmore that these circles were called "Venn diagrams".

Music wafting in from Cheryl's office was beginning to get on my nerves now. Concentration eluded me. A warbly voiced man and a country-sounding woman sang a duet about being lost in love but getting back on their feet again. It was disturbing my circles, this gushing stream of warbling pseudo-emotion, these mindless lyrics smeared on a nonexistent melody. "Smooth jazz and cool vocals" was how the station touted the stuff.

Slowly my Venn diagrams became covered with doodles. I still didn't have any idea how strong were the claims in Moon's patent. I suspected there might be a problem. Let's face it, I told myself, Dr. Moon had acted strange when I started asking him about the possibility of competing compounds. It would be bad, bad, bad, if someone else had already discovered other compounds that shrank tumors by inhibiting the protein kinase C enzyme. I made a note to do a literature search when I returned to my hotel room. I made another note to check whether Broadmoore's contract guarded him against failure of patent protection in the future.

After digging deeper in the cabinet, I found the file that Moon had been so nasty about — correspondence with the patent examiner. The examiner seemed to have done his work well. He had challenged the novelty of Dr. Moon's application, citing three other patents that claimed tumor shrinkage by compounds from sponges. But Dr. Moon pointed out that these compounds didn't work on protein kinase C. They worked on completely different enzymes. I didn't need Venn diagrams to understand that one: The other people's compounds weren't even on the same sheet of paper.

The examiner considered Moon's arguments and agreed that Moon's invention was novel. So far, so good.

"How's it going with the patent?" Cheryl was checking up on me like a car salesman in a showroom.

"Thanks for asking. It would go a lot better, if you'd turn down the radio."

"Sure."

She rushed off to fix it right away but returned a few minutes later. She caught me looking out the window again. I pretended not to notice her. When I finally turned around she was staring at my jacket, draped over the chair. "Nice suit. Herringbone weave and pinstripes. Subtle halftone weaved in. Must've cost a thousand dollars."

"Close," I replied neutrally.

"Well, it's clear you're a man who understands quality."

I made no reply. Then she asked the question I had hoped nobody would ask . . .

"Ben, when did you get your Ph.D.?"

GETTING TO KNOW ALL ABOUT YOU 15

How should I repulse Cheryl's creeping familiarity?

Oh, hell! Anyone would expect me to chat a little. "I got my Ph.D a couple years back," I fibbed. It made me feel uncomfortable, thinking about having to defend my dissertation in a few short days. Hell! Now I'd have to play the Bostonian and pretend that I hadn't been living in Miami for the last eight years.

"Which university?" Cheryl asked.

"Well, it was granted by Boston University, but it seemed like I worked at every university in Boston, including Harvard." The best way to fib is to keep it indefinite. "Where did you get your degree, Cheryl?" The best defense is a good offense.

Cheryl shifted her weight and turned an ankle. It had to be uncomfortable wearing high heels all day. "I got my Ph.D. at George Washington University. And I did a postdoctoral fellowship at the National Institutes of Health."

I pursed my lips to indicate approval. "Washington, D.C., and suburban Maryland. Nice area. Where did you grow up?"

"Silver Spring." A toss of the head sent a wave through her golden hair. It came to rest on one velvety shoulder, exposing a sensuous neck, framed by the overlaid collar of her silk blouse.

"Silver Spring, Maryland," I said. "Visited there once. Suburb of Washington."

"Famous as the hometown of the popular comedian Goldie Hawn," Cheryl added smoothly.

"She must have felt right at home there, being so close to Chevy Chase." I felt proud of my clever *double-entendre*, coupling Maryland geography with the classic television program, Laugh-In.

Cheryl didn't recognize it as a joke right away. Slowly her face transformed into a ripe smile. She shook her head and said, "That's very good, Ben." She took a step closer and tapped my stomach with a knuckle.

Was Cheryl being friendly or was her touch a power tactic? It wasn't easy to hold her gaze. "If you did your graduate work at George Washington, you didn't have to go far from home — "

"I did my undergrad at George Washington, too," she said.

"Who'd you do your dissertation with?"

"Abdul Moran. I did a project on smooth muscle for him."

Cheryl shifted her weight and inched a little closer — close enough for me to have reached out and put my arm around her. "And your postdoctoral fellowship?"

"Worked for Henk van Friesland on effects of cyclic nucleotide inhibitors on cardiac contraction."

Funny, telling me she had worked *for* these guys. Maybe it was part of the business mentality: Work for pay. When people ask me about my work, I start telling them about the *project.* Rebecca is the same way.

I didn't know either of Cheryl's mentors, but I'd sure as heck find out about them.

It was hard to talk at close quarters with a woman who could have been on the cover of *Vogue*. The close match-up of our ages and professions increased my difficulty. And she was still an enigma. What made her tick? Was she a scientist or a material girl? While I tried to concentrate on the actual exchange of information, my eyes took refuge on her velvety shoulder. But they kept sliding to the collar of her silk blouse. From there, it was a slippery slide down the velvet-lined V to the place where men's eyes are programmed to come to rest.

My voice probably sounded wooden. "When did you finish the project with van Friesland?"

Cheryl inhaled, creating small strain-lines in the fabric around the most interesting tension-bearing buttons. "Four years ago. After that, I worked for a Washington defense contractor for two years. The project was in medical contingency planning. I've spent my last two years with Bud King."

Ah, she had been a Beltway Bandit, working for one of those piratical consulting firms organized for the sole purpose of ripping off the Defense Department. "So you stopped doing bench science after your postdoctoral fellowship," I interpreted.

Cheryl's eyes sharpened for an instant.

My comment amounted to a value judgment: Desk science is inferior to bench science. That's what most of us believed, but it would be awkward to discuss it here. I stared back dumbly to avoid giving Cheryl any cue.

Slowly Cheryl's pupils reverted to placid, transparent green. After a long silence, she said, "I like science, but I also want to have a life."

I knew what she meant. Sure, I knew the delight of an experiment that starts delivering answers at four o'clock Friday afternoon. I also knew the regret that comes with it when you have to call off a date and work straight through until five o'clock on Saturday morning. Lab bench science is a lonely, demanding pursuit.

"How do you like working here at BIOTECH?" I asked.

"Great. It's fun to put a real project together," she answered with an amiable smile. My implied insult was obviously forgotten. Maybe she did have a passion for applied scientific projects. "But we've been talking about me too much. What about you, Ben? Where'd you get your B.S.?"

How easily she turned the tables. I thought rapidly and replied, "Boston U."

"You didn't have to go too far from home for your Ph.D., either!" Now she was all bubbly enthusiasm. She made it sound like our life stories were written together in the stars. "And I bet you grew up there, too. You look and sound so Boston." She searched my eyes. Silk moved under velvet.

I lied the easy way — with a nod of the head. "Yeah, you can always get a lot of good courses around Boston."

She drew closer to me. "Tell me about your research."

I took a deep breath and gave her a snow job, rattling off complicated mechanistic stuff about protein kinases, and positive and negative feedback loops in cell control. I drew freely on my dissertation research. It wasn't hard to shake her loose from the subject with such talk.

Actually I don't think she really cared for details. But every time I looked up from the floor, her green eyes responded, feeding back on my small enthusiasms. I couldn't say a dozen words without her face blossoming into a smile. It felt like speaking into a microphone, plugged into an overly amplified public address system where any word might trigger a feedback blowup that can burst eardrums.

While I was thinking about how to pull the plug on the conversation, our accountant stopped in the doorway. He gave me a broad wink. He'd probably been scoring points with Alma all day and figured I was doing the same. I just waved back, and he walked on by.

"Ben, you were telling me you worked at a lot of schools."

Now, Cheryl was interviewing me like a television reporter. She even looked the part.

I moved a couple feet away, leaned against the table, frowned and stared her in the eye. "You might not believe it, but I was at every one of them — at one time or another."

It wasn't hard to play the aimless student. For six years, after graduating from Swarthmore, I had been little more than a lab bum, biding my time at Dr. Westley's toxicology laboratory and pursuing dilettante interests in the evening.

Cheryl kept studying me. "Did you do a postdoctoral stint in Boston, too?"

"Yes."

"Tell me about it."

She sidled deep into my personal space. I would have to do something to shake her off. After all, my heart belonged to Rebecca.

"I could tell you some. But the most interesting part was classified. Then I started doing consults for local biotech companies." If you have to lie, make it a big one.

"Interesting work," Cheryl said.

"I've been doing well as a biotech consultant for a long time. The pay's much better than for a run-of-the-mill postdoctoral position. You know about the glut of Ph.D.'s on the market. I'm not sure that I want to get onto the academic treadmill where you have to publish three papers a year and write one grant proposal after another. Have to face it: The conventional academic career path is like going for a swim with a millstone around your neck. Consultative science works just fine for me."

It wasn't hard to speak that piece; a part of me really felt it. I even managed to keep looking at Cheryl while saying it. I really didn't know what I was going to do with the Ph.D. I was getting from Bryan Medical School.

Funny how interested Cheryl was in my spiel. She nodded.

Her face mirrored my words and expressions. And she stood so close that I could almost feel the pull of static electricity from her blouse. Thinking of Rebecca, I moved away.

"I know exactly what you mean, Ben. Tell me, what sort of cases did you consult on?"

This was getting out of hand. I shook my head, took a deep breath and answered gruffly, "Look, you know that most consulting work is confidential. Now let's get back to work — evaluating the patent." Green eyes flickered. "I've already seen the patent examiner's search. I want to see your own search of prior patents by other inventors. And get me the prior scientific literature, too."

She said, "Yes," and walked away, insulted, as if I might be sending her out to get coffee. But she was just stepping out to fetch the keys. She unlocked the third cabinet and pulled out a foot of files. She plunked them down on the table and didn't stick around for my reaction.

One file contained a dozen patents by other inventors who claimed to have compounds with anticancer properties. After a quarter hour's study, I was pretty sure that none of the compounds was close to what BIOTECH was extracting from sponges. I took the patents to Cheryl's office.

"Could you make me copies of these patents and the correspondence with the patent examiner?"

"Don't you think that would be confidential?"

"Patents are certainly not confidential. They are already published. I want to study them in my hotel room tonight. Sure, the correspondence with the examiner is confidential, and I'll keep it that way. I want to study it in my hotel room, too. It's getting late."

Cheryl didn't argue. She simply handed the documents to the secretary at the central work station. I glanced into Ahma's room. She was alone, standing in stocking feet near her window, looking far into the distance. The beautiful Trinidadian probably didn't like indoor air any better than I.

Back in my room, I lit into a second file containing published scientific papers on anticancer compounds. The papers closest to Moon's invention were three publications by a Japanese group. Their compound also inhibited protein kinase C. But it was a completely different chemical compound. And it was extracted from fungus. No problem.

I spent a quarter hour typing information into my laptop computer — authors' names, titles, and journal citations of the papers in the file.

I knew how I'd sum it up for Broadmoore: "So far, so good."

Moon's compounds shrank rodent tumors. Dr. Lau and Singh's work proved that Moon's data was not faked. Dr. Moon's patent was in good shape. The U.S. Patent Office had examined it thoroughly and said it was novel. The scientific literature in the file seemed to back it up. And from the looks of the draft IND document, BIOTECH wouldn't waste any time getting started with human experiments once the FDA gave them the go-ahead.

Yes, Dr. Broadmoore, everything is fine. It looks like it might be worth buying for $10 million and upgrading with another $10 million. It's just fine. Well, everything is fine — except for one thing. Dr. Moon has been acting extremely defensive, and I don't understand why.

I found myself doodling on a sheet of paper. Cheryl flickered in and out of my field of peripheral vision. I pretended not to notice her. When I finally looked up she did a parody of a school girl hovering on the threshold of the principal's office.

"I am sorry to interrupt your concentration, Inspector General, but I have an important message." She used a sassy tone that matched my impression.

I ignored her sarcasm.

Now came a faint smirk. "You are cordially invited to Bud King's tonight for cocktails and a cruise of Biscayne Bay."

CLEARING THE DECKS FOR ACTION 16

I acted like I had to think about this cocktail and cruise invitation. "I don't know, Cheryl. There's still plenty of work to do. On the other hand, it might give me a chance to talk with Dr. Moon under relaxed circumstances."

"I can't promise you that, Ben. But it would certainly be a nice chance to meet Bud — and the rest of the team."

Yes, I thought, business deals probably required this sort of thing — socializing over cocktails.

I stalled for a long time before saying yes. Cheryl told me King kept his boat on the Coral Gables Waterway. She gave me an address on Granada Avenue. With a 7:30 p.m. appointment, there was just enough time to return to the hotel and change. I turned down Cheryl's offer to call me a cab.

What a relief to be breathing outdoor air again!

The MetroMover station is one block inland from the high-rises of Brickell Avenue. It was nestled between 1920s vintage Florida Cracker houses made from "Dade County pine". The wood is naturally termite-resistant, but real estate speculators and high-rise developers had been gnawing away at the neighborhood for a couple of decades.

The MetroMover station was reminiscent of a French garden café, enclosed by a latticework of white bars. I deposited a quarter in the turnstile and rode the shiny escalator. The platform was about level with a sea of green — mango, papaya, live oak and royal poinciana. Through the tree canopy glinted an occasional solar reflection from a tin roof.

A faint electric whine announced the next rubber-wheeled, driverless vehicle. An automated voice invited me to step in and please stand clear of the doors. It was a Disney World ride, except that all the sights were completely authentic. After coasting several hundred yards through the treetops, we made a tight turn to round an old three-story hotel, now a flop house. I could look right into the bedrooms. It was like a lighted display on anthropological museum. All detail was completely authentic — the stain on the bare mattress, the peeled veneer of the dressers, and the ancient tongue and groove floorboards. A swarthy man in a white, ribbed undershirt was leaning through a termite-riddled window frame, smoking a cigarette.

I tried to shove all that from my mind, and I thought about how to summarize the day for Broadmoore.

Now our car was ascending the steep concrete guideway that arched high over the narrow Miami River. We passed the mast of a container ship. Standing next to me, a German tourist was enthusiastically videotaping our approach to Downtown Miami. "*Es ist so wie eine Achterbahn*," he told his wife.

Yes, it was like a roller coaster. And when we docked in a slot cut out high on the side of the NationsBank building, it seemed like *Star Trek*. Then we launched, gliding eastward past skyscrapers and northward past cruise ships, docked at the port terminals across from the bayfront park. Next we ducked into the center of old downtown, snaking around 1920s vintage buildings and along an occasional section of street with southern-style covered sidewalks.

The Omni station was only a one-block walk from my hotel. I called Broadmoore from my room. He sounded like I'd awakened him from a nap.

"Sorry to bother you, Dr. Broadmoore. I was just wondering if we would meet tonight. I want to report in."

"No formal meeting is planned. How did you fare today?"

"I couldn't find anything wrong with the rodent trials. And my search of the files supported the claims of Moon's patent. The correspondence with the patent examiner looked fine. The examiner's file didn't show any dangerous-looking prior art. But Dr. Moon, himself, was not very cooperative. When I tried to discuss the patent, he was surly — "

"Surliness should not protect him from a few well-placed questions."

"The tactic he used was to insist that the interview was redundant. He kept saying it was all explained in the patent files. You didn't supply them in the metal cases, so I wasn't able to see them — until after the interview. Moon acted like I was an idiot."

"Rather like cross-examining a hostile witness, I gather."

"You said that right!"

"But you will not let him prevail with that tactic."

"I won't let him get away with anything. I am compiling a list of specific questions that he won't be able to evade. Tomorrow I will pin him down like a chloroformed butterfly."

Broadmoore remained silent for an uncomfortably long time. "Is there more to be said?"

"I am invited to King's for cocktails and a cruise. I wanted your suggestion as to whether I should go."

Once again Broadmoore remained silent. He let me flutter like a pinned live butterfly. His eventual reply was a drawn-out monosyllable. "Well?"

He made me feel like a kid, asking permission to go out on a school night. Hell! Everyone knew these social meetings were important. First, the two groups have to sniff each other out. Then they create a bond, so that they can work together.

"Well, Dr. Broadmoore, are you going on the cruise?"

"No. I'm from the Midlands. I do not fare well at sea."

"I never get sick at sea."

I must have said it in Gilbert and Sullivan cadence; Broadmoore chuckled. "Well, perhaps you can learn something about the Captain of the Pinafore."

"Maybe I'll learn something about the *Pirates of Penzance*."

It was a complete shot in the dark; I knew absolutely nothing about the operetta.

"Quite, quite, quite!" Broadmoore said with a booming laugh. "Geoffrey said you were a bright lad. Keep your eyes and ears open. Cheers." (Click)

What to do now? I needed to double check that there weren't any patents out there that could be dangerous to Moon's invention. I remembered Robert, a reference librarian who had helped me to get information for the last job Dr. Westley gave me. I pulled out my little brown book and dialed Robert's number at the Miami-Dade County Public Library. Was he still working the night shift?

A middle-aged female voice answered in a strong Spanish accent. She listened to my request and laid down the phone without comment. In the background, I could hear Robert's high-pitched voice. He seemed to be helping a patron locate a manufacturing company in Brazil. He finished in three minutes and picked up.

"Robert. This is a voice from the past. Ben Candidi."

"Benjamin!" Robert exclaimed in his excited falsetto. "I haven't heard from you for a long time. Thought maybe you left town."

I told him about getting my Ph.D. in a few days. He told me about some courses he was taking as a hobby at Miami-Dade Community College. I would have liked to ask whether he'd discovered any new bike routes, but there wasn't enough time for his answer.

"Robert, I need you to do a special project for me. I'm going to pay two hundred dollars, and I need it fast."

"No, you don't need to pay me anything, Benjamin. I'll do it for free."

It was once again time to take Robert under my wing and serve up a giant helping of big brotherly advice. "Robert, don't you remember me lecturing you about not selling yourself cheap?" When I first met him he had been doing research for lawyers at eight dollars an hour. A guy pushing thirty should be making money at something. "Look, Robert, I'm on a roll. I'm getting paid big bucks for the project, and I want to spread it around among my friends."

"But Benjamin —"

"But nothing! Now take this down. I want you to do a patent search and give me anything on anticancer drugs and — either marine sponges or protein kinases or protein phosphatases." I spelled out all the terms. "Combine all the biochemical terms with sponges, using a Boolean 'OR'. Then combine the result with cancer, using a Boolean 'AND'.

"I've got you, Benjamin."

Although Robert probably didn't have more than a dozen college credits to his name, his general knowledge was greater than many profs. And he was a whiz at computerized information retrieval. He may have flunked high school algebra, but he took to the logical operations of Boolean Algebra like a duck to water. You didn't have to draw him any Venn diagrams. He always kept crisp mental images of each category and worked with great enthusiasm.

"Can you do the project tonight on your computer at work?"

"No problem. And if the library closes before I'm done, I'll finish it at home on Prodigy."

Robert lived in a second story garage apartment behind a Coconut Grove house owned by a middle-aged couple. They treated him like a son.

I said, "Give me full text of any hit. Give it to me on disk. And I want a photocopy of any hits where the anticancer compound comes from sponges. I'm staying at the Marriott on North Bayshore Drive. Please bring it to my room tonight. If I'm not there, leave it at the desk."

I started to give him directions to the hotel, but he interrupted, saying, "Sure, Ben. That's the one next to Trinity Cathedral. I can ride my bike there straight from work."

Now for a delightful evening cruise — or so I hoped.

THE MECHANIC'S TALE 17

Luckily I had packed extra clothes for not-so-rigorous occasions, and I had olive-green Dockers slacks, a white polo shirt and rubber-soled, canvas-topped slip-ons. Double-checked the ensemble in the full-length mirror. Curly black hairs over my sternum were enjoying their freedom, peeking through the V-neck of the polo shirt. It felt good to get out of that business suit. I locked my laptop computer in my attaché case and put it in a dresser drawer.

The Omni Shopping Gallery on Biscayne Boulevard was only a block away. It had a food court on the second level. I ordered a deli sandwich at the New York Subway, and I took it to a bench in front of a Radio Shack store. I listened to the Gallery's calliope and watched the kids on the old-time merry-go-round while I ate. Their little faces glowed as they rode through shafts of light from the slanting three-story window. After dinner, I took the escalator down to the cab stand in front of the Wyndham Hotel in the Omni complex.

I gave the driver instructions that would spare us the worst of the rush hour traffic — west through Overtown, skirting the Medical Center, south into Little Havana, west on Calle Ocho, then south, skirting the business district of Coral Gables, "The City Beautiful", and picking up University Drive. On the way to The City Beautiful, I thought about Bud King. Why does a construction tycoon get into the biotech business? Did he have any legitimate interest in this work? Did he really think he was helping to cure cancer? Or was he just a greedy developer who thought his methods would work just as well in science?

The stately mansions along Granada Avenue reminded me of George Merrick, the granddaddy of all developers. He's the guy who "invented" Coral Gables. Behind those mansions ran the canal that Merrick had blasted from coral rock back in the 1920s. Merrick dubbed it "Venetian" and lined it with pilings decorated like barber poles. He offered vacationing Northerners free gondola rides for listening to his real estate pitch. That reminded me of Bud King's flamboyantly choreographed luncheon. Maybe every good cause needs its snake oil salesmen and hucksters.

Today residential Coral Gables rivals Beverly Hills. And it would sure as hell beat out Venice, California, in a competition for the title of "Venice, USA".

Coral Gables is a class act. The only thing the Northerners get for free is a glimpse of the canal from the window of a tour bus when it stops on a strategically selected bridge. Now the charms of Merrick's canal system are reserved for those who are rich enough to afford a canal-backed estate.

It was a pleasant ride south along Granada Boulevard.

Where we crossed U.S. Highway 1, the canal widened and became the Coral Gables Waterway. We rolled into Bud King's area a good 15 minutes ahead of the appointment.

King's neighborhood also followed Merrick's plan — large, set back, two-story Spanish and Italian style houses with stuccoed walls, chimneys, bell towers, and complicated barrel tile roofs. Black cast-iron ornamentation and multifaceted outdoor lamps provided a final touch of charm.

As the house numbers got closer to King's address, I told the driver to slow down. King's house was a one-story red brick hybrid of colonial and ranch styles. Out front was a big silver step van. I told the cab driver to park in front along the road.

King's colonial-ranch stuck out like a sore thumb. The flat roof tiles were sheathed in a shiny-white, sprayed-on plastic material.

Six plain white, cylindrical columns rose from a concrete slab porch to support the low overhang of the roof.

The right end of the house served as a garage, judging from its large white door and the asphalt driveway. Immediately I recognized the feline backside of Cheryl's maroon Riviera. To the left of it was a big, white, late-model Cadillac. It had to be King's; it was parked closest to the front door. Funny, the resemblance between the siblings and cousins of the extended family of General Motors. Both cars had a rounded rear end — but the Caddy's was enormous and crass, while the Riviera's rear end was more inviting.

A forest-green Jaguar was parked a respectful distance behind. With two wheels resting on the grass, it left enough space for the Caddy and the Riviera to get out. The Jag just had to belong to King's lawyer.

As I stepped out of the cab, the statement on the silver van's bumper sticker caught my eye: "Maybe I voted for him, but I sure didn't vote for HER."

No, it couldn't be Sam!

I stepped back into the street to read the lettering on the van's broad side of shiny aluminum: Sam's Marine Engine Repair.

Sam was probably working on King's boat. From inside the van came the sound of metal clinking on metal.

"Sam!" I called in through the sliding door on the passenger side.

"Oh, don't tell me!" came a whiny drawl. A familiar blond-bearded face popped out of the doorway. "Ben! Ain't seen you in a month of high-tide, full-moon, fishin' Sundays. Got to thinking somebody musta run over you an' your bicycle." His chipped-tooth grin told me he wasn't insulted that I'd been neglecting him.

"No, Sam. I keep a good eye out for power-wagons." I approached, extending my right hand. "But what about you? You look fine, but let's see your other hand. Didn't saw off any more fingers, did you?"

Sam was proud of that story. He must have told it a hundred times sitting with his buddy Lou at Captain Walley's waterside bar. Any time the pair met someone new, good buddy Lou would say something about "The Finger", and the retelling of the story became as inevitable as another round of beer.

You see, one hot afternoon when Sam was down in the bilge, sculpting a fiberglass engine mount with his electric saw, something slipped. And off came the tip of his left index finger along with a sizable piece of bone. But Sam didn't cry out or faint. He just pulled off his headband and twisted it into a tourniquet to stop the bleeding. Then he groped around in the oily bilge water long enough to find his missing fingertip. He wiped it off and wrapped it in a paper towel soaked in beer. (According to Sam, beer has all kinds of medicinal properties.) Finally, he drove to South Miami Hospital, walked into the emergency room, and told the doc to sew it back on.

Now Sam had workman's comp, but he never filed a claim. Florida Crackers don't take much stock in bureaucracy — government or private. And the next day he and his reattached finger were back on the job.

"So — yuh remember that story, do yuh, Ben?" Sam's eyes twinkled behind his puffy bearded cheeks like a Christmas card Santa Claus. Then his smile slowly faded. "But yuh don't stop around Captain Walley's for a brew anymore. An' we never see you. Why it was just last week that Lou was sayin' you was probably gettin' too high-falutin' for us."

"Sorry, Sam. I've been hot and heavy with my girlfriend."

Sam scratched his pot belly and said, "So what'cha doin' here?"

"You might say I'm on one of my 'la-di-das'. I'm part of an inspection team they got up to look into a science company that a man named C.C. King got himself into. I'm working for a guy from Boston that King's trying to sell it to." I looked warily around the corner of the van toward the house. No one was coming out to greet me. Maybe Sam and I could chat for a couple of minutes in the shelter of the van.

"You ain't working for King?"

"No, I'm working for the guy from Boston. King thinks I'm from Boston. You might say I'm working undercover to check out King."

Sam reached in his shirt pocket and pulled out a Marlboro. "You always was mysterious — workin' for that medical examining place and doin' all them co-caine readings and such." He glanced, slant-eyed, toward the house and flicked his lighter. He squinted at me and asked, "So — what you figure you need to know about Bud King?"

"For starters, tell me what you think of him."

Sam took a big drag, rolled his eyes, and blew out a cloud of smoke. "The guy's a big asshole. He's just a big asshole that wants to be a bigger asshole."

"A big asshole — like a big show-off? Or big asshole — like he goes out of his way to give you a hard time?"

"Both," Sam said, exhaling another cloud of smoke. "Acts like he knows everything about boats. He don't know nothing. Fucking candy-ass. Got them twin two hundred horsepower eight-cylinder Chrysler gasoline burners. Hell, gasoline ain't meant to be out on the water. And he don't never run them 'cept when he's got some kinda' fancy la-de-da executive party. He leaves them settin' for a coupla weeks, but they's supposed t' be purrin' smooth as a pussy cat when he turns his key and slow-revs his boat outa his friggin' Coral Gables la-de-da Waterway."

"He doesn't know about moisture buildup on the plugs?" I asked.

"Wouldn't know if he had a plug wire dangling on his donk. That's what I'm here for today, Ben. To twist a fucking spark plug wire, so the jerkoff don't have the same trouble starting it up like he did last weekend. Lucky it was just a plug wire, 'cause he pulled his old trick again."

"His old trick?"

"Yeah, running his engines warm before I come. He thinks it's good, 'cause he can show me exactly what's wrong. Don't think about how I gotta crawl in there on top of a hot engine. I'd rather be humping the Devil's be-hind in Hell than go a'crawlin' on a hot engine." Sam's occasional grins told me it wasn't all that bad.

"Did you tell King not to run the engine before you came?"

"If I tol' him once, I tol' him a hunderd times. But that asshole won't listen. So — I don't mind taking his money to twist his spark plug wires — especially when he's paying me with a company check, anyhow."

"The guy doesn't have any mechanical sense — "

"Don't have no kinda sense at all. You know what that jerk did to me a couple weeks ago? He'd been reading his yachting magazine, and he went out and ordered his-self a top-of-the-line GPS satellite unit. The thing tells you exactly where you are and keeps a log on everywhere the tub's been for the last year. Says he'll pay me to install it. Had to spend an hour readin' the instruction book.

"That book had all kinds of instructions — like how it's always s'posed to be on a live wire so you don't lose your data, but you can disconnect it for short times 'cause it's got a backup battery. All that kinda shit.

"So — I read the shit and mount the unit right in front of his captain's chair where he can see it good. I turn it on, and it reads a longitude and latitude that ain't more than a tenth of a mile from his dock, if you can believe the chart he gave me. Then he wants me to prove it's accurate like it should be — down to fifty feet or something. Hell, the GPS was probably more accurate than his ol' chart."

"You're right, Sam. They're using GPS to correct the charts."

"So — I sit down and start writing up a bill. Then he comes over and shows me in the manual where his unit's supposed to record numbers for anywhere the boat's been spending more than ten minutes. Supposed to do that automatically. Supposed to help you get back to your favorite fishin' holes. Hell, Ben, I don't know how to pull waypoints out of that computer's ass."

Sam threw down his cigarette, stomped it, and lit another one. He was sounding whinier by the minute. "So — I tell him he's gotta read the manual his-self. The damn thing's three inches thick. So — he gets all huffy and says he ain't payin' for no installation, 'til he know's it's workin' right."

I looked toward the house, probably impatiently. I hadn't reckoned with a two-cigarette conversation.

Sam shook his head and said, "Then King shows me a section full of fancy technical stuff — where you can increase its accuracy down to five yards. He tells me I've got to do that for him, too. Or he ain't paying me. Hell, I can't figure that all out, sittin' in the hot sun." Sam's mouth was running belligerent, but his eyes were pleading for sympathy. He reminded me of a kid who has to stay after school until he straightens out his arithmetic problems.

"No, Sam, that isn't fair to withhold pay — unless you both agreed beforehand that programming would be part of the installation."

"Yeah. He did it to me after I'd got an honest bill writ' up. So — you know what I told him? That I'd pull the installation and he don't pay me nothing, but I'd never work for him again."

"Did that bring him to his senses?"

"Fucking A." For a few seconds, Sam chuckled over his triumph. Then his face clouded over. "Hell, I didn't never go to no electronics school, Ben."

Time to give Sam a pep talk. "Hell, knowing all about engines and busting frozen bolts without destroying the heads is enough to ask from one guy. Listen up: My friend Zeekie — Joe Kazekian —

runs ABBA Radio & Video, out west on Bird Road. The guy's a genius with electronics. You get King to agree to pay in advance, and you bring in Zeekie for one hundred bucks an hour as your special consultant. Then you split the fee. Make sure you get King to make notes in the manual on everything Zeekie shows him. That way you can say it's his fault, if he calls up afterwards — complaining it doesn't work."

"Ben, you's sharper than a riverboat gambler." Sam was all smiles again.

A cab pulled up behind us.

It was show time.

BARCAROLE 18

I took a couple steps back, pointed to the house, and waved to Sam like I was thanking him for directions. Sam understood and waved me off. Out of the cab stepped Elkins, our team's lawyer. His idea of nautical dress was a navy blazer and polo shirt over white slacks and oversized running shoes. He all but ignored me as I fell into step with him. I pressed the bell and a middle-aged Latina maid admitted us a few seconds later.

Passing through the hallway, I noticed a large portrait of a prim-faced woman, dressed and posed as a *grand dame*. She had to be Mrs. King. We entered an enormous living room where other guests were socializing. Cheryl rose from a chair to greet us. She looked sporty with her white canvas-topped shoes, dark blue slacks with slight bell-bottom flare, and loosely fitting white silk blouse. She said we should make ourselves comfortable and that Bud would be happy to fix us a drink.

I gazed across the room. "Is Mrs. King going on the boat?"

"No, she is out of town — visiting relatives. Just make yourself at home." Cheryl called to our accountant who was sitting alone at the end of a sofa under the oversized shade of a huge floor lamp. "Can I get you anything, Thad?"

I remembered his last name was Smith.

Mrs. King's interior decoration fit her portrait — lace curtains, massive chairs and sofas, and walnut-stained end tables. On a coffee table, copies of *Readers Digest* and *Modern Maturity* were arranged in neat little stacks. Copies of *Yachting* magazine, and *Field and Stream* were strewn on top.

At the other end of the sofa, our colleague Elkins was already seated and deep in conversation. He was talking with a dark-haired, bearded man who had the look of a brooding baritone villain in an opera. I later learned his name was Roger Black, King's lawyer.

King was mixing a drink at the bar. The arrangement stood on other side of the room before a sliding glass door that looked out on a patio and a pool. He was dressed similarly to Cheryl but with a heavy, loose-weave, boat-neck shirt. When he looked up and saw me with Cheryl he put down the glass and walked over.

"Bud, this is Dr. Ben Candidi."

"Nice you could come along," King said in a voice loud enough to get everyone's attention. He rocked me off balance with a handshake that was more like an Indian wrestling tactic. "Cheryl showed you the lab, huh? Pretty fancy — all those rats and belljars, calibrated instruments and everything."

Since all eyes in the room were on us, I didn't tell King the lab wasn't fancy at all.

King took a quick glance around the room and shouted out, "Well, I guess everyone's here that's going. You all put on your rubber-soled boat shoes. The *Ace* don't like scrapes. Just call him *Ace* for short. Real name's *Ace in the Hole*." King gestured toward the sliding glass door. "Go out to the patio and around the pool."

As the first man out, I was also the first to fall under the predatory stare of Diana the Huntress, stationed on the other side of the pool. Diana was a statue, bronze and life-size. She stood sideways in an archer's pose with her bow at full draw —pointed directly at me.

The guests were slow to get moving, so Diana had plenty of time to cast her spell over me. Her back described a sensuous arch with a nicely rounded fanny at one end and charmingly uplifted breasts at the other. Exquisite nipples hovered tantalizingly, but confidently, close to the draw of the imaginary bow string. Her face, perfectly aligned with the arrow, bore a close-lipped smile expressing confidence that she would strike home. I imagined a Roman senator's daughter, recently come-of-age, impetuously throwing off her wrap, and challenging a suitor to a contest of naked archery.

A name occurred to me for the work of art: "Soft Kill".

As guests emerged from the house, I stepped out of the line of fire and amused myself with their reactions to Diana. Thad Smith looked away quickly, then sneaked a second look. Roger "brooding-baritone" Black had obviously seen her before. Lawyer Elkins smiled slyly. "Nice piece," he told King.

"Picked her up at an antique shop at Twenty-Seventh Avenue and U.S. 1," King answered loud enough for everyone to hear.

"What did your wife say?" asked Thad Smith.

King half-muttered, "Says what she always says: 'I was so embarrassed.'"

The backyard had a good view of the canal, but I didn't see any *Ace*. At this point, the Coral Gables Waterway was about 70 yards wide. It was a good place to dock a cabin cruiser. Three blocks north, the low-lying bridges of U.S. Highway 1 would block a big boat.

King gestured for me to go to the side of the yard. I was first confused because that area looked like a storage depot for his construction company. A towerlike framework of aluminum tubes rose from behind a tall stack of cinder blocks. King pushed on by. After I followed him to the far side of the cinder block depot, it all became clear: The aluminum structure was a "tuna tower". It rose from a large, rectangular pit cut 15-feet deep in the coral rock. Nestled snugly in this pit was an ocean-capable, 36-foot cabin cruiser.

The yacht was moored tautly, nose-in. The bow had the curve and flare of a vessel built for rapid transit of high seas. Two anchors were fixed at the end of a foot-long bowsprit, hovering like steel bumpers a couple feet from the steep coral wall.

Everything behind the bowsprit was optimized for handling wind and sea. The forward deck started flat, then rose and curved gracefully to form the front wall of the main cabin. A windshield was built in to allow piloting from the main cabin in heavy weather. Above the windshield, the fiberglass wall continued to rise and curve, forming the base of the semi-protected flying bridge. Also called the "fly bridge", this was the piloting station for fair weather.

The flying bridge's roof came level with the patio. And high above, atop the tuna tower, was a third piloting station, useful for sighting and chasing schools of fast-running fish.

I followed King down a steep, narrow flight of stairs, cut on the side of the long wall of pocked coral. The stairs ended at the *Ace's* stern which faced the Waterway. The yacht's large aft deck — its "fantail" area — was set with canvas-backed folding chairs. Large letters on the stern announced: *Ace in the Hole.*

"Guess where the *Ace* rode out Hurricane Andrew?" King yelled out. Nobody answered his rhetorical question. "Right here," he said, waving a stubby finger in a circle above his head. "Didn't get a scratch. And you can see why."

The walls of the enclosure were lined by vertically mounted, rubber-coated four-by-fours. King tapped one. "I ain't in the construction business for nothing."

I was reminded of Captain Nemo in *Twenty Thousand Leagues Under the Sea.*

We boarded the stern over the starboard rail. I noticed deep scrape marks on this section of the rail. Apparently King had not always taken his own advice about wearing rubber-soled shoes. Some of the scrapes were deep enough to contain grit.

King pulled on a fiberglass seat that was molded into the outside wall of the cabin. He swung it open like a door. This was the access to the engine compartment. King reached in and flipped a switch, explaining that he was disarming the alarm. A small red light by the door of the main salon stopped blinking.

Yes, Sam was right: The compartment was just big enough for a man to lie down between the large gasoline engines. Underneath, a lot of space was occupied with water hoses and air vent ducts. King shut the seat-door, stepped to the door of the main salon, and opened it — after pushing a sequence of buttons on the combination lock.

King reached in and flipped on lights. "Go on in, Candidi, and take a look around."

I walked in and did a marine survey, paperless variety:

Main salon with sofas to the starboard side; teak rail along ceiling, providing hand grips; dinette to port; steering station to starboard; forward left of the main salon, a TV and VCR; three steps down to port, a kitchen area with sink, refrigerator and microwave oven; forward to the head on the portside and cabin with bunk-type berth arrangement for two on the starboard; and in the forward V, a master bedroom.

Returning to the kitchen area, I noticed a curious arrangement of several liquor bottles in a stand. From each bottle rose a thin polypropylene tube, leading to a small module that didn't look much different from the pump on Dr. Lau's HPLC instrument back in the lab. It was an automated cocktail mixer. On the bottom of the module were a series of buttons to select drinks. Above was a LCD screen like on a laptop computer.

I returned to the fantail where Cheryl was getting the guests seated in deck chairs. King was already sitting in the captain's chair up on the fly bridge. The blowers were running. A minute later he was turning the key. The two massive gasoline engines came to life, purring like contented lions and throbbing the deck under our feet.

King rose from his chair and cranked a winch mounted on the side of the flying bridge. Above his head, guy wires strained and the tubular frame of the tuna tower began to tilt back toward us. Smith and Elkins looked up warily.

"Don't worry, I ain't gonna bean you," King yelled. "Gotta take the tuna tower down. The Hardee Street bridge ain't no drawbridge."

Soon the tower was secured a few feet over our heads. King climbed back into his chair and called out, "Get ready to cast off."

Cheryl uncleated the stern lines, pulled them through the hawsepipes, and threw them on the dock. King applied a second's backthrust to keep the bow off the coral wall, while Cheryl cautiously made her way along the narrow strip of the deck between cabin windows and safety rail. She detached the two remaining lines on the bow. No question that she knew what she was doing.

King backed the boat out gently, touching neither the dock nor the coral-mounted fender bars. After clearing the dock, he glanced down as if to check that we were all safely seated in the canvas deck chairs that were placed along the rail and secured with rope. I remained standing near the port rail, holding the ladder that went up to the fly bridge. Out in the channel, King manipulated his throttle levers, skillfully turning the boat about its center. Soon we were motoring south along the canal.

It looked like a tight squeeze under the Hardee Road bridge. Its concrete arch couldn't have been taller than 15 feet at its apex. It couldn't have been wider than 30 at its base. The cars speeding across the arched bridge seemed to be tossed from one side to another. King made the final approach at five knots. I held my breath as we entered the concrete tunnel. The outgoing tide jostled and accelerated us to eight knots. But King held a straight course, and we emerged without a scrape.

"Like the tunnel of love at the county fair," our accountant said excitedly.

And like the carny who sits up there and runs the ride, King turned around and grinned down at us. What a funny picture he made with his big rear end framed in the cutout of his chair. His rear end was punctuated by the stern light, mounted a couple feet below. He made me think of a friendly farmer who hitches a wagon to his tractor and takes you out for a hayride. But when he squashed a microphone into his bulldog face, keyed down, and started talking to us over the loudspeaker, I started thinking of him as a tour bus driver.

"To the left, you see that property that looks like a Kennedy compound. On top of the coral bluff, behind the long tall wall with all them arched holes in it, there's a central house and two small houses on the sides. And on each side of the property there's a boathouse. If you look into them close, you can see that they carved inlets in the rock — just like mine."

King seemed to be enjoying himself up there.

"That house was the CIA's headquarters when they was trying to rub out Castro — back when Kennedy was president. So it really was a Kennedy compound — ha, ha, ha. The CIA gunrunners used to load their boats from this dock. And the agents debriefed them in that house when they got back. Too bad the CIA botched the job."

The canal broadened and curved to the left. On the outside of the bend, the coral bluff was 20 feet high. A row of park benches lined the crest. King keyed down on the mike and announced, "That's where Le Bus takes the European tourists to get a good look at our canal."

Above, a steady stream of cars rounded the "Cartagena Plaza" traffic circle. The bridge for LeJeune Road was much wider than the one we had transited at Hardee Street. King upped the revs and took us under without generating excitement. Here the coral walls rose 30 feet and the canal felt like a canyon. It was getting dark.

King stood, steering with one hand, while he vigorously cranked his tuna tower into a state of erection. Then he banged around for a minute, probably inserting retaining pins. I had to give him credit. It was an ingenious rig. After he'd locked it in place, the guy wires didn't even show.

The 20-story Edgewater Condominiums came into view.

King picked up the mike and announced, "Cabin personnel will serve drinks. And if anyone would like to visit the captain on the flight deck, please come on up."

I hung out on the port side, passing the time estimating how much gasoline we had guzzled since casting off a mile back. Looking through the glass, I saw Cheryl in the salon, punching numbers into King's electronic cocktail-dispensing gizmo. She came out to the fantail carrying what looked like a Tom Collins. She grabbed the other side of my ladder. King must have sensed her approach by telepathy: He turned just as she took her first step up the ladder. They both stretched a little, and the cocktail was smoothly transferred. King put it in a teak holder next to the wheel.

I had to admit, Cheryl moved around on the boat pretty well.

Cheryl stepped back down, locked onto me with a smile, and asked, "What are you drinking, Ben?"

"You can keystroke in a gin and tonic."

Cheryl threw her face to the darkening sky and replied with a breathless laugh. "Funny!" She swung to my side of the ladder and punched a knuckle softly into my stomach. "The machine is not programmed for G&Ts, but I'll be glad to do it by hand." She winked like she'd made a little joke. "I'm sure we have tonic water in the refrigerator. Meanwhile, the captain has invited you to tour the bridge. Go on up, and I'll bring your drink to you." She turned to our accountant who was seated close by and had been listening. "Mr. Smith, you are also invited to the bridge."

"No, thank you. With all the swaying, I think I'd be more comfortable down here." I could believe it of him.

Cheryl turned to me. "Why don't you help Mr. Elkins up to the second deck. He's invited too." Before returning to the cabin, she patted my shoulder as if I might be a trusted member of her team.

One glance to our illustrious John Elkins, Esq. told me that he had no sea legs and would not want to be helped up to the fly bridge.

I made a show of climbing the seven vertical steps like an old hand. King turned and locked eyes on me — like a destroyer captain waiting for his petty officer's report to the bridge. I pretended to be impressed with the pilot station's bank of instruments. After a few seconds, King unlocked his eyes and chuckled. He turned toward the fantail, looked down, and shook his head. "What's with your Mr. Elkins? Can't he climb ladders?"

"Doesn't seem to have the stomach for it, sir," I answered, smartly. The "sir" came out involuntarily.

Yes, it was like a scene from a B-grade World War II movie.

King smiled to himself and shook his head. His big hand made a curious gesture that started as a pat on the shoulder and ended as a dismissive left-handed salute. "Damn lawyers are nothing but a bunch of pukes anyway. Climb into the mate's chair, and I'll show you how to run this baby."

The Edgewater Condominium towers were behind us now.

Dwarfing us on the left was a city block-sized complex topped with two Italian-style turrets. On the right, darkened mangrove swamp glided by. I climbed into the mate's chair, placing myself elbow to elbow with King.

"You know anything about boats?" King asked

"A little — but nothing this size."

"Yeah, coming from Boston you probably know all about dinky day sailers and rowing races on your muddy Charles River. But up there they ain't got so many boats this size. Down here, we don't have to haul out our boats every September. Down here, it don't freeze. Hell, I could live on the *Ace* if I wanted to."

"If I owned this yacht, I'd have to live on it," I answered.

I sure as hell couldn't afford to run it. Probably cost $400 in fuel just to take it out for a few hours.

"You're one of those technical guys that likes to stare at instruments all day. Well, here's some instruments." King motioned to the panel of glowing orange and green dials. "Got it all. Tachometers for engine rpm, oil pressure, engine temperature. Even got a built-in fire extinguisher that will fill the engine compartment with Halon, if they catch fire. All I have to do is pull this knob. And it's got carbon dioxide backup. If you knew how much it cost me to get the system recharged, you'd fall out of your chair."

"Probably would."

"And, of course, I've got a depth meter, compass, radar, autopilot and a GPS for satellite navigation. You're even supposed to be able to hook them up together to — " He abruptly stopped talking, as if suddenly distracted. Then he shook his head and inched the throttles forward, speeding our progress toward open water.

I was curious to look at the GPS which had given Sam so much trouble. Its large screen shined iridescent green. The screen was big enough to display maps, but all it showed now was longitude and latitude numbers. The left-most digits didn't change, but the final digits whirled like the meter on the pump at the filling station. I estimated that we were passing channel markers at a rate of 50 cents per minute.

"It looks like a top-of-the-line GPS," I said, enjoying my advantage of special knowledge. "Does it have a lot of waypoints?"

"More than you can keep track of." Now King sounded almost defensive. He pulled his glass from its teak holder and took a big gulp.

"I hear that some of these units will record waypoints for you automatically," I continued.

King didn't respond. Should I tell him the theory of GPS?

Back on my coffee table, under Rebecca's picture, sat an issue of *Scientific American* with one hell of an article on the subject. Using so-called differential methods, engineers had overcome the tiny inaccuracy of the atomic frequency clocks that beep time-position signals from orbiting satellites. GPS receivers can now measure changes in position down to the nearest three feet.

In fact, geologists have bolted super-precise units onto rocks in the California desert to predict earthquakes. But King probably wouldn't want to hear a lecture from me. He'd lose the upper hand. I said nothing.

King must have been watching me while I contemplated his instruments. He let out a deep-throated laugh. "That's what I need — a smart young guy like you to show me how to use my equipment. I should get an electronics boy down here some time."

I sensed a soft tug on the back of my chair. I half-turned, touching Cheryl's breast with my shoulder. She didn't withdraw. She simply handed me a glass and said, "And a gin and tonic for the first mate." Our fingers touched lightly. "And another setup for the captain?" she asked.

"Maybe later," King said with a brief glance in our direction.

Cheryl remained, holding the back of my seat, fingertips of one hand resting lightly on my shoulder.

"Do you do much fishing?" I asked King, trying to be friendly.

"No. Don't have the patience for rod and reel fishing. I like to jump in and chase after them. I've got a spear gun and scuba equipment down in the locker. Do a lot better when I can see what I'm going after."

Then he gasped, as if he'd seen a piling dead ahead. Odd, I thought. We'd already passed the last pole, a two-second flashing red marker that had just switched on as we'd approached. We were now in the open water of darkened Biscayne Bay, heading south.

King turned to Cheryl and said, "Maybe I've been spending too much time up here." I felt Cheryl move back. "Maybe Dr. Candidi would like to sit in the catbird seat." He turned to me and asked, "You know enough about the rules of the road to be lookout?"

"I guess."

"Then I'll put her on autopilot. And I've got the radar alarm set for half a mile. That should be pretty safe. You just call down, if you think the electronics is missing something."

I nodded in agreement. The job wouldn't require that much vigilance. And it was pleasant up there, farther from the engine noise. The half-moon didn't give us much light, but I would be able to make out other vessels by their navigation lights. King had set the engines to push us along at a fast trawl. A collision at this speed would damage the boat but wouldn't kill anyone.

King followed Cheryl down the ladder. As King set foot on the deck, his lawyer Roger Black stood up, coming to attention. With an air of good-hearted friendliness, King circulated among his seated guests; he made a personalized comment to each. It was easy for me to hear; they had to shout over the engines. I inspected the autopilot and figured out how to deactivate it, if I needed to regain the helm in a hurry. Every once in a while, I turned in my seat and looked almost straight down on the fantail.

The guests had settled into a shouted group discussion about doing business in Boston and Miami.

High on the tuna tower, a set of downward-facing lights switched on. They lit the fantail up like a stage and made it hard for me to see into the darkness ahead. King was now standing right below me, back to the cabin wall, one hand grasping the ladder, and facing his audience. He held forth:

Business is the same everywhere. You have to know the territory. And most important, there must be a solid understanding between the parties.

Our accountant Smith nodded. Our lawyer Elkins sat rigidly in a deck chair along the stern rail, holding the armrests. Beside King sat his lawyer, Roger Black. He kept asking polite questions which King was always delighted to answer. Soon the group discussion had turned into a *Forbes* magazine interview on King's business philosophy.

The twin motors kept purring, and each sweep on the radar display showed nothing. I kept my eye on the horizon but couldn't make out a red or green running light for miles. Every minute or two, I sneaked a look down at the brightly lit fantail to catch visuals on King's blustery monologue. The longer he held forth, the more he sounded like General Norman Schwarzkopf bragging about how he kicked Saddam Hussein's ass:

In business, like in war, you've got to deliver. If your allies can't deliver, don't depend on them — just keep them out of the way. Your own team has to be superbly organized. You don't need the fanciest equipment. What you see is what you've got. Everyone you've got is there for a purpose. Don't waste personnel repainting the flagpole. Set up reasonable objectives, set up a budget for your project, and kick butt every time anyone gets out of line. And don't forget that your logistician and your cost accountant are as important as your frontline soldiers.

King concluded, "And you've got to fight all that red tape. It can bog you down as bad as an enemy's land mines."

Our accountant was shaking his head in disbelief. "How do you deal with red tape?"

"You cut it with your magic scissors."

There was no follow-up question. Our accountant just stared off into the darkness. I could imagine King buying off construction inspectors and calling up his buddy, Mayor García, for special favors.

King remained silent for half a minute before picking up his lost thread. "In construction, every minute you lose, you're losing money. Some damn traffic cop stops your cement truck, and you're behind schedule at the pour, then you wind up paying your men overtime to finish the day's work. The damn cop thinks he's so smart, I'll get his captain to send him to my mixer. We'll give him a jackhammer and let him clean it out himself. You see, I do a lot of charitable work. I might just happen to know the police captain socially."

The performance had run 20 minutes. King now seemed ready to cap it off — in a democratic tone. "Teamwork, that's what it takes to have a winning team."

Then he surprised me. "Hey, Dr. Candidi! Is everything clear from the bridge?"

I leaned over the back of my chair, squinted down, and hollered, "All clear, Cap'n."

"You see, folks, all the while we've been talking, Dr. Candidi's been up there navigating the boat — with a little help from the auto-pilot."

King's deep chuckle was audible over the throaty engines.

He picked up a few laughs from the audience, too. But the laughs were followed by a full moment of silence. Cheryl broke it by asking for orders from the bar. King, who was on his third drink, put in a grunt for another Tom Collins. Elkins looked like he could have used an antacid. He grimaced, then asked King what was his worst logistics problem.

"It was a shopping center project outside of Atlanta. Roger, you remember that damn mess you had to get me out of."

Roger Black piped back a leading answer, setting the stage for another monologue. Before settling down to hear Act Two, I placed a hand over my brow and did a careful 360 degree search. There were no other boats on the Bay — just one boat, so far away that its stern light seemed yellow and intermittent.

King told an interesting story. He had been building a shopping center outside Atlanta. Halfway through the project, the corner of the newly poured concrete parking garage started sinking. It turned out he was building on a Civil War trash pit. The "damn engineering company" he'd paid to take soil samples had bored in the wrong places. King had to tear down the parking garage, compact the ground, and start all over again. And he narrowly missed having his construction blocked by the Georgia Historical Society. King wrapped it up, saying, "Boy, I'll never get burnt like that again. It was like that Clark Gable movie — *Gone with the Wind*."

"Oh, shit!" I heard myself yelling, loud enough for everyone to hear.

"Holy shit!" I screamed again.

The other boat's stern light was dead ahead, not more than 50 yards away. I grabbed the wheel, but it wouldn't budge. It was a small motorboat. We were closing in on them fast. They were shouting frantic warnings in Spanish. I groped for the autopilot, pushing buttons until the wheel relaxed. I threw it over hard to starboard, narrowly averting a collision.

The *Ace* lurched hard. Cups and glasses clattered to the cockpit floor. Our bow was almost past the small craft when I had to throw the wheel hard to port to keep from swiping them with our stern. The small boat was at anchor. Our wake lifted them almost three feet and rocked them, sending their dim lantern flying around their short mast like a tetherball. That's what I mistook for a stern light. The small boat almost swamped when it slid off our stern wave. A woman clutched two small kids. A man held on with one arm and shook his fist with the other.

Aboard the *Ace*, everyone was knocked to the cockpit floor — everyone except King who was hanging onto the ladder. "What the hell!" he shouted. Then he yelled at the rocking motorboat, "Fucking shit. Water-lice!"

Then he yelled to us in explanation: "The radar didn't beep."

He hollered up to me: "Where in the hell did they come from?"

"Sorry," I called down. "But our fantail lights —"

"That's okay, Candidi. You didn't have any chance of seeing them. They aren't showing any navigation lights. You folks all see that? That boat doesn't have any navigation lights. Now, Candidi, take a good look. Any more of them out there?"

"Everything is clear for miles around," I announced.

King climbed up to the fly bridge and displaced me from the captain's chair. He picked up the microphone and said, "This is the captain speaking. We had a little turbulence back there, but it's going to be clear running from now on. I'm going to turn off the seatbelt sign." Polite laughter filtered up from below. "And as an apology, I am instructing the cabin crew to bring you a free drink of your choice."

I started to go down, but King gestured me back onto the mate's chair. "Stay here. I can use a copilot." Hand on the wheel, squinting into the darkness, he muttered, "Damn greaseballs. Don't know nothing. I won't have them in my crews. Always breaking out to drink *café cubanos* on company time. Don't give a shit if they get the job done or not." He looked at me and added, "No, you've got to stick with the rednecks — Joe Sixpacks. There's a special type of them. When you tell 'em they ain't man enough to do the job, they take it personal and work twice as hard for you. Like the guy I've got repairing the *Ace*. If he was a greaseball, the *Ace* would have sunk in its berth by now."

Of course, I disagreed with King. At that moment, I couldn't find the moral strength to contradict him.

King squinted into the distance. "Hell, I see why you were having trouble. The deck lights are strong enough to blind you." He picked up his microphone again and boomed over the P.A., "And we are going to turn down the cabin lights."

He flipped a switch, and the boat was suddenly dark. The only illumination was the lights of Key Biscayne. As my eyes slowly dark-adapted, stars appeared overhead. The only remaining distraction was the noise of the engines. But King seemed to draw strength from their vibration. He upped the power, raising the *Ace's* bow. The ride became faster and rougher.

The orange and green glow of the instrument panel gave King's face a hard, demonic quality. But his voice was gentle. "You know, Candidi, I find out a lot about people by taking them out on this boat. It's like one of those executive training courses where they take the guys out and make them climb cliffs together. Challenge your people and find out what they're made of. Now look at your lawyer-puke down there. Elkins?" He turned and looked down. "Hey, that's what he is actually doing right now — puking over the side."

A quick backwards glance confirmed King's observation.

"You see, Candidi, the only place a fellow like him is any good is behind a desk. I know a lot about lawyers. Even Roger, the one down there scratching his beard, ain't much better. You got to keep them on a short leash, or they'll make things so complicated that you don't want to get out of bed in the morning." He chuckled. "Turn your back on them, and they'll bill you for expenses faster than Goldfinger ran all that gold out of Fort Knox."

"I don't have much of an opinion of lawyers, either," I said truthfully.

"I know you don't." King glanced at me. "You don't look it, but you're really a take-charge guy. You think with your hands. When something's wrong, you fix it before it gets worse. You don't send me no memo and wait for an authorization. You just punch out the autopilot and turn the wheel. 'Cause of you, those greaseballs and their boat are still floating. We just shook them up a little bit."

I should have called him on his "greaseball" statement. It was a mean-hearted description for a humble family of Cuban-Americans fishing for their next dinner. But while sitting elbow-to-elbow with King, it was impossible to contradict him. His will was too strong — a Darth Vader force field. It had the power to paralyze at short distances.

"I do share your opinion on red tape and bureaucracy," I volunteered.

"Fucking waste, nine times out of ten," he spat out. "Only one time out of ten that bureaucracy can be good. You know when that is, Candidi?"

"Can't say I do."

"Give up? Okay. It's when I've been grandfathered in for years, and when a new guy is trying to weasel his way in to compete. I've got my approvals, but he needs a variance to get his project going. Then the bureaucracy works for me by holding him back. Like when the FDA approves my drugs but gives the other companies a hard time. It's like in construction. You've got to know how to get approvals."

Now was my chance to test his mettle. "But you don't have any FDA approvals yet." I said it with all the firmness I could muster.

"I know how to handle Washington bureaucrats," King answered gruffly. "They still need to look good. And the only thing they have to give anybody is their goddamn approvals. They ain't got no cure for the cancer that killed my grandmother. When they see what we've got, those FDA bean-counters will have to approve us."

This was his idea of male bonding between our companies.

"I haven't seen any human data that can shake up the FDA. Maybe you could tell me — "

"The *Ace* ain't a good place for scientific discussions."

King looked over his shoulder. "He'll see some data tomorrow, won't he, Cheryl?"

"Yes, certainly," Cheryl said. She removed our glasses, set two

Styrofoam cups of coffee in the teak holder and disappeared as silently as she came.

So much for my chance to pin them down on what BIOTECH data the FDA would find compelling.

"Look, Ben," King said, adopting a fatherly tone. "We'll do fine with the FDA bureaucrats. I've been dealing with bureaucrats for years. You've just got to have some of your own bureaucrats to talk to their bureaucrats. Usually I ain't got no use for them in my own organization. But you were just looking at someone that knows how to beat the bureaucrats at their own game."

"Who?"

"Cheryl. That gal isn't just a scientist. She knows all about the FDA. She'll be good at moving our stuff through that organization."

I made a mental note to find out what our unctuous "regulatory affairs" man thought about Cheryl's expertise. Too bad he wasn't along for the cruise. I guess that water and unction just don't mix.

King pushed the throttle forward, causing the stern to dig in. He pushed the throttles forward more, and the yacht started climbing out of its own wake. After we were riding on plane, King executed a broad turn and set course for the entrance of the Coral Gables Waterway. He leaned over the wheel like the conversation was over.

Despite his rude manners and tedious style, there was something I had to admire about King. He seemed to have a strong work ethic. And what he lacked in grace and talent, he made up with persistence. Maybe there was something to this bonding-between-companies thing. Bond tonight; work out the problems tomorrow.

A few minutes later, King powered down, and we entered the Waterway. He picked up a flashlight, trained a beam on the base of his tuna tower and showed me the braces he wanted unlocked. Then, once again, he manned the crank while steering the *Ace* through the narrow coral canyon. He got the tuna tower folded back just in time for the LeJeune bridge. He pulled out a cellular phone and called a taxi.

The houses along the big bend were charmingly lit. As King lined up his shot under the narrow Hardee Road bridge, I went below. The second transit went as smoothly as the first. Cheryl worked her way up to the bow, carrying a boat pole. Yes, I had to admit that she moved around the boat very well. Of course, powerboats are less challenging than sailboats. She probably didn't know how to handle sails like Rebecca.

King maneuvered the *Ace* so adroitly into his coral-lined slip that all Cheryl had to do was hook the loops on the cleats.

King killed the engines, climbed down, and extended his hand to me. "Nice working with you on the bridge tonight, Candidi." He said it loud enough for everyone to hear. "See you tomorrow. And you let me know if my boys don't give you everything you're looking for."

Cheryl had already gone ahead to turn on the lights that marked the path. I followed our lawyer and accountant as they slowly climbed the stairs. Cheryl took us to the driveway where a cab was already waiting. My two colleagues took places in the back and slammed the doors shut. As I opened the front passenger door, Cheryl gave me a kindly smile and said softly, "It went very well tonight, Ben."

Creeping familiarity.

The backseat duo gave the driver orders for the wrong Marriott, then threw up an impenetrable wall of Boston insider chitchat. I told the driver the right hotel. He answered, *"Oui."* In polite Creole-accented English, he assured me he knew how to get there. The lighted card on the dash identified him as Jean-Pierre Dubois.

We traveled north in midnight traffic along U.S. Highway 1, maintaining tempo with timely changes in lane. Apparently the sway of the loosely sprung Ford wagon reminded Elkins too much of the yacht. "Please drive like an American," he demanded.

When Jean-Pierre started to take offense, I told him, *"Il a un peu mal de mer."*

Elkins cleared his throat and shook his head like I'd committed a breach of protocol. I was in no mood to apologize. Thus I lost all the chance to compare due diligence notes with my colleagues. As a result, J.-P. and I brushed up our French for the rest of the way to the hotel. When the cab came to a halt deep in the Marriott's yawning mouth, my colleagues jumped right out, leaving me to pay the fare.

They probably went straight to bed for a good night's sleep.

But I couldn't. I had work to do.

20 AND MANY BYTES BEFORE I SLEEP

I checked for messages at the desk. There was an envelope from Robert, containing only a diskette. Up in my room, I popped it into my laptop and flipped through a dozen screens. Robert had delivered just what I'd ordered: a thorough patent search. His high priority list included only three patents — the same three I'd already seen in the examination file. And I already knew that the U.S. Patent Examiner had decided that these three did not interfere. So far, so good.

Robert also included a broader, less selective list. Just to be thorough, I studied it too. After an hour, I was sure that Dr. Moon's patent property had no encroaching neighbors. None of the other patents was even close.

No question about it: Dr. Moon had given King a solid title to the ground on which BIOTECH was building. But could an uncompacted Civil War trash pit lurk below the ground's surface? Could someone have written a scientific paper on the same thing five years earlier, robbing Dr. Moon's patent of its novelty?

Another hour's work before I could sleep.

I pulled out the phone and plugged my computer into the phone jack. I modem-connected with the medical library's computer and selected the Medline database. It has the summaries of all the papers published by every important biomedical journal since 1964. I selected "cancer" AND "sponge" and got a list of 53 papers. I pulled down the abstracts, one by one. Most of the articles were about "surgical sponges". Only two of them were even close. They didn't have anything to do with protein kinase C or even cancer for that matter. They were the Japanese publications I'd seen back in Cheryl's office.

By two o'clock, I knew that no Civil War trash pit lurked below the surface. King had built BIOTECH on solid ground. But that one gnawing question remained:

Why had Dr. Moon been so nasty?

By now, my brain was low on oxygen and high on metabolic waste. I drew open a curtain and discovered a sliding glass door and small balcony. What a relief to breathe outdoor air. I leaned over the rail and gazed down on the residential islands lying before Miami Beach. Everything was nice and quiet down there. The narrow Venetian Causeway carried no traffic. Occasionally a pair of headlights flashed on the six-lane MacArthur Causeway.

To the north, along the shore, a mobile construction crane towered over a building that was sprouting like a mushroom. Once-charming 1930s houses and two-story apartment buildings were making way for high-rises. The crane's blinking red aircraft warning light reminded me of King's construction business and of his ingenious tuna tower. By leaning far over the rail, I could see around the edge of my building and could make out the concrete bunker that housed BIOTECH's lab.

Why, my brain demanded, had Dr. Moon been so nasty with me?

Things were going well for him, weren't they? He had started out with a $50,000 idea. Then came King who liked the idea so much he founded BIOTECH. King even spent a million dollars on Moon's idea, if Cheryl was telling the truth. And now Broadmoore was planning to invest $20 million on Moon's invention.

Why wasn't Dr. Moon happy?

Was he boxed too tight in his prefab office enclosure? Was he becoming claustrophobic? Had the promise of imminent success triggered a panic attack? Or was there no harmless reason?

I couldn't rest easy until I had the answer.

What also bothered me was the *Alice in Wonderland* quality of Broadmoore's leadership — or lack of it. Ditto for our team's organization. Broadmoore ran his team like a Greenland Eskimo runs his sled dogs — a separate line to each and all fanned out in a 60-degree arc. What a terribly inefficient method to navigate a complicated landscape! Or was I missing some essential feature of Broadmoore's logic?

Be a good team member, Ben. Keep straining on the leash, investigating BIOTECH. Bust your brain to make sure it's a real company and worth the money. But B.M. Capital wasn't a real company, either.

B. M. Capital was a virtual company. And we were a pickup team of hired consultants. Each of us was good within his area of specialization but useless for anything else. Maybe that was why Broadmoore kept each of us on a separate line — so he wouldn't have to stop his sled to cut loose a faltering dog or two.

How was Broadmoore going to make the decision three days from now? Would he ask for each consultant's vote and decide by a simple majority? Or would he ask for each man's degree of enthusiasm and factor it into a complicated formula? Or would he apply stricter criteria where a single vote of "no" would nix the whole deal? Hopefully, everything wouldn't depend on me.

Suddenly I was fighting for air. I was experiencing a panic attack myself from all this unbridled speculation. I tried to calm myself down. Maybe Broadmoore didn't need absolute assurance that the three compounds would cure cancer. Even if the compounds proved mediocre, he'd probably find some way to dress up BIOTECH and turn a profit selling its stock. There was no law that you have to prove to the FDA that you can cure cancer before you can sell your company's stock. Maybe Broadmoore knew he'd make a profit in any case. Maybe that was why his due diligence on BIOTECH was so relaxed and disorganized.

And what was I to think of King? Despite his chest-thumping, posturing, and generally bad manners, King did inspire trust in his ability to get the job done. Maybe anyone will turn out gruff, if he spends his life bootstrapping his way up from a lawn mowing service.

Maybe King's life experience had made him a master of "fuzzy logic" — the only type of logic that works when the categories are fuzzy and half the data isn't in yet. He'd named his boat, *Ace in the Hole*. Maybe poker playing had given King a sixth sense for avoiding disaster. I really did hope that he could charm the FDA as easily as the Miami city bureaucracy.

Still, the nagging question kept coming back: Why was Dr. Moon so nasty when things were going well? Without the answer, I hadn't earned my $6,000 today. I stepped back into my room, phoned the front desk, and asked for a wake-up call. Then I plugged my computer back in, dialed my Internet access server.

I http'd Miami's Strategic Biomedical Alliance using the address that Rob McGregor had given me. Yes, their Website listed BIOTECH. It also gave a 300-word sketch of the company. But what was more interesting was their hypertext link to Dr. Moon's company. This had information dating before BIOTECH had bought Moon out.

Moon's company was called "Biosynergy". The summary described it as a "natural-products-based drug discovery company". The text was largely an egocentric description of Dr. Moon's expertise in identifying drug actions of natural products. Still restless, I roamed the Web, jumping across hypertext links like a sheep jumping over a fence . . .

. . . until I was most rudely awakened.

WEDNEJDAY'J WOEJ 21

"Mister Candidi!" shouted a muffled voice in the distance. A door rattled in its frame. I sat up quickly. Had to free myself from a tangle of wires before I could get up and open the door.

It was a bellhop. "Your phone was off the hook; I'm delivering your wake-up call personally."

I reached into the pockets of my rumpled slacks and pulled out a $10 bill. "Thanks. You saved my life."

Thus began day two of the project. Three days were left to complete my work.

I untangled the cords from the sheets and unplugged the phone line from my computer, hoping I hadn't damaged the modem socket. I plugged the phone back into the wall. A few minutes later, the phone summoned me from the shower.

It was Cheryl. "I'm sorry to have to call, Ben. Something came up."

"Something came up?" I said, with preemptive irritation.

"Yes. With Dr. Moon. We have to cancel your appointment with him." She said it casually, as if it were a dental appointment cancellation.

"And why?" I asked, growing madder by the second.

"He called and said he had to cancel it."

"What's his excuse today? Cramps in his anal sphincter?"

"I'm sorry, Ben. But I can't tell you."

"Can't or won't?"

"Can't. He just left a message on my machine that he couldn't come in this morning. I don't like it either, Ben."

"It's irresponsible. Especially after yesterday's performance. And because . . . Look, damn it. According to your contract with us, I'm supposed to have ready access to the inventor during the due diligence phase." I couldn't cite her chapter and verse, but my chosen words had the right sound.

"Ben, please be patient. I'll look into it and try to reschedule the appointment for this afternoon."

She sounded like an airline reservation clerk apologizing for a cancelled flight and promising to do her best to book me on the next flight out — if only I'd be patient.

I might have put her through another round of cross-examination, if I hadn't been standing wet and naked in front of a full length mirror. "I'll be at your Brickell Avenue office by nine-thirty this morning. I'll want to look into the relationship between BIOTECH and Dr. Moon's company. Can I expect to see you there?"

"Yes, Ben."

"Good," I said.

The minute I hung up, I phoned Broadmoore's room. No answer. But I caught up with him in the hotel's restaurant.

It is a terraced, two-level affair projecting from the side of the building and facing the Bay, designed for a Continental look: external walls and ceiling of greenhouse glass, dramatically suspended brass fans, potted palms, and wicker furniture. Appropriately it was half-filled with leisurely European and Latin American tourists. The other half of the fill was hectic North American tourists, apparently waiting for cruise ship connections and vans to the airport.

In a corner, oblivious to it all, Broadmoore was eating a hearty breakfast while giving instructions to assistant Sally. She was leaning over a steno notebook, perched on the edge of the table. Judging from the movements of her pen, she was capturing his every word and perhaps even his thoughts.

She must have captured my thoughts, too. She rose immediately and made an excuse about having to go to the "powder room," which was odd since she didn't use powder or lipstick. Broadmoore's greeting was a couple degrees below lukewarm.

I blurted out, "We have a real problem. I got a call from Dr. Cheryl North that Dr. Moon has cancelled my appointment."

Broadmoore showed no surprise. "How could he do that?" He watched me carefully.

"He put it on her answering machine."

"Yes. What a boon to obfuscation, these answering machines. It is rather like throwing a note over the garden wall."

This was not the time for wry, detached humor. "Dr. Broadmoore, it's more like the garden path, and Dr. Moon is leading us down it. If I can't see him by this afternoon, I won't be able to do my job properly."

Broadmoore shook his big head and clicked his tongue like I was overreacting. He gestured for me to sit down. "Perhaps you could tell me about your scholarly investigations of his patent."

This calmed me. "The patent checks out fine. Dr. Moon has built a wall around anticancer use of those three compounds. And no one else even comes close." I briefly described the last evening's patent and Medline searches.

"You did accomplish a great deal last night besides your heroics at sea," Broadmoore said this with a knowing smile. Then he leaned back, waiting for my reaction.

"Yeah, man," I answered sassily. "It was a real dangerous cruise. Your legal eagle refluxed his cocktail and your accountant — what's his name? Thad Smith? — got salt spray on his glasses. Where are those guys, anyway?"

"Self-deployed in their separate directions, pursuing their individual pursuits," Broadmoore said with a sly smile.

Talk about obfuscation!

A waiter was coming my way with a coffee pot. I eagle-eyed him and turned up my cup. He poured, then slipped me a "guest check" for eight dollars.

Broadmoore noted my reaction to the high-priced cup of coffee. "Perhaps you would like to get a bowl of cut fruit at the buffet."

"Back to your question," I said. "Dr. Moon checks out okay on paper. But in person he does not inspire confidence. He's uncommunicative, as if he has something to hide. The only way I can assure you that everything's right is by sitting down with him and having a long conversation. Eyeball to eyeball." I was starting to sound like King. "I must see how he responds when I subtly probe him."

"Maybe he feels he has been subtly probed already."

That was the opening I needed. "How did he feel about my predecessor, Dr. Yang?"

Broadmoore's left cheek twitched. He quickly scooped up a large forkful of scrambled egg and made a big show of having to chew it. He took a sip of coffee and muttered into his cup, "I would not know."

It wasn't orneriness that started me interrogating my new boss. It was curiosity. No one had volunteered a word about Yang. Not Cheryl, not Dr. Moon, and not Broadmoore. "Then you're saying you don't know whether Moon was cooperative with Dr. Yang."

"No," Broadmoore muttered; he cut off a large piece of pork sausage.

"It would bother me if he had uncovered something that I have overlooked. It's strange. I found very few notes from him."

"Yes, I can see that you consider the inventor-access problem very upsetting," Broadmoore replied. "I will personally insist that Moon see you this afternoon." He raised the sausage to his mouth, as if to signal that the conversation had come to an end.

"Thanks. But I still need to know: Did Dr. Yang leave you any kind of note before you started missing him?"

Broadmoore lowered his eyes and mumbled, "No, he just disappeared."

"How did you get his metal briefcases?"

Broadmoore's eyes followed a woman walking by. She wore rope sandals and a short silk blouse over a Brazilian tanga. "He left them in his room."

"He abandoned his rooms!"

"Yes, his briefcases were found by us in his abandoned room."

"He didn't check out of the hotel?"

"No."

"Did he leave any personal belongings — like his clothes?"

Broadmoore glanced again at the woman. She was now sitting with a man who acted so indifferent that he could only be her husband. "Yes," Broadmoore answered quietly.

Why the hell hadn't I asked these questions earlier?

"Did you contact the police?"

"Yes, of course."

"What did they say?"

"They considered the disappearance nothing out of the ordinary — a routine Miami disappearance or mishap, so to speak. Naturally we persisted in having them investigate. And we notified his next of kin, a sister in Taiwan. We couldn't locate any friends in the U.S. He wasn't very social, I understand. I must admit that I didn't know him very well."

"Were the metal cases locked?"

"Yes."

"And you opened them up without checking for fingerprints?"

"No, the police checked them when they examined the room — to rule out foul play."

"And?"

"They found no sign of foul play."

"And the cases?"

"And the cases bore no fingerprints."

Broadmoore's stonewalling was making me impolite. "And what do you make out of that fact?"

"I shouldn't know what to make of it."

"The cases should have had Dr. Yang's fingerprints. Someone must have wiped the cases clean."

Broadmoore first acted surprised. Then he lifted his huge head and studied me carefully. "Aren't you being a little melodramatic?"

"No. I'm being methodical. I understand from Sally that Dr. Yang used a laptop computer. Did you find it in his room?"

"No."

"So it could mean that they took —"

Broadmoore snapped, "It could mean that he was carrying the computer when he was waylaid by Latin street toughs." His eyes flashed.

"I'm going to keep an open mind on this," I snapped back. "Maybe Dr. Yang found something wrong with the patent and Dr. Moon killed him — to keep him quiet." I thought for a second and asked, "Have you checked your room for bugs?"

"Bugs?"

"Not insects. Listening devices."

"No. I hadn't thought to and — "

"There's twenty million dollars at stake. If they bug your rooms and listen while you talk to your experts, that might give them the edge they need to outsmart you."

"Now, now . . . I really don't think we could justify the expense — "

"This one's on me. I'm putting my own man on this at my expense. If he doesn't find a bug, I pay for it. If he finds one, you pay him."

Broadmoore reluctantly agreed. He said I should report to him in his suite at seven that evening. I laid eight dollars on the table and grabbed a couple of Danish pastries on the way out.

An escalator led to the meeting room level where there was a bank of pay phones. If our rooms were bugged, now was the time to start acting on the suspicion. I stuck in 35 cents and punched the number for ABBA Radio & Video. Old Mensa buddy Joe Kazekian could help me out on this one.

"Ben, it's good to hear you. And thanks for that Edmund Scientific catalogue. I bought the Russian night vision scope and four of their camera boards. But my wife hates you. Says you're helping to keep us poor."

"Tell her I'm sorry, Zeekie."

"She's given up trying to change me. She just calls me an electronics nerd. But that's okay; it keeps her from getting jealous of my wedding gigs. Boy, you ought to see some of those honeys on those gigs. Want to come along Saturday and help me with the videotaping?"

"You're into that stuff pretty heavy, huh?"

"You ought to see my van! That's where I've really been spending money."

"You plushed it out to make it a nice place to invite girls for a quickie," I teased. I could imagine that my dark, curly headed, hairy-chested Armenian friend was a real turn-on for a lot of blond-headed chicks — and for Armenian chicks, too.

"No, you've got it all wrong, Ben. I catch their essence with my video cameras — remote. You really ought to see my setup."

"You can show me tonight. I've got a job for you. I want to find out if a certain businessman is being bugged."

"Sure, Ben. You looking for audio or video bugs?"

"Probably audio. It would be industrial espionage, not sexual blackmail." I told Zeekie about the situation. He agreed to meet me outside the Marriott at 6:30 p.m.

The morning sun sparkled nicely on the Bay as I rode the Metro-Mover to BIOTECH's Brickell Avenue office. Toward the end of the ride, I saw another collapsible construction crane. Of course, it reminded me of King and his tuna tower. The rig was hoisting a two-ton bucket of liquid concrete 400 feet in the air. A new layer of channelized cement would be poured as fast as the underlying layer could harden. Pretty soon there would be another story.

The workers — "Joe Sixpacks", King had called them — were crawling around the top level, tying together rebars and putting up molds. They were probably just one step ahead of the concrete truck schedules. After the process was repeated 40 times, they'd have 40 stories roughed in. Then they would fold up the crane like a carnival ride and drive it down the road at 40 miles an hour to its next job. And no doubt about it, King was a master of that art.

I walked into the office to find Cheryl standing by the secretary's workstation. She glanced at me, then at her watch — to let me know I was late. She ushered me into my room and said in a hushed voice, "Ben, I followed up on our phone conversation. I spoke to Dr. Moon at his home. He's acting up again. He said he isn't sure he's coming in today. He made it sound like he was sick but said he might be in the lab late this afternoon. But I think he is just having a mood."

Had Dr. Moon gotten a "mood" when my predecessor disappeared?

I frowned. "This is no good. I will have to see King to complain."

"He's very busy today, but I will see if I can get him."

"Last night, King made me a personal guarantee. I'll have to talk to him by noon at the latest."

Cheryl nodded, then gestured to a stack of patent and scientific files that she had laid out for me the day before. Hell, I'd spent all of yesterday afternoon on them. Did she think I'd be only too happy to bury my face in them again?

What I needed was an interview with the inventor. In absence of that, I needed all I could learn about the things that were motivating him — money and contracts.

I drew a deep breath and tried addressing Cheryl in an even voice. "I want to see all your files on the relationship between Dr. Moon's company and BIOTECH."

"I don't know what you mean by 'files on a relationship'," she answered.

"Sure, you do. Let's start with the contract that gave you Moon's technology."

Cheryl replied, "Don't you think this is a matter for a lawyer?"

"Just get it." I was mad at myself for not asking Broadmoore for lawyer Elkin's opinion on the contracts.

Cheryl talked to the secretary at the workstation outside my door.

138 ❖ Biotechnology Is Murder

They found the file of correspondence. But they had some difficulty locating the contract between Moon and BIOTECH. Then the secretary remembered the contract was in the refiling bin. Didn't Dr. North remember Mr. King asking for the contract when Roger Black called yesterday? Cheryl told the secretary, no, she did not remember. The secretary started acting defensive.

I sat down with the contract and a two-inch file of associated correspondence. It fleshed out the story I had learned from the Website the evening before. After an hour of study, I knew the formal history of King, Dr. Moon, and his sponges.

Dr. Moon's small company, Biosynergy, had been "incubated" by the Miami Strategic Biomedical Alliance, the "SBA". King sat on the board of directors of the SBA. When Dr. Moon discovered the anticancer properties of the marine sponge compounds three years earlier, King became interested and started negotiating to buy into the action.

King founded BIOTECH. He located Cheryl through a recruiting firm in New York that specialized in scientific executives. He hired her two weeks later for $70,000 a year. Lawyer Roger Black negotiated an agreement giving BIOTECH full rights to the technology in exchange for giving Dr. Moon one-quarter of the profits that BIOTECH would make from the technology.

The buyout contract was complex and 43 pages long. It locked in the rights of each party solidly. BIOTECH got full and irrevocable rights to the three compounds; Dr. Moon got irrevocable rights to a share of the profits. Moon also received a guaranteed salary and stock options.

The contract required BIOTECH to finance one hell of a lot of lab work. Memos in the file told the rest of the story — how BIOTECH hired Dr. Lau, Dr. Singh and a new technician, and how BIOTECH took over Dr. Moon's lab and expanded into adjoining space in the warehouse. And, yes, I saw the work orders for constructing Moon's air-conditioned office and private toilet, not specified in the contract. Adding up all these numbers, I estimated that King had put about $600,000 into the technology.

BIOTECH's contract with Dr. Moon also revealed how much King thought the technology was worth: $5 million. That was the amount of life insurance that BIOTECH was entitled to take out on Dr. Moon.

I double-checked. Yes, the contract gave BIOTECH ironclad rights to the three compounds. They belonged to BIOTECH; Dr. Moon could never sell them to anyone else.

Perplexed, I wondered why in the hell Dr. Moon was acting so dissatisfied? Why had Cheryl watched him like a hawk when I talked with him? Was she there to keep Moon from administering a karate chop to my neck when I found flaws in the technology? Is that what Dr. Moon did to Dr. Yang?

Nonsense! Well, I hoped so . . .

Dr. Moon had no reason kill Yang to cover up defects in his technology. The contract guaranteed Moon $90,000 a year salary for six years, regardless of how well the three compounds tested out. He would make out well even if Broadmoore didn't buy, and BIOTECH fell flat on its face.

Was there any reason why Dr. Moon wouldn't want us to buy into BIOTECH? No, he had every reason to want our money to go into the technology. Big bucks had to be put in for the clinical trials. If the human testing went well and BIOTECH started making money, Moon's cut would be fabulous.

Blood shifted from my brain to my unused legs. I struggled with mid-morning drowsiness. I went to the secretary's workstation and poured myself a big cup of coffee. Thadeas Smith, our accountant, had the same idea. "Taking a little break?" he asked.

It turned into my first candid conversation since hiring on with Broadmoore.

HEAVY HITTER 22

Here was a chance to make Thad Smith talk shop. "I was just reading the correspondence. It gives me an appreciation of the big numbers you are working with. Looks like Bud King spent six hundred thousand dollars on the technology."

"It's probably more like eight hundred thousand, depending on how much value we assign the hours he's billing for professional effort. He's billing a lot for use of employees of his construction company." Thad Smith looked to see if the secretary might be listening. "That's my only remaining issue. Say, Ahma's had to step out. Let's go into her office."

It was directly across from Bud King's office where the door was shut. Secure within Ahma's four walls, Smith seemed ready to give me information. I primed him with a statement: "King spent eight hundred thousand on this deal, and he will get ten million plus ten percent of the action. That's not bad."

Smith sat in the guest chair beside Ahma's desk and stretched. "No, it's not bad. He's sharing some of it with Dr. North. But I don't know how much. Roger Black knows the details of BIOTECH's shareholders agreement — their pre-organization agreement."

"That reminds me. I have some questions for our legal eagle Elkins on Broadmoore's contract with BIOTECH. How can I get hold of him?"

"He spent most of yesterday with Roger Black. Today I think he's standing by in his hotel room." Smith smiled like he was starting to enjoy our conversation. "But you've done lots of jobs for Brian; you know how he works. We don't talk much to each other — just to him."

It was a relief to know that I was not the only one in the dark. I tried to act casual, half-sitting, half-leaning against the edge of the desk. "Yes, Brian's methods are very efficient — for him. I couldn't reach Elkins on the phone this morning."

A little smile formed on Thad Smith's face. "Talking about Elkins — you really pinned his ears back last night!"

"Oh?"

"Talking about him in French to the cab driver."

"What did I say?"

"I don't know, but it sure made the driver laugh. Of course, you probably know you've got a lot of people spooked on both teams."

"Spooked?"

"Everyone knows that your opinion is the one carrying all the weight around here." I tried to not act surprised. Smith glanced toward the open door, as if checking whether anyone was in earshot. "And, of course, you've got Dr. North waiting on you, hand and foot. How is she, anyway?"

"Dr. North is hard to fathom. How's your liaison with BIOTECH?"

"That's exactly what I'd like to have with Ahma — a liaison. I've often wondered — "

Thad never got to finish his question; Ahma returned. I slid off her desk and moved to the side to let her in. I offered to leave. But Ahma was hospitable. I stood in the doorway and chatted with her and Thad for a while.

After a few minutes, I heard rumblings coming from behind Bud King's closed door. I nodded at everything Ahma and Thad said but gave my full attention to what King was saying. He seemed to be on the phone with a colleague, talking about someone neither of them liked. It had to do with what was spelled out in a contract. After a long silence, I heard a greasy laugh. His next words were completely audible. "What you're saying is that his lawyer got too fancy — doing a fancy dance that got so fancy he stomped his own cock!"

Just then, Cheryl came out of her office and asked if she could help me with anything. I told her she could help by arranging an appointment with Moon. She said that she was working on it.

Now King's conversation seemed to be over. Or maybe he was speaking too softly to hear. Well, I wasn't getting paid enough to put my ear to his door. I refilled my coffee cup and returned to my room.

Unable to think, I spent the next moments looking out on sunlit Biscayne Bay — viewing paradise from a skybox in hell. Of course, my damnation was voluntary. Succumbing to the lure of a $6,000 a day consultancy, I'd buttoned myself tightly in a thousand-dollar suit that straitjacketed my every thought. How did Cheryl manage to walk around all day in high heels? Had she dressed that way when she was a bench scientist?

My thoughts drifted back to Broadmoore's motley crew — the pickup team assembled to render multimillion dollar advice to a guy who had invested $160,000 in pork futures. And I was the pivotal member of his team . . .

I rested my eyes on the sparkling green of the Bay where a large sailing yacht was moving slowly in a lazy sea-to-land breeze. A mile oceanward, a big cabin cruiser was plowing water and moving fast, probably at 25 knots. In a few minutes, his wake would rock the sailboat. Why did I think "his" wake? Probably because making waves is a masculine activity. But many women go for power yachting, too. In fact, more of them go for power yachting than for sailing.

Last night's cruise had revealed the essence of power yachting.

For King, boating was a turnkey operation. Climb aboard, turn the key, keystroke in everyone's favorite cocktail, and glide down the Waterway, drink in hand. Don't bother pulling halyards and setting canvas. Just get out there and make the engines roar.

The difference between the powerboat and sailboat cultures had been made clear to me many years ago at the Miami Boat Show. It was actually two boat shows — a powerboat show at the Miami Beach Convention Center and a sailboat show on Watson Island — as different from each other as Saks Fifth Avenue and L.L. Bean. I can still feel the sting when the sales representative regarded me aloofly and asked if I was a "serious buyer" before allowing me to climb aboard her powerboat. Oh, how that Barbie Doll personified that $300,000 cabin cruiser. I've never had much use for Barbies.

The sailing Betty is the exact opposite. Sailing Betty greets you with an open face and expressive eyes. She reminds you of the girl you met at the last Sierra Club outing. When you ask her to tighten your jib line, she never complains about busting her fingernails. She never puts on airs. And she always holds up her end of the conversation.

Cheryl came in wearing a strained smile. "How are you doing?"

I said, "Fine, if I have an appointment with Dr. Moon for early this afternoon; lousy, if I don't."

In now familiar flight attendant style came the answer that she would do everything possible.

After Cheryl returned to her office, it occurred to me that it was time to check her out as a scientist. I asked the secretary for permission to use the phone in my room. Yes, of course. Was the line shared with any other office? No, it wasn't. So I pulled out the phone cord and plugged in my laptop. It took only a couple of minutes to establish a modem connection with the medical library and bring up their Medline database.

I selected "author" from the menu, and typed in "North CW."

Cheryl had six multiple-authored publications for the six years she was in academic science. One per year wasn't bad, but you would expect twice as many for a hustling academic scientist. Half of the publications were from her dissertation and the other half were from her postdoctoral work. She was listed as the first author on each of them. Predictably the last author was either her Ph.D. advisor, Abdul Moran, or her postdoc mentor, Henk van Friesland.

What made me wonder was that every one of her publications had at least one middle author, sometimes three. This meant that other people besides her advisor had contributed to her work. This raised the question whether she had ever done an experiment by herself. Was she qualified as a stand-alone scientist?

And what about the quality of the work? I pulled down the summaries of the papers. It seemed like solid work that was part of her advisors' ongoing research programs.

Might as well check out Dr. Moon, while I was at it. I did a Medline search on him and came up with 28 papers in the last six years. I had seen full copies of many of them in the two metal cases. The abstracts of the remaining papers revealed nothing new. The guy was a published expert on biosynthesis of natural products by plants and primitive animals like sponges. But maybe he didn't know much pharmacology. Maybe that was why he didn't want to talk to me.

Dr. Lau, the second lab bench scientist, had a good string of publications in pharmacology. Dr. Singh's publications were mostly in Indian journals. He was an expert on the effects of drugs on blood pressure in rats.

There was every reason to believe they were all respectable scientists. I really couldn't imagine them conspiring to pull off a scam. This led me back to the gnawing question: Why was Dr. Moon so hostile to my inquiries?

Cheryl stuck her head through the doorway and said she was leaving. She would be back around a quarter after one. I nodded but moved closer to the door. I would collar King when he came out. I caught a glimpse of Tony Altino walking to King's office. A few minutes later, all three of them came out, looking like they had some serious business to do — elsewhere. But I wouldn't let them get past me.

King read me like a road sign. "I know what you want, Candidi. And I'll have the problem solved by one o'clock." He hardly broke stride as he passed by.

Ahma Sharma and Thad Smith seemed to be out to lunch. I asked the secretary to order me a ham and cheese sandwich, then started a couple of little projects. Dialed up my Internet access. Sent Rob McGregor an e-mail that something came up, and I would be unavailable for a couple days. Asked him to write me a couple of lines describing the laboratories of Abdul Moran and Henk van Friesland. Thought it would be useful to know about the labs where Cheryl did her Ph.D. and postdoctoral work.

It was a good idea to communicate with Rob through cyberspace. That way he couldn't trace me. He was probably mad as hell that I'd taken off.

Tried calling Broadmoore at his room, but there was no answer. Called Dr. Moon's office and got only an answering machine.

The secretary went to lunch and left the workstation in the hands of "Jenny" who seemed a teenager and new to the company. I handed her Dr. Moon's contract with BIOTECH and asked her to make me a copy. She did it without asking a question — a cog in the wheel, a link in the chain.

That's what a contract was — a document that chained us all together — even if we weren't cooperating. Moon was chained by his contract with King. And King was chained by the option contract he signed with Broadmoore. Or was he? Had my predecessor, Dr. Yang, looked into this? He left no notes; and, by now, my imagination was at free reign. What had happened to Yang?

I pulled from the file a copy of Broadmoore's option contract with BIOTECH. One paragraph said that BIOTECH and its affiliates must cooperate with Broadmoore in due diligence, making "freely available" all files, corporate records, key personnel and patent attorney. BIOTECH would be in breach of contract if Moon kept refusing to talk to me. I looked down at the two-foot stack of patent files. Then a little light bulb lit up in the back of my skull.

Interrogate the patent lawyer.

I opened one of the patent files, found letters from BIOTECH's Washington patent lawyer and punched up his phone number. According to the contract, he'd have to talk to me, too.

"Luskin, Daper and Luskin," answered a middle-aged female voice.

"This is Dr. Ben Candidi, calling from BIOTECH Florida, a client company of yours. I'd like to speak to Mr. Eddington."

"I'm sorry, but he's in Japan. He won't be back until the middle of next week. Is there anything I can help you with?"

Should I insist that he call me from Japan? Or should I try another approach? I had another flash of inspiration. I would join the BIOTECH team. "Yes, please. We have a big problem here. Actually I'm the one who has a big problem. I've lost some important correspondence, and Dr. North needs to show it to B.M. Capital Company today. It's that due diligence thing."

I dropped my voice like the due diligence thing was the biggest pain in the ass that I'd experienced in my short career. If BIOTECH could play tricks on me, I could play tricks on them.

The Washington patent-legal secretary responded cautiously, "Well, you could check with your Mr. Roger Black. He receives all the originals."

"That's just it. I'm afraid I lost his only copy when I was going through the file."

Did she have heart enough to rescue a careless young man who'd gotten himself in deep shit?

"Which letter was it?" she asked.

"That's the other problem. I'm not sure what it was — just that it was sent to us in the last two weeks." If BIOTECH was in trouble, it probably happened recently.

"Humm," the secretary said disapprovingly. But she softened. "I'll get the file and see what we can find."

I quickly flipped through the files, looking for any correspondence as recent as the last two weeks. I found only one letter, written for Broadmoore's sake, expressing an opinion that everything was right with the patent for the three compounds.

My concentration was broken by the deli delivery boy; he came with my sandwich. I pulled out my money and found nothing smaller than a $20 bill. I gave it to him and waved him off just as the Washington secretary returned to the line.

"Dr. Candidi, I've found it. It's an opinion letter on the patent. We sent it last week."

It was the letter I had in my hand.

"No, I have that one. There was supposed to be something else."

"Are you sure you lost anything? I don't find anything else from the last two weeks. There are some handwritten notes for a memo that Mr. Eddington started to draft last Friday. But then your lawyer called us back and said the letter wouldn't be necessary."

"That must be it!" I said in mock relief. "I almost knew Mr. Black was wrong when he said I lost it. Just to be sure, what did the memo say?"

"Let me see. It deals with the law on continuation-in-part applications. It's hard to read. Oh, here's something about multiple inventorship."

"Right! That's it. And what else is in it?"

"Nothing, really. There's a note about post-H patenting. But you must understand, Dr. Candidi," she said in formal tones now, "this is work product. I really shouldn't be reading it to you."

"No, I understand. That's fine. Thanks again. You got me off the hook. I'll just tell Mr. Black that he remembered it wrong. Thank you again."

"And thank you."

"Just one more thing I need to check. Excuse me, but I'm new here."

"Yes?" she said, sounding impatient now.

"Besides the patent that Dr. Moon already has, are there any more that have been filed?"

"No. I'm quite sure of that, Dr. Candidi. Will there be anything more?"

"No. And thanks again."

I hung up. Good that the patent lawyer was in Japan. He wouldn't have tipped me off about BIOTECH's last-minute inquiry. I just prayed that nobody from BIOTECH would find out about my call.

That wasn't all the praying I did. I used to be an altar boy. I am unable to lie without experiencing strong feelings of guilt and memories of the confession booth.

I got another cup of coffee to steady my nerves, then sat down and scribbled notes about multiple inventorship, continuation-in-part applications and "post-haste" patenting. Why had BIOTECH called its patent lawyer last Friday? Were these important issues? Or were they just dotting their i's and crossing their t's? And if this stuff wasn't important, why would it have to be done post-haste? I would have to ask our lawyer about this.

I ate my sandwich, then spent some time walking around the offices of King Construction. None of our team members was around. Some of King's employees eyed me like I was trespassing. I called Broadmoore's suite and still got no answer. Left a message at the desk: "Still no interview with Moon. Major problem. Can't do my job."

It was almost two o'clock before Cheryl and Bud King returned. King looked as serious as when they left. He stomped in — right past my door — without saying a word. Cheryl put on a worried look and walked up to me.

Cheryl pretended she'd been trying to help me out of a jam. "I'm sorry, Ben. Dr. Moon won't see you today."

"Well, who the hell does he think he is? The King of Siam?"

"Unfortunately, yes." She laid her green eyes on me and put on a face expressing sympathetic concern. Funny how a woman can disarm you by agreeing with you.

"As you probably know, Ben, Dr. Moon is not an employee of BIOTECH. We licensed the technology from him. There is no way we can force him to have another appointment with you."

"Another appointment," I practically shouted. "I didn't even get a first appointment. He was totally uncooperative."

Cheryl stepped back and shook her head like I'd been rude.

"The best we can do is maybe tomorrow morning at nine."

I wasn't going to stand for that. We went through several rounds of thrust and parry:

I said the option to buy was a ticking clock, and they were depriving me of valuable time. She replied that we still had plenty of time. I said the option contract required BIOTECH to cooperate with B.M. Capital. Cheryl replied that BIOTECH had been cooperating. I reminded her that today was Wednesday. I might not be able to complete my evaluation by Friday afternoon. If things kept going like this, we might not be able to buy BIOTECH.

"Well, Ben, I guess you are aware that your colleagues have found other problems. I'm sorry if we won't be able to do business." How strangely she intoned these words. She could have been telling a boyfriend that their relationship wasn't working out. "And yesterday I was so hopeful. Maybe if you had approached Dr. Moon differently — "

"Like hell! From the start, he was acting like a villain in a B-grade karate flick. He *kiai'd* me out of his *dojo*. And you told me yourself, he was a pain in the ass."

"Ben, I don't know what to say."

I snatched up the phone and held it at eye level. "I insist on talking to Moon — now. Please punch in his home number."

"No, Ben. Don't try. It will only make matters worse. Go see Bud, if you feel you have to."

I did just that. King glanced up from his desk for an instant as I crossed his threshold. Then he kept me waiting a full two minutes while he pretended to be working. Finally he stared up at me like a bulldog daring me to climb over the fence.

"Well, Candidi! Come on in. What can I do for you?"

"You can pick up the phone and tell Dr. Moon that he is going to see me in one hour."

King grimaced. "You know, I'm really disappointed. I thought scientists were supposed to get along. I really don't know what you guys have got for a problem."

"For starters, he doesn't like to answer questions. And I've still got a load of them. And we'll have to be getting answers soon, or I won't be able to complete my scientific evaluation before the deadline."

"And Cheryl couldn't take care of you?"

"The answers have to come from Moon."

King set his jaw and locked his eyes on me. "Well, I don't know what to tell you, Candidi." His brows narrowed, and he continued to stare until I blinked.

He won. I lost.

The rush of dumped adrenaline hit me seconds later. The brute actually thought he could win on raw willpower. It took great effort to speak with a steady voice. "Mr. King, I am sorry to tell you that BIOTECH is in violation of the option agreement. You are in breach of contract with B.M. Capital."

"That's your duly considered opinion? Then you can talk to my lawyer."

"If that's what's needed to convince you, set it up. I'll be there as fast as a taxi can bring me."

King waved his hand as if to dismiss me. Then he picked up the phone and started punching numbers. As I turned to leave, he called out, "Hey, little guy, don't be so impatient. I'm setting it up." Into the phone, he said, "Roger, I've got Dr. Candidi here, blowing his stack that he can't get another shot at Dr. Moon. Now he's spouting off something about us being in breach of contract . . . Of course, it's nonsense. Look, I'm going to send him over. Can you read him some law? . . . Elkins? Yeah, I know he took off back to Boston. Ain't that a pisser? Anyway, just read Candidi some chapter and verse so he don't go off doing nothing rash."

King dropped the phone into its cradle and told me, "My lawyer, Roger Black, is expecting you as soon as you can get there. Get Roger's address from my secretary on the way out."

Roger Black's building was three blocks south on Brickell Avenue. His building adjoined a long parking garage which extended all the way to the Bay. At eye level, the building wore a thin veneer of quarried stone over poured concrete. Above, it was the usual steel and glass. I walked up an array of marble steps. The steps were edged with nonskid insets, the perfect defensive arrangement for a building that houses lawyers.

The marble statement was blemished by a set of plastic Cheapo-Mart patio tables and chairs standing near the entrance. It was easy to deduce the purpose of this retrofit: Seated there was an elegantly dressed businesswoman about my age — nursing a cigarette.

The express elevators, serving floors 25 and above, had full-length windows facing outside. My touch of button 53 triggered a metallic voice that reminded me to stand clear of the doors. The ascent was rapid and viscerally stimulating. My stomach tugged on my diaphragm as poincianas and palms diminished below me. The acceleration maxed out just as the expressway emerged from behind the trees. Then the whole city appeared before me as a green, textured gridwork.

At the pinnacle, the elevator doors opened to a reception area. At first glance, it could have been mistaken for the street-level foyer of a cozy but elegant London hotel. The law firm occupied the whole floor.

I gave my name to a prim, dark-haired woman in her early thirties. She lifted a brass and porcelain receiver from its French Art Deco cradle and announced to Roger Black, Esquire, in ersatz English accent, that a Mr. Candidi was here to see him. Then she informed me that Mr. Black was with a client and could I please be seated.

I chose the first convenient grouping of sofa, coffee table, and opposing chairs. Their legs ended in talons clutching glass balls that pressed into a Persian carpet covering a long expanse of marble floor.

I was not impressed with their kitschy ibis-shaped umbrella stands or the weakly refracting pseudo-crystal chandelier hanging overhead.

That was not to say that the interior designer hadn't tried hard. There was wood veneer and marble at eye level, and painted plaster above. They even framed the elevator entrances with dark-stained wood. But it was a bad choice to cover the sliding metal doors with wood veneer. And the false wooden doors seemed silly when air wooshed through the cracks, as the elevators whizzed up and down their channels at express speed. If I got a chance, I'd tell these people that they would have done better to have riveted on some hammered brass with a textured geometric design. These new rich should take a trip up north and see some old-time elevators.

After a quarter of an hour, the receptionist indicated Mr. Black was free. She led me to his office at the end of a long hallway that displayed gilt-framed, color lithographs of English foxhunts, Alexander von Humboldt botanical illustrations, and Audubon birds.

Dressed in a white shirt, broad tie and red suspenders, Black sat behind a mahogany desk, talking on the phone. It had something to do with delivery of documents in a civil case. With a flick of the hand, he indicated that I was to sit. I pretended to not notice and amused myself looking out his window.

I knew the game he was playing. He was using the home court advantage, making me wait around in his space and trying to impress me with his furniture.

I mentally rehearsed the opening moves of the game. He'd probably make a half-assed apology for keeping me waiting. I'd tell him that was okay and that I knew a brass worker who could replace the phony veneer on his elevator doors. After we got down to business, he'd probably tell me I didn't have any business complaining about their impediments to due diligence, since I was not a lawyer.

I wouldn't look at his furniture, and I would look out his window. He had a breathtaking view of the Bay, now hued in pastel aquamarine and sparkling in the mid-afternoon sun. A couple of miles to the southwest I could make out the anchorage at Coconut Grove, a sprinkling of moored sailboats, and the Australian pine inhabited spoil islands. Layers of built-up humidity blurred all detail like the over-wash in a watercolor painting.

It seems to be a major personal shortcoming with me that I look out windows and daydream when I should be thinking about the game. But what more should I be thinking about? How do you prepare for a pissing contest?

Roger Black was still haranguing his adversary. I moved a couple steps and looked out his landward window. To the west, a traffic-jammed U.S. Highway 1 cut a jagged swath through the tree canopy. The asphalt groove was filled with hydrocarbon aerosol that forward-scattered the sun's longer wavelengths, producing a layered brownish tint.

Roger Black shifted to a summary tone. "So they will be on my desk tomorrow, Goodbye." Black locked me in a narrow-eyed stare, then jerked his head toward the guest chair to indicate that I should have already been sitting in it. "Dr. Candidi, what can I do for you?"

No apology for keeping me waiting; no chance to insult his elevator door. And what an irritating choice of words: He knew damned well what I wanted. I moved the guest chair a foot closer to his desk before sitting down. And before speaking, I brushed aside his brass business card dispenser with the back of my hand.

"Mr. Black, you already know that Dr. Moon is not cooperating with the due diligence. He has denied me an opportunity to receive his answers to questions necessary for us to evaluate the technology." Black just sat there glaring at me. "It is my opinion that his lack of cooperation puts BIOTECH in breach of contract with B.M. Capital Company."

"Dr. Candidi, I must apologize. I didn't know that you have a law degree."

"I have read the contract, and —"

"Firstly, I would not agree that Dr. Moon is being uncooperative. Secondly, you have been given copies of the patent and access to all the supporting documentation. Thirdly, your own lawyer has received an opinion letter from our patent attorney stating that the patent is secure. Your lawyer appears to be able to make his own determination." Black smiled, as if he had an ace up his sleeve. "And, fourthly, I do not know how your team is dividing up its work — but with respect to legal matters, don't you feel a trifle far afield?"

While he was reciting, I moved a silver-framed picture to the side of his desk, as if it had been obstructing my view of him. I took a deep breath before answering. "Regarding your fourth point, it is no concern of yours how my team divides up its responsibilities.

Regarding your first three points, you are not a scientist — and your opinion carries no weight. One does not have to be a lawyer to understand the contract's plain language on the requirement of co-operation. As the expert responsible for evaluating the scientific validity of your drug compounds, I hereby protest the lack of coop-eration from your inventor. He has refused to give me more than ten minutes of his time. How can we make a twenty million dollar de-cision — based on a ten-minute interview?"

"As BIOTECH's counsel, it is not my duty to schedule meetings or predict —"

"Maybe you wouldn't mind writing us a letter of assurance that Moon will be fully available after the deal is closed, whenever we need him. And write in a money-back guarantee against defects that we may uncover in the next three months."

"I cannot be responsible for producing unpaid opinion letters or assurances against undefined events. I was not retained to make my firm a potential target for litigation. In this litigious climate — "

My smirk brought this remark to an abrupt halt.

"Dr. Candidi, you may find it amusing, but you are not a lawyer. I must refuse your naive request for assurance on scientific ques-tions you may invent in the next three months. Now — is there anything else I can do for you?" Black composed his narrow-eyed face into a condescending smile, comprising equal parts of white teeth and black beard.

"Okay, Mr. Black. Let's restrict the question to legal ramifica-tions you should be able to understand." I'd show him I could also toss a word salad. I thought back to conversation with the patent lawyer's secretary. "Could you tell me what would be the effect of Dr. Moon's noncooperation if a 'continuation-in-part' patent appli-cation were necessary?"

Black's eyes widened. The teeth disappeared from his smile. He made a throat-clearing noise and pressed the fingers of two hands into a triangle.

Allow your enemy no respite. "Mr. Black, this doesn't require complex judgment, so please answer."

"It is my informed understanding that a continuation-in-part is not necessary to secure your licensed rights to the technology. You already have optimal patent protection." Black seemed to be quickly regaining confidence. "You must tell me if you wish to pursue this question in terms of the real facts of the case — or in the hypothetical. A full answer would require your statement of what you consider to be the facts in the present case."

I wouldn't let Black escape into a thicket of legalisms. I'd follow him in like scrappy terrier, even if it meant getting a nose full of thorns. "Mr. Black, please answer non-hypothetically with all the facts of the present case. Will a continuation-in-part be necessary to perfect the rights to the three compounds for use in treatment of cancer?"

Black rocked forward. He rubbed his beard and looked down at his desktop. Breathing deeply, he got up and faced the window. Obviously I'd asked an important question.

"Well?" I coaxed.

"Based on all the information that has been made available to this office and to you, the answer is no. Further patent applications should not be necessary to secure the technology granted in your contract." Black said the last words ever so carefully.

It was, nevertheless, a very encouraging answer. I needed to cap it off. "So, if Dr. Moon were hit by a car tomorrow and died, our rights would still be secure."

"Yes, your defined rights to the three compounds will be as secure as the Rock of Gibraltar."

"And I can quote you on this?"

A sarcastic grin took form on Black's face. He pushed the intercom button and said, "Miss Steadman, could you prepare Dr. Candidi an opinion letter stating that if Dr. Moon is hit by a car —"

"That's okay," I said. "We will send you a memo tomorrow with my understanding of what you said. If I express it wrong, you will be welcome to correct it."

"I'd be most happy."

"Good. I feel that we've made some progress."

Black smiled.

"But I still expect a three-hour interview with Dr. Moon tomorrow morning to answer my remaining scientific questions. Otherwise, you will receive a hand-delivered letter stating that BIOTECH is in breach of contract."

"I cannot promise you the interview, but I will prevail on BIOTECH to do everything possible." He sounded almost friendly.

There was nothing more to say. I would either get the interview, or I would not get it. I thanked Mr. Black coldly and left his office. I walked slowly down the hall, pretending to look at their botanical pictures.

As I passed a secretary's office, Roger Black's voice echoed on an intercom speaker. "Penny, please get me Mr. King."

Deep in thought, I walked slowly back to BIOTECH. Perhaps my forcefulness would make BIOTECH cave in. Black was ready to go out on a limb, assuring us that the three compounds were okay. In that case, BIOTECH's last-minute questions to the patent attorney on "continuation-in-part" were probably just dotting their i's and crossing their t's.

But why had Roger Black's mouth dropped open when I mentioned the term 'continuation-in-part'? And why had Cheryl started acting like we wouldn't have a deal. It was as if they had decided they didn't need our money.

I went back to BIOTECH. Their secretary told me that both King and Cheryl were gone. I put things away and went across the street to a Cuban café. Put my briefcase down on a table next to a pay phone. I ordered a *con leche* and gambled some pocket change on Broadmoore. This time he answered. I briefly recounted my day's efforts, including the pissing contest with King and the half-promising outcome of my sparring match with Roger Black.

Broadmoore said he was now having his own problems with King and had just finished complaining to him. Broadmoore's lawyer, Elkins, had taken a 12:30 p.m. flight to Boston but would be available on the phone this evening. We would all participate in a conference call from Broadmoore's suite at 7:30 p.m. Yes, he agreed with my assertion of "breach of contract". No, I didn't need to confer with him or his lawyer before the conference call.

I took the MetroMover to the Marriott. It was nice to get out of my suit and into normal dress slacks and a shirt with an open collar. I went to the food court at the Omni Gallery and ate a steak and cheese sandwich while watching the children on the merry-go-round. Then I walked out to the street for my appointment with Zeekie.

A hand waved from a white, late-model van with tinted windows. "Right here, Ben," boomed a loudspeaker apparently mounted behind the grill. "Step right up to Zeekie's wedding van."

I didn't see Zeekie in the driver's seat. "Do you perform weddings in here?" I shouted through the open passenger-side window.

"No, I document them," answered the loudspeaker. I stuck my head through the window and looked toward the back. The walls were lined with TV screens, VCRs and electronic equipment. Joe Kazekian sat at a large mixing console with several rows of sliding levers. Next to him, a pair of headphones dangled from the ceiling.

"Gee, Zeekie. This looks more like a surveillance command post."

"Well, you can think of it that way, but the people pay me good bucks to be surveilled. I know we've got to see your friend but give me a couple minutes to show you my setup. Can't turn on everything; we're on battery power. But just watch the monitor. I've got it cued up at an interesting spot."

He flipped a switch, and the van filled with Middle Eastern music. The video monitor lightened. In a couple seconds it was running in sync with the tape. A middle-aged, semi-bald, Anglo-looking guy was making soprano sax quaver in Middle Eastern vibrato. Behind him, a curly-headed teenager was running half-tone riffs on a synthesizer keyboard. The screen quick-switched to an overhead shot of the floor covered with a swarm of animated dancers.

A chorus of female and male hips gyrated in synchrony with the music. The camera zoomed in on one couple. The man shed his necktie and bound it around his partner's hips. The necktie seemed to increase the amplitude and frequency of the woman's gyrations. This couple was not the first. Several other women were competing to blur their husbands' colors over the broadest arc.

The quavery sax/oboe tapered off and a throaty female voice cut in. Her first phrase provoked whoops from men in the crowd. The female singer repeated the phrase again and again, working it up to an orgasmic pitch. The screen switched back to the stage. The singer's long black hair moved in waves from one shoulder to the other. Her body writhed in unison with her rhythmic moans. She concentrated her full passion into the microphone.

"Pretty hot stuff, your Armenian weddings. Where did you do this gig?"

"Right here in the van. See these four joysticks. They're for controlling the cameras. Set them up in the hall on poles. The cameras work on batteries and send back video signals by short-range wireless transmission. But look . . . here's where it really gets good."

The screen returned to the overhead shot. The dancers were turning in two concentric, counter-spinning rings.

"Look at the one in the white jacket, Ben."

The camera zoomed in and followed a black-haired, dark-eyed beauty in a tight purple skirt. Her white suit-jacket was held together with a couple of pinned-on gold chains. After several second's watching, I was sure: She had absolutely nothing under. The camera stalked her as she snaked in and out between the oncoming dancers of the counter-flowing ring. Her breasts jiggled with every step.

"Boy, Zeekie! She doesn't leave much to the imagination."

"No, and I caught her at least half a dozen times in full profile using freeze-frame — right down to the nipple."

"Did she know that the camera's iris was dilating on top of the pole?"

"After she saw the playback, she wanted me to dilate *her*. But I was too busy selling videos."

"Selling the video at the same wedding?"

"Yeah. I master the tape in real time and play it back while the guests are lined up, waiting for the valet parking. Make them order up front before they drive off. I roll their plastic." Zeekie pointed to a credit card machine. "But this gal, she wanted a custom order — all the outtakes of her. Look, here's her business card." He handed it to me proudly. She was a commercial real estate broker in Boca Raton.

I joked, "If Rebecca doesn't come back soon from Jamaica, you can take me on one of these jobs. But right now, we have to see if my client is bugged."

Zeekie nodded. He flipped off the video and picked up a canvas bag full of equipment. As we made our way through the hotel lobby, I told him what I found suspicious about BIOTECH.

Up on the 28th floor, I discovered that Broadmoore's Greenland dog team had shrunk: Just gal-for-everything Sally and accountant Thad Smith remained. Broadmoore had cut loose the oncologist and the FDA expert. Sally said they had left for the airport that morning. And, of course, lawyer Elkins had taken an early afternoon flight. After looking once more around the room, I realized that I was the lead dog.

Broadmoore walked up, shook my hand, and patted me on the shoulder. He nodded to Zeekie, already in the corner and unpacking his bag.

"Ben, you should leave all the talking to me, unless I indicate otherwise with a pointed finger."

The guy was actually capable of giving directions.

Sally picked up the phone and started talking. She gave the operator instructions on which parties to add to the conference line first. Elkins answered at his home in Boston. Then they got Roger Black at home in Miami. Next she put on Bud King at his office and Cheryl at her apartment. Now Sally flipped on a speaker phone.

Broadmoore took over and went through the ritual of calling names and asking if they could hear. "And do we have Dr. Cheryl North?"

"Here," she said distantly. "Hi, everybody. Hi, Ben."

Bud King's voice came through the strongest. "Okay, now that you finished your roll call, can you tell me what this is all about?"

"You know, just as well as I," replied Broadmoore in the tone of a schoolmaster. "By denying us access to your inventor and by denying us certain financial information, you are making it impossible for us to complete the due diligence. You must correct this immediately and extend the deadline, or you will be in breach of contract, and we will be forced to sue."

"Nobody's suing nobody. We sent you the financials two months ago. And your man's been crunching numbers with Sharma for two days now. I pulled her this afternoon. I need her on another project. I'll send in a backup tomorrow. Does that take care of it?"

"Unfortunately it does not. There is the more serious matter of Dr. Moon's refusal to meet with Dr. Candidi."

"Let's don't talk about anyone who can't find his ass with both hands. Moon didn't refuse to see Candidi. He saw him yesterday afternoon. Isn't that right, Cheryl?"

"That's right," Cheryl chimed in. "I took Ben over there right after the luncheon."

Damn her creeping familiarity.

"So what's the beef?"

I answered King faster than Broadmoore could raise a finger. "What's the beef? There wasn't any damn beef in the hamburger! Moon wouldn't answer my questions. He said the answers were in his patent. But they weren't. Then he got surly and practically kicked me out of his office."

Cheryl jumped in, "That's not true, Ben. You agreed that I would show you the data." She made it sound like a domestic dispute.

"Dr. Moon was so overbearing, he left me no other choice. But, Dr. North, you will remember that he promised me an interview for nine o'clock this morning. You called me at eight this morning and cancelled it."

King grunted, "Candidi, did you ever think that the poor guy might have gotten tired of answering the same questions for you guys? He spent the whole goddamn last week answering questions for your buddy. What was his name? Young?"

"Dr. Yang," I said.

"And then you show up and start asking the same damn questions all over again."

Broadmoore was now hovering over the speaker phone. His face bore a pained, hopeless expression. When I had tried to get his attention he turned his back to me.

I snapped an answer back at King. "They weren't the 'same damn questions'. I picked up where Dr. Yang left off. I have my own questions." Broadmoore turned to me and smiled. "It might seem as simple as pouring concrete to you, Mr. King, but antineoplastic pathways are complicated. Like electronic circuits are complicated. Dr. Moon thinks the target enzyme is protein kinase C. But there are at least eleven different forms of this enzyme."

My voice was echoing nicely off the walls, and Broadmoore was giving me thumbs up. "It is imperative for us to have more information on what Dr. Moon does and doesn't know. We have to judge the strength of the patent protection. And we have to assess the probability that the three compounds will receive FDA approval as cancer therapeutic agents."

I was starting to feel pretty proud of myself.

The line was silent for several seconds. When King answered, he sounded deeply offended. "What you seem to be saying is that you're getting cold feet. Maybe the technology doesn't look so good to you."

"I'm saying that I need straight, forthcoming answers from Dr. Moon on the mechanism of action, or we don't know what the hell we're buying."

When King didn't answer Cheryl chimed in, "But, Ben, I showed you the mechanistic data yesterday afternoon and this morning."

"You showed me nothing of the sort. You showed me perfect bean counts on mouse mortality."

"Oh." How vividly she made this single syllable express her emotions — disappointment curdling into contempt — insulted — as if I'd suggested that she go on a diet.

Bud King came back gruffer than ever. "Roger, do you think we are in breach of contract because Moon can't tell Candidi what he wants to know about his eleven brands of protein 'kind-naze'?"

Roger Black assured us all that they weren't in breach of contract. Then Elkins jumped in and said that they most assuredly were. Thus, the next event was a prize fight with the lawyers shadowboxing in legalese for $300 an hour. Roger Black's technique was scrappy and ornery. Elkin was more suave. He hung back until Black threw himself out of balance, then counterattacked, plastering him with jargon and peppering him with precedents.

Thad Smith was busy making notes on everything. Sally was recording the conversation on a hand-held tape machine. Zeekie stood by, holding his gizmo. He was glad to get my attention. He motioned me over and showed me that the light was flashing. I gave him a nod.

In a whisper I told Sally to have Zeekie check our other rooms. They left to do it and returned in a quarter of an hour. Zeekie signalled me a "yes". By this time the lawyers had duked it out for 10 rounds. They'd danced across the canvas, forwards, backwards, clockwise and counterclockwise.

Even King was getting tired of the prize fight: I heard him grunting in the background. He broke in a few minutes later. "Okay, its clear who's won. You Boston guys won't get very far down here with your fancy arguments. Take your demands and stuff them. Let's say goodnight to them, Roger."

Broadmoore answered in a scolding tone. "If that's truly your final position, we'll be in court tomorrow seeking an injunction to prohibit the sale or licensing of the technology to any other party. It may cost me a pretty penny, but I will tie you up for years."

"Finally showing your true colors, are you?" King sounded sinister. "Taking the low road. Okay, Roger, we'll give them what they want. Candidi sees Moon nine o'clock tomorrow morning at the lab. Dr. Broadmoore, you got any more bugs up our ass?"

"No, thank you. And I am delighted that you were able to pull out your own cork . . . although I do not wish to know how many hands you required to do it. Mr. Black, Dr. North and Mr. King, I wish you good evenings."

King replied with a grunt and a click. Mr. Black and Cheryl said goodbye. Then Broadmoore told Elkins to check back the next morning. Sally deactivated the speaker phone.

I went to the desk and wrote, "Room is bugged," on a notepad. When I handed it to Broadmoore he frowned but showed no surprise.

"What an uncivilized bunch, this Miami company," Thad Smith said, polishing his glasses.

"What happened to you today?" I asked.

"They started dragging their feet about letting me see the books for the first year of BIOTECH's existence. It shouldn't have been any big deal, but they said 'no' very abruptly."

"When?" I asked.

"Right after lunch."

"Who said 'no'? Ahma Sharma?"

"No, she's always been nice. It was King. He marched in and told her she had to do something somewhere for the construction company. He made it sound like I was wasting her time. Sounded like he wasn't interested in the deal anymore."

"Hard to understand," I said. I walked to the door and signaled Broadmoore and Zeekie to follow me. I took them down the hall and through the fire door to the enclosed stairwell. I introduced Zeekie and asked him to give his report.

Zeekie got right to the point. "All your rooms are bugged. Your phones, too."

Broadmoore didn't waste any words, either. "Thank you, Mr. Kazekian. Please give your bill to Ben to pass on to me." He turned to me and said, "You have won the bet."

I thanked and dismissed Zeekie, promising to call him at the shop the next morning.

The air in the stairwell had an unwashed, unsealed concrete smell. But I couldn't leave, yet. Needed to exchange a few more words with Broadmoore. "What do you think now?"

"I think that you are a bright lad with talented and well-connected friends. The fact that BIOTECH is eavesdropping is not in the least bit surprising."

"Not surprising?"

"It happens in one out of every four deals valued at twenty million. In and of itself, it doesn't prove a thing about BIOTECH — except that they don't trust their own judgment."

"You aren't going to take countermeasures?"

"My dear boy, I have done so from the very beginning. I never made significant judgments for all to hear. No top-secret utterances were ever made in that room. All my significant communications have been with isolated individuals in secure locations, phone calls included."

Not only did he string the dogs to his sled individually, he put blinders on them.

Broadmoore concluded, "Anything top secret exists solely within my cranium."

"But it makes me feel creepy. First your Dr. Yang disappears, then BIOTECH bugs your rooms."

"If Dr. Yang hadn't disappeared, I should not have had to engage you, and the rooms still would have been bugged."

Broadmoore's logic was difficult to argue against.

"Okay. What do you want from me?"

"Find out if Dr. Moon has anything to hide with respect to the patents."

In essence, Broadmoore was concerned that he might be buying a Civil War trash pit. And I was his principal geologist.

"And happy hunting tomorrow." He turned toward the fire door, indicating that the interview had come to an end.

He got away before I could ask him about my predecessor, Yang. But somehow I had the feeling he wouldn't give me a straight answer. In fact, it was even possible that he told Yang to disappear to Key West because he wanted to send in a second man — Ben Candidi — to confirm his suspicions.

It was getting late. From the bank of pay phones, I called our empty apartment. Punched in the code for a playback of our answering machine. There were no messages, just hang-ups.

I went back to my hotel room and plugged in my computer to check my e-mail. I hoped Dr. Rob McGregor might have answered my query on the scientists Cheryl had "worked for" back in Washington. Instead, I had a message from Richard Bash, old roommate from my Swarthmore days. Richard came from eastern Tennessee. His defining characteristic was an overripe sense of humor, based on crude homilies and pseudo-intellectual hyperbole. He built every joke on the premise that he was just a dumb hillbilly trying to figure things out. He was actually one of the brightest guys I'd ever known. And now I was laughing tears by the time I'd gotten to the third line:

From: rbash@x1.esvax.umc.dupont.com
Copy:
Subject: Hard-fucking male spiders
Message: ******************************

Dear Ben:

Long time, no write. Finished your dissertation, so I have to call you "doctor" now? My heart bleeds for you, but an M.S. will be good enough for me. I don't mind staying an analytical chemist here at DuPont. As the saying goes, "If you can stand the smell, you've got it licked!" Which reminds me, are you still shacked up with your beautiful med student? Thanks for the picture. She looked nice, and your boat didn't look bad either. If you're planning a June wedding, let me come down and throw you a bachelor party. I'll make it so obscene she'll change her mind, and leave you a free man.

Which reminds me — did you see that piece in Science Magazine (M.C.B. Andrade, Science 271:70 (1996)) about the hard-fucking male spiders? The hard-fucking trait is genetically determined. The males that give the old mamma spiders the hard fucks, they do it by positioning their heads over the old lady's jaws. Better penetration that way — but they invariably get their heads bitten off when she comes. In contrast, the poorly penetrating pussyfooting males keep their heads out of harm's way, don't always get eaten, and thus sometimes live to fuck again. The thing about it is that the hard-fuckers pass on their genes better than the pussy-footing pricks. Now isn't that a bitch!

So why is Mother Nature such a prick tease? Well, it's all what's best for the survival of the species. It seems that when old mamma spider gets a hard fuck and gets to eat her old man for dessert, she don't want nothing else for a long time. And she chases all the pussyfooters away.

Some theoreticians came up with a mathematical theory that shows that it takes MUCHOS pussyfoot fucks to equal one good hard fuck when it comes to making spider-babies. I'm sure that this has something to do with marriage, but I'll let you figure it out for yourself. One last word of advice that my old man used to give me:

> If you don't want to get bitched,
> Don't get yourself hitched.

Yours truly,
Richard (Unbashful) Bash

That was old Richard! — the only guy who could get me laughing so hard my ribs hurt. After drying my eyes, I realized I was tired. I plugged in the phone, ordered a wake-up call and dozed off. Spent the night dreaming about webs, spiders and social Darwinism.

HARD BOILED   25

I climbed out of bed in time to see the sun rise from the Atlantic near the mouth of Government Cut. It was Thursday morning: my third day of the project — less than two days to finish my work.

BIOTECH's lab was within walking distance of the hotel. But by the time I got suited up and made it out to the pavement, the sun had already done its late-Spring magic. In consideration of the heat and humidity, I opted for a cab. Why arrive dripping in my expensive threads?

A buzzer unlocked the door half a minute after I pressed the button, admitting me into BIOTECH's dingy reception area. As I entered the lab, Dr. Singh greeted me with a pearly white smile, then returned his attention to an unconscious, cannulated rat. The door to Dr. Moon's office was closed. What a funny-looking office — that windowless module crowned with an octopine tangle of flexible air conditioning ducts.

Singh said, "Dr. Moon is not here. Dr. Lau is not here, either."

I walked up to Moon's door and knocked anyway. No answer.

Late for the interview. Funny that Cheryl wasn't here to monitor it. Grabbed a lab stool and sat down, leaning against a makeshift lab bench. Watched Dr. Singh working on the limp rat with ghoulish intensity. Crazy excuse for a company, this BIOTECH: crazy, unapproachable inventor. Wouldn't let me ask a logical series of questions.

Crazy liaison arrangement they had for me: good-looking female administrative scientist, deployed like a corporate *geisha* to wait on me hand and foot, and exert influence on my due diligence. Well, it had become damn clear who she was working for — after she opened her mouth last night.

No question about it, this morning's interview with Dr. Moon was much needed.

For an eventless quarter of an hour, I waited and mused over BIOTECH. Every couple of minutes, the technician poked his head through the doorway of the back lab like he was looking for someone. Finally Dr. Lau walked in the front door. He glanced at me in surprise.

"I'm waiting for Dr. Moon," I said.

"He should be here," Lau answered.

"You can say that again."

Before I could say more, the technician interposed himself between us. He looked worried. "Dr. Lau, there's no way I can quick-freeze the cell cultures this morning. We're all out of liquid nitrogen. We're almost out of dry ice, too."

Lau grimaced. "This early in the week? I don't understand how you could run out."

"I don't, either. I didn't waste any." The technician sounded defensive. "I need your permission before putting in a rush order. There'll be a surcharge."

"It cannot be avoided. We have to freeze the cells now for Dr. Moon's kinetic — " Lau stopped in mid-sentence. The technician hurried off to make his call. Lau turned to me. "Why are you not speaking with Dr. Moon?"

"Because he isn't here."

"No, he must be. I saw his car in the parking lot."

"Well, his door is shut, and he didn't answer when I knocked. Does he do this often? Locking himself up in his office?"

"Yes, when he is working hard and not want to be disturbed."

"Maybe I should knock again."

"Yes, knock hard. His air conditioning is noisy. He might not hear you — if he is in the toilet."

It was hard to suppress a smile while knocking on the door of anally retentive Dr. Moon. Beginning with a series of polite taps, I progressed steadily to the level of solid raps. After a minute, I was knocking with theatrical intensity. Soon the tightly sealed door was literally rattling in its frame. I turned and threw a questioning glance at Lau. He nodded in consent. I tried the handle. The door opened with no difficulty. The small room greeted me with a rush of cold, moist air. No sign of Dr. Moon.

"Dr. Moon," I called in a voice loud enough to carry into Moon's private toilet. I waited for a polite interval, taking stock of the room. Humidity had curled the calendar on the wall. The desk was surprisingly clean — no papers left out for me to snoop through. On the edge of the desk, the word "sponge" was written with felt-tipped pen. Neither of the computers was on, but the laptop was plugged into a phone extension.

After a couple minutes, it seemed curious that I hadn't heard any plumbing noises from Moon's private toilet. It should have been time to flush by now, unless he really did have a cramp in his anal sphincter.

"Dr. Moon?" I called. I knocked on the bathroom door, slowly building up to frame-rattling intensity. The doorknob would not turn.

Dr. Lau appeared at my side. "This may be serious," he said. "Maybe we need to get a locksmith. But there is no hole for key."

I said, "No, it's a bathroom doorknob. Has a punch hole in the center for emergencies — like when a kid locks itself in. Could you get me a large paper clip?"

A few second's poking around yielded a satisfying click as the thumb button popped on the other side. The door opened easily the first couple inches but offered stiff resistance to my efforts to open it wider. After several hard pushes, I got it opened wide enough to get my head in. The small room had a moist, fecal odor. Moon lay crouched on the floor between toilet and door.

"Dial nine-one-one," I yelled to Lau.

I reached in and tried to pull Moon forward. My fourth try cleared the door enough that I could squeeze in. Had to crawl over Moon's back to get a look at him. No sign of consciousness. Couldn't judge his condition in the bad light. Manhandled him into the corner to get the door open. Dragged his upper body into the office where there was space to lay him out.

Moon's pants were down around his legs and his shorts were loose at the bottom. Couldn't feel any breathing. Eyes closed. Couldn't get any pulse on his neck. But I was never very good at that. Felt my own heart racing, though. How long had I been fumbling?

"Call nine-one-one," I screamed out the door.

"They're coming," Lau called back from the lab.

I tore open Moon's shirt and put my ear to his chest.

Couldn't hear anything. Chest wasn't moving. What did they teach us in Basic Rescuer? Fifteen compressions and two breaths? Sensed a crowd behind me. I must have looked idiotic. Started chest compressions. Lot of resistance below the rib cage. Tried to give him respirations. Lot of resistance from his jaw. Grabbed hard and forced his mouth open. Cold and clammy. I breathed out hard, but my exhalations wouldn't take. Now I realized — his whole body was cold and stiff.

Stiff arms at his side wouldn't bend. Heard sirens. Pulled back Moon's eye lids and saw death. No pupil reflex, even to the fluorescent lights overhead. Tested it by moving my hand in front of his eye.

Footsteps and two-way radios were coming near. I jumped up and blurted out to the lead man, "No respiration — can't hear a heartbeat — gave fifteen compressions — couldn't establish airway —no pupil reflex."

The paramedic knelt over Moon. He placed a thumb on Moon's neck while visually inspecting him. He tried to bend Moon's right arm at the elbow. It didn't budge. He shot a glance at his number-two man carrying the defibrillator and shook his head. He turned to me and said, "Okay, you did fine, buddy."

Bumped into the wall when I tried to step back. Was a lot clearer when I could see it from a distance under good light: Moon's face had an ashen hue. Such a sorry sight — hairless chest framed by a torn-open shirt. At the junction of his short, bare legs, a small patch of dark hair hid a penis the size of a child's thumb. Bunched pants and undershorts bound his legs at the ankles. Leading to the bathroom was a thick fecal trail, marking my frantic attempts at extraction and rescue.

The lead paramedic said, "Run a strip." The number two man straddled Moon, holding two paddles to his chest. I expected to hear the thing charging up with a high-frequency whine, then a click, releasing a kilovolt pulse. But the paramedic just held the paddles on Moon's chest for a long time.

"Okay. Flatline," said the lead paramedic. He reached down, tore off a narrow strip of chart paper coming out of the unit and attached it to his clipboard. Then he pulled a radio from his holster and keyed down. "Rescue Two to dispatch. We have a '45'. Request PD."

I was pretty sure of one thing: There was no way that Moon's death could be a coincidence. I went to the outer lab and dialed Dr. Westley's office. His secretary, Doris, remembered me from when I used to work in Dr. Westley's lab. She put me right through.

"Dr. Westley, we need a medical examiner at the BIOTECH lab right now. I found Dr. Moon, BIOTECH's inventor — dead — in his office. There's a good chance he's been murdered." I stammered out the word "murder" before looking around. Luckily nobody was near me. They were all gathered outside Moon's room.

"Ben, calm down. Describe to me the circumstances."

"No time for that. Dispatch a medical examiner and a homicide detective immediately. I'll call you back after they've secured the crime scene." I made Westley take down the address, then hung up before he had a chance to protest.

I elbowed my way past several onlookers and into Moon's office. Put a finger to my lips and whispered to the lead paramedic, "Treat this as a crime scene. A medical examiner and a detective are on the way."

The paramedic looked down at me, shaking his head condescendingly. "Come on, buddy," he answered in full voice. "Just chill out."

I returned a look that must have convinced him I wouldn't be an easy case.

He answered it like he was reciting from a procedure manual.

"There's no bullet holes or blunt force trauma."

I grabbed his upper arm and pressed a thumb into his hypertrophied biceps. I spoke softly but looked him square in the eye. "I just got off the phone with Chief Medical Examiner Geoffrey Westley. Those are his orders. I used to work in his lab."

I made a bigger dent in his logic than in his biceps. "Okay, you got me listening. Where do you come into this?"

"The story is too long to tell. The body is not to be moved. According to procedure, you need to secure the area." I was making it up as I went along.

The paramedic turned and hollered out the door, "All right, everybody. Go back to your places. If you don't have any business here, you gotta leave."

Employees from the other companies did as they were told. Lau, Singh and the technician grabbed stools and sat at the lab bench.

I stepped up to the paramedic. "Thanks. You did it right. Now please don't say anything to those guys about my Medical Examiner's connection. Any of those three might be a suspect."

The paramedic wrinkled his nose and stepped back. I finally realized what was wrong. I excused myself and went to the men's room by the common reception area. Took off my pants and shoes, and gave them a thorough soap and water treatment. Got them back on and returned just in time to find a medical examiner and a detective at the scene. The M.E. was at Dr. Moon's side, inserting a rectal thermometer. A core temperature reading would help him establish the time of death. The M.E. wasn't that much older than me — probably just a trainee.

The detective was a good 20 years older than either of us. He looked like he'd inspected thousands of crime scenes and wasn't particularly impressed with this one. He just stood there clicking his tongue, as if he might be dealing with a kid who'd pulled the fire alarm for the smoke coming from a neighbor's barbecue. He was probably convinced it was just a heart attack. To deal with this guy, I'd have to play the Westley angle for all it was worth.

I ignored the detective and squatted next to the M.E. "I'm Ben Candidi. Formerly of the M.E. tox lab."

"Jeff Powell," he answered. He glanced at his latex-gloved hand, as if to apologize for not extending it.

"Dr. Powell, you were told by Dr. Westley to treat this as a suspicious death. Right?"

"Right," he answered.

I told him about the locked door, the position of Dr. Moon's body, and how I had dragged it out.

The detective chuckled and said to himself, "Ain't no '31.'"

I ignored him and made a big deal out of showing the M.E. the toilet. Moon had dumped half his load there, and the other half on the bathroom floor. No paper had been used. What a cold, disgusting sight. Occasional droplets of condensation fell from the overhead vent and splattered on the befouled floor.

From his corner, the detective kept looking on. He had the appearance of a guy who'd seen it all and done it all: heavy jowls sagging from large cheekbones; probably once played football as a lineman. Hoped I could get him on my team; he would be a hard guy to play against.

I concentrated on the M.E. "Medically there isn't much more I can tell you. The two scientists working here didn't see Dr. Moon in the lab when they came in this morning. I didn't have any chance to ask the technician." I turned to the detective and asked, "Did you learn from the technician when Dr. Moon arrived?"

He scratched his flat forehead couple of seconds, then smiled. "Not yet." His spoke with that tight-jawed intensity you hear around the streets of New York — when New Yorkers are dealing with New Yorkers. "I thought you guys could tell me when his old ticker stopped ticking — whether he was working late or coming in early. Hey, I thought you could figure that out by just sticking a thermometer up his ass." Yes, he sounded contentious enough to be from the Big Apple.

For my reply, I adopted an insistent but polite tone. "Well, perhaps you can corroborate one theory or the other by interviewing the three witnesses"

The cop settled his slow eyes on me and grimaced. Probably too much trouble to tighten his throat and growl an answer.

I would have to push him hard. "Dr. Lau out there told me he saw the deceased's car parked on the lot. If you want to get really fancy, you might go out there and stick your finger up its tail pipe. Then you could give us your opinion about when its old engine stopped ticking."

The M.E. cracked up. He hid his face by turning toward the stinking toilet. The detective's eyes smoldered. His throat engaged. "I don't need any wise ass — "

"I'm not telling you how to do your job. But I am telling you that Chief Medical Examiner Westley considers this a high-priority case and —"

"Okay, I hear you talking, buddy." He pushed off the wall and walked out to the lab.

M.E. Trainee Dr. Jeff Powell grinned as he packed up his field kit. "That was pretty good — telling Sergeant Cordova to go fuck himself and take a rectal temperature on a car. You handle homicide detectives real good. You must have gotten around."

"No, I was just a lab rat at the M.E. Office. But when I was about thirteen years old, I read a lot of hairy-assed L.A. detective novels."

From then on, Jeff Powell and I got along just fine. I told him about my consulting job. Told him that my predecessor had disappeared, and how Moon had been acting strange. Powell promised to order a complete toxicology screen. They would also look carefully for signs that Dr. Moon might have been smothered. He reached into Dr. Moon's pocket and pulled out a key ring. "I'll give this to Sergeant Cordova for his automotive core temperature determination."

I stepped out to the lab and found Detective Sergeant Cordova; he was gruffly interviewing Dr. Lau, Dr. Singh and the technician. He kept eyeballing Singh like a suspect. Maybe Cordova didn't trust guys who wore turbans.

I didn't think any of the three could have done it. But maybe a couple people working in a Brickell high-rise office had wanted Moon dead. I picked up the phone on the other side of the lab and called Cheryl. Hoped to catch her by surprise, but I was too late. "Ben. I just heard. Lau just called and gave me the bad news. It's so horrible."

She spoke quickly and convincingly, but that didn't mean anything now. Too bad I didn't get to her before Lau. Now I'd have to push her hard to learn the truth.

"Yes, Cheryl, when anyone dies it's horrible. It's time for you to tell me what this is going to do to the company."

"Like I said, Ben. It's horrible." She had answered slowly.

Inarticulate. Mushy. But how should I interpret that? I would have given a thousand bucks to see her on a video link.

I couldn't let up. "But yesterday you were telling me you had the technology under control — you said I didn't even need to talk to Dr. Moon. Which is it? A minor setback or a complete derailment?"

Cheryl answered my question with complete silence.

"Tell me — now," I demanded. "Which is it?"

"Oh, Ben. It's always bad for a company when an inventor dies. The investors are always afraid that — "

"Bullshit! Broadmoore and I are the investors. We can think for ourselves, once you give us the facts. Yesterday you and your illustrious Roger Black, Esquire, were telling us the patent is airtight. You guys were arguing the technology was so good that your inventor could get away with playing lunatic. Now you're telling me it's horrible that he is dead. Please do us both a favor. Tell me which of your statements is right."

"Don't you have any sympathy? Can't you tell what I'm going through?"

"No. And if you can't give me a straight answer, then put me through to Bud King. Right now."

My demand was met with a long silence. A sudden absence of office noise in the background told me Cheryl had cupped her hand over the transmitter.

Across the lab, Cordova had just finished with the three lab workers. He was walking out the door with Moon's keys in his hand. The phone rang on the other side of the lab. Lau picked it up. He nodded immediately. Unfortunately his phone and my phone were on separate lines with no transfer buttons. No way for me to listen in.

After a minute, office noise returned to my receiver. I heard breathing. A second or two later, Cheryl answered in an carefully controlled voice. "I'm sorry, Ben. Bud is not here at the moment."

"Then have him call me as soon as he pokes his glazed head in the door." I hung up and meandered across the lab to eavesdrop on Lau.

"Long weekend? Yes, I see. I tell them no one works on Friday. Yes, lock up the lab. As soon as police tell me they are through . . . Yes, he is here . . . I don't think I can say that to him . . . Yes, I understand. Okay."

Lau must have sensed that I was listening. The closer I got, the more softly he spoke, until he finally turned his back and cradled the phone as if protecting a baby in a storm.

"Hey, is that King?" I demanded.

"Yes," Lau answered, half-turning toward me.

"Tell him I want to talk to him. Right now."

"Dr. Candidi here, want to talk to you." Then Lau faced me and said, "I am sorry. He just hung up."

"He hung up after you told him I wanted to talk to him?"

"Very sorry."

Cordova came back and bellied up to the sink. He used a generous helping of liquid soap to remove engine grime from both hands. But the soap didn't remove the yellow stain from the tips of the index and middle fingers of his left hand. I considered my intended words very carefully.

"Lieutenant Cordova?" I asked meekly. It wouldn't hurt to give the sergeant a field promotion.

"The engine wasn't warm when I touched it," he answered. "Was probably off for four hours or more. And Moon was here before any of those other ginks came in."

"Thank you. Could I ask you a little favor?"

"Not today. I'm fresh out of favors for wise-asses." He chuckled and threw a glance toward Dr. Lau across the lab.

"I'm sorry. Trying to do CPR on a dead man must have really shaken me up. I haven't smoked for years — but could you lend me a cigarette?"

My fake admission dissolved Cordova's crusty shell like a sugar cube tossed into a cup of hot coffee. "Sure, buddy. I thought I'd kicked the habit, too. Then one night the going got rough." He pulled out a soft pack — dark red background bearing the white outline of an armored, helmeted knight flanked by two rampant lions. He shook out a filterless cigarette. I plucked it up like an old pro. But Cordova stared at me as I held it between my fingers at waist level.

Cordova's left hand was twitching near his pants pocket, as if receiving contradictory orders on pulling out a lighter. He frowned and said, "But it didn't shake me up so bad that night that I forgot how to put the cigarette in my mouth and smoke it."

"I'm sorry, Lieutenant, but they probably won't let me smoke it in here with all the ether they're using to knock out the rats. Maybe we could smoke one together outside."

"Sure, why not?" The sugar cube was completely dissolved.

We did the nicotine thing on the south side of the building in the shade of a live oak. Sergeant Cordova pulled out a Zippo lighter, and I hunched over its blue, hydroxyl-radical flame, catching a whiff of alcohol. I pulled hard on my borrowed high-tar and nicotine cigarette. It would be important to inhale deeply. Then, I started coughing.

Cordova whistled and said, "Boy, you really musta kicked the habit a long time ago, if a cigarette gets you coughing like that.

My world turned gray, and for a second I thought I'd have to grab the tree.

Cordova pointed with his cigarette toward the parking lot where two men were loading a body bag laden stretcher into a M.E. station wagon. "Yeah, that's where strong cigarettes will put you. Throws your lungs topsy-turvy." He looked down at the cigarette. "Guess that's why they call them pell-mell's. Now what do you want to talk to me about? What is it the Chink scientist and his Hindu buddy aren't supposed to hear?"

"I'm working for a Boston company, checking out a drug that the deceased Dr. Moon is supposed to have discovered. If I decide the drug's all right, I give the Boston company the go-ahead, and they can invest in it. But the Miami BIOTECH company that's selling the invention didn't want me to get near Moon. And when I did he acted funny."

Cordova rolled his eyes, wrinkled his nose, and blew out a cloud of smoke. "You think someone might have poisoned him with his own drug?"

"Exactly," I answered. Of course, it wasn't exactly what I suspected, but I couldn't afford any negative salesmanship at this stage. I took a deep drag on my cigarette and blew it out through my mouth without choking this time. "What makes it really suspicious is what happened to the guy the Boston company sent down before me — he disappeared last weekend without a trace."

"Okay, Candidi. I get your drift. And Chief M.E. Westley is tuned into all this?"

"Very much so. He's been interested in the deal since the other guy was missing."

"What does Westley have in mind?" Now Detective Cordova's throat was relaxed and his voice had broadened. He was sounding "New York friendly". Maybe it was the nicotine molecules binding to their receptors in his brain.

I improvised a wish list. "Work up the scene so you know whether physical assault or subjugation can be ruled out. Then get the lab sealed off as a crime scene. Take the keys to Dr. Moon's house and look for evidence of a break-in or a search. And look to see whether he has any documents or reports lying around, — dealing with cancer drugs from sponges. When you're done looking have the house sealed as a crime scene, so that no one else can come in and disturb it."

"And why do you want that?"

"Because he may have been killed for his data. Because his scientific notes and reports might offer a clue to why he was murdered."

"You mean, if he was murdered, Candidi." Cordova's cigarette was burnt down to a stub. He threw it away. "And while you're at it, why don't you ask me to bring back a pizza. Look, I've got too many files open as it is now — including a double homicide from last night. A guy doesn't get points doing favors for that windy old Brit. And he's working for the County, and I'm working for the City of Miami."

"If you do what I'm asking, Dr. Westley will owe you a favor."

"Like what? A discount seat on British Airways?"

I tossed away my cigarette. Thought for a few seconds.

This called for one hell of an answer. "I really can't promise you anything for sure. But when I was working in Westley's lab I heard a story about how a cop was put in a tight spot about shooting a 'perp'. Shot him in the back during a drug bust. The cop said it was dark, and there was sudden movement. He got lots of trouble — Internal Affairs, newspaper reporters and lawyers for the family — all that kind of stuff. Well, what I heard was that Westley stepped in and personally reinvestigated the case. Westley found that the junior M.E. had gotten the entrance and exit wounds mixed up."

I was sorry I'd thrown the cigarette away. I could have used it to distract from my nose — which had just grown a foot. I finished by saying, "You never know when you might need a favor."

Cordova eyed me carefully while lighting another cigarette.

"And when I talk to Dr. Westley, everything you say is going to check out?"

"Sure. Talk to him about Dr. Moon and the suspicious cancer drugs and how my predecessor, Dr. Yang, has been missing since last weekend. Let him know that you're working hard to do him a favor. But don't say anything directly about a payback. If you try to make him come out and say it, he'll draw the line — and you'll be on the wrong side of it. You just have to trust him and me. And the favor's not transferable. No 'friend of a friend of a friend.'"

Cordova thought for a second. "Okay, Candidi. You're on."

He reached into his pocket. "Moon's got five keys. These two are to his lab. This one's his car. These two must be to his house. I'll get his address from one of scientists in there —the one that isn't wearing a turban. I'll get a crime technician to work the office up for prints in case Westley needs them later."

PICKING UP THE PIECES 26

I gave Cordova the phone number of my apartment, saying he could leave messages for me there. Also told him I'd return to the lab after making a couple of phone calls. The burger franchise, a few blocks away on Biscayne Boulevard, seemed like a convenient place. Dr. Westley accepted my call without delay. He was pleasantly surprised that I had recruited Detective Cordova to search Dr. Moon's house — until I told him about my fib and the promise I made in his name.

I went to the counter and purchased a 99-cent "Super". It effectively removed the taste of the cigarette but didn't replace it with anything better.

For the price of some more pocket change, I was able to transfer some of Westley's disdain to Broadmoore. How dishonest of him to downplay the danger in this assignment. Assistant Sally answered the phone at his hotel suite and left me dangling for four minutes.

"Ben, I have heard the news already. You have performed admirably. Geoffrey will do his — err — own due diligence in sufficient depth." Broadmoore's choice of words reminded me that his line was bugged. "For the remainder of the day, you could continue your — err — due diligence with the laboratory notebooks and computers, if you catch my drift."

Did he expect me to say "aye, aye, sir" and hang up?

"I would like to talk to you face-to-face." He owed it to me. When someone is missing that's one thing. But when someone dies, that's another thing. "Maybe we could meet in the Omni Center near the merry-go-round."

"Ben, that would be premature. I want you to devote the next precious hours to determining the value of the patented technology and any trade secrets the company may have."

"Talking about assigning value to the company, did they insure Dr. Moon's life for five million dollars with themselves as beneficiary?"

"The contract allowed for it. I am in the process of finding out whether they actually insured his life."

"Good. And do we still have Friday evening as a deadline for making up our minds? That's little more than a day."

"I requested an extension, and King denied it. Just got off the phone with him, in fact."

"What do you make of his behavior."

"Inappropriate to discuss now."

"Why so? If you want me to figure this thing out — "

"Ben, I find this irritating — or how does the American expression go? You are bugging me."

I'd almost forgotten that the phone was bugged. "Okay. Have it your way," I answered, pretending to be irritated myself. "Leave word at my room when you want to see me."

Back at the lab, I found Detective Cordova giving instructions to a crime scene technician. Dr. Singh and the lab technician were gone. Dr. Lau sat in the corner of the lab, acting like he was afraid Cordova would steal something. Cordova turned to me and said, "We're doing a quick search for prints. Dr. Lau, over there, says that no one ever came in Moon's office except Moon himself. Should be done here in an hour or so. Then you can look over his papers and computers. Looks like the little one is plugged into the phone line."

I did as Broadmoore told me. Spent a lot of time going through the notebooks in BIOTECH's outer lab. Cheryl was right when she assured me that everything was in order. I found hundreds of pages of experiments supporting the patent. And there were thousands of pages supporting the chemistry section of the IND document they were going to submit to the FDA. If BIOTECH had any fault, it might be over-organization.

The animal experiments were all properly referenced to the analytical chemistry experiments. And the chemistry pages were referenced back to the extractions from sponges. Everything was just as required for the FDA. Their records probably surpassed FDA standards. And Moon had apparently ordered Lau and Singh to do a lot of control experiments, using encoded standard compounds sent from a laboratory in Oregon. The only glitch I found in their Good Laboratory Practices work was that these extra control compounds were not completely identified.

Around four o'clock, the crime technician told me he was finished. I went into Moon's office and snapped on the two computers. The laptop didn't contain much data. If I could get it out of the lab, I could explore it at leisure. So when Lau wasn't looking, I packed the laptop into an evidence bag and told the crime technician to take it to the M.E. office. After the crime tech left, Lau started to get assertive.

"How much longer you stay here?"

"At least another hour, 'til five o'clock. Since I didn't get my interview with Dr. Moon, I can at least look over his papers."

"He doesn't keep many papers in his office."

Lau was right. There weren't many papers in his desk.

The file cabinet in his office didn't have any personal papers, either. It contained mostly copies of scientific articles on natural product chemistry and metabolism — articles by other scientists.

I spent the rest of the hour with Moon's desktop computer, going through the directories and files. Most of them dealt with lab management. The computer contained minimal correspondence. It had no Internet access or FAX capabilities. I got up and took a little walk around the lab. Time to sum it up.

To sum it up, the afternoon's dig in BIOTECH's files revealed nothing that I didn't already know about the technology. Moon had left everything so well-documented that his death would not threaten the project. Either the technology was solid like a rock, or everyone in that lab was a fake, including the technician.

There was no reason to stay longer. Lau followed me out, activated the alarm and locked the door behind him. He said that no one would be working in the lab tomorrow, Friday. If I needed to get back in, I should make arrangements with Cheryl.

I called Westley from a pay phone near the merry-go-round at the Omni Mall. I asked about the autopsy.

"No sign of wrongdoing on the corpse. If it were a death by smothering, it must have been done with velvet gloves in a padded room. There were no defensive marks. Nothing revealing under the fingernails. To wit, no sign of a struggle. It might be fatal arrhythmia while he was straining at stool. Could have resulted from vagal stimulation. There were, in fact, certain malformations of the heart."

"What about poisoning? Maybe he was drugged."

"No, Ben. The blood analyses failed to turn up anything. In absence of information to the contrary, we will have to list this one as sudden death resulting from arrhythmia."

After hanging up on Westley, I called Broadmoore's room.

Nobody answered. I bought a Philadelphia steak and cheese sandwich at the food court and sat down with it near the merry-go-round. It was nice to see the smiling faces on kids enthralled by the sound of the calliope, enchanted by fleeting images in the turning mirrors, and challenged to stretch for the brass ring. The smiling kids were still young enough to pretend that their painted horses were real.

I did not realize that I'd be riding a merry-go-round myself, before the night was over.

27 ONE ENCHANTED EVENING

I returned to my hotel room around 6:30 p.m. My first order of business was to give the expensive pants a second soap-and-water treatment and hang them up to dry. My second order of business was the blinking message light on the phone. The front desk gave me a message consisting of a telephone number and a single word: "Cheryl." They said the message was taken an hour earlier. Good! I would get another crack at her. I would ask her the same questions I was going to ask Dr. Moon.

I opened the sliding glass door before punching in the number.

Cheryl answered on my second ring with a distant, "Hello."

I played hard to get. "This is Dr. Ben Candidi. I had a message to call this number."

"Oh, Ben," she said, warmly now. "Thanks for calling back."

"Well, here I am." I tried not to sound too friendly.

She said nothing for several seconds. "I'm sorry I wasn't making any sense when you called this morning. It was such a horrible surprise to learn Dr. Moon died so suddenly. You can only imagine how I felt."

How quickly she turned the tables.

"Can only imagine?" I mocked. "There are too many things I can only imagine this last three days."

"Oh?" She could pump so much expression into a monosyllable. This time it was disappointment and disapproval. She followed it up with a dramatic pause, then continued in a soft style: "I was also calling to find out if you had any idea what Dr. Moon died of. I mean, it came as such a surprise. We didn't know that he had anything wrong with him — except his personality."

She might have been speaking naturally; she might have been reading from a script. I certainly wouldn't forget how she had put me on hold with her hand over the transmitter, so that Bud King could get a head start on talking to Dr. Lau.

"Look, Cheryl, I don't know what Moon died from. He was dead when I found him. Probably long-dead. Could have been a heart attack. How should I know?"

"You discovered him. You were with the paramedics. And they say that a medical examiner investigated it. Do you know why?"

I moved with the phone toward the balcony and looked out across the Bay.

"The head paramedic radioed it in. They sent out a medical investigator right away. It's probably standard procedure when they find a relatively young man dead for no apparent reason. Moon wasn't much over forty-five, was he?"

"I see," Cheryl said, dropping her voice. Then silence.

"So, Cheryl, where does his death leave you?"

"Can't you imagine?"

"No, I can't imagine. A lot has happened that I can't imagine. Like I can't even imagine why BIOTECH wouldn't give us an extension of time when Dr. Moon refused to see me yesterday. And now you won't give us an extension after we found Moon dead. We need time to evaluate the effect of his death on the technology." I laid in a long pause and scowled at the telephone. "Well?"

"Well, I'm sure you can see we were getting other problems."

"What other problems? That we were taking too much of Alma Sharma's time? No, I'm afraid I don't see." Again no answer. "You are acting like the deal's off. I get the feeling that BIOTECH has changed its mind and doesn't want to be bought. And I'd like to know why."

"Ben!" she exclaimed, as if she was trying to stop me from swearing in church. But she didn't follow up on her monosyllable; she gave no explanation. Waiting her out must have taken half a minute. I just stared across the Bay at a lone condo building on San Marco Island.

"Ben, this might be complicated. Maybe there was a misunderstanding. Maybe if the two of us got together, we might be able to break the logjam. Maybe you and I could talk, and find out where our two companies stand. Could you come to my apartment? We could sit out on the balcony and talk it through."

I hesitated. "It couldn't hurt."

I would go over there and interrogate the hell out of her. I'd ask her about the eleven types of mechanism and find out why the were inquiring about "post-H patenting". I'd question her about the whole works.

Cheryl gave me the address of a condominium on San Marco Island. It was the building I was staring at. I said I'd be right over. After I climbed into the cab, it occurred to me that I should have suggested meeting in a neutral place, say, the cocktail lounge in my hotel. But it was too late now.

The ride was so short that the driver grumbled about losing money. San Marco Island was a straight shot due east along a two-lane road that crossed the Inner Bay on a palisade of concrete pilings. The taxi chugged up the gentle rise to the low drawbridge where its tires sang on the metal gridwork. Then came a gentle descent to San Marco, the first of the low-lying, man-made Venetian Isles. The Venetian Causeway connects each of these two-by-six block islands like beads on a string.

Back in the days when Al Capone lived on neighboring Palm

Island, the 1930s vintage houses were rated as mansions. Today they seem small and crowded together on the little islands. The old timers probably don't agree with that, but Father Time has been working against them. One by one their houses are being sold and torn down to make way for mansions which do a better job of expressing their owners' grandeur in the vertical direction.

Showing off her expensive apartment was probably part of Cheryl's strategy.

I thought about Cheryl's style of argumentation — suiting up, acting businesslike but using familiarity to win a losing argument. It went against my training — candidly talking through the problems and letting logic work it out. Rebecca agrees with me on this. I remembered the story of Rebecca's patient interview with the assistant dean for curriculum when the third-year rotations were making trouble for everyone. She didn't suit up for the interview. She just went in there and told the guy where the problems were and how they could be fixed. She didn't even try to take credit for it afterwards.

The cab took the first turnoff on the right and approached Cheryl's condo building. With only 14 stories, it was small for a condominium but big for San Marco Island. The old timers in the neighborhood association had probably kept them from building a taller one. Probably trying to protect their little tropical isle from the condo-and-concrete disease infecting Miami Beach.

Despite its moderate stature, Cheryl's building strove for grandeur. Built on a broad base, it used terraced stories to achieve maximal exposure. Little sister strutted her stuff with all the architectural requisites of her big sisters on Miami Beach — elaborate landscaping, under-lit palm trees, and an elevated, semicircular motor entrance.

I would use Cheryl's pseudo-business logic against her.

I tried hard to get into a corporate state of mind. Told the driver to keep the five-dollar bill for the two-dollar fare. My blue blazer, purposeful stride and my "don't-bother-me-I-know-this-place" demeanor got me past the valet station and doorman without insult. Off to the side, the concierge didn't bother me, either. I stepped directly into the marbled and mirrored elevator, and punched number 13.

As I stepped out into her hallway, it occurred to me that I should have invested more thought on my face-to-face cross-examination of Cheryl. Her apartment was on the south side of the building at the end of the hall. I pushed the button and heard a klutzy pair of chimes ring inside the apartment. A few seconds later, the peek hole flickered dark, then the door opened.

"Ben!" Cheryl exclaimed with mock surprise. "They usually call to the apartment."

"They must have figured I belong here."

She was still in business clothes, elegantly cut from velvety cloth, dark cherry red. No blouse, structured jacket with top button undone affording a good peek, short tight skirt, and nylon stockings. She seemed a bit shorter without heels. She leaned forward, deeper than necessary to close the door as she moved it past me. "Make yourself at home." As I stepped inside, she patted my elbow. It would have been a lingering touch, if I hadn't withdrawn immediately. "Let me show you around," she said.

The apartment was a standard product of an expensive but unimaginative interior decorator. The living room didn't seem lived-in. The oversized, white-upholstered couch presented its backside to the sliding glass balcony door, thus ignoring an excellent view of a small strip of Bay and of Miami beyond.

The couch faced a wall of black plastic shelves displaying four equally black devices: A three-foot TV screen, a VCR, a stereo tuner and a CD player. Between the black wall and the couch stood a white marble coffee table, exhibiting a half-sized female African head carved from ironwood. And scattered around at the carving's base, like slabs of ironwood, were several black plastic remote controls.

How long had Cheryl been living in this apartment? Did she own it?

To the right was a kitchen and bar area. To the left was a short hallway, through which I caught a glimpse of two bedrooms. One was dominated by a designer bed, its mattress covered with a tightly tucked sheet with a bold zebra-skin pattern. It rested on a flat base of shiny, chromed steel — the type you see at upscale discos. The second bedroom contained an exercise cycle and a stair climbing machine. A tubular-frame writing table, devoid of books and papers, was the only furniture in that room.

"Nice setup for corporate entertaining," I said.

"Yes, it can be nice for entertaining. You should see the view from the balcony." She stepped behind the oversized couch, opened the sliding glass door, and indicated I was to follow her out. I leaned with both hands on the rail, looking straight ahead, west, toward the Miami mainland. Cheryl pointed to the south; cruise ships were lined up at their terminals. "They call it 'Government Cut' for some reason," she said with a distant voice. Her hand came down on mine as if by accident.

"Maybe the government cut the channel." I removed that hand from the rail and shifted my weight away from her.

"That's good. What would you like to drink?"

"Anything. Specialty of the house. Something that goes with the decor."

"Coming right up," she said, this time with girlish enthusiasm. "First, I'll slip into something more comfortable," she added in a husky voice that reminded me of an old movie from the 1940s. "Why don't you slip out of your blazer? This isn't Boston, you know. Down here we're less formal." Cherry's velvet swished against blue polyester as she moved past me. The touch of fabric produced no sparks.

I dropped my jacket on the couch, then returned to the balcony. The sunset over Miami was a three-dimensional Rorschach pattern. Its inkblots were woolly white, backlit in cherry red, orange, and purple.

The blast of a foghorn interrupted my contemplation. A cruiseliner was leaving the dock. Its four open decks were lined with passengers anticipating a fun-filled evening en route to Nassau. Or maybe it would be a three-day "Caribbean Adventure". With all that pre-programmed fun, the liner was less a ship than a floating Disney World.

Yes, I had also cruised to the Bahamas — but much closer to the water aboard my sturdy two-masted *Diogenes.* For the price of a commercial three-day cruise, Rebecca and I had roamed the Bahamas for weeks on end. At the thought of her, my right hand lifted from the rail, seeking Rebecca's angular shoulder to draw her into a familiar embrace. Rebecca was the one I wanted to share this sunset with. But she was still in Jamaica. Before I'd met Rebecca, the *Diogenes* had served as my apartment. Hell, I'd bought the boat for less than Cheryl's interior decorator bill.

But enough of this! It was time to focus my attention on wringing information out of this woman. I would pull three sheets of blank paper from the inside pocket of my blazer and would question Cheryl. I would question her on the newly arisen "issues" between our companies.

Then it occurred to me that the "issues" came up right before Dr. Moon's death. Could there be a connection? A part of me thought the answer was yes, even if Westley couldn't find any evidence for murder. Five million dollars of insurance money would provide enough motivation, particularly when the inventor had already completed his duties and was starting to become a pain in the ass. Moon was as lovable as a foulmouthed parrot.

But five million from the insurance company is a lot less than $20 million from Broadmoore.

Time to check your premises. My murder theory was based on suspicion, aroused by the earlier disappearance of Dr. Yang. Was it possible that Yang had "fallen victim to street toughs"? Could my training in statistics and probability be any help?

When you added Broadmoore's group and Bud King's team together, you had maybe 30 people. What was the probability that in the space of five days one of them would disappear without a word, and that another would suffer a fatal heart attack? Pretty small, I thought. And there were no fingerprints on Yang's steel cases; it was as if they had been wiped clean.

But maybe these premises were false. Was it so unusual to replace a consultant? Maybe Broadmoore was lying to me. Maybe he had some reason for replacing Dr. Yang. Like I was thinking before, maybe he sent him on vacation, lied to BIOTECH about it, then sent me in to get a second opinion. What was the probability of that?

Was there anything else that was improbable? Every week there were probably hundreds of tricky venture capital deals going on in Miami. A few of them might be in biotechnology. And if this one hadn't been a biotechnology deal, I never would have been selected. I had to face it: My probability calculations didn't prove shit.

What do you do when your upper brain is putting out confusing signals? You fall back on gut feelings, the most primitive of your God-given survival instincts. What was responsible for my negative gut feelings? The manipulativeness of Cheryl? BIOTECH's creepy lawyer? The hidden microphones? Broadmoore said the microphones were common tactics, so I shouldn't count them. Ditto for the creepy lawyer. That left only Cheryl as the unfathomable one.

What about BIOTECH's erratic behavior? The sudden lack of

cooperation and tough words from King? Maybe that, too, was just par for the course — standard tactics designed to wring last-minute concessions from Broadmoore.

I would have to put the conspiracy theory on hold. The most important thing to do was cross-examine Cheryl on the science.

The Rorschach kaleidoscope in the sky had darkened and matured. On the edge of my peripheral vision, a shadow moved slowly, tickling my retinal rods. It was two images: Cheryl and her reflection in the marbleized mirror that covered her kitchen and bar area. She was putting together a couple drinks. A quintessential yuppie setup. She wore a silky black kimono. A little too casual for my taste, even for an informal meeting. It could have been a pose for a *Sharper Image* catalogue.

Cheryl picked up a remote controller lying on the bar. The living room flooded with sound — orangish synthesizer tones, moving slowly through aimless chord changes. Against this fuzzy background, a male falsetto sang about achieving the highest high. A couple gooey measures later, his female counterpart echoed him with a throaty country warble. Her tones were actually deeper than his.

It was the same "smooth jazz and cool vocals" station Cheryl had played in the office — corporate Muzak by day and bedroom Muzak by night. "Covering all phases of your lifestyle" was the station's motto.

Cheryl looked into the gold-veined mirror just in time to catch my glance. She responded with a comely smile. But tonight feminine charm would not be part of the equation. Once I got that inverted unisex music turned off, once I got her sitting across the table, the cross-examination would begin. I'd find out what she knew about the eleven protein kinases and how well the compounds targeted each of them. I'd make her explain their last-minute inquiry with the patent lawyer, even if they were just dotting their i's and crossing their t's. I'd find out if this change in attitude was just playing hard to get.

By now, I had figured out all Cheryl's linguistic tricks. Dropped voices and tactical pauses would have no effect on me. I smiled back to her, then turned my face toward Miami. The city was now transformed into an endless grid of sodium lights.

Had the waning half-moon emerged from the eastern horizon? Was Rebecca watching it at this moment?

The clinking of ice cubes against glass announced Cheryl's approach. Staring off into the distance, I said, "You must have seen a lot of nice sunsets from this balcony."

"Yes," she said.

I turned. Her dark kimono clung silkily. A knotted sash held it together at the waist. Shawl-like, it draped from her soft shoulders. It rearranged subtly as she handed me a glass. "Here's the special of the house for very special guy." Her voice was as silky as the fabric. "You've heard of a tequila sunrise? Well, this is a Miami Sunset. Rum and coke, Colombian style. Confectioner's sugar on the rim — not salt like tequila. You're supposed to hold it on your lips."

A puff of wind blew a wisp of hair over her cheek, and the shawl fluttered. With quiet insistence and exasperating self-confidence, she held me with her eyes. I hate it when they try to charm you.

"To business," she said as we clinked glasses. "Our business."

I'd soon cure her of this creeping familiarity. I used my first sip as an excuse for not looking at her. The sugar dissolved at the touch of my lips. Was it like inositol sugar? The cocktail tickled my taste buds. It went down with considerable sting and left a tart aftertaste. My second long sip tasted as strong as the first. "We have serious problems to face," I said.

"Yes, I know," she said, now with a purr. The cleft widened in the polyglycine fabric as she cupped her drink in both hands. It was hard to keep from looking down. Light green eyes searched me placidly. Reflecting the indoor light, they seemed almost transparent. It was hard to return their gaze at any depth. As a defensive reflex, I took a long pull on the drink. Then my lips really went numb.

Cheryl inched closer. "Ben, maybe we all need to take things slower. Maybe you've been working at this too hard. I know you're a real smart guy, but sometimes it's not smart to be so smart."

What was coming over me? It couldn't be the height that was making me dizzy. The cocktail couldn't have had that much alcohol. I half-turned, half-stumbled toward the balcony table. "Cheryl, we'd better sit down — "

"Not here. Let's sit on the couch." She grasped my upper arm with surprising firmness. She steered me toward the couch, supporting much of my weight.

What was wrong with me?

I dived for the couch and landed soft. Landed on a web of chords spun by a fuzzy orangish synthesizer. A tide of ambrosia welled up, starting in my thighs, swelling my crotch, then percolating in my abdomen and chest. Pleasantly it lapped against my lower brain. Too bad if it wet my cerebrum. But it already had. Half-formed thoughts were floating around, trapped in the upper regions of my skull.

Pectoral muscles tightened across my chest. My shirt felt tighter than the heat-shrunk plastic sheathing on a CD case. I moaned as Cheryl unbuttoned it.

"Here, Ben. This will help you to breathe better." She said it like an ER nurse. Could she keep me from drowning in this dreadful ecstasy?

"What did you do to me?" I moaned.

"Nothing really, Ben. I'm just putting you in contact with yourself. And maybe with me, too — if you want."

Spiked drink. No brain function left to resist. Just the sensation of floating in a sea of molasses, lifeless limbs at my side, a growing tumescence about my center, my brain spinning uncontrollably in outer space. Out of the dizzying swirl, I caught freeze-frame images of Cheryl hanging over me — a framed half-moon breast before a silk screen — the breast in crescent profile, charmingly punctuated by a craggy nipple, hanging gently in empty space like a little curved ski jump.

I was skiing down smooth white slopes toward an alluring siren call, my skis picking up speed until there was no stopping — nothing left but to take the jump.

"Oh, I feel so . . . " echoed an inarticulate, disembodied voice through a thick fog. The voice was my own.

A silvery female voice echoed down from a misty mountaintop. "Now we're finding our centers."

Pressure lessened around my waist. It felt like popping out of a G-suit.

"Clothes are so confining," echoed the Greek goddess. "There! I knew that was the way you felt about me." Tiny fingertips entered my nostrils, massaging from the inside. "The nose is an erogenous organ, too — especially when you give it candy."

The gel liquefied like confectioner's sugar and infused my nasal membranes. My nose became numb and cold. I breathed through my mouth and snorted to keep the substance from working in deeper. But it broke through in a numbing postnasal drip. Would I soon be choking on my own saliva?

A portable telephone hovered overhead. "You can come now," echoed the voice. Time became sticky and semi-elastic like taffy on a pulling machine. Half-formed thoughts funneled down my spine, then welled back up in a tidal surge.

"What do we have here, Ben? Here, Tiger," she mocked. "I know you're lurking in the bushes. Come on out and get tamed."

Chimes rang in the distance. I felt Cheryl moving away. Neuro-chemical sensors predicted an impending dopamine dump. Writhing on the brink of the ultimate spasm, I was beyond either help or shame. I was propelled into outer space.

My frame-grabbing electro-optics captured images of a dark-haired woman in a beige raincoat. In an instant, she jettisoned the coat and transformed into a belly dancer with long, flowing hair.

Cheryl purred, "Tonight you get to live the ultimate male dream — private dancing with two women."

A small red light hovered and blinked over my swimming head. The black sound-wall filled the room with Arabian music. The dancer undulated behind filmy, transparent silk. Her fascinating dance captivated me like a charmed snake which she stiffened, sheathed and then captured with her gyrating hips.

In tandem, danced Cheryl to the accompaniment of the slinking oboe and to the rhythm of her partner's finger cymbals. She held high a small dark case with the blinking red light. Black silk sailed across the room, sleek white skin flashed and her hips moved softly, approaching boldly.

It had been a lifetime of one woman at a time. Now it was two women simultaneously. Had this step taken me halfway to infinity? Was I now coupled to half the women who had ever lived? My blinking eyes delivered snapshots. The long-haired brunette danced on me like a six-armed Indian goddess. And the blond mountain goddess held up the smooth, black, magic stone which was capturing these moments to be played back forever.

Suddenly Cheryl was also astride me, delivering a labial kiss. I returned it with mammalian fervor. Caught in Cheryl's sticky web and in her partner's grip, my captive brain stem delivered a massive efferent discharge down my spine. It flowed like a swollen river into the sea. The ultimate expression of male and female complementarity had been rendered; Parvati had extracted the essence of Shiva.

Above, Cheryl's voice echoed, "Oh, Ben, you found me." Finger cymbals crescendoed and faded. Parvati disengaged from a shrinking Shiva. And robbed of its strength, my body swayed like a marine sponge in a sea of soft convulsions.

For an eternity, I gasped for breath.

"How did you like that, Ben?" Cheryl coaxed.

No, I could find no words or actions to protest her logic.

"I . . . I . . . "

The snake-charmer music stopped abruptly. In the distance, a door slammed. After a second eternity, the fog lifted. Slowly an image of Rebecca emerged through the mist. Deep within me, something silently moaned. A disembodied voice wailed, "I didn't . . . I didn't . . . "

"Yes, you did, Ben." Cheryl was sitting next to me. "And we can prove it. The pictures didn't show my face, and my body was a little out of focus, but you and the exotic dancer came out nicely."

"Why?" I managed.

"Because I thought you would like it. Because it will help us to work together. I need your help with the deal."

My spirit plunged into the darkness of a bottomless well. "What will become of me?"

"You'll be my special friend."

"Is that all?"

"Who knows. We could fall into some kind of love. I know what you like. And you want me." She said this matter-of-factly. Then she teased. "Unless there's still someone else that you like better —"

I held my body still and my eyes shut, and willed my face to not betray me.

"Few men have ever gone as far as you tonight, Ben. You stretched yourself." Cheryl seemed to have moved back. "And now we're going to have a little talk. And then I'm going to show you how to stretch yourself a little more." Her voice sounded more formal now.

Slowly I turned my head toward the sound of her voice, then opened my eyes. She was back in the kimono, sitting in a nearby chair, her legs crossed at the knee. Resting on her lap was a small, black, hand-held video camera. Its eight-inch stainless steel antenna was pointing toward me. With a knowing smile, Cheryl looked down and caressed the antenna tip with two fingers. The red light was not blinking. "It's so handy," she said. "It doesn't need a cord. It sends the picture to a receiver that can be in another room or in another apartment. Let me show you the nice pictures."

From under the ironwood statue, she picked up a remote controller. In the wall case, the oversized TV screen lit up and the VCR whined in fast-rewind. Cheryl pushed the button again, and the screen filled with images of a veiled belly dancer writhing over my midsection as my head flopped back and forth. In high-definition video, I was instantly recognizable. Cheryl fast-forwarded to a close-up shot where my face shared the screen with her pubis. I sucked in my breath and turned away.

"You really know how to whip a guy with a camera," I whimpered.

"But you liked it, Ben. I can always tell. Your face came out very nice. But no one can tell that it was me."

My body tensed. "The tape. Do you have other copies?"

"Yes. If you're thinking of knocking me down," she mocked, "and tearing it out of the VCR, you'll just make things more difficult. So use your good brain, Ben."

Then she switched to a tone of mastery. "Darling, we are going to have a little talk. Here's the story: BIOTECH isn't as good as you and Broadmoore thought. You have discovered that the patent isn't really airtight. You will tell Broadmoore that the data doesn't support the patent. You'll tell Broadmoore that BIOTECH is a waste of money. You're smart. You know how to make convincing arguments. It will be easy, especially since Broadmoore doesn't understand science very well."

Why had BIOTECH changed its mind?

She picked up a piece of light-green rectangular paper. "When it's all over you can take this to the bank. It's a cashier's check for ten thousand dollars. Payment for consulting for us for giving us the use of your good brain." Cheryl smiled sweetly. "You're going to do it, Ben. And then we're going to have a real nice ongoing relationship. Bud likes you. If everything works out, he may offer you a place in the company."

"And what if I can't find something wrong with the patent?"

"Oh, you will, Ben. With that good brain of yours." She put her hand on my forehead. "I can feel it warming up now."

"What if I won't, Cheryl darling?" Slowly but surely my head was clearing up and making sense of things.

"Well, some mean old person is going produce the video and make a nice story board — and send it to a certain Miss Rebecca Levis."

"Rebecca! How do you know her?"

"Oh, we know a lot about you, Mister Ben Candidi who is not from Boston. We know that Mister Candidi has been stretching himself these last few days — learning how to play the company scientist. And he doesn't even have a Ph.D. yet." For this, she used a weak, high-pitched voice, as if she reading a nursery rhyme to a child — the little kitten that lost its mittens. "But he'll get his Ph.D. soon — if his professors don't find out he's been starring in porno videos. But, Ben, we really don't want to waste time talking about bad things that aren't going to happen."

She switched to an earnest tone. "I want you on my team, Ben. We're glad you aren't from Boston. We won't have to pay relocation costs to hire you."

The mist was evaporating rapidly now. I was afraid of what my arms might do when they found the strength. I forced my numb brain to work through the logic of sexual blackmail. Must keep control. Shut your eyes. Keep your face limp. Think it all through before saying anything.

"Cheryl. You've got to tell me one thing."

"Yes, Ben."

I stared at her with unfocused eyes and gushed, "What do I really mean to you?" I let my voice break into a sob. The thought of Rebecca was enough to produce tears.

"You're real good, Ben. You make a nice playmate. And we're going to have some real good times together."

"But — "

"Don't spoil it with talk about vine-covered cottages. I found out myself the hard way. The world isn't like that any more."

"Then how's it going to be, Cheryl?" I pleaded, reaching out to her with both hands.

She grabbed one and stroked it like a big sister calming little brother after he'd fallen off his bicycle. "I can't predict your future. You've still got a lot of changes to make. But I know this, Ben, dear. You're on your way. Just like I was a few years ago when I learned the important things about the world."

"But you — "

"All I did, Ben, was puncture an overinflated super ego. It was getting in the way of what you really wanted. We're going to grow together, and learn together, and get rich together. Bud is making it possible. He's showing us the way." Cheryl's face seemed to glow with the vision of a promised land. "And your brilliant scientific mind is going to help us to put all the pieces together. That's what the ten thousand dollars is really for. It's your retainer."

She paused for a while, as if to think. "Ben, I'm sorry I had to push you over the edge tonight. But you wouldn't have made the jump yourself. And now you know how to do it — any time." She looked down on me searchingly. "How do you feel, Ben? Can I call you a cab?"

There was only one way to escape from her web. I closed my eyes and pleaded, "Cheryl, kiss me." As I felt her lips on my cheek, I turned my face upwards and kissed her mouth hungrily, thrusting deeply with my tongue and pulling her down. "Darling," I gasped between breaths. Her tongue returned in kind my fake passion. But when my hand slid into her kimono, she quickly disengaged.

"Oh, Ben. You are a real tiger. No, this is enough for tonight. Fix yourself up. I'll call you a cab."

She handed me my clothes, half-turned and picked up her portable phone. The number must have been pre-programmed because she pressed only two buttons. I removed the latex sheath, knotted it at the bottom, turned it inside out, and stuffed it into the pocket of my pants. Thank goodness, the dancing whore had thought to use that thing!

When I was dressed Cheryl gently pulled me to my feet. She brought my jacket, inserted the check in the breast pocket, and helped me on with it.

As she led me to the door, I asked to stay the night. She said no. We would see each other at the office the next morning. As she started to close the door behind me, I jammed it with my foot. I demanded a goodnight kiss and made a play to come back in.

"Ben, if you don't go back to your hotel room tonight Broadmoore might think something's funny. But you've probably figured that out already."

Nodding, I turned and headed for the elevator on unsteady legs.

I avoided my reflection in the elevator mirror. Walked right up to the concierge desk, pulled out the sign-in book and wrote down my name and the time — 10:30 p.m. Wrote with a lot of pressure to leave a deep impression on the underlying page.

The fat, uniformed doorman eyed me with a sly grin and said my taxi was waiting. Told him I didn't need one. Walked past a black and yellow heap idling in front of the door. After I waved it off, a dreadlocked driver slipped out and ambled behind me. He protested in Jamaican-accented English. "Hey, mon. De lady called me for you and said I was to take you to the Marriott downtown."

"Sorry, it was her mistake. I'm planning to walk."

He stiffened as if I'd delivered an insult. Then he pleaded. "Hey, mon. That is not fair. De dispatcher give me this one, and I be waiting just for you." I turned and looked him in the face. His eyes had no *ganja* glaze, just the hardness of willpower. I shook my head and resumed walking. Turning plaintive, he said, "Okay, mon. I take you there off the meter, flat rate — five dollars."

"I'm really sorry, but the lady gave me such a delightful night that I really have to walk this one off." I grabbed my crotch and tossed in a couple wide-legged steps.

Turned my head to throw him a smile but used the glance to memorize his face and license number.

Why didn't BIOTECH want to be bought? Why was I getting the feeling this guy might try to kill me?

DAMAGE CONTROL 29

The walk along the Venetian Causeway took 15 minutes. It gave me plenty of time to think about how I'd left myself wide open, about how I'd been sucker punched, and about how it wouldn't have happened if a part of me hadn't found Cheryl attractive. I also thought about the cab.

It passed me twice — once at the center of the drawbridge and once as I passed Trinity Cathedral near the hotel. I tried to act happy and pretend not to notice the driver. Tried to think about Rebecca and what I would tell her. Tried to think of my dissertation and whether my profs would accept it after Cheryl mailed them a video supplement. Thought about this crazy assignment that had suddenly turned vicious. Tried to think what the cab driver was telling someone on his cellular phone. Thought about the only one who could rescue me. As I walked past Trinity Cathedral, I fixed my eyes on the flood-lit mosaic of Christ the King.

Safely inside the Marriott, I took the elevator to the 28th floor and went straight to my room. Rattled coat hangers in the closet, slammed drawers, and turned on the shower, but I didn't go under it. Did spend a lot of time brushing my teeth, though. Wrapped a change of clothes in a bundle. Turned the clock radio on loud. Set it to go off early the next morning. Drew the curtains. Took the phone off the hook. Turned off the lights.

Bundle in hand, I left the room, closing the door ever so quietly. Ran down the hall and the fire stairs to the third floor ballroom level. Exited to the pedestrian bridge that crossed over the street to the big parking garage of the Omni complex. I stayed low to keep from being seen from the street. Traversed the Omni parking garage at the second level and entered the Wyndham Hotel. Exited through their ground-level motor entrance on Biscayne Boulevard.

Took the first cab in line. "To the Dade General Hospital complex," I told the driver. Sank back in the seat. Tried closing my eyes and resting, but I couldn't trust myself. The knockout drink and nose candy started to take over again. I fought it and concentrated on the outside world.

Poor old historical Overtown was an ugly sight under the yellow-orange sodium lamps that evening. At every corner, a $40-a-throw streetwalker was showing off her stuff. Share a couple lines of coke with her, and you could probably get the trick for $20. How much had Cheryl spent on her hired exotic? Probably a thousand bucks.

My dirty old cab threaded its way under ribbons of expressway. Next came a couple of decrepit Baptist churches and a small women's prison. Finally the medical center. I got out in front of the Medical Examiner's Building, conveniently located across the street from the Ryder Trauma Center. I rang the bell to roust the guard. He remembered me from the old days when I'd worked for Dr. Westley as a lab technician. The M.E. on call that night remembered me, too — but not well enough to grant my request on his own authority.

Dialed Dr. Westley's home number. He picked up on the seventh ring.

"Dr. Westley, I'm at your facility. I need your approval. Need to have a medical examiner take blood samples from me. We need to establish drugs of abuse. We also need swabs of my pubic hair for vaginal secretions."

"But — whatever for? You are clearly not dead."

"No. I've been raped — chemically and physically — by Dr. Cheryl North. She's BIOTECH's chief scientist. She lured me into her apartment. Her pretext was breaking a logjam in the negotiation. She slipped me a Mickey. She brought in a belly-dancing prostitute to mess around on top of me while she videotaped the whole thing."

"Have you been blackmailed?"

"Yes."

"I would gather she wants you to advise Brian to buy the company, despite Dr. Moon's untimely death."

"Negative! She wants me to advise Broadmoore not to buy the company."

"How curious!" Westley lapsed into silence for a few seconds. "Of course, the blackmail attempt has failed, now that you have told me its particulars. So you have properly discharged your obligations to Brian."

"Yes, above and beyond the call of duty. I will have to explain it all to Rebecca before they get to her. Then I'll worry about getting justice."

"Justice, yes. But after the business deal is completed — and not before," Westley said, firmly.

"Right now, they think I'm going along with them. And I'm going to keep it that way."

"Quite." Westley fell silent for a long time. "Well, then, bring to the phone whichever examiner we have on duty this evening."

I handed the phone to the M.E. who was standing by. It was a two-minute conversation in which the examiner said nothing but "yes." Then he handed the phone back to me.

"Ben," Westley said, "my instructions will lead to the forensic documentation of the episode, as you have requested."

"Thank you," I said.

Once again, Westley's end of the line was silent. He must have been thinking. "Ben, if Rebecca must learn, I am sure she will stand by you. Behind her shy exterior you will find a resolute lass who can deal with adversity and setback. Regarding the entrapment — under the influence of psychotropic drugs, free will is but a weak, philosophical concept."

My throat tightened. "I should have seen it coming," I croaked. "I should have resisted — "

"Ben," Dr. Westley began sternly, as if lecturing a son, "you were a victim of one of the oldest deceptions in the history of mankind — subjugation by pharmacology. Every culture has developed it to a fine art, although I rather suspect one of the most refined examples was in eleventh century Persia . . . with Hasan ibn as-Sabbah. He brought young men to his hilltop fortress, fed them meals laced with a goodly quantity of hashish — until they were hopelessly entranced. Then he brought out scantily clad dancing girls. The next morning, he told his youthful male guests they had experienced a fleeting vision of heaven — a heaven which they could earn for an eternity by plunging daggers into the hearts of Hasan's political enemies."

As Dr. Westley got into a groove with this monologue, his voice took on a lecture hall quality. "So from Hasan, we have, perhaps, the most nefarious example — akin to the present one — from which is derived the word assassin. Of course, the word is the French transliteration of the Arabic term *hashishi* which means hashish-eater. The French began using the term assassin around the time of the Crusades."

I couldn't blame the Old Boy for escaping into pedantry. It was the only way he knew to express sympathy. I said, "Speaking of assassins, can you prove that Dr. Moon was assassinated?"

The Old Boy cleared his throat. "It remains as I told you before. There was no evidence of foul play. There were no poisons or drugs of any kind. No sign of a struggle. No blood. No foreign skin under the fingernails. No crushed larynx as seen in strangulation. And no pulmonary edema or any other manifestation of respiratory distress. We were left with no alternative but to postulate a sudden death heart attack — a fatal arrhythmia. This hypothesis was supported by malformation of the S-A node found at autopsy. From the circumstances, one would be forced to conjecture that it was brought on as he strained at stool."

"You could say that about Dr. Moon — if you didn't know that Dr. Yang was missing. How do you explain him?"

"Questions concerning Dr. Yang would require untethered conjecture."

My mood turned sarcastic. "Of course. And although you are a good friend of Brian Broadmoore, you probably don't have the foggiest notion why BIOTECH doesn't want to be bought out."

Westley cleared his throat again, louder this time. "That's the job for you, his highly paid due diligence expert."

"Well, thank you. This due diligence expert is going to have his blood drawn before his liver cleans the drugs out of his system. Maybe we can finish before midnight."

"Yes, my laboratory is at your disposal."

"Be careful in your conversations with Dr. Broadmoore. His hotel suite is bugged. Mine too."

"Godspeed."

"Cheers," I replied, distantly.

The M.E. gave me a case number supplementary to Dr. Moon's. His assisting technician drew my blood and took urine samples which would be tested for cocaine and other illicit drugs, and for prescription drugs. They also sampled by nasal swab. They swabbed in other places, too. They cut off samples of my hair for reference. And they took my clothes for the same purpose. I told them to examine the female-facing surface of the knotted prophylactic in the pants pocket.

Naked, but with my bundle of fresh clothes in hand, I walked to the employees' shower, where I washed away the last external traces of the evening. Then I sat at a vacant desk and wrote an affidavit describing everything that happened at Cheryl's place. Photocopied the $10,000 check. The technician returned to tell me they'd found foreign hairs — one blond and one dark. I got him to countersign my affidavit. I sealed it in an envelope and asked him to give it to Dr. Westley.

I called Detective Cordova's extension. I wasted some time with his voice mail and pager before it occurred to me to check my own messages.

I called home and punched in the code for playback. First, the answering machine played a lot of hang-ups, spread over the last two days. The first message was from Rebecca. The girl I'd chosen to last a lifetime sounded like she wouldn't last another minute. Her voice jittered like she'd been waiting in a cold wind. She sounded close to tears. I thought of all that I'd have to explain to her.

"Ben, I am really getting worried. I've tried calling you collect around midnight for the last two evenings. You weren't there. It must be that job you're doing for Dr. Westley. But why would that keep you out past midnight?"

How hopeless her recorded voice sounded, played back by the heartless answering machine.

"Forgive me for worrying, but the more I think about it — the job couldn't be safe if they are paying you so much. And the man working before you disappeared. You remember what happened the last time you did a job for Dr. Westley."

Yes, I remembered. I remembered how I had had to disappear for two months, leaving her to take the heat.

"I had to get special permission to charge this call to the hospital. I can't imagine you'd just be out partying. I need to know that you are okay. Please call me at the critical care ward. I hope you aren't mad because I wasn't sure about coming back for your dissertation defense. But that isn't a reason to not sleep in your own bed." Her voice cracked. "It was one-thirty when I called last night. Please let me know everything is okay. I love you, Ben." (Click)

The electronic voice said the call had been at one o'clock Wednesday — about 24 hours ago.

Rebecca's recorded message was followed by an angry-sounding Dr. Rob McGregor.

"Okay, Ben. I got your e-mail message about how something came up. You had to make yourself scarce for a couple of days. You didn't say what you were going to do. I'm assuming it wasn't anything like a death in the family or you would have told me. Now, if you check your own e-mail box, you'll find a curt message from me saying get your butt back here."

On the answering machine, McGregor sounded especially gruff.

"Please excuse me for playing Mother Hen, but I checked with Audio-Visual Service. They told me you didn't send them any figures to make slides from. What are you planning to do for your dissertation defense? Wave your hands over the screen? They can still do a rush job — if you get in tomorrow morning. And I want to go over your presentation with you so there won't be any mistakes."

Then came such a long silence that I thought McGregor had hung up. But finally came a chuckle, and Rob reverted to the affable tone that was his trademark.

"Now that I've vented my spleen, I remember you wanted some information on a couple of Washington scientists — Abdul Moran and Henk van Friesland. Now why the hell do you want to know about those guys? Their stuff doesn't have anything to do with your dissertation. Abdul's working on smooth muscle physiology and Henk's working on cardiac. You thinking of switching fields?

"Hopefully you aren't considering post-doctoral work with one of those clowns. There are better choices in the Washington area. The only thing they excel in is womanizing. In fact, you just named the most notorious butt-pinchers in the Federation Society Directory. Rumor has it that no female gets out of van Friesland's lab without getting fucked. Moran's just as bad.

"Incidentally his male students get fucked, too. They get fucked over. After you work in van Friesland's lab two years, he takes your manuscript and slaps the name of his latest girlfriend on the front page. That leaves you only a middle author on your own paper. No credit for all your hard work. You better think twice before postdocing for van Freesen or Moran. Just listen to me . . . No, enough friendly advice. Now get your butt back here. You understand?" (Click)

The automated voice told me the message was from yesterday morning.

The next recorded message was from Detective Cordova.

"Dr. Candidi. Here's the report. And don't forget to tell Dr. Westley he owes me a favor. We looked over Dr. Moon's house and didn't find no atomic secrets lying around — no secret recipes or nothing. But you wouldn't believe what I saw. He had aquariums all over the place. But nothing swimming in them. Just sponges. And his kitchen's full of chemistry stuff. If I didn't know he was a legitimate scientist, I'd say it was a cocaine lab."

"He was doing research at home," I said to myself.

"And he had some of those long glass tubes with numbers on them."

Graduated cylinders.

"And a blender, like for making mixed drinks."

A Waring blender for busting up sponge cells.

"And on his kitchen counter there was a long line of those funny glass wine dispensing doo-dads — the kind you see at them fancy fondue restaurants. But instead of metal needle valves on the end, they all had glass knobs."

Separatory funnels to extract anticancer compounds.

"But the scientific notebooks you wanted me to look for? Well, I went through the place with a fine tooth comb, and didn't find anything like that."

Moon was hiding information.

"Just a little book that looked like a diary; it was written in Chinese. Would have guessed it was a diary, except for all the numbers in it."

Probably Moon's short notes to himself.

"What was surprising was that he didn't have any computer there. That's real surprising. Judging from his office, it seemed like he really was into that shit." (Click)

Yes, it was strange that Moon didn't have a computer at home. Maybe his private computer was his laptop. Good that I'd told the assistant M.E. to take it with Moon's body.

I asked the night technician to get me the evidence bag containing Dr. Moon's laptop computer. Once in hand, I plugged it in and booted up.

30　ENTRAINED ON TRANE

Dr. Moon's laptop wasn't a bad piece of hardware — internal modem, ball cursor driver, and 250 megs of hard drive. But only four megs were in use. After completing the boot, it gave me a "C>". Moon had been using DOS. I selected his word processing program and found nothing — just executive programs. Where were the files of data and notes to himself? What had he used this computer for? I remembered him doing something with it on the day of the fire-breathing interview. He was probably using it right before he died. I'd found it plugged into the phone jack.

I brought up the file manager and looked at Moon's communications programs. The fax-modem directory had nothing but executive files and 1.5 Kb of data buffers. Wouldn't find any big scientific secrets there.

In front of me on the desk sat a radio. I flipped it on. Then I sat back, shut my eyes and tried to put the info together. So Moon had been doing secret experiments at home. He extracted compounds from sponges in his own kitchen. BIOTECH's second lab scientist, Dr. Lau, probably didn't know about that work. Lau just thought he was analyzing compounds received from — from a reference lab. In Oregon! That was it! After Moon secretly extracted compounds at home, he sent them to Oregon, where they were remailed. That explained all the "reference" assays I'd found in BIOTECH's lab notebooks that afternoon. Moon was developing a secret data set — of new compounds. New candidate anticancer drugs! And that's why the BIOTECH people killed him.

The radio was set to an easy listening station. The music wasn't that bad, but the zonked-out D.J. got on my nerves. She giggled and talked breathlessly about love in the night. Took dedication requests from listeners who were also giggly and breathless. The power of suggestion is strong. I changed the dial to classical WTMI.

Where did Moon store his data? Why wasn't it in his laptop? It made me dizzy, teetering on the verge of discovery. Had to check my logic carefully, or I might climb down the wrong side of the mountain.

I held a conversation with myself:

Either Moon didn't store data on the computer or his murderers removed it all.

But your argument is based on presumption. How do you know that he was murdered?

He died under unusual circumstances.

But Dr. Westley said Moon was predisposed to fatal arrhythmia.

Then how do you explain Dr. Yang disappearing several days before? It's just too improbable — two deaths in such a short time.

No, Ben. Your assumptions are improbable. Your reasoning is nothing but a house of cards.

That's how it always comes out when you try to conduct a scientific dialogue in your head. One side of you plays explorer. The other side turns into an obnoxious parrot that perches on your left shoulder and keeps saying you've taken the wrong path. The shitty bird doesn't stop squawking up until you find the proof.

Every time I shut my eyes, Cheryl's drugs threatened to take over again. WTMI was playing a willowy-sounding piece — Ravel or Debussy.

"Hey, Shit-Bird! How do you explain the blackmailing and bribing? How do you explain that BIOTECH suddenly changed its mind and *doesn't* want to be bought?"

The Bird never answers when you try to make *him* do the work.

A soprano chorus was singing a stream of undulating ahs. A soft complement of tenors overlaid it with ripples.

I scored another point against The Bird.

"There must be a lot at stake for them to use psychotropic drugs and hire a private dancer. Tonight's performance wasn't just Cheryl's version of an Adlerian power trip."

The music billowed insistently like gentle waves on a foggy sea. It was a musical portrait of creepy, lethal seduction: The type of charm that makes you drop the lodestone. It was the lure of a siren call that grows stronger by the minute, making you forget your wife at home and finally becoming irresistible — a strengthening wind that accelerates your boat through the mist toward that moment of terror when it's too late to throw over the tiller. You break up on the rocks. And as you grope helplessly in the wreckage, your muscles weakening with each futile grasp, she sings to you her enchanting song of self-serving loveliness, ending when she salutes you, baring her tits, as you go down for the third and final time.

It wasn't an hallucination. It was the memory of a turn-of-the-century French painting I'd seen in a cyber-art gallery on the Web.

So I'd just had another brain-fade. Well, at least it had been useful. It had told me how to get the truth out of Cheryl tomorrow. But how to get the truth from Moon's computer tonight?

Could I find the siren painting on the Internet using Moon's computer? No, Moon's computer didn't have Netscape. His communications program couldn't do graphics. But I ran it anyway.

David Connor was now announcing, in his unmistakable Walter Cronkite voice, that we had just heard *Three Nocturnes* by Debussy, concluding WTMI's program. Then, in unflappable Cronkite style, he read three minutes of national headlines. I unplugged the line from the phone and plugged it into the computer.

Connor invited us to stay tuned for China Vallas' "Jazz Thing". Why not? I'd developed a taste for straight-ahead jazz seven years ago, after Mike Cook's presentation at a Mensa meeting. He brought in vinyl 33s, played segments, and explained to us what the guys were really doing on those cuts.

"Good morning," greeted China in his usual gravelly voice. In the background, a jazz piano was modulating a complicated chord in tidal rhythm. Within a dozen beats I had it identified: McCoy Tyner's lead-in for John Coltrane's rendition of *My Favorite Things*. The cut would be 15 minutes of high-flying, free-spirited delight.

And that was when it came to me!

Dr. Moon's computer was one of his favorite things. He was a two-computer man. This was the computer he liked to plug into the phone jack. And that was how I would get my answers. By plugging his computer into the phone jack and playing it like one of his favorite things.

Obnoxious Shit-Bird had flown from my shoulder. He was replaced by the image of a Canadian goose, flying with steady wing-beats and gaining elevation over a lake. That's what the fluttering soprano sax reminded me of. Trane played it straight for the first chorus of the Pollyanna song. The squawky horn, the familiar melody, and my memory of the song's words all came together in a beautiful metaphor: wild geese that fly with the moon on their wings.

Trane laid down straight melody in the first chorus and jazzed it up on the second. I clicked on the dial-up option in Moon's communication program. The on-screen menu showed two local numbers: One labelled "Internet Server" and the other unlabeled. The Canadian goose quavered in soprano and honked in alto. The song of joy rose high above the pine trees. It was time to launch. I clicked on the Internet Server. Moon's computer joined the session with a noisy sequence of dial tones, rings and 19.2 kilohertz modem handshake.

The screen asked for a password. I couldn't let the charm of the moment be broken. I shut my eyes and imagined myself as Dr. Moon, sitting at his desk and playing with his favorite computer. What would be his password? What was Dr. Moon's favorite thing? I looked down at the desk. I remembered the six letters written on Moon's desk with felt-tipped pen: "Sponge." I typed in the word and hit Enter. The screen flashed a welcome message saying that Dr. Moon had no mail.

Now to check what was behind the second door. I exited and clicked on the second, unlabeled number. I didn't need my brain now. My fingers were doing the job in synchrony with the sax, piano and goose. My feathered friend didn't need to flap with heavy downbeats to climb into the sky. He used thermal updrafts to soar, rising from the heat of McCoy Tyner's glowing chord patterns, stoked by the relentless beat of an insistent bass and a shimmering high-hat cymbal. The laptop's modem answered the high-hat in 19.2 kilohertz emulation, and we came to the last line of the verse.

The screen flashed — and there it was! Dr. Moon's cache — his trove of scientific treasure hoarded in a hidden computer at a secret location.

The screen displayed two full two columns of named data files. With his laptop computer and office phone line, he had added to and accessed his precious files with all the confidentiality of a Swiss bank account.

I selected a file labelled NEW-PATENT and flipped through screens describing his favorite things. How can I describe my state of mind? Did Trane click my brain onto a poetry program which automatically rhymed the captured text-bits as fast as my optic nerve could fire on them? Or did his music cast a posthypnotic suggestion that made me translate the screens into verse, hours and days after reading them?

Enzymes do magic when you squeeze them from sponges.
Shelves full of compounds to test out your hunches,
Separatory funnels all set up in rings,
These are a few of my favorite things.
Old books that tell you the likely reactions,
Columns that separate the products in fractions,
BIOTECH testing what the courier brings,
These are a few of my favorite things.

New compounds outshining their three simple cousins,
Methods to make them cheaper by the dozens,
Infinite structures from aliphatic rings,
These are a few of my favorite things.

Now my spirit was soaring up there with Trane. I exited NEW-PATENT and retrieved a file named CODE.

Testing by BIOTECH disguised as control sample,
Drugs slow down the kinase, the evidence is ample,

Dozens of products await in the wings,
These are a few of my favorite things.

Coltrane was winding down, but my flight was far from over. I
retrieved a file named BUSINESS.

Lawyers who agree that it's outside the contract,
Investors with money to put it on fast track,
Millions of dollars that come with few strings,
These are a few of my favorite things.

With fluttering grace, Coltrane landed his goose on a lonely lake.
I flipped off the radio just as China Vallas launched into a retrospec-
tive. He'd probably say something about hearing an early Coltrane
performance of the song at Philadelphia's Showboat Jazz Theater
back in the early 1960s.

It was time for me to come back to Earth. I went back to the point
of discovery. I proceeded methodically this time, interpolating the
actions that lead to murder. BIOTECH learned very recently that
Moon had a shit-load of new compounds that were more valuable
than the original three. It probably came out during Dr. Yang's due
diligence. Dr. Moon probably told BIOTECH he wouldn't share the
new compounds unless they paid him more money. He might have
demanded $20 million. Of course, BIOTECH didn't have this type
of money. They were probably sick and tired of Moon anyway. But
they wanted his new compounds.

So BIOTECH probably started thinking that their inventor
might be more valuable to them dead than alive. The $5 million
life insurance would help them develop their three compounds.
After they got Broadmoore to drop his option, he would have
absolutely no claim to the new technology. Later they could find
a new investor and work out a much better deal. Right now, they
would patent the new technology in their own name and keep
everything for themselves. That's why they called their Washington patent lawyer last week — to find out about "post-H"
patenting.

It wasn't "posthaste" patenting. The "H" stood for something
else. I worked through the possibilities, using systematic vowel sub-
stitution: Post-Ha. No. Post-He. No. Post-Hi. No. Post-Hoc. No. Post-

Hu. Yes! Post-Humous. They would kill their inventor. The patent would be granted posthumously. It all fit.

My predecessor, Yang, must have gotten wind of the second invention. BIOTECH killed him before he could report the news to Broadmoore. Next they had to worry about what Ben Candidi might learn. They probably instructed Moon to say nothing to me about the new technology. That was why Cheryl was always listening in. When I pressed for a second meeting with Moon — they stalled. They were trying to get him to back down on his demand for more money or to moderate his demands. When Moon wouldn't agree — they killed him.

And when a dead inventor didn't discourage us from the deal, Cheryl lured me to her apartment and used blackmail. And she sweetened the deal with $10,000. She was probably figuring on using me to put together the patent application, once Broadmoore gave up and went back to Boston. Cheryl was either a murderer or an accessory after the fact. What about the other two scientists, Drs. Lau and Singh?

The image of Coltrane's goose subsided along with my thrill of discovery. My body was weak. A hollow feeling hung in my gut. My ideas were right, but something was wrong with my images. I grabbed the sides of the desk and shut my eyes. It was the image of a solitary goose that had been wrong. Geese come in pairs. They mate for life. I had been flying without my Rebecca. I opened my eyes, picked up the phone and dictated a telegram to Western Union. Had to tell Rebecca that everything was all right.

Necessary manual work helped to steady my nerves. I retrieved and downloaded all the files from Moon's remote computer. Made a double set on some diskettes borrowed from the technician. Sealed one set in an envelope for Dr. Westley. Kept the other set for Dr. Broadmoore. Unplugged the computer and placed it in an evidence bag, along with one set of diskettes. Asked the technician to give the stuff to Dr. Westley.

I hailed a cab at the entrance of Dade County General. Made the guy drop me off at the parking garage near the Omni Gallery. Crossed over to the Marriott parking garage through the second-story skybridge. Took the hotel elevator to the 28th floor. Silent entrance to my bugged room required careful handling of the door. Didn't turn on any lights. Undressed to my undershorts and lay down in bed.

The message light on my off-the-hook phone was blinking like a red channel marker. It flashed through my eyelids, making it hard to fall asleep. Worse still were the luminous green letters of the pay TV box. They shone over my head like a beacon from the land of casual entertainment.

The box's options probably included a soft porno channel. Cynical thoughts welled up in my brain. One push of a button and you could see the 90-second preview. But don't forget to push the deactivating button in time, or they'll count it as a purchase. And since it would be such a shame to waste the six dollars after the box sent its little digital signal down to the main desk, you keep watching the video moves and maybe even participate — until the busty blond M.C. shows you her mammaries and smiling face — one last time — and says she hopes that you, her tiger, liked watching the show as much as she liked putting it on. And the next morning at checkout, your bill shows a six-dollar item, generically labelled "entertainment" which you don't dispute. Transaction hermetically sealed in plastic for your own protection.

I would have to forget about Rebecca for the next 24 hours. Tomorrow I would do battle. I slept the night inside a rigid body, hardening myself for the day before me.

MORNING REPORT 31

I woke early, well ahead of the clock radio. I rose from the bed like a zombie, bleary eyes reporting gray images to a deadened brain. A sleep-deprived body resisted orders sent down the spinal ganglia. It was the fourth and final day of the project. I had less than twelve hours to complete my work.

For the microphones, I uttered a big exclamatory, "Ahh," before putting the phone back on the hook. Punched the number for the hotel operator and asked for my messages. There was one from Cheryl, received at 12:30 a.m. I thanked the operator. Went to the sink, splashed my face and got things working with a couple dozen deep-knee bends. Returned to the phone and punched the number for Cheryl's condo. Sure, I'd tell her what she wanted to hear.

"Hello," she said expectantly.

"Cheryl, I got your message this morning. What gives?"

"Nothing, Ben. I just called to be sure you got back to your room all right."

"I did, thanks."

"But first they said you weren't in, and then they said they couldn't reach you."

"I walked back to the hotel. Had to be out in fresh air — in Nature. I guess you can call me a nature boy." I laughed heartily. It helped to ventilate my lungs. "Took the damn phone off the hook so no one could disturb my sleep. I've got a big day in front of me, Doll Babe. Just getting ready to go over and break the bad news to Broadmoore." I was starting to feel better already.

"Do you feel you can handle it okay, Ben?"

I put on a cocky attitude. "Piece of cake. Figured out exactly what to do last night on the walk home."

"Well, that's good," she said, trying to sound assuring, but actually sounding incredulous. Face-to-face, an interrogation by her would be overwhelming. But confined to the oral channel and robbed of the use of her searching eyes and animal magnetism, Cheryl was quite disadvantaged. Actually, this was like a boxing match with a blind man.

"Look, I'll keep my end of the bargain, and you make sure you keep yours." I dropped my voice. "Never a word of this to Rebecca."

"Of course. Never," Cheryl protested.

"Someday you may meet her. She mustn't get the slightest inkling. She's real intuitive. She picks up on things fast — like when another girl is acting too familiar."

"I understand."

"Good. Because she wouldn't. She's kind of Victorian and a little inhibited. She doesn't think much of threesomes and alternate lifestyles."

"I understand."

"Good," I said brusquely. I let Cheryl dangle for a couple seconds, then I came back with bravado. "Listen! Taking care of Broadmoore shouldn't take me longer than this morning. Think you could get yourself free this afternoon? We could get together somewhere away from the office, and I could . . . ah . . . debrief you."

"Sure, Ben."

"Good. Just sit tight at your desk and wait for my call." I hung up first.

I showered and shaved. My thousand-dollar suit passed the sniff test and the right knee wasn't too wrinkled. I suited up. Wrote a short note and stuffed it into my suit pocket. Grabbed the two metal brief cases as well as my own and walked down the hall. Set the stuff before Broadmoore's door and knocked. He seemed surprised to see me.

"Dr. Broadmoore, I'm sorry to barge in on you. But I have to give you my report. It's got to be face-to-face. And it's got to be now."

I put a finger to my lips and handed him a slip of paper. It read, "This is for the microphones. I tell you not to buy. You argue with me, but eventually agree."

Before I could pick up the metal cases, Broadmoore was already doing a good job of playing his part. "Yes. I understand you had some reservations about the technology. And as a perfectionist, you want to make a clean breast of your reservations. But I don't really think — "

"I've done some hard, accurate thinking on this," I said slowly and steadily. "I've got bad news. You'd better sit down. The patent is weak. It doesn't stand up to a prior art search of the open scientific literature. If you invest $20 million in that project — it would be like building a shopping center on land you don't have title to. Worse yet, it would be like building on a trash heap that has never been compacted."

Broadmoore launched a windy counter-argument based on the integrity of the U.S. Patent Office. I cleared my throat in disagreement, rattled the metal cases and pulled out papers. Finally I interrupted. "The examiner didn't consider the prior art closely enough. Look at this paper. It describes the same type of thing. Moon's claim to novelty is shot. And I can show you six separate instances where Moon argued falsely against the other patents cited as prior art."

We argued for the better part of an hour. Gradually Broadmoore's counter-arguments softened and dejection crept into his voice. Our moment of role reversal came when I said, "Look, you have only a couple hundred-thousand dollars in the project. Cut your losses and get out."

Broadmoore argued back that the science was so promising.

I delivered the *coup de grace*. "I don't think the three compounds will cure cancer. There's no human data. For decades, scientists have been finding compounds that have worked on rats and have fizzled on humans. The odds are against BIOTECH."

Broadmoore's reply was so inarticulate that I actually felt sorry for him. Yes, we had improvised a good little radio drama for Bud King and his gang. I handed Broadmoore a note saying to meet me in the fire stairwell in five minutes. To the microphones, I said, "If you need me in the next half hour, I'll be in the dining room."

Broadmoore arrived punctually. I put a finger to my lips and walked him up a couple dusty flights of stairs to where the rumbling of the heavy air conditioning machinery was quite loud. "Sorry to put you on the spot. I was afraid you wouldn't be able to play your part if you knew the whole story."

A broad smile slowly took form on his face. He chuckled. "Well put, my good lad. I will remember those words." Then the smile subsided. "I learned from Geoffrey what befell you. He used a well-placed historical illusion to alert me during innocuous conversation. I called him later on a safe telephone line, and he gave me some detail."

I had no time for tea and sympathy. "Dr. Broadmoore, let me tell you the reason they don't want to sell. Moon invented a follow-on technology that runs circles around the old one."

"I suspected as much."

"The technology you were buying is only for three compounds — three stars in space. The new technology covers a whole galaxy of related compounds. Each new star shines as bright as the original three." I shifted metaphors. "The new technology's got the old one surrounded — like in the game of Go."

"Surrounded?"

"Yes, surrounded. Moon figured out how the enzymes work to close the multicyclic aliphatic rings. He figured out how to manipulate the precursors. He could produce rings with between five and eight carbons. He can place reactive groups almost anywhere along the way. And he has a big set of data on how protein kinase inhibitor activity depends on molecular architecture. He has extensive data on charge modification and side-chain branching. And some of the compounds stimulate protein phosphatases."

"Amazing — "

"What's really amazing is how he got most of the work done in the BIOTECH lab without them knowing — until recently. He cooked up his enzyme soups at home, extracted them, and sent them to BIOTECH, after remailing by an accomplice in Oregon." I paused to let Broadmoore digest this.

"Sneaky, inscrutable Asiatic," he said under his breath.

I continued. "Moon probably demanded more money. He probably blew up at them. And they probably gave up on him. Last Friday they were thinking he might be more useful dead than alive. I know that because they were asking their Washington patent attorney about the law on posthumous patenting. I tricked the patent lawyer's secretary into telling me. BIOTECH also inquired about continuation-in-part-applications. I'm very sure of this: They now think they have enough information to do a posthumous filing on the new technology. They know the technology's worth much more than what you're paying. And they want it all for themselves."

Broadmoore did not seem the least bit surprised at any of this.

"And that's why they killed Dr. Moon," I concluded.

Broadmoore shook his head vigorously. "Now, now, now. One should not let oneself get carried away with thoughts of murder." He stared at the raw concrete wall. "Geoffrey told me there was no evidence that Moon's death was anything other than an anatomically predisposed fatal arrhythmia, probably triggered by straining at stool."

Broadmoore repeated Westley's words so fluently, I wondered if he'd practiced them. I also felt a threatening undertone.

"Dr. Broadmoore, there are twenty million dollars hanging on this. Ten million to buy ninety percent of BIOTECH's stock, and another ten million that you must invest in the company. I've experienced BIOTECH's methods of operation firsthand. They would not stop at murder to achieve their ends. Dr. Moon's contract with BIOTECH did not automatically grant them rights to any new technology. If he had said one word to me about the new technology, we would have negotiated with him directly. And that would have rendered worthless BIOTECH's million dollar investment. That's why BIOTECH wouldn't give me any time with Moon. That's why Cheryl drugged me and blackmailed me last night."

Broadmoore didn't bat an eyebrow. He used a new tactic —

making a show of stuttering an answer, as if my assertion was so ridiculous as to put him at a loss for words. "Well . . . well, well . . .

"*Well*," I interrupted, "they want me to tell you the three compounds are worthless so you won't buy in. *Well*, if you don't exercise your option, they can now have the whole thing to themselves. *Well*, Moon got in their way, and they decided to rub him out. *Well*, the life insurance policy will reward them with five million dollars. *Well*, that was reason enough to kill him. *Well*, that's all the more reason why they wouldn't need you."

Broadmoore cleared his throat and looked down on me like a headmaster dealing with a sassy student. "The question of murder and the five million dollar insurance policy are sensitive subjects. It would be unwise to pursue them at this time. I am rather more interested in your scientific due diligence report for which I am paying you." He clenched and unclenched his big hands and moved his heavy, muscular body closer to me.

I cleared my throat, too, and scowled up at him. "Okay. Here's your due diligence report. Listen up. The old technology is worthless, if it must stand alone. The new technology is worth many times the price of the old one. Make sure you can take it over after you buy BIOTECH. Have your three-hundred-dollar-an-hour lawyer check out the contract situation. Be sure you can do the posthumous patenting yourself."

"Very well."

"My guess is that we know a hell of a lot more about the new technology than Cheryl North and Bud King." I opened my briefcase and handed Broadmoore two diskettes. "This is all the information that Moon was keeping on a remote computer. It's somewhere in Coral Gables, judging from the phone number where the computer answered. King doesn't know about the remote computer. Otherwise he would have already turned it off."

This softened up Broadmoore right away. I gave him the phone number and suggested that he take control of the computer immediately after buying the company.

Once again, Broadmoore stared at the rough concrete wall, apparently lost in thought. Slowly a smile broadened his face. Now he seemed the epitome of North Country sociability. "Yes, Ben. You have acquitted yourself well. You have fully earned your pay You can consider yourself dismissed." He was cutting another dog loose from his sled. "I will set the process in motion. I will do what must be done. You are free to go back to your dissertation."

"Does 'setting things in motion' include a police investigation into the disappearance of Dr. Yang and the murder of Dr. Moon?"

Broadmoore stiffened. I flinched when his right hand leaped from the railing. It came to rest at chest level. The issue was clear to both of us. If Moon had been murdered, the life insurance company would not pay off. Then Broadmoore's newly acquired BIOTECH would lose its five million dollar dowry. Broadmoore's face was flushed. "Ben, we have been over this ground before. On Dr. Yang, there is absolutely no evidence of wrongdoing. Regarding Dr. Moon's body, Geoffrey can find no evidence of foul play. You should not dirty the pools by stirring up needless speculation." He made it sound like I'd driven a flock of sheep into his "pools".

"What about the sexual blackmail? Cheryl drugged me and black-mailed me. She even bribed me. To sweeten the deal, she gave me a cashier's check for ten thousand dollars."

"If you fell for the charms of the young lady scientist, you do not have me to blame. Regarding the ten thousand dollars — take it. You are hereby dismissed from my service. You are now free to accept the money from BIOTECH. You no longer have any conflict of interest."

"Thanks." That was all I could think to say.

"But you must maintain the confidentiality of B.M. Capital's business interest, as described in the secrecy agreement you signed before I hired you. You must not breathe a word to BIOTECH of your new knowledge. And you shall take no steps which will cause them to gain this information, particularly before our deadline for signing — which is five o'clock this afternoon. Have I made myself clear?"

"Yes," I said. He was probably right about my business obligations.

"Then I will thank you for your good work and wish you well. For appearance's sake, keep your hotel room until this evening. I will instruct Sally to wire-transfer twenty-two thousand dollars — the remainder of your fee — to your account within the hour. Now if you will please forgive me, I have much to do."

He descended the stairs with surprising agility and rushed back to his room.

I walked down 20-some flights to the meeting room level and the bank of phones. I punched in Detective Cordova's number. His voice mail said that he was either on the phone or away from his desk. I left a short message about needing to talk to him, saying I'd call back in a few minutes.

Grabbed a quick breakfast at the buffet, then returned to the phone bank. This time Cordova's voice mail said he was not available. I left him an urgent message and the number for the pay phone right next to me. Then I called the central number for Miami P.D. Homicide. A man's voice answered. I identified myself, said it was urgent, and asked to talk to Cordova immediately. The guy told me Cordova was on leave for a week. No, he didn't know who was handling his cases. No, he could not help me any further.

"Could you please take down a message for him?"

"If I have to."

"Tell him that Ben Candidi knows why C.C. 'Bud' King and Cheryl North murdered Dr. Tehong Moon."

The man took the message unenthusiastically. The Miami Police Department was giving me the stonewall.

Secretary Doris answered my call to Dr. Westley's office. Yes, Dr. Westley was in, and she would get him. She returned to the phone a couple minutes later and informed me that "Dr. W." was very busy. He would not be able to speak with me until Monday. Yes, she had told "Dr. W." it was important. No, he was quite firm about not having time until Monday.

The Old Boy was giving me the stonewall, too. That really disappointed me. He obviously didn't want his Cambridge buddy to lose the $5 million. It wouldn't do to let Ben Candidi muddy the pools and confuse the insurance company.

But I would do what had to be done — with or without Westley's help.

I deposited more coins and punched the number for ABBA Radio & Video. "Zeekie, this is Ben. I'm ready to take you up on your offer to bug the bad guys."

"Sure, Ben. How many locations does your English friend have in mind?"

"He's out of the picture now. It's my own private affair. I want the BIOTECH offices bugged — two separate rooms. Also, two cars, a condominium apartment, and a house on the Coral Gables Waterway. In an hour or so they're going to start squawking, and I'll want to know what they're saying."

"It sounds like a big job, boss. Too much for a amateur like me. I can fix you up with a private detective, but he'll probably charge you several thousand dollars."

I figured I had $10,000 to spend.

"Do whatever it takes. The shit's going to hit the fan soon. We need to get everything on tape, starting today and ending late tomorrow afternoon."

"Good. I've got a wedding gig on Saturday night. I'll need my equipment back for it."

We talked briefly about the details of the job. Zeekie would meet me in an hour. I went back to my room to change into my expensive suit. Pulled out some paraphernalia, including a hand-held tape recorder, and wrapped it in my empty valet pack together with my boat clothes. Placed my laptop computer in my attaché case, closed the latches, and turned the combination wheels. With bundle under one arm and attaché case in the other hand, I went down to the lobby. At the hotel gift shop, I got a fancy shopping bag and stuffed my clothes in it. I left the attaché case with baggage check, being careful to get a receipt.

My bank had a branch in the Omni Center. The teller took a second look at the nicely dressed young businessman presenting a $10,000 check for deposit. She was doubly impressed after confirming that I had just received a wire transfer of $22,000. Broadmoore had kept his end of the bargain.

I took the MetroMover to the Brickell Avenue financial district and got off at the station near King Construction. Zeekie's van was where it was supposed to be. Behind it was parked a decrepit BellSouth van. As I climbed in the passenger seat next to Zeekie, I sensed someone behind me.

"Ben, let me introduce my friend, Johnny."

I turned around and saw a uniformed BellSouth repairman.

"That van behind us belong to you?" I asked.

"Yes, sir," Johnny said in a Cracker drawl. "I'll admit it to you." He broke into a shit-eating grin and added, "It gets more curious looks than me."

"I didn't know BellSouth was letting their fleet go to pot," I said, trying to be funny but sounding nervous.

"Bought her at an auction for two hundred bucks. Never thought to touch up the paint. Like Pa used to say, 'Don't haul shine in no vee-hickel you cain't walk away from.'"

After a good laugh, we got down to business. I gave Johnny and Zeekie a list of locations to bug and the phone numbers to tap. Suggested they do the offices first, then Cheryl's condo and finally King's house. "Their cars should be in the parking garage of BIOTECH's building."

"Well, it looks like we can do half our shopping with one stop," Johnny said. "I'll follow you guys." He climbed out the back door.

I watched through the sideview mirror. The little van emitted a puff of black smoke and flashed one headlight. Zeekie drove the three blocks to the parking garage and took a ticket from the machine. The faded BellSouth van lagged behind. Neither vehicle seemed to make much of an impression on the parking attendant.

Locating King's white Cadillac wasn't much of a problem, since it was parked next to Cheryl's Riviera. The yellow hard hat on the back seat removed any lingering doubt that we had the right Cadillac. I didn't see exactly what Johnny and Zeekie did to the cars. I loitered, far away, holding my breath and hoping they wouldn't set off any alarms. A few minutes later they walked up to me.

Johnny handed me two black boxes, each the size of a thin pocket calculator. "Could be I can't get into the utility closet to tap them office phones. It would be good to have some backup for the offices. You push this little button when you deploy it. Tear off this here adhesive covering and plant it under a desk drawer or maybe behind a file cabinet. It's voice activated. Can record twelve hours' worth of conversation. But don't put it close to no noisy equipment, or it'll use itself up faster."

"Fine. I'll do it."

"Now you just remember — each unit costs seven hundred and fifty dollars. You can't retrieve it, I put it on your bill."

"A deal." I stuffed the units in the bottom of my shopping bag.

After Johnny and Zeekie drove off, I found a phone by the door that linked the parking garage with the office building. Called up Elegant Baskets. Used my American Express number to order a Cambridge Punting Basket to be picked up by me in about an hour.

Suddenly I had to turn my back and bury my face in the phone enclosure. Bud King walked right past on his way to the garage. He looked very preoccupied. Not having him around the office would be just fine with me.

It was now around one o'clock. I hoped Cheryl was hungry. I pushed the button, and the elevator took me to the 21st floor. Strode proudly past the cubicles to the King's side of the building. Winked at the secretary as I walked past her station and up to Cheryl's office.

I just put on a big smile and stood in Cheryl's doorway, until she looked up.

"Ben!" she exclaimed. She sounded mildly embarrassed, as if I had brought her flowers.

"Just dropped in to say goodbye," I said, debonair as they come. I stepped closer and whispered, "And to rescue you from office drudgery this afternoon."

"Well, sure," she said cautiously. Then she whispered, "Is everything all right?"

"Of course," I boomed out. "Can I sit down? I also wanted to give my regards to Bud. Wanted to shake his hand, wish him well. Wanted to thank him again for the nice boat trip."

"I think he stepped out," Cheryl said. She didn't know quite what to make of me.

"Well, maybe he stepped back in, and you didn't notice. Could you go over and check for me?"

Cheryl shook her head, as if she thought the drugs were still affecting me. "I'll see if he's here."

Her walk to the adjoining office gave me just enough time to reach into the bag and fix a recorder under her desk drawer. I slipped the second unit in my suit pocket just as Cheryl returned to the doorway.

"He really isn't here, Ben."

"Hell. Well, maybe I can leave him a note. Can I use this sheet of paper?"

Cheryl waited impatiently in the hall while I leaned over her desk and wrote a gracious note. When she momentarily disappeared from the doorway I stripped the adhesive from the second unit and returned it to my pocket, cradling it with my left hand. I walked out and entered King's room. Planted the unit on the back of a credenza before Cheryl could follow me in. I was in a feisty mood. Made a big deal about centering the note on King's desk.

"This just about takes care of it," I told Cheryl, loudly. I wanted the secretary to hear it. Then I whispered, "Meet me in the parking garage in five minutes. Tell them you're taking the afternoon off. If you don't come, I'll return and make a big scene — like the jealous lover that I am."

"Sure," she said.

Ten minutes later, Cheryl came through the door to the garage. She glanced to the left and right, as if worried that she might be observed. She didn't recognize me at once.

"Ben, you've changed clothes."

"Yeah. Did my Superman act in your first floor men's room." I glanced at the valet pack I was hanging over my shoulder, airport style. "Except I'm not flying anywhere. Thought we could spend a delightful afternoon together. You're probably assigned to keep track of me anyway. Til the witching hour of five p.m., that is."

Cheryl frowned. "But we couldn't go back to my apartment."

"Cheryl, you insult me as untrusting and unimaginative," I joked. Then I added a touch of Mel Gibson gallantry. "I invite you to an elegant picnic on the Bay in gratitude for your expanding my horizons."

"Did you cash the check?"

"Yes. And I thank you. As the old hippie expression goes, 'Today is the first day of the rest of my life.'"

Cheryl relaxed visibly. She smiled at me like an older sister. "Well, it is nice when you can bring a person good news." Then a wrinkle came to her forehead. "And you are sure Dr. Broadmoore is going to turn us down?"

I cranked up my Mel Gibson impersonation. "When I left Broadmoore he was crestfallen. His eyebrows were sagging to his lower lip. I'll bet that right this minute he's flying back to Boston to lick his wounds."

"Where are we going for lunch on the Bay? What about Sundays on Key Biscayne?"

"No. I've got a better idea. We're going Cambridge Punting. Now don't spoil the surprise by asking me questions about it. Just give me the keys to your car. I've always wanted to drive a Riviera."

Cheryl's face went through many expressions before stabilizing in an incredulous, semi-enthusiastic smile.

I don't know where I found inspiration to sustain my continuous levity. But it didn't fail me for a second. Not on the way to Elegant Baskets at Five Points near U.S. 1; not while we stood at the counter awaiting our Cambridge Punting, a fine wicker basket provisioned with a bottle of port wine, and a selection of cheeses and delicate sandwiches under a checkered tablecloth.

Like sparks from a van de Graaff generator, gallantry came to me in flashes — like when I told the counter clerk to convert the $45 deposit to the purchase of the basket as a present for 'my ladyfriend'. Nor did I admit the slightest degree of embarrassment about popping into Crook and Crook Marine Supplies and returning with a macramé bikini in a tube — one size fits all. "In case the afternoon sun becomes irresistible," I told Cheryl.

The drive past Coconut Grove's outdoor cafés reinforced the mood. I even turned to my advantage a frustrating traffic jam on narrow Ingraham Highway. How romantic to be sitting with an upscale lady at my side in plush, air-conditioned luxury, amid a tropical forest of sensuous trees with dangling air roots. Just think of those French paintings of elegant couples visiting a greenhouse. "Our greenhouse is just inside-out, Cheryl."

Yes, it worked. By the time we passed the gate of Matheson Hammock Park, we'd clocked a full hour of sustained levity. Only a couple hundred yards more to the marina carved out of mangrove swamp.

But I must admit that my skills of persuasion were heavily taxed when it was time to get Cheryl out of the car and moving down the concrete dock. I could not twist her arm. I was carrying the wicker punting basket, on which teetered my shopping bag full of paraphernalia. Sandwiched in between was one neatly folded garment bag containing the expensive suit. But Cheryl did follow me.

I put down the load at the end of the dock. There, the *Diogenes* was bobbing and pulling gently on its six lines.

"Behold, my oversized punting boat," I said.

"But don't you think it would be too warm?"

"No, it's three in the afternoon. There will be a nice breeze when we get out on the Bay."

"But don't you think it will be complicated getting out there? We'll have to put up all those sails."

"No, we'll motor out a ways, then drop anchor."

"Oh, does your sailboat have a motor?"

"Of course. It's a thirty-six footer. Has a big auxiliary motor."

"Okay. But don't expect me to swim. I've just had my hair done."

No, blond, sleek-skinned and buxom Cheryl would not be a good swimmer — not like my dark-haired, bony but lithesome Rebecca. I'd once joked to Rebecca that she was a maiden of Phoenecia, not a daughter of Israel.

"Cheryl, I promise that you won't be required to swim." With a hand on one arm, I gently moved her toward the boat. The *Diogenes* seemed to pull harder on its lines like a faithful horse shying from a stranger.

With my assistance at the elbow, Cheryl stepped out of her high-heeled shoes. She gracefully lifted her high-hemmed, sculpted skirt and let herself down into the cockpit.

I breathed a sigh of relief. Brought aboard her purse and heels. Then I carried on my bag, valet pack, and the punting basket. Opened the cabin and took the stuff inside. In the shelter of the wet locker, across from the head, I quickly opened Cheryl's purse and removed the battery from her portable phone. I returned to the cockpit, started the motor, and cast off the lines.

The fun was about to begin.

WHAT'S GOOD FOR THE GANDER IS GOOD FOR THE GOOSE 33

As promised, the wind picked up as we exited the channel. I told Cheryl to make herself comfortable below and stow her jacket. Maybe she could look on the towel rack in the head and bring my swimming suit.

The gentle rocking of the boat against small incoming waves was like a massage of my soul — a soul too long imprisoned in man-made spaces and crushed by reams of gray-paragraphed abstraction. Why have we sentenced ourselves and fellow inmates to tortured days of scheming in power clothes — clothes whose only real power is to straitjacket the body and torture the spirit like an iron maiden?

At the last channel marker, I turned the *Diogenes* to the southwest, running parallel to the mangrove-lined shore.

Cheryl looked up from the companionway. "I found your swimsuit, Ben. When will we get there?" Gone was the self-assuredness with which she had slinked across the carpeted floors of her condo. Gone was the confidence with which she had negotiated the throbbing deck of Bud King's 36-foot motor-barge.

"It's okay, Cheryl. We'll be there in about fifteen minutes." I'd already stretched it out to almost four o'clock. I was starting to feel sleepy. Couldn't afford that. Had to keep my brain in gear. "It must be hot below. But the air up here is salty. Not good for your clothes. Try the bikini on for size. I promise not to look until you tell me it's time."

Cheryl leaned forward in the companionway, making a calculated presentation of velvet-framed cleavage. A wrinkle appeared on her flat forehead. "You know, Ben. I'm starting to develop feelings for you. You're so subtle. You probably know that a girl like me has to work hard to keep looking good."

I made a show of opening my eyes wide. "Well, you seem to have a knack for it."

The wrinkle disappeared. She shook her head and smiled. "Thanks. I spend a lot on clothes. Did I tell you I have a private tailor?"

"No. He seems to know a lot about plunge lines and strategically placed buttons, though."

Cheryl giggled, tossed her head, then stretched closer and deeper; now I could behold her at a still more provocative angle. "He does what I tell him. And I get a lot of good ideas from magazines."

"Sounds like you've made a study of it."

"Promise not to tell? I was a fashion model for a while."

"I promise not to tell. What was it like?"

She smiled to herself. "It was hard having to strike the right pose. You have to strike the right attitude so the picture will sell the product. You have to make them look twice." The wrinkle came back to her forehead. "Life is hard. Especially for a girl. Especially if you want to rise above it all. It isn't easy to live your dream."

I tried to keep my eyes above the companionway, looking at the horizon and cottony clouds. I hoped Cheryl would change into the bikini.

"What's your dream, Cheryl?"

"Oh, you know. To have it all. To live in elegance. To not have to put up with the things I had to — when I was getting started."

"Do you like material things?"

"Yes. I like things that are real — things that will always be there for you. Like my car. It isn't the latest model, but we've traveled a lot of miles together. I guess that's why I keep him around. You see, when I was living in Washington and when I got my first chance to make some money, well, considering all the things I had to go through — I just decided that I owed it to myself to have a nice car." She tossed her head, sending a wave of hair over her left shoulder. "Rivi's been a good friend. Just sitting there patiently in the parking lot at the Dulles Airport, waiting for me to come back from those military conventions. We had to work an exhibit for a whole week. It got irritating, all those cocktail parties. You know what I mean."

"Yes, I do." I stopped the motor and threw the bow into the slow wind. "I hope you're ready to model the bathing suit. I'm anchoring."

It was close to 4:45 p.m.

I walked to the bow and threw out an anchor. I also pulled up all the fenders and made sure no lines were dangling over the side. I remembered how Rebecca had once jumped from the boat — naked — and how she had dared me to do the same. I remembered how she had called me a scaredy-cat when I asked for a minute to set the swim ladder. I recalled all the fun we had, working as a team to get ourselves back on board without the ladder. What a shame it would be to desecrate that memory.

When I got back to the cockpit, Cheryl called out, "Get your camera ready now, if you want to click off some shots. But don't be too critical. I don't specialize in swimsuits."

When I looked down the companionway and saw Cheryl sitting behind my dinette table, I responded with a genuine "Ah." Leaning forward, she had created a stunning pose, her splendid breasts amply filling the macrame cups, the bottle of port wine and two glasses arranged to either side. Above this plethora glowed a comely smile.

"Is that all you can say, Ben?" Her smile faded as she searched my face.

Memories of an old James Bond flick came to my rescue. I imitated early Sean Connery's thick northern English accent and exclaimed, "Miss Rebecca Moneypenny! You aren't your angular self. No, it's you, Pussy! What gracious curves you have."

"Oh, Ben!" Cheryl gushed. "Where do you get all that stuff?"

Now it was important that my eyes never leave her. Bathing her in a constant stream of silent admiration, I descended the ladder and retrieved the corkscrew from a galley drawer. I uncorked the bottle and filled two glasses. She probably thought I was going to make a move on her. And she probably didn't feel ready for it. Fine.

I held the two glasses at chest height and continued my James Bond conceit. "I propose a toast on the deck." I climbed the ladder and moved to the end of the cockpit. Cheryl followed me. I threw a glance over my shoulder. Everything was fine: No other boats around and half a mile from the deserted mangrove shore. Now I would bring the scene to its proper conclusion.

"To our mutually agreed-upon future," I offered. We clinked glasses and drank, she lightly, and I deeply. I put down my glass, stepped close to her and placed a hand on each of her shoulders.

At my touch, the wrinkle reappeared. Cheryl stared down at her glass, apparently deep thought. "You know, Ben, I've been thinking about us and . . . "

And I would never know what she had been thinking. I pushed her back with all my might, sending her spinning out of the cockpit. She hit the water upside down. Came up gasping and flailing. As the bubbles cleared, I noticed one breast had popped out of the bikini top.

"Ben!" she screamed, half beseeching, half enraged. "Why did you do that?"

"To find out the truth." I turned my back to her and went below. To the accompaniment of her screams, I hurried to the wet locker and retrieved the small tape recorder from my bag. Snapped it on and returned to the cockpit, holding it out of sight.

"Ben, help me up. I'm drowning."

"Then you'd better answer my questions quickly and truthfully. What did you put in my drink last night?"

She didn't argue. She searched the hull for something to grab. But ocean-wise *Diogenes* offered nothing but a stubby finger-sized exhaust port. Cheryl lunged for the stern rail and came a foot short. Three and one-half feet of freeboard doesn't seem like much in high seas, but it's quite formidable when you're in the water looking up. The six-inch waves added to her confusion. It was enough to panic Cheryl. She didn't think to swim to the bow and grab the anchor line.

"Ben, let me up."

"First — tell me what you put in my drink."

"What?"

"In my drink."

"*Dantrazopam*. It's like 'ludes. It didn't hurt you."

Dantrazopam is an experimental anxiolytic/sedative which the FDA refused to approve because of its side effects and abuse potential.

"Throw me a life saver."

"Not yet. Where did you get the drug?"

"From the manufacturer. Said we wanted it for animal experiments."

"What did you put in my nose?"

"Coke. You liked it, didn't you? Come on, Ben, let me back up."

"Not 'til you've told me everything. Where did you get the belly dancer?" For the tape recorder, I added, "The belly dancer that danced on top of me as I lay on your couch zonked — after you spiked my drink."

"Exotic Escort Service," she gasped. Flailing her arms in a useless attempt to keep her head high was costing her a lot of energy.

"What is her name?"

"Called herself Habibi. Don't know her real name. Not one of their regulars. From out of town. Come on. Let me up." The rhythm of panic was setting in — mouth below the surface, then clawing water to rise a few precious inches, gasping for air, then sinking all too early. She was still doing her best to answer me between breaths.

"You must know her real name. You wrote the check."

"Paid for the trick with cash."

"Who made the second video tape?"

No answer. Just flailing arms and gasps. I'd have to play tough. Turned my back and moved out of sight.

"Ben," she screamed. "Don't leave me here. I'm drowning."

"Who made the tape?" I called over my shoulder.

"Tony Altino. In the company apartment . . . next door."

Returning to the transom, I saw she was really on the verge of drowning. I'd have to get it all on tape quickly.

"So you lured me to your apartment on the pretense of talking business, and you spiked my drink. You drugged me so I couldn't stand. You stuffed cocaine up my nose and stripped me. You made a videotape to blackmail me into giving a false report to Broadmoore."

"You know all that already. Let me back up."

Good. The blackmail was documented. Now to get the rest of the story. I locked on her angry eyes and shouted down, "Did you make a tape of Dr. Yang, too?"

Surprise drove away anger and quickly turned to panic. She looked away and renewed her struggle. I couldn't give her time to work up a lie. I reached down and pushed the starter button. The engine chugged to life. Cheryl screamed in terror when the exhaust and cooling water spurted out the little hole in the back. I threw the motor into gear. The *Diogenes* pulled away at idle speed.

"Tell the truth or drown," I shouted.

She answered me quickly, between breaths and plunges. "I invited him . . . He wouldn't come . . . Would talk only in the office. Then just disappeared. Come back! I'm drowning."

I threw the gear lever into neutral and let the boat drift back slowly with the wind.

No, I couldn't be so simple. Dr. Yang didn't "just disappear". If

I went along with that, I'd be blaming myself for the rest of my life. My next step was inevitable. Perform a dehumanizing interrogation. Cheryl would experience mortal terror, and I would inhabit the soul of Heinrich Himmler.

On an intellectual level, I knew the techniques well. I had read about the theory in scholarly magazines; I had seen case studies in documentary films; I had seen enactments in movies. The interrogator uses escalating terror to demand honest answers. He punishes lies with near-death experiences. And he always allows his victim to recover, to be put through the cycle again to extract the next round of answers. I was glad that Cheryl was a poor swimmer. I could never have done it, threatening her with a knife.

Cheryl was struggling harder and harder, each time clawing higher and sinking more hopelessly. I told her that I knew all about Moon's second invention. I demanded to know who killed Dr. Yang. It was hard to listen to her gurgled protestations of innocence and then watch her drown. I finally rescued her by throwing out a length of flag halyard. She could use it to hold her head out of water, but it was too thin to climb.

At first, she didn't want to talk. But she started talking when I uncleated the halyard and gave her three feet of slack.

It was a long interrogation, negotiated with three-foot increments of line. In bits and pieces, she told me that Dr. Yang had been getting wise to Moon and was getting wind of the new invention. She and Bud couldn't keep Moon under control. He was demanding $2 million up front. They couldn't come up with the money. Moon was impossible. He threatened to tell Yang and start his own negotiation. She had to be with Yang all the time to keep Moon from getting to him.

"And then what did you do?" I paid out another three feet of line.

"Then Bud said he took care of Yang. He didn't tell me how."

"Bud murdered Yang to keep him from telling Broadmoore," I said matter-of-factly.

"I thought he just bribed him." The lie gurgled in her throat.

"Impossible. Then Yang wouldn't have disappeared."

"Persuaded him, then . . . maybe to go on vacation . . . to disappear for a little while."

"Impossible." I uncleated the line, tossed it overboard. "Who killed Yang? Bud?"

"Ben. I don't know — "

"You have to know that Bud did it. You've been sleeping with the guy."

A Bayliner rode by on high plane. Cheryl turned, screamed for help and waved frantically to them. They waved. I just smiled in their direction and waved back. Five seconds later, they were long gone.

Cheryl whimpered, "Tony Altino is the enforcer — for the construction business. But I don't know anything."

I had to let her go through another drowning cycle. I rescued her at the last minute with another length of flag halyard.

"Don't lie to me. I know you asked the Washington patent lawyer whether you can get a patent after the inventor is dead. I know you decided to murder Dr. Moon — "

"No, Ben. We never talked about killing him. Two nights ago — Bud and Tony — said they'd take care of things. Nobody shot him or beat him up. Probably argued. Heart attack. I was surprised . . . when the lab called . . . and said that he was dead."

"Was Bud surprised when you told him the lab called and Moon was dead?"

She didn't answer. She stalled a long time. Finally she managed, "How could I know? Bud never looks surprised. He's a poker player."

I tossed out the line, threw the engine into gear and gave Cheryl a poker-faced, French Connection bye-bye wave, as I glided away. She shrieked and tried to swim toward the boat, losing strength with each hopeless stroke. Then she gave up. "Ben," she screamed. "I really don't know."

I guessed the odds were two to one that she was telling the truth. More time in the water wouldn't improve my estimate. She looked so pitiful. She had lost it completely. Probably inhaled water. A few seconds longer, and I might not be able to rescue her.

I took the motor out of gear. Opened the hatch to a cockpit locker. Grabbed a big rubber fender and threw it overboard. Secured its line on an aft cleat. Killed the engine.

She'd lost it, all right. It was pathetic. The fender could float maybe 20 pounds, but she tried to mount it. She tried to stand on it and climb the rope. When she finally came to her senses, she said things that were painful to hear.

That I was a dumb bastard who was ruining everything, just like

Moon. That all they wanted to do was market a cure for cancer, and all Moon wanted was more money. That Moon wouldn't listen when Roger Black tried to talk sense into him. That Moon was going to bankrupt them. That I could still be part of their team. That they could make me rich.

I sat down on the bench, out of sight, and plugged my ears. It became siren call — a series of promises. That she'd tear up the video tape — both copies. That Rebecca would never know. That she'd be my special girlfriend anytime I wanted. That she'd make love to me in ways I'd never dreamed of. That we would get rich together. That she would teach me to make money with my excellent brain. That the seduction had actually been good for me.

"Ben, think of the first girl you made it with. Didn't she — "

"Shut up!" I looked at my watch: 5:20 p.m. "I've told Broadmoore everything. *Everything.* He's buying. And I've been recording all your words on tape."

I held up the tape recorder high for her to see.

She cried, first angrily, pouring forth a litany of dirty words worthy of a 40-dollar whore. To steady my nerves, I gulped down a glass of port. It made me dizzy as fast as it settled in my empty stomach. I went below and took a sandwich from the wicker basket. My hands trembled as I stood in the cockpit, eating the sandwich and looking down at Cheryl. She was crying and clutching the fender like a heartbroken teenager sobbing into her pillow.

I felt just as sick myself. For Cheryl's sake, I tried not to let it show. "Cheryl, listen up. I'm towing you to shore. You'll have to make a decision. You are an accessory to two murders — Dr. Yang's and Dr. Moon's. I've got your statements on tape. At nine o'clock tonight, I'm taking the tape to the Homicide Division of the Miami Police. Only one thing will stop me — if you go to them first, if you tell them everything, and don't warn Bud. They should be lenient. But if you don't go to the police by nine o'clock, the tape's going into evidence. And you'll be named accessory to murder."

The ultimatum delivered, I felt limp. This wasn't my style; but I hadn't known what else to do.

Cheryl didn't answer. She just sobbed.

I went below and found a plastic trash bag. Stuffed it with Cheryl's shoes, clothes, and purse — minus her cellular phone. Knotted the bag and brought it to the cockpit. The labor at the bow, pulling up the anchor, helped me to ignore a new round of pleading — Cheryl's assurances that all was still salvageable, new protestations of burgeoning love, and promises of additional four-figure payoffs for my cooperation.

Back in the cockpit I pushed the button, and the motor snorted to life. Threw it into gear and headed toward shore at moderate speed with Cheryl in tow. Aimed straight toward the middle of a long stretch of mangroves separating Matheson Hammock on the north and the Gables-by-the-Sea development to the south. Slowed to a dead crawl about 150 yards from shore when the depth meter started reading six feet.

"Ben," she yelled. "I'm not a bad person. I had a lot of bad breaks when I was young. Abusive Father. Demanding Mother. Now I'm a woman in a man's field."

"I'm dropping you off here. The water's almost shallow enough to stand. Swim toward shore. Another fifty yards, and you can wade. Matheson Hammock and your car are to the right. Gables-by-the-Sea is to the left." I tossed over the side the stuffed trash bag. It floated next to her like an oversized black pumpkin. I uncleated the line to the fender and motored off toward Matheson Hammock. I looked back once but lost Cheryl in the low six o'clock sun. I just prayed she would make the right decision.

WHAT YOU CAN DO WITH AN OLD KAZOO 34

This time, the motion of the boat didn't relax me. It only distracted from necessary thinking:

My audio tape would neutralize Cheryl's video tape — with my profs for sure, with Rebecca, maybe. Well, I hoped it would never come to that.

I had discharged my duty to Broadmoore. He had his scientific answer. No doubt, he had just plunked down the $20 million. Congratulations, Broadmoore. You just bought yourself a couple fine technologies — and a couple of murderous partners in the bargain.

Bud King would be surprised. With a little luck, my bugs might catch him saying something incriminating. But the tapes would probably not be admissible in court. Still, I couldn't think of a more fitting way to spend Cheryl's bribe money.

From here out, doing the right thing would require no more physical involvement than walking into the police station at nine o'clock tonight. But the more I thought about it, the clearer it became that I must do more. Without Cheryl's confession, no one would be tried for murder. For Dr. Yang's murder, there was no body. For Dr. Moon's murder, there was a body but no evidence of wrongdoing. How unfair for Bud King to get away with it — murdering a guy just because he was costing money. And I didn't want Dr. Westley to get away with putting a blind eye to the microscope. Couldn't let him get away with saying that Moon died of natural causes just to save his Cambridge buddy $5 million.

Yang's murder seemed a bigger tragedy than Moon's. I'd never met Dr. Yang. Hadn't even seen a picture of him. But his death was more real to me than any horrible murder I'd read about in a newspaper. My predecessor was an innocent human being. That's what was so troubling for me: Yang's innocence.

It could just as easily have happened to me. I felt guilty — like the quick-minded guy when he remembers shouting, "Yes, I'll give up my seat on Flight 350 in exchange for a guaranteed seat on the next flight out *plus* a free ticket to anywhere" — like when he remembers the congratulatory smiles of fellow passengers as he marched up the aisle with his carry-on — like when he remembers the nod of gratitude from that final passenger hurrying down the jetway toward the overbooked plane — like when he learns the next day from CNN News that Flight 350 crashed, leaving no survivors.

Yes, I owed Dr. Yang a debt. No way I would turn my back on him.

Then an idea hit me like a bolt of lightning. I slowed the engine to idle speed and went below. Grabbed Cheryl's cellular phone and replaced the batteries. And, yes, aluminum foil was on board. Tore up a roll of toilet paper to get the cardboard tube. Went back to the cockpit and killed the engine. Wrote a script and practiced it a couple times before pulling out the pocket tape recorder. The aluminum foil, wrapped over the end of the tube, gave my voice a fine metallic sound. I disguised it further by pinching my nose.

"You have reached the cellular voice mail box of telephone FIVE . . . SEVEN . . . ONE . . . SIX . . . THREE . . . TWO . . . TWO. The telephone is temporarily out of service. Please leave a message of up to ten-minute duration at the tone."

I laughed while playing it back. My machine-generated, unmodulated numbers were a nice touch. I cued the tape to the beginning of the message and reactivated the phone.

After restarting the motor and pointing toward Matheson Hammock, I sank into thought. With or without bugs and tape recordings, everything depended on finding Yang's body. And it could be anywhere within a 50-mile radius. Well, that was comforting! Just 400 square miles of Biscayne Bay and Atlantic Ocean on one side. On the other side was another 400 square miles of shopping strips, Everglades, and rock pits.

How to find Yang's body? My mind whirled with the countless possibilities. Had to narrow it down. What were the general ways? Couldn't think well, standing at the helm and piloting the boat. Needed to sit down and doodle on a piece of paper.

A few minutes from the Matheson Hammock Channel, Cheryl's cellular phone rang. I killed the motor, pressed the phone and tape recorder together, and flipped their switches. After the tape recorder played my message, I pushed one of the phone keys to deliver a beep. Almost forgot to change the tape machine to "Record". Tried to listen in real time but couldn't make it out. Got it all in playback, though. It was Bud King.

"Cellular voicemail? Look, I've been trying to get you for the last hour. You still babysitting that Candidi runt? Well, forget about it. Forget the whole damn thing. Little bastard must have double-crossed us. Should have taken care of him like . . . And Broadmoore came up with the money. We've got our ten million but not the big money. That limey bastard's over here, walking around, making decisions, and acting like he's carrying on a board meeting. His little butch is following him around, taking it all down. Got a moving company taking out all the files. Says we're barred from the lab. Must have gotten wind of the . . . You and me gotta talk. But nothing on the phone." (Click)

I restarted the engine and headed into Matheson Hammock. Chose an empty slip at another dock. Didn't want them to vandalize my boat. Scraped it once before I could get it tied securely to the dock.

Lost in thought while adjusting lines and straddling between the dock and boat, I almost fell in as the boat moved away. I rescued myself by jumping for the boat. And a grade school thought popped into my head, By land or by sea? Which way would the Redcoats march? That was my question: Did King dispose of Dr. Yang's corpse by land or sea?

I sat in the cockpit with a sheet of paper. Drew a vertical line, dividing the sheet into halves. Wrote on the left side: The Corpse. Wrote on the right side: Bud King. Now to start filling in details that would reveal the connections between the two. Write down the facts and probable actions that will *equate* the two. It was like the "identity problems' in college trigonometry where we had to equate complicated functions of "sines", "cosines", "tangents", and "secants". I had been really good at that stuff back in Swarthmore.

Soon I had filled the sheet of paper with logic. But inspiration did not come. That's just like you, Ben, always trying to go back to school where they always gave you gold stars. Wake up. This is the real world, and there isn't any textbook. Get a grip!

I gripped the bottle and poured another glass. Drank half of it in two gulps. I shut my eyes. I always keep going back to school because it was one of my favorite things. Then the answer came to me — clear as day.

When facing the problem of corpse disposal, Bud King would use his favorite thing. He wouldn't take the chance of having any Park Service ranger or Highway Patrol smokey catching him, while dragging Yang's corpse from his Cadillac's trunk to the Everglades swamp. And he sure as hell wouldn't dig a hole for Yang in the coral rock behind his house.

No, King would use his favorite thing. And if some damn Coral Gables Marine Patrol officer asked him why he was going out at midnight, he'd tell the bastard he wasn't paying $20,000 a year in taxes on waterfront property to have some seagoing flatfoot tell him when he could use his boat. And if the flatfoot thinks he's so smart, he can ask the Coral Gables mayor, who King happens to know socially.

Once out in the Bay, there would be no witness to King's dumping a heavily weighted corpse over the side. Fish and crabs would pick a corpse clean in a couple of weeks. The cartilage would rot. The bones would scatter in half a year. And there was too much Bay for anyone to search.

Yes, it all fit: the pile of cinder blocks in King's backyard and the ugly scrape marks on the *Ace's* starboard rail.

But King would be smart enough to scrub down the boat to remove all traces of Yang's blood and hair. To prove he did it, we would have to find Yang's body — an impossible task because the Bay is so vast.

Deep in thought, I sipped on the Port wine left in the last. Then . . . EUREKA!

The answer was sleeping in one of King's favorite things. In one of his favorite things that he really didn't know how to use. But he would think of it now. He would pull the plug on it first chance he got. I had to get there before he did.

WATER WORLD 35

A bike would be as fast as a cab and more practical. I went to the V-berth and manhandled out one of the small-wheeled collapsible bicycles we had used on our Bahama trip. Unfolded it on the dock. Crammed my pockets with the tape recorder, Cheryl's telephone, and a penlight.

A few minutes later I was pedaling top speed along the arrow asphalt bikeway that snakes through the mangrove swamp of Matheson Hammock. Several minutes and a couple squashed crabs later, I was up on the Atlantic Costal Ridge, pedaling along Old Cutler Road, dodging ficus air roots and twilight Rollerbladers. Another 15 minutes, and I reached the traffic circle that links Old Cutler with Sunset and LeJeune Roads.

It was high-calorie exertion. I stopped to catch my breath on the park bench at the scenic overlook by the LeJeune bridge. Looked down on the Coral Gables Waterway in the direction of King's house. My action on his boat had to be carefully planned and quickly executed. By the time my respirations were back to normal, I had it figured out. My heart beat rate was another matter.

I pedaled three blocks north on Granada, parallel to the canal. The bushes under the Hardee Road bridge made a good hiding place for my bike. Thought for a second. Stashed Cheryl's telephone with it. Emerged on Granada Avenue, looking like a normal Coral Gables resident out for a stroll in the dark.

Luckily there was no sign of King's Cadillac in front of his house. Blue light glimmered in a room off to the side — probably the maid watching black and white TV. Skirted the side of the house and descended the carved coral steps to the *Ace*. Ran a finger over its fiberglass rail. Yes, the cinder block scrape marks were still there.

Remembered the boat's alarm system. Also remembered how the door to the engine compartment doubled as a built-in fiberglass chair. A sliding latch was all that secured the hinged door-seat. I opened it and flashed the penlight around inside. Found the deactivation switch on the inside wall above a small pile of snorkeling gear. Held my breath and flipped the toggle switch. Thank God, the alarm didn't go off.

Quickly climbed the ladder to the fly bridge. Took the cover off Bud King's prized satellite Global Positioning System unit — the GPS gizmo that he liked to brag about but didn't know how to operate. A click of the switch and the green LCD screen lit up almost as strong as the maid's TV set. Luckily the screen was facing away from the house.

The GPS screen presented two long numbers which I recognized as our latitude and longitude. Yes, there were enough numbers behind the decimal point to fix our position to the nearest several feet. Six buttons controlled the display. That made for a lot of possible combinations of keys. So it was a long time before I could bring up the date-time group on the screen. Unfortunately the latest date was two years ago. I pondered this discrepancy for a long time before realizing that no one had ever set the date on the GPS. The latest date was really today.

Soon I was pushing buttons, sending the time numbers whirling back to the evening of our yachting party. Finally longitude and latitude numbers also began to spin. This marked King's Norman Schwarzkopf speech on the fantail and our close encounter with the Cuban-American fishers. Then the numbers reversed and came to rest at the longitude and latitude of King's dock.

Now to find out what the boat had been doing around the time Dr. Yang disappeared. I threw the time machine into fast reverse. The time numbers whirled backwards faster than I could read them, but the position numbers stayed constant. Then longitude/latitude numbers started to move down the canal just like before. I stopped, read the date, and did some mental arithmetic. They'd taken the *Ace* out the previous Saturday night.

I held down the buttons again, setting in motion the time-date and latitude/longitude numbers. Then I found it — a little blip where the time kept moving and the position didn't. The *Ace* had stopped, probably somewhere out in Biscayne Bay, probably long enough to dump Dr. Yang's body. I recited the longitude and latitude into the tape recorder. Then a white light flashed in my face. Damn! Car headlights turning in and pointing right at me. I dropped to the floor and snapped off the GPS. Bud King was coming home.

Several seconds later, car doors slammed. I replaced the cover on the GPS. I would have to get out of there quick. What else had I disturbed on the *Ace*? Trudging footsteps approached, and I heard labored breathing. Then the car lights went out. Delayed automatic on those Cadillacs, I now remembered.

"Hold your end. Don't let it drag." They were already on the patio and approaching the steps. I scrambled down the ladder. Was about to slip off the stern and into the canal when I gasped: The door-seat to the engine compartment was halfway open. Just as I got into position to close it, a head appeared over the ridge. One turn of the head — and he'd spot me. No time to think it over. I just did it. I crawled into the engine compartment, pulling the door shut behind me.

On hands and knees between the two massive engines in the small, dark chamber, I knew it was the wrong choice. Couldn't change anything now. Would they notice that the door wasn't latched? Would King notice the alarm was already deactivated? If I stayed in the center, he'd find me for sure. But where to hide? Penlight in hand, I crawled over the top of the port engine and wedged myself between it and the firewall.

With my ear to the fiberglass their conversation came through like on a tin-can-and-string telephone — lots of muttered directions and heavy breathing. They clomped around like furniture movers. A muted thud told me they'd dropped a soft but heavy object on the deck. No, it couldn't be.

"Bitch is heavy," whined a high-pitched voice that sounded vaguely familiar.

I started to feel sick as I realized what they had done. Groped around and found the tape recorder in my back pocket. The little red light was still glowing. I'd forgotten to turn it off. I pressed the end with the built-in mike against the ceiling

"Shut your fucking mouth. Don't call her a bitch. Get the tarp off the barbecue." It was King.

Footsteps left the boat and it was silent for a long time. King began muttering, then whining, "Goddamn." The footsteps returned.

"Now get me a dozen cinder blocks," said King.

"Yeah, but you gotta go up and help me."

"Like shit. You shouldn't have done it. I say you shouldn't have done it."

"You know I had to. She got diarrhea of the mouth."

"We could have popped her a *Valium* and talked reason into her."

"Like shit. The police would have cracked her. With all that stuff she told Candidi."

"She didn't have to be — "

"I did you a favor by taking her out. You were getting pussy-whipped. It wasn't love. Don't kid yourself. She was playing you as hard as you was playing her."

"Just shut up," King spat out. "And fix the alarm so it don't go off and rouse the whole neighborhood. And get those goddamn cinder blocks."

The door opened suddenly. My testicles shriveled as I heard a hand fumble for the switch.

"Up is off. Right?"

"Yes, you jackass."

"But — "

The door slammed shut. I didn't hear him click the latch. Maybe I could bust out and make a break for it. But after a couple minutes, it was clear I would have no such luck. One of them was always climbing around on the boat or cranking down the tuna tower.

Then came a rush of air and the whine of the blowers in the next compartment. In one minute they would be starting the engines. Would have to get out of that corner, or I'd be cooked. The port engine started cranking just as I began to crawl over it. It shook, then roared under me as they fired it up. Watch out for the rubber belts on the alternators, I told myself.

Suddenly my left leg went stiff. Was getting tetanizing shocks from the spark plug wires. The shocks went up my sweaty body, tickling my fluttering heart. They made my fingers curl around the edges of the motor block. It took the full weight of my body to tear my hands free. Felt like I broke my kneecap when I landed on the floor.

A strobe light flashed and a whip cracked in synchrony with the motor's unsteady roar. A dislodged plug wire was arcing onto the engine block. My numbed hand seemed to work in slow, jerky motion as I fumbled in the pile of diving gear and grabbed a rubberized glove. Gingerly I picked up the dangling wire and snapped it back on its plug. Darkness again. Over the engine roar, I heard only the thud of footsteps. I prayed they hadn't noticed anything wrong with the engines. If they opened my door, I would shoot out and dive over the stern.

The engines slowed to dead idle and a lever clanked. We were backing out of the slip. Cautiously I pushed the door. The only resistance was from the spring catch. After opening it an eighth of an inch, I could peek out and inspect the fantail. No one was back there. In the dim light of city glow and an occasional backyard spotlight, I could make it out — a tarp covering a small mound of what had to be Cheryl's body surrounded with cinder block.

Bud King and his accomplice would be high above me on the fly bridge. Chances were they wouldn't look back much. I would escape by diving over the stern.

Open the door slowly so they won't notice a change in engine noise. I'd just started when a pair of legs came into view. I quickly closed the door. A minute later, I eased it open to a narrow crack and peered out.

A man was sitting in a deck chair next to the mound. King probably sent him down to make sure the tarp stayed on. I recognized Tony Altino's face as he flicked a lighter and pulled on a cigarette. By the time he'd finished it, a flashing green channel marker glided by to starboard. Then engines went into high rev. I shut the door and tried to relax. We were too far out for me to swim back, even if I could jump off undetected. Just have to stay put and ride it out.

After another 10 minutes the engines slowed to an idle and stopped. The boat rocked erratically in moderate waves. I heard King come down the ladder. With my ear against the door, I could just make out their conversation.

"Just like before, but put the tarp down. Don't mar the gelcoat this time." It was King. "The rope's in the side compartment."

Tony Altino grunted something. They stumbled and thudded around for 10 minutes.

Then King said, "One, two, three." There was a horrible banging and a splash.

"I told you not to tear up the gelcoat," screamed King. "Now get a bucket and brush. Can't leave a speck of blood. Not a single hair."

Altino said, "I'm going to sit down for a smoke first."

The door banged against my ear, then swung wide open with Altino riding on it. Suddenly King and I were staring at each other. I froze. He gasped.

King screamed, "Shut that door." Altino rolled off the door-seat and slammed it in my face. "Latch the fucker tight," ordered King. "Did you see that? That damn Candidi. In the engine compartment — spying on us."

"Said you shouldn't have thrown the gun away so soon."

"Ah, shut up. We don't need no gun to kill off that bilge rat. Let me think." I stayed frozen, my ear against the door. "We'll do it just like we did with Moon. We'll suffocate him. Except this time it won't be liquid nitrogen. This time it'll be *Halon* and carbon dioxide."

"*Halon* and carbon dioxide?"

"The fire extinguisher system, you dumb shit."

My brain raced. I turned on the pen light. The blowers were in another compartment. They blew air in and out through long flexible ducting. Another pair of flexible ducts supplied outside air to the engines.

"Candidi," King yelled. "Yuh think you're so smart — giving me a hard time. Well, you did fuck me up. Just like that smart-ass Moon."

How could I get air from the flexible ducts?

"But we killed him. And nobody could figure it out. We know all about you, Candidi. Your coroner buddy couldn't figure out how we killed Moon without leaving a mark. All you fancy doctors and Ph.D.s with your fancy theories. You couldn't see the answer right under your nose — even when it's written on the damn tanks. 'Nitrogen does not support life.' But the label didn't say it was dangerous to go around jabbing the nozzle into air conditioning ducts. So you couldn't figure it out. Could you?"

My killing gas would probably come from the blower ducts. I'd go for the engine air intakes. I tore away at the four-inch diameter, metallized, plastic and wire tube. Finally made a thumb hole.

King was really running at the mouth. "Yeah, that Asian rat, Moon, went to sleep without a fuss. Just like the rats in Punjab's bell jar. Except Punjab let his rats wake up. We didn't let Moon wake up, did we, Tony? And we won't let Candy-Rat wake up, either."

I grabbed the snorkel from the pile of diving gear, inserted it in the hole and breathed through it. The gasoline odor was unpleasant but preferable to what would come.

"Say your prayers," King called out smugly.

Jets of gas hissed through small holes in the ceiling. A cool and eerie fog descended on me. By mistake, I took one breath through my nose. It stung my nasal membranes like a combination of operating room anesthetic and soft drink burp.

I pounded with my foot against the door. Made like a dying rat, thrashing and scraping. I pulled deep breaths through the snorkel, then screamed into the compartment, begging for mercy. Altered gas physics gave my voice a strange sound. The hissing of the gas jets stopped a couple minutes later. Gradually I slowed my hammering and finally went still. They were quiet too, obviously listening for sounds of life from inside the death chamber.

"I'll go in there and finish him off," said Altino.

"No, give him fifteen minutes. That'll be more than enough. I'll turn on the blowers before you go in."

I pulled the tape recorder from my pocket, turned it on, and hid it behind the port engine. What a shame I'd been too excited to tape King's tirade about asphyxiating Moon. The silence was ghostly. The only sound was the waves lapping on the hull.

What were my strategies for the end game?

Option Number One: Rush out past them, jump in the water, and swim away like hell. But I couldn't avoid checkmate. They had searchlights. They had mobility. My only hope would be to hide under a patch of seaweed.

Option Number Two: Come out fighting. Push one overboard and fight the other one to the death. Slim chance of winning.

Option Number Three: Keep them thinking I was dead and let them throw me overboard. It might work, if they didn't knock me unconscious before dumping me.

I reviewed the decision tree several times. If the deck lights were on, I'd take my chances with Option Number One or Two. Under bright light, there was no way I could convince them I was dead. Involuntary pupillary response would give me away.

If the lights were off, I'd go for Option Number Three and play 'possum. I'd watch them through partially opened eyes to make sure they weren't going to bash or stab me. I'd let them weight me down. But if they started making the knots too tight, I'd get up and jump overboard.

The fans came on. I counted to 20 and took one last deep breath. Dropped the snorkel into the pile of diving stuff. Leaned against the door, so that I could fall out onto the deck when they opened up. Less chance of getting my head banged that way. The residual gases were making me light-headed but maybe that would help me stay limp.

The latch clicked. The door opened to a dark cockpit. I dropped my torso onto the deck, banging my head convincingly in the process.

"Look," said Altino. "Just like a Jew-boy at Auschwitz."

I made myself limp like a sack of potatoes as they dragged me and pulled me up by my shoulders. They dropped me backwards onto the bench along the port rail.

"Get me the plow anchor," ordered King. "And I want all its chain." Altino took a long time. King was sitting next to me. After a while, he started muttering, "Dumb bastard — goddamn — goddamn dumb bastard . . . "

Thank the good Lord, the moon had waned to a thin sliver. King wouldn't make out much from my face. The angle of my head kept me from seeing him. It sounded like he was too far from the edge for me to surprise him and push him overboard. We were definitely in Biscayne Bay, not the Atlantic. The ride had been too short and the waves were too gentle. The average depth of the Bay is 15 feet. I would stick to Plan Three — take the plunge and wiggle out.

Altino stumbled around with a plow anchor. It nearly crushed my rib cage when he dropped it on my chest. They pushed my head and shoulders overboard to make it easier to wind the chain around my body. They started wrapping my neck, then three times around my chest, and four times around my legs.

I had to concentrate on breathing slow and shallow. The edge of the rail came a couple inches below my shoulder blades. It hurt, letting my head dangle and my back droop. We were in the Bay, all right. Off in the distance loomed Miami, upside down. Altino wrapped the last of about 15 feet of chain and tucked the free end under the loops at chest level.

"Shit," whined King. He pulled out the loose end of chain and threw it down so it clanked against the hull. "You didn't even put a knot in it. You think that's going to keep this piece of shit from coming up, once he starts bloating?"

"Fuck, you can't make good knots with chain."

"I've got some scraps of rope — in the locker across from the head. Bring me a few feet. And don't take a knife to any of my good anchor line."

Altino stomped off. King resumed his whining litany of "shits" and "goddamns". They got louder and more frequent with each repetition. Then he started talking to me like I was alive. "You thought you were smart — college boy — telling the detective to take the body to the coroner and have him look for poison. But you didn't think of the simplest poison of them all — taking away the oxygen. Snotty-nosed science boys. Think you're so smart. And that goddamn chink thought he could squeeze me for two million, did he? Thought he could just shut the door and get rid of me, did he? Thought I was dumb, did he? He was gassing rats in his lab every day. But he never thought I'd shoot liquid nitrogen into his air conditioner. I put that rat to sleep. No dumbshit chink's going to make me buy the same thing twice.

"And you, you little runt. You cost me fifty million. Thought you was pretty smart, bird-dogging me for your Boston limey. Even after Cheryl puts herself out for you, gives you ten grand, and offers you a place on the team. But, no, it was more important to you to get a pat on the back from your limey boss." King was sounding increasingly nasty. "Did Broadmoore tell you that you're a nice Harvard bright boy? You ungrateful, double-crossing, snot-nosed pencil-dick."

The force of the unexpected blow to the face caused my limp body to teeter. I would have fallen naturally over the side, if King hadn't grabbed my leg.

"Tony, you found the rope, yet?"

"No. Come over here and show me."

King responded with a hollow laugh. "You couldn't find your own cock, if they painted a yellow line down your chest." Footsteps told me he'd moved away. Lights flipped on in the main salon.

Now was my chance, if I could make it sound convincing. Inside my chain cocoon, I wormed a couple more inches outboard. The anchor was breaking my back. Tried doing a little sit-up, which brought my chest up three inches. Now or never. I let go completely and almost popped a vertebra. Chain clanked on fiberglass. My body slid down several inches. The cocoon skipped a couple chain-widths, then came to a stop. Then the anchor slipped and hit me in the chin. I used all my strength for another sit-up and let go. Clanked overboard and hit the water faster than I could gasp for my last breath.

Tried to twirl against the wrap of the chain as I sank. Loosened up few feet before I hit the sandy bottom. Arms were still wrapped tight to my side, but both legs were free. Rolled over and over, stirring up so much sand I was afraid to open my eyes.

After a chest-heaving eternity, my hands were free. Got my neck out of the last loop when it hit me right through the eyelids — daylight. It came from all directions, as if I might be inside a luminous cloud. They were training a spotlight down on me, and the cloud of sand was scattering the beam. White glow was coming from all directions. I wiggled my hips free, dug my toes under the anchor, and pushed off horizontally with all my might.

I shot out of the cloud and breast stroked along the bottom as fast as I could. Some 15 feet above, the Ace's hull was illuminated in the spotlight's backscatter. My lungs had given up heaving. My breathing reflex had died. My throat was burning from carbon dioxide. And I was graying out. Try not to faint during ascent! Pushed off hard from the bottom and shot up toward the dark side of the Ace.

Halfway up, everything went black. Was I clambering through water or clawing air? Must have broken the surface because there were no bubbles when I blew out. The exhalation burnt my nose worse than the killing gas. And my lungs couldn't suck air. Felt like an asthma attack. Leaned a shoulder into the hull for something solid and willed my lungs to suck their first milliliters of oxygen-bearing air.

Slowly my lungs relearned how to breathe. Slowly black turned to gray. Then gray turned to diffuse yellow — the yellow of distant sodium lamps. Soon I was sucking sweet air so hard that I had to concentrate on keeping quiet.

For a partial repayment on the oxygen debt, Nature reconnected my sense of hearing. King and Altino were arguing. Where should they point the spotlight? How fast were they drifting away? Was the cloud drifting, too? Should they trawl against the drift? How could they make sure my body was down there?

I concentrated on blowing off carbon dioxide. As my blood pH started to return to normal, Mother Nature thanked me by giving back my sense of vision. Slowly I started making out details of the Miami skyline. We were far out in the Bay, south of Coconut Grove. Swimming to land would take eight hours, if my strength held out.

"Look," said Altino, "if you want to be sure he's dead, put on your diving gear and jump in."

Their argument gave me a chance to check out my options. From the bow, a loop of anchor line dangled where Altino had removed the plow anchor. I reached up and grabbed. Luckily it was secured at both ends and held my weight. The *Ace's* prow was nicely protected from sight of the fly bridge by the curvature and flare of the bow. If I had the strength to hold on, I'd have a ride back to shore. Could let myself back into the water when they slowed down. But what if they saw me?

They started their motors with a roar. No time to ponder the question. Couldn't give them eight hours to destroy the evidence. As they threw the motors in gear, I pulled myself up. Was high out of the water when they started to move. The line was too high to hook my legs on. I wrapped each arm in a segment and hung like a prisoner in a medieval dungeon.

Soon the boat was riding high on plane. For me, straddling the bow, it was like riding the underside of a bucking bronco. On each side, streams of water shot up with the force of a fire hose, holding my legs in place. But every twentieth jounce dumped me into a speeding wall of water that swatted my butt like a giant hand. It took all my strength to keep my body high. After several minutes, my arms started cramping, and it was pure agony. I wouldn't make it.

Looked over my shoulder to sight land. Coral Gables was maybe five miles ahead. And before it was a small white light that was getting bigger by the second. It was a gasoline lantern on a fishing boat. The *Ace* was bearing down on it, almost on a collision course.

Do it now, Ben! Plan the jump. Do it hard to the side so you don't get chopped up by the props. Which side to take? Portside is more shielded from the helmsman's view. I crawled along the galloping bow to my right. I said a little prayer as we closed at about 50 yards. Pushed off hard with all fours. Cleared the port side. Snapped into the fetal position just before I hit the water.

36 IN THE CORAL CORRAL

The water spun me hard. Stayed below in the *Ace's* turbulence as long as possible. When I surfaced, the *Ace* was hundreds of yards away and still hauling ass.

Two fishermen were cursing in Cuban Spanish. *"¡Cuidado pa!"*

I yelled for help at the top of my lungs. *"¡Ayudame!"*

One of them crossed himself in reflex. He searched the darkness in the wrong direction. *"¿Quien es? ¿Donde estas?"*

"¡Detras de ti!" I yelled with all my might.

Slowly the man turned around.

It was just an old wooden shrimp fishing boat, not much longer than 20 feet. But after the *viejos* hoisted me aboard, its rotten wooden deck felt as solid as the Rock of Gibraltar.

Thank God I'd gone to the trouble to become fluent in Spanish. I told the fishermen that the people in the other boat had tried to murder me. I offered them $100 to take me straight to the Coral Gables Waterway. The captain had no trouble understanding or believing me. He pointed the bow toward the glow of Coconut Grove and pushed the throttle to full power. We maxed out at a disappointing six knots.

The *Ace's* stern light kept receding toward the middle of the Bay. Under the shrimper's wheel was a rust-encrusted VHF. I couldn't call the Florida Marine Patrol on Channel 16; King might hear us. I hailed the marine operator instead. When she finally answered, we both switched to Channel 17 where I requested a 911 call.

"Captain, we are not allowed to relay nine-one-one calls. Please switch to Channel 16 and hail the Florida Marine Patrol. Over."

It did not impress her when I explained that I was trying to report a crime. She was more impressed with her rules than with my arguments. She suggested that I pay with a credit card. I reached in my shirt pocket for the little brown book containing my credit cards. Must have lost it while playing Houdini. Searched my memory for the card number and gave the lady my best guess.

"Captain, did you say three-eight-two-zero-seven-zero-eight-eight-two-three-one-two- zero-one? Over."

"Yes. But don't call me Captain. I've been rescued by a fishing boat. They picked me up after a couple gangsters dumped me in the Bay. Over."

"The number cannot be correct. It is missing a digit. Over."

"Which digit is missing? Over."

"That's what you're supposed to be telling me. Over."

I agonized over my next guess for a long time. "Make that one-two-zero-one-one. Over"

"Please wait a minute, Captain."

All the time the *Ace's* stern light had been growing fainter. Now it disappeared like they'd darkened the boat. They were probably scrubbing down the fantail.

After an eternity, the marine operator came back on to tell me that my number was not valid. I said many unrepeatable things before keying down and transmitting. "My name is Ben Candidi. My phone number is five-four-seven-two-eight-nine-three. Isn't there any way I can make this call? Over."

"Do you have True Calling, U.S.A.?"

"Yes," I said, not knowing what it was.

"What is your P.I.N.? Over."

I gave her the four digits that Rebecca and I always used.

"I can now place your call, Captain. But not to nine-one-one. Do you want the Miami Police or Metro Police?"

I selected Miami Police. When they answered I asked for Homicide and was left holding for at least five minutes. But I was more patient now. Our boat kept chugging toward the Coral Gables Waterway, and the *Ace* still had to be out in the middle of the Bay.

"Homicide, Davis."

"This is Ben Candidi. I have been cooperating with Detective Cordova on a suspected homicide in the case of Dr. Tehong Moon."

"Sir, can you call back? We have a bad connection and the line's full of static."

"I can't call back. It's already taken me half an hour to get patched in. I'm on a small fishing vessel in Biscayne Bay. Marine Operator. Marine Operator! Please check the squelch on your receiver. Over."

"Sir. You're breaking up all over the place, and I'm getting only half of it. With all due respect, sir, can I suggest that you wait until you get back from your fishing trip. Over."

It was an exercise in patience to recapitulate my story. I chopped it into bite-size chunks. By the time we were closing in on the Coral Gables Waterway, I had managed to spoon-feed half of it to Detective Davis.

Off our stern, a pair of green and red navigation lights appeared from where I'd last seen the *Ace*. The lights grew closer and brighter.

Then Davis interrupted me. "Sir, if the guy pushed you off his boat, you can come down to the station and file assault charges."

"There's more to it. He murdered his chief scientist Cheryl North and threw her overboard. Please write this down. He is C.C. "Bud" King. He lives at 6099 Granada Avenue, Coral Gables."

I repeated how I'd stowed away and how King had thrown out Cheryl's corpse. I said the murder was related to Dr. Moon's murder. It went painfully slow. As we entered the channel for the Coral Gables Waterway, I finished by saying, "King is out in the Bay removing the last traces of evidence from his boat. You need to apprehend him before he gets back and removes the victim's blood and hair from the trunk of his car. Over."

"Sir, only half of what you said came through. What did you say your name is?"

"Candidi. Ben Candidi."

"Just a minute. I want to look on Detective Cordova's desk."

The navigation lights were much closer now. I made out the oncoming shape of a large cabin cruiser getting bigger by the second. Down the narrow channel it came, still riding high on plane and barreling down on us.

I yelled to our man on the wheel, *"¡Es el! Echa el barcola al lado."* I let go of the microphone and snatched the partner's straw hat. *"Para cubrirme la cara."* Covered my face more by dipping the brim and kneeling over the bait chest. Just in time. The cruiser switched on its spotlight and lit us up like it was daytime.

Over the radio came the detective's voice. "Mister Candidi, Detective Cordova left a note asking that you come in Monday. If you are ready to sign an affidavit for what you have alleged . . . Mister Candidi, are you still on the line?"

It was surely the *Ace* and I couldn't let them see me. I kept the hat brim down over my eyes and kept digging in the cooler.

"Mister Candidi. Mister Candidi. We seem to have lost the connection. I'm hanging up." Then came a dial tone. The cruiser roared by, passing us at less than 20 feet. Its stern bore no surprise — *Ace in the Hole*. Its wake bounced us so violently that we lost control, almost hitting a piling.

The *Ace* didn't power down until it was abreast of the big condominium. I told the captain to follow it. Tried to get back the marine operator. The *Ace* disappeared behind a bend in the coral canyon. A couple minutes later, I caught sight of it once more, loitering in front of the LeJeune bridge. They were cranking-down the tuna tower. Then it transited under the bridge. By the time we motored under the bridge, the *Ace* was out of sight, well beyond the next bend in the Waterway.

"Turn back," ordered a loud metallic voice, coming from the shadows behind us. It was a Boston Whaler with an array of lights and sirens mounted over its steering station. As it pulled along side of us, I read: Coral Gables Marine Patrol.

I called out, "You have to stop that boat. There's been a murder — "

"Turn back or you will be boarded," came the only answer.

"Tengo que obedecer," my captain said.

I couldn't ask him to disobey, but I did ask him to go close to the bank when he made his turn. Couldn't find a pen or pencil. Used my finger. Wrote my phone number in the grime on the gas tank.

"Llama a este numero para pagarte."

The debt will be paid. No time to say more. I jumped overboard and swam the few yards to land. Scrambled up the steep embankment to the scenic overlook. From it's western-most edge, I could see that the *Ace* was halfway to the Hardee Road bridge. And the damned Marine Patrol Whaler was still loitering at the spot where they'd intercepted us.

I started running up the street. Had to get to King's house before he did. Couldn't let him drive his car to an all-night gas station and vacuum out the trunk. I'd let the air out of all his tires, that's what I'd do.

Ran at top speed up Granada Avenue, paralleling the canal. Couldn't see or hear the boat because the mansions were in the way. I ran all the harder. After a few hundred yards, I had to slow to a jog. My lungs were threatening to burst. I cursed the setback sidewalk and the broad curving street. The wide vista made my progress seem slow like in a drawn-out, scary dream.

If only one of those mechanized gates would open to let out a Jaguar. Its upper-class driver would react to a fellow human in distress. He wouldn't ignore my plea for a quick lift three blocks up the street. Please, gentle neighborhood, I'm running myself to death.

But my pleading was not answered. Behind coral walls, charming outdoor lights cast their rays over vast, manicured lawns. I might as well be pleading to the stars. Is anybody out there? There must be humans somewhere. I can see televisions flickering behind your curtained windows.

By the time I reached the first bridge, which crossed a sidearm of the Waterway, my lungs were as acid as vinegar. I put both hands on the stone rail, gasped for breath, and looked off toward the main canal. No sign of the *Ace* . . . just a property that looked like the CIA/Kennedy Compound on the far side. King was probably way ahead of me.

I pushed off. After another several hundred yards of flat-out sprint, my muscles were cramped with lactic acid, and my blood was fouled with carbon dioxide. No glucose to run my brain. I was graying out over stumbling legs — a panicked horse running itself to death, pushed only by that small part of the brain for which God programmed that last trickle of blood, offering to the will of survival the last molecules of glucose.

Mercifully the rise of the Hardee Road bridge came into view. King had probably cleared it already. From its center, I would be able to see his backyard. But how strange. The entrance to the bridge was blocked by squad cars. Same for the northern leg of Granada Avenue. Several darkly dressed figures stood near the top of the bridge. As I ran up to them, I recognized SWAT uniforms.

One of them showed me the bottom of a flattened palm. I slowed to a jog. "Sir, I must ask you to vacate the area. We have an emergency situation."

"But you've got to stop that boat; they just murdered — "

"Sir, if you do not vacate the area, you will be taken into custody and — "

I walked away long enough to convince the cop I was going. Then I doubled back through the bushes along the north side of the bridge where the coral slopes to the water.

The *Ace* was loitering in the middle of the canal about 50 yards from King's dock. Tony Altino stood on the bow with a boat hook, and King was up on the fly bridge, cranking the last few turns on the winch to re-erect his tuna tower. Then, with military precision, he slowly glided the *Ace* toward its grotto-berth. Altino jumped off and attached a dockline.

When the *Ace* was halfway in King pointed his face to the sky like an animal sniffing for a scent.

Then a spotlight snapped on, shining down on him from the top of the grotto. A tinny voice boomed, "Police! Clarence King, you are being taken into custody in connection with a murder investigation. You will be boarded. Remove your hands from the controls. You! Man on dock. Do not move."

King bent over slightly. A metallic click told me he'd keyed down on his mike. He boomed over his P.A., "Option bravo. We are not in violation of any Coral Gables code concerning boating at this hour. If you object, I suggest you take it up with the mayor, who happens to be a good friend. And if you don't believe it, call him up at two-eight-four — "

"Turn off your engine and put your hands over your head. If you resist, it may be necessary to use deadly force."

A line of sharpshooters popped up along the ridge of the grotto.

"You fucking, fuzzy-toed, flatfoot — "

"Don't lose your head, Bud!" cried Altino's unamplified voice.

The *Ace's* engines snarled and the yacht moved backwards. It accelerated, slowed momentarily, and lurched backwards again with even greater speed. Something shot from its bow, and Altino fell backwards on the dock.

Then came muzzle flash. Chips of white fiberglass flew into the air before the *Ace's* fly bridge. The sound of the shots arrived a split-second later. The motors slowed, then revved, and the yacht shot forward, aiming for the bridge.

It felt like standing at the side of a narrow underpass while 10 tons of Mack truck comes barreling down. The *Ace* accelerated and its bow climbed high, throwing up two continuous curtains of water that framed the fly bridge and King's grimacing face. Hypnotically the picture grew before me. Then shots rang out over my right ear, and the boat veered straight at me.

I willed my legs to move. The *Ace* crashed and skidded up the coral bank faster than my legs could jump for the sky. To the sound of a 10-car collision, I grabbed the concrete railing and scrambled over. I rolled on the pavement. The bowsprit poked its horn over the rail like an angry bull in the rodeo. The twin motors screamed like banshees; airborne propellers wailed like air raid sirens.

Then the bowsprit receded. I peeked over the rail. The full length of the yacht was out of the water. The yacht was sliding back toward the canal to the sound of grating fiberglass and crunching rock. The vibration of ungoverned motors and screaming propellers greased the skid. A cloud of rock dust rose in the air. Next the high-pitched ensemble decelerated like a wood-chipping machine devouring a tree limb. A micronized spray of salt water filled the air. And then came gasoline vapor.

"Get down! It's going to explode," I yelled and pressed my body to protective asphalt below the bridge's high sidewalk. But it didn't ignite. The glacial crunching of fiberglass reported that the *Ace* was returning to sea. As the propellers dug deeper, the motors slowed. Exhaust bubbled and gurgled sporadically. When the engines finally choked and died I found the courage to look between the concrete pillars — just in time to witness the *Ace's* final launching. The sinking stern dragged the bow across the last outcrop of coral rock. The yacht looked as helpless as a Canadian moose that had broken through the ice. It was sinking fast.

The evidence! Over the concrete railing I leaped, crashing through broken bushes, half running, half falling down a slag heap of broken fiberglass, cushions and solid foam, twisting my ankles and cutting my legs as I raced toward the receding bowsprit. I lunged for the pulpit and gripped the stainless steel tubing just in time pull myself up on the bow.

I slid across the sinking deck and leaped over the shattered front window. Pulled myself high onto the bullet-pocked front wall of the fly bridge control console. Clattered over the top and into the chair, where my crazed, unbelieving eyes verified that the iridescent screen was still flashing longitude and latitude numbers. Miraculously the Satellite GPS Unit had survived the rain of lead.

While the *Ace* pitched, rolled, and sank, my hands found their way under the control panel. Flesh stripped from my frantic fingers, as I attempted to loosen Sam's workmanly installed mounting bolts. Ex-altar boy Candidi prayed to God. I prayed for Jesus to preserve against harm the life in this box — the silicon wafer bearing the microscopic labyrinth. I prayed for the Holy Spirit to preserve the wafer's life principle of steady regulated voltage. And I prayed to God in his infinite wisdom to spare these blessed megabytes that would grant me digital omniscience. Oh, Lord, I beseech you, do not send into oblivion the secret locations of Cheryl's and Yang's bodies.

The yacht was being dragged by an outgoing tidal current and was listing to port. A heavy cushion was pushing against my ankle and trickling warmth. I looked down and saw King, riddled with holes. Blood was welling up through his unmoving chest in the rhythm of arterial spurts. His heart was still beating, but he was beyond help.

Was the GPS also bleeding out its last ampere of strength? I switched off the screen to cut the current drain. Did the unit have a small internal backup battery that would keep the bits alive after salt water shorted out the Ace's batteries?

Above me, the tuna tower rang out like a clock tower chime. The boat stopped with a thud. The tide had jammed it sideways between the two bridge abutments. My panic lessened; peripheral sensation returned. I looked up into a bright light shining down from the bridge.

Like a chorus in an ancient Greek tragedy, two-way radios beeped and blurted, reporting in abrupt staccato that the area was secured, that an attempted escape was foiled, and that it had been necessary to use deadly force when the escaping yacht imperiled the crew of Coral Gables Marine Patrol Vessel Number 24, pre-positioned under the bridge to block such escape.

Backlit by blinding light, like an emissary angel, an officer descended on me, climbing down the tuna tower.

With extreme concentration, I could force half-formed words from my mouth. They came out like balls of cotton. "Quick. Help me. We have to unbolt the Sat-Nav unit. Needs twelve volts, or it's going to die. It's got all the information where the bodies are. It proves those guys are the murderers. Anyone! A small adjustable wrench. Or a buzz saw. Don't just stand there." I punched the officer's shoulder with my left hand.

"Hey, buddy. You better chill out fast, or we're going to have to Baker Act you."

He thought I was off my rocker. "But you don't understand — "

"Do what he says, Ben," said another voice — one that I immediately recognized and trusted. My sigh of relief was so deep that my heart missed a couple beats. It was Zeekie. He was calling down from somewhere behind the blinding lights.

"Ben, the boat isn't going anywhere. I've got all the stuff in my van — wrenches, wire, and a small twelve volt battery. I'll have the unit out in a couple of minutes."

"But, but, but — "

"You've got to learn to trust your friends!"

A second cop had climbed down and checked out King. He called out, "Lost all his blood from the looks of the deck. Probably'll be a D.O.A."

The two cops helped me climb up 10 feet of tuna tower and onto the bridge. Even with both feet planted on solid ground, I was still shaking. I sat down on the high curb. Still couldn't make enough saliva to unglue my tongue. Could only croak.

Zeekie put his arm around my shoulder. "You had me worried for a while, Ben. You should clue your friends in on your plans. My video camera caught you sneaking onto the property. With the Russian nightscope, I could see you working on that box, even from across the canal. But when those guys came down the steps carrying their load, I lost track of you.

What really got me suspicious was the enchilada they made with the blue tarp. When they started loading cinder block, it removed all doubt. After they shoved off and I couldn't find you, I knew you must be on board. You really put me on the spot; the Marine Patrol and police wouldn't respond at first. I had to do some fancy talking. I got the number of your coroner friend. He didn't want to do anything, until I told him your life was in danger. His buddy Broadmoore was at the company he just bought, directing a little army of Wackenhuts."

My words came out as a dry whisper. "You were watching me? I didn't see you — "

"And King didn't, either. I set up shop on the other side of the canal. One of the houses is empty. I pretended to be working on their satellite dish. As soon as I get your GPS out, I'll take you over to the van and show you the pictures."

"Careful, you don't want to dump the memory."

"Hey, man, you're not talking to a ordinary high school dropout. I dropped out to go to electronics school. Don't worry. I haven't forgot the basics — make before break!"

I felt a rush of emotion. "How am I going to repay you?" Then I said stupidly, "And I owe you and Johnny a lot of money."

"Make you a deal. You don't owe us anything, but we get to keep the video footage. I want to sell it to that TV show, Hard Copy. Call it a deal?"

We shook hands on it. Then Zeekie frowned.

"Hey, Ben. You'd better do something with those fingers, or you'll get a bone infection."

The Fire Rescue people removed King's body. Then the police let Zeekie recover the Satellite GPS unit. A paramedic bandaged my fingers and treated the more serious lacerations he found on my legs. I asked him what happened to Tony Altino.

"The guy on the dock was dead when we arrived. A boat cleat was drove six inches in his skull. The SWAT guys said the line stretched like a bungee cord before the cleat pulled out. Came flying back like a slingshot."

I asked the policeman in charge to get divers to retrieve my tape recorder from the engine compartment. Introduced him to Zeekie. Told them both how to find the locations of the bodies from the coordinates of the *Ace's* stopping points. The rest of the evening was a blur of police radios, boats, helicopters and TV news cameras. All I really remember is that I found my own bed sometime around midnight.

I had trouble getting to sleep, after remembering something else I had to defend — my dissertation.

37 DISSERTATION TIME

The seminar room was packed. Dr. Rob McGregor introduced me. At a table on the side sat the examining committee — five of our professors and a prof from Yale. It was hard to keep a warble out of my voice as I started with my introduction. It had been a scramble to get my presentation together. I had to compose the slides on my computer, using Power Point. I had connected the computer to a hastily borrowed color LCD display on top of a transparency projector.

Held my breath while clicking the keyboard to project the first slide. It came out fine on the screen. Pressed more buttons to bring down my introductory bullets. The software was working fine. The audience reacted like it was real high tech, and everyone got into the groove.

I told the audience how I'd been suspicious of a transient liaison between tyrosine phosphatase and calmodulin. Told them I'd set out to chemically handcuff them together. Talked about the low probability of any two molecules staying together — if they lacked affinity for each other. Conversely when two molecules stay together a long time they must like each other a lot. And that made them good candidates for chemical handcuffing. I had used the detective analogy in a seminar a year earlier, but it still produced smiles and whispers around the room. Despite all attempts to downplay my role in last Friday's police action, the word had gotten out.

I regained control over the proceedings by stepping up the pace. A brisk march through a complicated figure is a good way to get everyone's mind back on the experiments.

As for myself, I do have a bad habit of day dreaming through seminars — even ones that I am presenting. As the march returned to a comfortable pace, my mind soon started to drift. It occurred to me that criminal investigations aren't that much different from scientific investigations.

The subjects of your investigation, human or molecular, have only done what came natural to them. You, the detective, spend time speculating on their methods of operation. You make some guesses and set up some hypotheses. Then you spend the rest of the time testing these hunches. Your test usually isn't any more complicated than seeing which way your subjects jump — after you apply a test stimulus. I gave Cheryl and Bud a test stimulus, and they jumped.

In retrospect, King's boat was the obvious choice for disposing of Dr. Yang's body. It was there. King and Altino had taken it out hundreds of times. It should also have been obvious to me that the Satellite GPS unit was the best way to find Yang's body. The unit had been staring me in the face on the cocktail cruise for the whole evening.

Call it a hunch; call it an hypothesis. But it was easy enough for Zeekie to use the GPS to guide the Marine Patrol to the latitudes and longitudes — accurate to the nearest 50 feet — where the *Ace* had paused this week and last. And it was easy enough to send divers straight down to check the hypotheses.

Zeekie took his video camera along to record it. I first saw his footage on the Saturday evening news. And Sunday evening he gave me a private viewing of the outtakes. When we got to the part where they brought up Cheryl, I buried my hands in my face. Dressed in the business ensemble she'd worn on my boat, she looked sodden but serene, as if she would never again fear the water. Zeekie said she had been shot through the heart.

Dr. Yang's body hadn't fared as well. The Bay doesn't have any sharks, but it always has lots of sea turtles. They take out big chunks of bloated flesh.

My audience remained attentive as I pressed on with figures describing the calcium dependence of the tyrosine phosphatase reaction.

After hearing King's tirade, it was easy for me to picture the murder of Dr. Moon by asphyxiation. King and Altino argued with Moon one last time. Moon said his final "no" and sequestered himself in his office. King and Altino wheeled the liquid nitrogen tank over to the flexible air conditioner duct that supplied air to the office. They punched the tank's spout into the duct and turned the valve wide open. As liquid nitrogen boiled away in the duct, it made nitrogen gas. Soon all the oxygen was displaced from Dr. Moon's office and private john. My observation that the overhead vent was dripping fit with this. The supercooled ductwork would condense water vapor and collect plenty of ice.

Yesterday I had made some calculations, using Boyle's and Charles' Laws together with the molecular weight of nitrogen. According to the "PV = nRT" calculation, 100 pounds of liquid nitrogen would have been enough to fill Moon's office many times over. Moon wouldn't have known what was happening to him. He probably got drowsy, then faint, and finally fell over unconscious. Fatal arrhythmia or outright heart stoppage would occur a few minutes later.

The warning sign on the tank had been apt — "Nitrogen does not support life". King was right when he screamed that you didn't have to be a scientist to understand this. In absence of oxygen you die. It happens when pilots lose cabin pressure. It happened when the NASA technicians went into a nitrogen-purged room. It's even happened to sailors who crawled into the holds of ships filled with respiring grain.

There were still loose ends to tie up with Moon's murder. I would have to show Westley the hole in the flexible duct. Up to now, Westley had not made himself available to me. And the police still needed to locate King's self-incriminating words on the tape recorder I left in the engine compartment.

I continued presenting the seminar on mental autopilot, until someone distracted me by opening the door. Rebecca! She did make it back from Jamaica. A couple of graceful steps and bounces of her ponytail, and she took an empty seat toward the back. The audience tittered. And she blushed — when I blew her a kiss.

I went back to talking about the relationship between calmodulin and tyrosine kinase. I reexplained how calcium flowing into the cell puts the enzyme in high gear, attaching phosphate groups to numerous proteins in the cell and giving the cell memory of recent events.

My hard work had rounded out the story — the striking similarity in the calcium dependence of cell activation and the calcium-calmodulin binding; the enchanting "S"-shape revealing cooperativity between the calcium ions while binding; and the resulting "all-or-nothing" behavior in cell activation. No, the cell doesn't tolerate rogue molecules turning it on and off haphazardly.

The same type of logic fit the BIOTECH venture. A multimillion dollar biotech company cannot tolerate a rogue scientist haphazardly turning it on and off. But BIOTECH was never set up for teamwork; the venture was probably doomed from the very beginning. Bud King didn't have any respect for Dr. Moon. He just wanted him for his "magic key". Too bad that it takes more than stare-them-in-the-eye forcefulness to cure cancer. And Cheryl North couldn't call herself a scientist, either. She knew some science, but her heart was never in it.

The detectives and the state attorney had spent a lot of time grilling BIOTECH's number-two scientist and ranking survivor — Dr. Lau. It was he who had discovered parts of Moon's draft patent application. He had gone to Cheryl and King with news of the second invention. King told Lau to keep quiet about it and stay out of it. Then the Neanderthal obviously confronted Dr. Moon and asserted rights to the new invention. He probably never even considered giving Dr. Moon more money for the extra work. Much tragedy is born of greed.

I was toward the end of my presentation. It was now time to discuss the implications of my findings for cellular control. Each cell has to control its internal reactions and manage its assets efficiently. And colonies of cells, like sponges, require symbiosis to survive. In higher organisms, some cells must be outright subservient to others. You probably can't maintain any productive system without establishing hierarchy. The back of my brain kept throwing up images of King, North and Moon, and of the big mess they made of BIOTECH. Where do you draw the line between symbiont and parasite?

Should I have expected King, North, and Moon to cooperate any better than sponge cells cooperate to make a colony? I had a lot of disorganized thoughts about cells controlling each other. Were Moon's compounds — the little molecules that stimulated and inhibited protein phosphatase — were they messengers for cooperation between cells? Or were they just poisons that teach the fish not to nibble?

How did Moon's sponges know which molecules to make? After they made some molecules that were especially effective, things got better for them. This was probably their go-ahead to start making a host of new drug compounds. Of course, sponges never consciously thought that it would be good to produce these molecules in such a variety of shapes and forms. They just did what they did, and their success reinforced the behavior. Give bio-molecules enough ways, and they may actually seem to have a collective will.

But with people, it's still, "Where there's a will, there's a way." Once we colonized each other and developed civilization, we quickly learned how to amplify our desires. After we discovered antibiotics to "cure" death by infection, we demanded a "cure" for cancer. It's easier to order someone else to do something than it is to do it yourself. And since most physicians don't know much chemistry, and since the federal and university labs often aren't imaginative enough to produce fundamental medical inventions, it's up to entrepreneurial types like Dr. Moon to come up with the test compounds.

Society threw the problem of drug discovery into the open market.

Of course, our collective could not allow for anything to go wrong. The entrepreneur-scientists' test compounds must not show any serious side effects, even in the first dozen patients to be tested. So the FDA throws up requirements for tons of paperwork, making the first human testing very expensive. And the little Korean scientist has to go begging for money. He has to beg awfully hard to a lot of people.

In drug development, you can't survive as a little fish. You have to be gobbled up by the big fish. To survive, Moon's discovery had to move up the economic food chain.

But after King gobbled up Moon, he needed help digesting the scientific information. He needed someone who could explain it to him the way he liked it. In stepped Cheryl, ready to turn her knowledge and charm into a supercharged career. Cheryl had already used the principles of symbiosis to work herself quite a way up the food chain without having to dirty her hands in the lab. I was sure that Drs. Abdul Moran and Henk van Friesland would still be willing to help her with anything for old time's sake.

But this was only the beginning. Moon's scientific discovery had to go still higher up the food chain to survive. King needed $20 million to have his newly acquired sponge compound tested in man. Up stepped Broadmoore with ready cash, planning to make hundreds of millions of dollars. That broad-shouldered, broad-assed, entrepreneurial Brit played the octopus, burying himself in the mud, stretching tentacles in all directions to feel out information. When he was attacked, he confused the water with a cloud of ink.

When his hired-actor Yang was killed, Broadmoore found himself shorthanded in the due diligence department. In stepped Ben Candidi — high-paid consultant — ready to stretch himself in all directions.

Who said that life is a stage?

It's funny how a newly bankrolled play will attract actors like chum attracts sharks. And they will act out any script you give them. That must have been what Luigi Pindaro had in mind with "Six Characters in Search of an Author". Or take "Rosencrantz and Guildenstern are Dead" — where the guys were even ready to kill Hamlet.

Maybe that's the trouble with modern life. Too many sorry actors on call, too many bad scripts floating around, and too much cynical money running the show. I had dark thoughts of wannabe stars playing in the schlocky Sunday night docudramas, financed by committees answering to Madison Avenue. Glumly I remembered the TV commercial where the imperious, tuxedoed pseudo-Englishman berates you for not driving his fine automobile. Cut corners, cheat or lie, if you have to, but, above all, win — so you can afford this symbol of high status.

And if your soul is already beyond redemption, wait a couple months for the new commercial where the actor walks up through the fog like a character in a John le Carré novel, and tells you sympathetically — like the controller bringing the spy in from the cold — that the reason you did it all was because you *deserve* the luxury automobile.

Little wonder that cheap, commercial fiction feeds back on real life, and that people start acting out the docudrama. And C.C. King becomes a Concrete Castle King who pulls out a gun and shoots out the heart of the due diligence inspector who got in the way. And an intelligent, attractive woman who wants it all, slips drugs into a man's drink. And the exotic call girl will dance on anyone's lap for the right price, just as she's been doing for centuries. And you can't find anyone this side of Peoria who will stand up and say it's wrong:

"I want to have it all, Ben."

While going over the slide listing the implications of my findings, I noticed Rebecca wrinkling her nose. Others were viewing me with curiosity as well. Maybe I'd been getting too philosophical. I took my mouth out of autopilot and changed to the last slide. My scientific presentation was in "end game".

The end game with Cheryl had been quick, too. My Humphrey Bogart confrontation left her with two choices. She took the wrong one and died. It made me so sorry. But I had no tears for Tony Altino — that get-rich-quick man. Somehow I felt sorry for King, though. Despite his gruff manner and go-for-the-throat reflexes, I sensed that a wide vein of good ran through his soul. He'd wanted to do something against the disease that had struck his family. His last words to my "lifeless" body were his expression of regret for having to kill me.

I tried to conclude my seminar with a flourish. The audience clapped enthusiastically.

Dr. McGregor announced that the general audience could ask questions. There were a few, and I politely fielded. Then McGregor dismissed everyone but the committee, and the examination began.

The outside examiner from Yale did not understand some of my logic. I reset my computer and went through a few screens, repeating my arguments. I answered several minor questions.

After seeing that everything was under control, McGregor puffed up his chest and asked a question. "Ben, there was something in your presentation that I didn't understand. You were speculating about 'actors fulfilling a need'. You said something about 'inappropriate stimulation by functionally parasitic molecules being a drag on the cell.'"

Jeez! Had I babbled my philosophical daydreams in front of the audience? I would have to fix that right now.

"Actually, Dr. McGregor, now that I think about it, it doesn't make any sense to me, either." My timing was right, and laughter exploded around the table.

The external examiner asked the last question: "What are your career plans?"

"Undecided as yet, but definitely nontraditional."

Everyone around the table shook my hand and pronounced me — Dr. Candidi. The outside examiner rushed off to catch a plane. Other committee members went back to their experiments. Dr. McGregor took me back to our lab where Rebecca and several of my fellow students congratulated me in unison. I touched Rebecca's hip as she gave me a delicate, congratulatory kiss. It fulfilled the promise she made in our dreamy conversation when she called me from Jamaica seven short days ago. My enchantment turned to passion. Nimbly Rebecca disengaged her lips from mine.

Someone brought an ice bucket with two bottles of champagne. Rebecca and I made a show of clinking glasses for the crowd. Our backdrop was the Miami skyline.

McGregor's technician flipped on his boom box, firing us up for a noisy party. Soon the social temperature in the room had climbed so high that we ignited a second party out in the hall. And our noise level was so high that McGregor almost didn't notice the lab phone ringing. He picked it up and gestured to me.

It was Dr. Westley. "In celebration of your dual success, I would like to invite you and Rebecca to dinner tonight with Brian and myself — if you could spare the time. Say around eight. Meet you at the club — you know the place." That was vintage Westley, issuing commands disguised as invitations.

"We would be most delighted."

"There are other matters which could be discussed most expeditiously right now, if you can spare the time. Can I assume there are no other phones connected to your line?"

"Correct."

"And can I assume that the line is secure?"

"Incoming, yes. Outgoing, no."

"Why, of course. You are in the midst of a noisy celebration as I can plainly hear. Well, to the point: I should inform you of certain serological findings which we made on Dr. Cheryl North."

"Yes, please tell me." I pulled over a lab stool and rested one foot on it. Westley's voice was difficult to hear over the background noise.

"Venereal diseases were negative. Hepatitis negative. Herpes negative. And most importantly, anti-HIV antibody was negative. Of course, we have nothing on the exotic dancer. But she is of minimal concern since you told me she applied a condom."

Long black hair caressed my shoulder. Rebecca kissed my ear and whispered, "Don't stay so long on the phone, Ben."

I nodded in agreement and slipped my free arm around Rebecca's slim waist. She broke loose and went back to partying.

"Would you like me to repeat the results?" Westley asked.

"Yes, please."

Westley repeated them slowly; I listened carefully, a finger stuck in my free ear.

"Thanks, Dr. Westley. It was a concern."

"As you know, it is possible that Dr. North could have been carrying the HIV virus but had not seroverted. A newly infected individual can be infectious to others but not yet produce her own antibody against the virus. The blind period lasts six months."

My mouth felt dry. I gulped down my second glass of champagne. "Yes, I am aware of that and will act accordingly."

McGregor called from across the room, "Hey, Ben, you aren't supposed to be getting into heavy-duty discussions now."

Westley continued softly, "To be certain, you must wait for six months and be tested again. But, Ben, the odds of your being infected are very small. You described the contact as female genital on oral and without cuts or abrasions. Statistical studies suggest such contact has lower probability of infection. Some researchers even speculate that the virus is neutralized by saliva."

I glanced around the room and then asked Westley, "Have your colleagues in the other branch uncovered any anecdotal data that might be useful in calculating probabilities in this particular case?"

Westley interpreted me correctly. "The 'other branch', meaning police, of course. Cheryl North was arrested once in Washington nine years ago for soliciting for prostitution."

I gasped.

Dr. Westley continued. "The charge was reduced to a misdemeanor. She was an undergraduate in college then. It would seem to have been an attempt at raising money for tuition — at least she so pled."

"Come on, Ben," McGregor yelled across the room.

"Excuse me, Dr. Westley. I have to sit down."

"I shouldn't make much of it now, the prostitution angle, that is. It was long ago. The detectives' interviews of her San Marco Isle condominium neighbors and inferences drawn from colleagues at BIOTECH suggest that she confined her . . . err . . . attentions to C.C. King during the last year. He also tested negative. So your chances of being infected must be vanishingly low."

Typical Westley, saving the best stuff for last.

I said, "Thank you, Dr. Westley, and we'll see you tonight."

"One other matter. The detective recovered two video tapes of the incident. There was no evidence that other copies had been made. From our casual viewing, it is clear that you were drugged. Our workups of your blood leave no doubt. The detectives have turned over the video tapes to me for safe keeping. After everything resolves itself, the tapes can eventually be destroyed."

"Thank you, Dr. Westley."

"Cheers." (Click)

As I hung up, McGregor said, "Ben, you look like you've seen a ghost. Lighten up."

"Sorry. The champagne must have got to me."

It wasn't only the champagne. The video tape problem was spinning in my head. Would it come out in the coroner's inquisition on the murder of Dr. Moon? If Westley didn't pursue it, maybe the life insurance company would. And how to explain it all to Rebecca?

DE CAPO 38

An hour later, the party was behind us, and we were back in our apartment. The champagne was still sloshing around in my brain. While I sat on the couch with eyes closed, fighting the effects of a week of sleep deprivation, Rebecca was changing clothes. She came out wearing her little black dress, the one that showed off her legs so nicely. She looked so delightful as she walked toward me from across the room. Around her delicate neck rested the gold necklace I'd given her last year. If she hadn't been wearing red lipstick, I would have kissed her. We rushed off to catch a cab.

We held hands during the ride. I told her that I'd made something over $24,000. I gave her the bare outline of what had gone on during the last week but avoided the heavy-duty stuff with Cheryl. I skirted all parts of the story involving physical danger — and physical proximity. The twenty-minute ride didn't give Rebecca a chance to ask many questions.

We arrived at the restaurant in the Faire Isle complex 10 minutes late. The maitre d' said that we'd have no trouble finding Drs. Westley and Broadmoore in the back. That was quite true. The two guys had polarized the room like a magnet under a sheet of paper sprinkled with iron filings. The closer we got, the stronger everyone's attention seemed focussed on them. A middle-aged woman with a New York accent told her husband, "He's singing something about being an English gentleman."

And that was what Broadmoore was actually doing, although the Gilbert and Sullivan lyrics declared him a "Major General". Seated, but pushed back a comfortable distance from the table, he was half-singing, half-reciting the patter song in a broad baritone that carried throughout the room. Westley sat next to Broadmoore, his face ruddy with excitement, not embarrassment:

"I am the very model of a modern major general,
"I've information vegetable, animal and mineral,
"I know the kings of England, and I quote the fights historical,
"From Marathon to Waterloo, in order categorical . . . "

Broadmoore pattered on about matters mathematical and equations quadratical. Then Westley joined in, echoing the last line:
"With many cheerful facts about the square of the hypotenuse."
Broadmoore swaggered through the next verse while Westley took a last sip from his martini, then stared down at the glass, as if contemplating whether to remove the olive. Four glasses stood empty. Broadmoore passed through all the wickets — differential calculus, scientific names of animal-culous, mythic history of King Arthur and Sir Carodoc, hard acrostic paradox and the crimes of Heliogabalus.
When Broadmoore stumbled on his conic sections and peculiarities parabolus, Westley jumped to his aid. Soon they were galloping together through the undoubted Paphaels from Derard Dows and Zoffanies. And in splendid solo, Broadmoore crashed through the croaking chorus from the "Frogs" of Aristophanes . . . humming fugues of which he'd heard the music's "din afore" and whistling all the airs from that infernal nonsense Pinafore.
Half the restaurant caught the last line and broke out laughing. It changed to applause as Westley jumped in to echo the chorus:
"And whistle all the airs from that infernal nonsense Pinafore."
Then Broadmoore made a broad sweep of his hand which caused a dramatic hush to come over the audience. He was letting Westley take the next verse. Westley began cautiously and Broadmoore supported him in *sprechstimme* — partly speech, partly song. Soon Westley was soloing through the gauntlet of washing bills in Babylonic cuneiform and details of Caractacus's uniform with such grace that he too seemed the very model of a modern major general. Broadmoore joined him on the last verse. Together they accelerated steadily through the mamelons and revelins, chassepots and javelins, and the skills of gunnery learned at a nunnery.
(A few days later, my friend Robert and I looked up the lyrics at his library. We had a lot of fun deciphering all these terms.)

Broadmoore and Westley crashed into the final chorus at bebop tempo.

Yes, the English duo's performance ran deep and true — like Robert Louis Stevenson's description of the bagpipe duel between Alan Stewart and Robin Macgregor at the smoky Highland cottage in *Kidnapped.*

The room broke into wild applause. Red-faced from the physical and mental exertion, the pair stood up and took a bow. In a flash, it became clear to me why all the well-heeled patrons were applauding so unreservedly. In their own club, they had finally experienced the real thing. For them, this snippet of English tapestry was the culmination of hundreds of thousands of dollars spent on expensive condominiums and luxury automobiles. Broadmoore's and Westleys' offering of lifestyle vindication was thousands of times more real than the flickering image of the screen Englishman and his expensive, fancy automobile.

"Bravo, Bravo!" I applauded along with the rest. Even Rebecca thought it wonderful.

Still bathing in glow of the moment, Broadmoore caught my eye and signalled us to approach. With a sweeping gesture of a broad hand, he showed his appreciation to the audience and indicated there would be no encore. Then the hand came down on my shoulder, and he ushered us to the table of honor.

Westley addressed his partner. "General Broadmoore, you already know newly minted Dr. Candidi. May I now present the soon-to-be minted Dr. Rebecca Levis."

"I am ever so pleased," said Broadmoore.

Rebecca smiled, cocked her head and offered her hand. "You are a wonderful singer."

"Well, thank you. Like Geoffrey, I had early musical experience as a cathedral choir boy."

"Did you actually perform Gilbert and Sullivan?"

"Yes, while in public school. When we put on the *Pirates of Penzance*, I was given the blustery role of the Major General. It may have been the definitive experience of my life, for I have been blustering ever since." He caught my eye and said, "Although Ben might say that up to now I have been amazingly silent in Miami." Beaming at Rebecca, he went on, "Now Geoffrey found his defining role as the Captain of the Pinafore, also as a public school performance. You might say public school was a seminal point in his life as well."

The two grinned at each other like a couple of prankish schoolboys.

Then Westley turned to us, furrowed his forehead, and said, "Although one must keep in mind that — "

I interrupted quickly, " — that public schools in England are not to be confused with the truly public schools of this country."

Westley was nonplussed. Broadmoore also caught my meaning and broke into a jolly laugh. Rebecca joined in with a pearly string of laughter. Westley's and my laughs were quickly recruited, and the table shook for several seconds.

Dinner was ordered, served and enjoyed to the accompaniment of amusing conversation, orchestrated by the two gentlemen and conducted at the leisurely pace of a cruise around the world. Our conversational cruiseliner departed from multicultural, subtropical Miami for the nearby Bahamas. Then we sailed south to another famous ex-colony — the one in which the delightful young lady had been practicing medicine — a young country in which cricket was played with greater ardor than in the worn-out country of its origin.

Rebecca thrived on the courteous attentions of my elderly and learned colleagues.

It felt good, being treated as an equal. I also felt proud as Rebecca told my two learned colleagues of the latest developments in tropical medicine. She really knew her stuff. They listened with interest, interrupting only for an occasional clarifying question. She could hold her own against those two better than I.

Next our party set conversational sail for points north, spending much time in Boston, tracing the origins of New England industry and recounting the city's incredible feat of creating a half-dozen major universities.

"What an incredible technological powerhouse — Boston," Broadmoore intoned. "Of course, the much-touted Yankee Ingenuity had its roots in England."

Could there now be any question as to the next port of call for our conversation? We set sail for England. Over dessert and coffee we visited the Cornish coast, sailed past the Cliffs of Dover, and up the Thames Estuary to London, whence to the inland waterways and motorways of that charming country, which is, always was, and always will be, the center of our cultural universe. After this verity was affirmed and reaffirmed by all, we collectively realized it had become late. Time to fly back on the Concorde.

But I was not yet ready to call it an evening. I had not heard a word about how the BIOTECH deal worked out. "Dr. Broadmoore. Now that you've bought the company, what are you going to do with it?"

"Have it make money, of course." Turning to Rebecca, he said, "I engaged your fiancé for advice on buying a pig in a poke. He urged me to buy it. He discovered that the company was something of a magic poke, capable of producing many pigs." Broadmoore explained to Rebecca the usefulness of Dr. Moon's follow-on inventions. "And we would not have known — if it hadn't been for your intended's clever detective work."

Rebecca's eyes sparkled. I had never seen her so proud of me.

"So you are going to file the continuation patents?" I asked

"Yes. The copy you uncovered is quite good, although it must be audited and improved. Dr. Lau will be listed as a co-inventor. Over the weekend, the detectives roasted the poor chap like Charles and Mary Lamb's piglet — thirty-some-hours all told — a real 'barn burner'. They concluded that he was innocent of any complicity in either of the murders. We are retaining him in his present position. As you may appreciate, it is easier to prosecute a patent application with at least one live inventor — although the posthumous filing mechanism would have worked in a pinch." He winked to me and smiled benevolently at Westley and Rebecca.

I asked, "Did you find the computer where he was storing the data?"

"Yes. We secured it, too. It was in a small rented room over a cinema in a strip mall along U.S. 1 on the south end of Coral Gables. Not too far from King's house, actually. The Riviera Theater, I think they call it. Have you heard of it?"

"Yes, we've been there."

"Good." Broadmoore smiled at me. "Unfortunately Dr. Lau is not very articulate. I would appreciate, over the next several weeks, if you could go over the computer's files and offer us some help with formulating the application. You could search and read the prior art. And we would appreciate your advice on how to navigate around any obstacles you detect."

I wrinkled my brow like this might be a problem. "Well, I still have a series of experiments to do, and I'm not sure that — "

"What I am proposing is a two hundred dollar per hour consultancy. The immediate phase of the project would require about one hundred hours."

Rebecca tried hard to contain her excitement.

"Well, yes," I said matter-of-factly. "I'd be most pleased. I'll just make the time."

"I thought it appropriate to give you first choice — easy duty after hard combat, so to speak."

Rebecca exhaled sub-audibly. She understood Broadmoore's meaning.

Broadmoore went on to say, "You see, Ben, your archangelic — well, I should actually say — your Gabrielic efforts during Friday's waning hours not only unleashed the sword of justice, they also simplified the playing field, as seen from the business sense, that is."

No one interrupted Broadmoore.

"Of course, there could be no question that BIOTECH was mine after I presented the check for ten million dollars. But Mr. King had raised considerable objection to our hastily but appropriately convened Board Meeting held at five minutes past five. Of course, my first act as majority shareholder was to vote him out of power. I became Chairman and President." Broadmoore smiled slyly. "Although he provided a surfeit of oral rantings and ravings, he left no recorded objections."

Rebecca listened carefully, not seeming to know how much was hyperbole.

"Also, the Board of Directors of the company reviewed the extra ten thousand dollar payment made to you by Dr. North. It was a lawfully contracted payment of the company. We decided that you had no conflict of interest in accepting it. Thus, the Board begs you to keep the money as a token of our good will."

"Well, thank you," I said.

Rebecca's eyes were wide with astonishment.

"Of course, the company can well afford the token of gratitude. The death of Dr. Moon has left us five million dollars richer." Broadmoore said this smoothly — too smoothly.

I asked then, "You don't think there will be any problem with the legality of accepting the insurance money?"

Dr. Westley didn't wait a millisecond to jump in. "The autopsy of Dr. Moon was inconclusive." His tone was autocratic. Gray irises expanded, narrowing his light blue pupils. Unfortunately your most important revelations were not captured on the audio tape. They were inaudible. And it would not be possible to consider any portion of that tape without bringing into formal investigation the whole tape — and perhaps other tapes as well."

Rebecca looked quizzically from Westley to me and back.

"I understand." I said it without croaking.

"We all find ourselves limited by technicalities," Westley said, now in a fatherly tone. "A formal proof of murder of Dr. Moon would be impossible to make."

Yes, everyone will find ways to cut corners when his personal interest is involved. But I would have to wrestle with this particular question for days.

Sensing that I was deep in thought, Dr. Westley shifted back in his chair and said, "Brian, I think that we should cease imposing ourselves on this young couple and leave them to their own devices."

Broadmoore nodded, understanding perfectly. "Quite right."

Westley continued, "They should be singing songs of Nanki-Poo and Yum-Yum, while we remain here and sing the 'Lord High Executioner'." Westley punctuated this dubious witticism with a sinister working of his eyebrows. The two Englishmen broke into hearty laughter. Rebecca and I laughed at their irrelevancy.

"I will call a cab," said Dr. Westley.

"No, I've already made arrangements," said Broadmoore.

His arrangements were a towncar limousine and uniformed driver who tipped his hat to us as he opened the door. While we rolled along Bayshore Drive, I told Rebecca that we would apply the $34,000 to her tuition loans. Her first kisses painted my mouth with lipstick. The kisses that followed were deep and hungry. They lasted the whole ride home. Rebecca's hands were bold and arousing. This aggressively female side of Rebecca surprised me. Sure, our lovemaking had always been daring and inventive. But the soul I had known was as chaste as Jane Austen.

Though a thousand miles away, my ex-Swarthmore buddy Richard Bash was still able to pop into my thoughts with a sarcastic interpretation of Rebecca's affection. No, Richard, it couldn't be as moronically simple as hard-fucking spiders and power trips.

As the limo approached the Medical Towers and I wiped red lipstick from my mouth, I remembered Westley's telephone lecture on saliva and the immunology of oral mucosa. No harm so far, but I would have to tell Rebecca the whole story before the evening progressed to its logical conclusion.

And how rapidly we accelerated toward that moment: Limousine quickly dismissed, the apartment door closed behind us, Rebecca's lithe, angular body molding to mine as she unbuttoned my shirt, her lusty rejection of my offer to uncork a bottle of wine, her naked and willing 120 pounds pulling me down to bed — and the moment was there.

A quavering voice called from behind me. "Rebecca, I need to tell you something first."

Surprise overthrew passion. A wrinkled forehead told me that the left side of Rebecca's brain had taken over.

"Ben, what kind of 'something' could be important now?"

Sitting together naked on the bed, I told Rebecca the whole story — up to the invitation to Cheryl's apartment. There my voice stumbled and faltered. And at that moment, the truth became clear to me: My refusal of the first brush of Cheryl's charm had not outweighed my acceptance of her cup. And it was clear to Rebecca, too.

Rebecca sat cross-legged next to me on the bed, listening quietly with all senses, one hand on my knee, her back straight, her shoulders square, her small but exquisite breasts hanging loosely, as I blubbered the story of my drugged orgy, the accepted kiss and the blackmail tape. I ended by saying that we would now have to take precautions.

Rebecca's eyes were full of sympathy, but her voice was clinically analytical. "If you'd feel better about it, we could use a prophylactic for a few months. But what you are really telling me, Ben, is that you were attracted to this woman."

I had no ready answer for Rebecca. I thought of how Cheryl had challenged the very foundation of my beliefs and how she had tantalized a part of my psyche that I'd never permitted to unfold. Tears dropped from my chin. I answered Rebecca truthfully with the first image that came to mind: "She shot in and out of my life like a comet."

Rebecca sighed. "I understand. A near miss. But you do bring it on yourself when you let your eyes wander. Yes, I know that men's brains are wired up differently from ours. Oh, Ben, you must watch yourself when I'm away." She signed. "I love you so."

Her sigh turned to a hug, which turned into a kiss, which deepened, evolved and transformed until reaching its ultimate expression — the act performed first as a happy reunion of our bodies, and then performed once more as an act of joyful rediscovery, until we had plumbed the depth of our love and lay expended in each other's arms. Candidi and Levis — he, a onetime altar boy, and she, a reader of sacred scrolls — two little people who had decided to live their lives together.

Nestled at my side, Rebecca's body gradually stilled with sleep. Mine stayed restless. Like stray film clips from an action movie, like flashes from a video CD player gone berserk, visuals of the seven days flashed before my closed eyes. Visions of Cheryl posed before her maroon Riviera, of the gray interior of BIOTECH's office, of sheets of faceless gray paragraphs piled high on tables, of turbaned Singh, of belligerent Moon, of pugnacious King, and then, again, of Cheryl.

I slipped from bed and looked out the window. The moon was still just a sliver, though waxing.

Yes, I had given Rebecca my most truthful answer. Cheryl had shot through my life like a giant comet — a wayward ball of ice and rock snared by Jupiter's sling. Cheryl had closed on me in a single, tight, elliptic orbit. She had shone many times brighter than the moon. Her close approach had wobbled my axis and raised thousand-foot tides. And my reciprocal action had deflected her course and sent her crashing into the sun.

The tidal attraction had created fractures. It had crazed the mantle of my soul. Rebecca would help me seal the cracks. I would prove to Rebecca that my love flowed from a spring called agape, the spring of pure love — sweeter and more constant than the River of Eros.

POSTLOGUE

With the exception of the blackmail and murder, the conflicts depicted in this novel are not atypical for a preclinical or early-clinical pharmaceutical technology transfer deal.

ABOUT THE AUTHOR

PHOTO: DOUG BECKMAN

Dirk Wyle in Little Havana.

Dirk Wyle (nom de plume) is a 30-year veteran of biomedical science and longtime resident of Miami. His novels deal with the why's and how's of crime involving biomedical scientists and physicians. Considering guns and bullets to be overused devices, he gives literary preference to methods that could fool even a coroner. His free-spirited protagonist, Ben Candidi, accepts the dual challenge of finding the murderer and discovering what made him do it in the first place.

Dirk's interests also include the South Florida waters, technology's impact on human psychology, the business applications of science, multiculturalism — and the telling of a good story. He has received the Icon Award from the National Writers Association (S.FL Chapter), he is a member of the Mystery Writers of America, and his first mystery novel, *Pharmacology Is Murder,* was selected as the Best First Mystery of 1998 by Joe's Detective Pages.

Dirk invites your visit to http://www.dirk-wyle.com. He is hard at work on two more Ben Candidi mysteries.